PRAISE FOR

The Breadwinner Trilogy

"Stevie Kopas continues to hone her surgeon's eye for detail and her sense of the heartbreak of everyday post-apocalyptic life. Rich with character and eerie with the kind of scares that get under your skin rather than nauseate you."

- Jay Bonansinga, *New York Times* bestselling author of *Robert Kirkman's The Walking Dead: Descent*

"A gruesome, fast-paced story which ticks all the boxes whilst avoiding the usual zombie clichés. Kopas puts her realistic characters through hell!"

- David Moody, author of *Hater, Autumn,* and *Strangers*

THE BREADWINNER TRILOGY

THE BREADWINNER • HAVEN • ALL GOOD THINGS

STEVIE KOPAS

A PERMUTED PRESS BOOK

ISBN: 978-1-61868-645-9

THE BREADWINNER TRILOGY
The Breadwinner, Haven, All Good Things

Cover art by Christian Bentulan

Permuted Press, LLC
275 Madison Avenue, 14th Floor
New York, NY 10016
permutedpress.com

THE BREADWINNER

BOOK I

IN THE BEGINNING

I

Samson Eckhart tugged at the sleeves of his gray designer suit jacket, brushing himself off and adjusting his tie. He checked his Rolex again and sighed, returning his gaze to the entrance of the courthouse. Outside the doors stood an army of reporters, impatiently waiting for him to make his grand exit after news had spread of his case being delayed. *Again.*

The sudden onslaught of a mysterious illness tearing its way through the country had finally made its way to their sleepy beach town in northwest Florida, and it was really starting to become an inconvenience for Samson. He overheard voices down one of the corridors. The courthouse was unusually empty, creating an eerie atmosphere, and the voices were a welcome distraction from the hungry news teams at the entrance.

He crept toward the source of the voices and peered around the frame of an office door. Two officers stood in front of a messy desk talking to a clerk.

"I'm tellin' you! I saw it with my own eyes, the fucker took a chunk right out of his cellmate's neck!" one of the officers exclaimed. "Had to put the whole fuckin' place on lockdown after we finally put the crazy son of a bitch down."

"And you expect me to believe one of your jailbirds tried to eat someone?" the balding clerk asked the short cop.

"Fuck yeah, I do. And he wouldn't die either. Shot him four times before he finally stayed down. Had to shoot him in the head." He jabbed at his own forehead, "Right between the eyes."

The clerk rolled his eyes, "And then the guy with the chunk missin' out of his neck, he came back to life?"

The cop nodded, "I'm tellin' you, I don't care how bat shit crazy it sounds, it happened! Just this morning."

The other officer, a tall black man, furrowed his brow. "Sounds like we don't have the whole story about what's really goin' on out there. Makes you wonder." He ran a hand over his slick, bald head. "Been hearin' crazy reports from the surrounding towns. Rioting, looting, the hospitals hitting max capacity...just a matter of time before they call us in to help out in the city. And if you ask around, nobody has a damn clue what's goin' on or what this *sickness* is."

"Well, whatever it is, it's here, and it ain't good." The short cop turned and spotted Samson eavesdropping in the doorway. "Hey! Get outta here, ambulance-chaser."

Samson scoffed, "I was just leaving. Pig." He pretended to tip a hat at the men and walked away.

Samson wasn't sure what he'd just overheard, but he didn't like it. The conversation left him with an uneasy feeling and he noticed a thin film of sweat had developed on his upper lip. The loud clicking of heels turned his head and his blue eyes brightened at the sight of his assistant Rochelle, walking beside his high-profile client at the other end of the corridor.

"Finally," he called out to them, "the natives are getting restless out there." Samson turned his nose down at his client as the three met in the entryway. He was a twenty-something redneck who liked guns and drugs. *A little too much.* He'd snorted too much coke and ended up murdering his girlfriend and her two friends a few weeks back. If it weren't for his daddy owning the largest sporting goods chain in the Southeast, there would have been no way he could have afforded an attorney like Samson.

Rochelle attempted to hand Samson a stack of paperwork but he waved her off, "Let's get out of here first, it's too hot for this shit." Samson stole a glance back toward the offices and shook his head before turning his attention back to his client. "Remember what I said, keep your head down, let me do the talking, and wipe that smug look off your fat face."

Rochelle stifled a giggle as the rich kid stammered a "Yes, sir" and stared down at his feet. Samson led the way to the door and prepared a big, fake grin for the crowd of reporters. He nodded at the guard on his way out the doors and an eruption of questions from dozens of mouths filled the air. Samson chose the most attractive woman in the crowd and gave a brief yet charming interview before ushering Rochelle and his client forward and away from the shouts and microphones. All the while, the overheard conversation echoed through his brain.

They parted ways in the back parking lot after agreeing to meet at the office in the morning. Traffic on the bridge was at a standstill and Samson had no intentions of spending the remainder of his afternoon stuck in a vehicle on his way back home. But after the conversation he'd listened in on, Samson wasn't too sure he had any intentions of doing that in the morning, either. The trial had been delayed, the kid could wait a few more days to meet with Samson.

"At least you're out on bond," Samson told his client before opening the door to his Range Rover. "Rochelle, you'll see him home?" She nodded and cracked a smile before heading off toward her vehicle with their client.

Samson settled into his truck and fastened his seat belt. "Call Moira," he instructed the Bluetooth.

A second passed and the Bluetooth responded, "Call Failed. Try again?"

Samson sighed, "Yes."

A ringing filled the car, and satisfied, Samson pulled out of the parking lot and headed home.

"Dad?" Samson's daughter answered.

"Hey baby girl, what are you doing home? Where's your mom?"

"She's next door, talking to Tracey. Mom wouldn't let us go to school. Lots of weird stuff going on."

"Yeah, tell me about it. Do me a favor hun, go get your mom and tell her to stay in the house. Make sure your brother's there, too."

"Alright." Keira's voice wavered. *"When will you be home?"*

"I'm on my way now."

The familiar tones of a dropped call sounded through the speakers and Samson cursed under his breath. He pressed his foot down on the accelerator, making the turn onto the main road toward Franklin Woods. The road was clear so he sped up, he was a mere five miles from home.

He turned on the radio and began scanning the channels, ignoring music; he was looking for information. In the few seconds that he took his eyes off the road, a Honda Civic flew through a stop sign and Samson's truck caught the tail end of the car.

The Honda spun and skidded backwards down into the drainage ditch. Samson barely felt the impact in the Range Rover, but was none the less shaken up.

"Fuck!" He shouted as he jumped out of the truck and sprinted toward the Honda.

He dialed 911 on his cell phone multiple times but the call refused to go through. The driver was unconscious, but he heard the woman in the passenger's seat moaning. She looked confused, blood ran down her chin from her mouth.

"Shit. Ma'am, you alright?" Samson called out to the woman.

There was no response, but she looked up at him and Samson recoiled.

Did she just fucking hiss at me?

He squinted and stepped forward. Her eyes didn't look right to him. There was a milky haze to them and they just seemed so...vacant.

Samson tried 911 again and got the same outcome. The woman thrust a bloodied arm through the open window, her fingers twitching and stretching. She groaned as she fruitlessly reached for him.

"Look, someone will be here to help you." He looked around. No witnesses. "I'm sorry."

He backed away from the Civic and the woman moaned again. Samson wouldn't risk getting closer to her, she could be sick. He had his family to think about.

"Shouldn't have run the damn stop sign," he said to himself as he got back into his truck and sped off toward Franklin Woods.

Samson pulled up to the enormous gates of the secured community. The guard poked his head out and waved to Samson as he pushed a button and let the man through.

"Bill," Samson nodded at the guard, rolling down his window.

"Looks like you had yourself a fender-bender, Mr. Eckhart."

"Yeah," Samson paused, thinking of the woman in the car. "No big deal. All sorts of crazy goin' on out there."

"Oh, yes sir, there sure is." He motioned toward the neighborhood, "Few of the residents were attacked out there today, came home seein' better days." Samson frowned at Bill's statement. "Oh, don't you worry sir, they'll be fine. Lucky for y'all, this is the safest place in the whole town, nothin'll get through these gates. In or out." Bill smiled proudly.

Samson didn't return the smile. "I'll take your word for it. Take care, Bill." He pulled his car through the massive entrance and headed for his driveway.

II

"Hansen, what's your location?"

The radio on Officer Andrew Hansen's hip crackled to life.

"I'm at the courthouse with Wake," he spoke into his shoulder mic.

"Hank said to tell you to get your ass down to the high school. They've got a situation."

Andrew looked down at the clerk he'd been talking to in the office and said, "This is where we part ways, my friend. Take it easy, man. Doesn't look like anybody else is coming to work today, you should sneak outta here."

The balding desk clerk nodded, "I think I just might. You two be careful out there."

Andrew and Wake rushed out of the clerk's office and toward the back of the building where their cruiser was parked.

"What exactly is the situation down at Franklin High, Betty?" Andrew spoke into the mic again.

"More rioting I suppose." The dispatcher's voice was shaky. *"Some reporter got attacked. I think a couple of kids are hurt, too. EMTs were en route but,"* Betty paused, *"they haven't arrived on scene yet. They're not responding. What's your ETA?"*

"Alright, don't worry, B. Give us five."

The cruiser sped out of the back, siren blaring, like a bat out of hell. There was a ton of chatter on the radio; fires had broken out all over the city, people were fighting in the streets. It was complete chaos.

"Man, they need to get the National Guard down there. What the fuck's goin' on?" Andrew's partner remarked.

"I know about as much as you, man. I just hope Hank's got shit under control at the school. I don't like hearing about kids gettin' hurt."

"Whaddya think, school shooting?"

"Nah, not in Franklin."

"Where the fuck are the EMTs?" Wake frowned, trying to wrap his head around the situation.

Andrew shrugged. "I don't know, man."

The cruiser pulled up to Franklin High School; the place was a mad-house. News vans lined the curb, parents screamed at school officials, while, teens snapped photos of the turmoil with their cell phones. Andrew jumped from his vehicle and didn't even bother closing the door. He spotted his LT, Hank, amidst the crowd and made a beeline for him.

"Hank!" Andrew shouted.

"Hansen!" The older man ran toward him. "Thank God! Look, I need you to get these fuckin' parents out of here. Tell them to get their kids and go. I don't even know why the fuck any of 'em are still here." He tilted his head toward a reporter lying on the sidewalk curb behind him, "Get over there and help her. Where the fuck are the EMTs?" Hank shouted into his radio as he walked off.

The two officers rushed to the reporter's side.

"She's losing a lot of blood," another officer said to them as they crouched down beside the wounded woman.

"How did this happen?" Wake asked.

"Some fuckin' nut job, came running out of the woods like somethin' was chasing him. This lady ran over tryin' to help him and he fuckin' bit her! One of the kids got involved, punched him in the face, guy bit him, too." He motioned to a teen standing nearby, his hand wrapped in a bandage. "But the kid beat him senseless. Dude's dead." He pointed to a sheet that lie over an unmoving body."

Wake and Andrew locked eyes, their faces grim. They had seen this before.

"Get these people out of here. I'll handle this," Wake told his partner.

Andrew stood up and looked around, the place was a mess. He attempted shouting instructions over the crowd, ordering people to return to their vehicles and leave the premises. Even with fellow officers trying to set up barricades and push the protesting parents back, it was useless. It was as if the hoity-toity residents of Franklin were more concerned about getting someone on the board of education fired for not cancelling school than they were about getting their children home to safety. He hopped on top of one of the nearby cars and put his hands over his head, getting everyone's attention.

"I need you all to find your child and return to your vehicles. You have five minutes before crowd control measures are taken!" he shouted to the parents.

A cameraman focused on Andrew while a reporter attempted to narrate the unfolding events.

Andrew pointed at the cameraman, "That means you, too! Outta here, now!"

Nobody listened. Teenagers giggled and chatted, Instagramming photos of angry parents. Many of them took pictures of Andrew on top of the car, others took selfies with him in the background.

A blood-curdling scream sounded off to Andrew's left and he drew his weapon.

"Jesus Christ! Wake!" Andrew leapt from the vehicle's roof and charged toward his partner, shoving people out of the way.

The reporter, who just moments ago had been very much alive, was latched on to Wake's neck. The other officer pulled the woman off, but the end result was fatal as she lost interest in Wake and set her jaws on him, instead.

The parents, now witnesses to the blood bath, began screaming and running around. Wake lay dying on the sidewalk, a chunk of his throat ripped out. The teen with the wounded hand jumped in, attempting to help once more, but the reporter claimed her third victim as she leapt from the officer's motionless body.

Andrew fired two rounds into her head, obliterating her skull. The teen stumbled back and dropped to his knees; blood spurting from his severed artery. Parents rushed to the kid's side.

"Get back! Get away from him!" Andrew screamed, but they didn't listen. He still didn't know why this was happening, but he now knew for sure just *how* things were escalating so quickly.

Wake leapt to his feet with a ferocious growl, grabbing a teenage girl as she ran by. The girl's scream was stifled as Wake closed his jaws around her throat, savagely feasting. Andrew's stomach turned, but he bit back his bile. He raised his gun, but before he could fire, Wake's head exploded.

"It's time to fall back," Hank said, his weapon still trained on Wake's now-unmoving corpse.

The howls of the dead and the screams of the living mixed together as Andrew ran for his cruiser, Hank following closely behind. Officers, parents, reporters, teachers…all too caught up in the moment to make a run for it themselves, fell victim to the rapidly growing mob of *eaters.*

"Floor it, Hansen."

"Hank," Andrew started, his hands shaking. "These people." He looked on in horror through his windshield.

"I said floor it, that's an order!"

Andrew shifted the cruiser into gear and slammed his foot down on the accelerator. He fumbled with his phone as he drove. He punched his brother's number in and thanked God when the call went through, but then cursed that same God when it went to voicemail.

"Clyde, I don't know where you are, but you get your ass home and you stay there. I don't know what's going on but it's bad. I'm on my way." Andrew ended the call and tried his girlfriend's cell. This time, the call failed.

Andrew returned the cell phone to his pocket and pulled the cruiser into the station. The two men rushed inside with their weapons drawn, but to their surprise, the place was empty. They heard whimpering under one of the desks.

"Betty?" Hank called out.

The overweight dispatcher poked her head out from under the desk.

"Go home," Hank ordered.

Neither man had seen the woman move so fast in her life as she grabbed her purse and hauled ass out the front door.

Andrew and Hank headed to the armory and made haste creating a necessary stockpile of weapons that Andrew loaded up into the back of his cruiser. They left the station behind and high-tailed it for the bridge that lead to the city.

The route to the interstate was thick with cars and pile-ups and Andrew considered himself lucky that he wasn't headed that way. As they drove onto the bridge, his eyes went wide with the number of cars on the opposite side of the road. "Everybody's tryin' to get out all at once."

Hank nodded. "Only us fools tryin' to get back in."

The people on the bridge were frantic. Those that tried to ride the shoulder only ended up crashing into other vehicles, blocking the way. Others that had tried desperately to make it to the other side of the highway only ended up getting their cars stuck on the median, or worse.

Andrew tried again to reach his girlfriend, but when the call finally went through, Juliette's voicemail picked up. Frustrated, he threw his cell phone out the window along with a string of curse words. He slammed on the brakes as all hell broke loose on the other side of the bridge.

"Oh, my, God," he muttered.

The people, if he could even call them that anymore, were attacking one another on the bridge. Those who fell victim rose soon after and joined in on the cannibalism, others, who'd had enough sense, threw themselves from the bridge in hopes of making it out alive, or at least suffering a lesser evil.

"Andrew," Hank spoke. He never used first names. "We need to keep moving."

Andrew's eyes filled with tears and he reluctantly continued. "All those people."

"Listen to me." Hank placed a hand on Andrew's shoulder. "You worry about you and your own. We just entered the Twilight Zone, buddy, and it ain't pretty."

The cruiser soon pulled up to Hank's house; the coast was clear.

"Stay here." Hank sprinted from the cruiser and popped the trunk of his car. He returned to Andrew with an immaculate golf club. "Take this. Just in case things get too close for comfort."

Andrew nodded. "You sure you don't want to come with?"

Hank lowered his eyes. "I gotta find my wife." He sounded so unsure. "You be careful, you hear me? Get your girl, get your brother. Keep them safe."

Hank disappeared into his home and Andrew sped off toward Juliette's.

III

Salvador Roja had just finished closing up one of his restaurants. The city was falling apart, he needed to get back to Franklin Woods. He jumped into his Lincoln and dialed his friend Ben's number.

"How are things at the pizzeria?" Sal asked.

"I've got it under control. Shit's gettin' crazy out there. I told the employees they could stay at my place for the night." Ben was the manager of Pisano's Pizzeria, one of the restaurants Sal owned.

Sal made his living flipping defunct restaurants and growing them into something they never could have been without him. He could take any other man's trash and turn it into treasure. He was a charismatic business man with three different degrees who'd moved from Mexico fifteen years earlier. Ben was an old friend whom he trusted with one of his businesses and rented the apartment upstairs to him, at no charge. He was a bright young man with no family. Sal met him at a VFW charity he'd catered a few years ago and they'd become fast friends. He often thought of Ben as he did his own son.

"Good, thank you, Ben. I'm headed home. Stay safe."

"You got it."

Sal took one last look at the lock on the security gate and nodded in approval. He wasn't sure how long it would be until he came back once he left the crumbling city. His phone rang and his wife, Lucy, was in a panic on the other end.

"People are attacking each other in the parking lot! I had to leave work. The bridge is all backed up, there are accidents everywhere! I can't get home!"

Sal pulled his phone back away from his ear and shook his head.

"Mama, lower your voice. Where are you right now?" Sal maneuvered through the city streets, dodging people and cars in his Lincoln Navigator as he spoke to his wife. He frowned at the thought of his only route home being blocked.

"I turned around before even getting on the highway when I noticed traffic wasn't moving. What am I supposed to do? Where are you?"

"Panicking is not going to help, especially if you're driving." Sal slammed on his brakes. A man in the street stopped dead in his tracks for a mere moment in front of the truck. He briefly locked eyes with Sal. It looked as if the man was saying something to him, but the screaming of two crazy-eyed women interrupted him and he took off running again. Sal narrowed his eyes and contemplated following them, but figured the police could handle looters.

"Salvador!" Lucy screamed through the phone, he had forgotten he was talking to her.

"Okay! Yeah! *Dios mio,* listen, you're going to end up hitting somebody. I don't need my insurance premiums any higher than they already are. Meet me at the pizzeria, we can stay with Ben." He changed course and headed toward Pisano's Pizzeria. "We'll try getting home in the morning. We'll figure something out."

He hung up the phone and sped toward his destination. As he got closer to the pizzeria, the streets seemed pretty clear compared to what he'd just driven through. He pulled up and killed the engine, craning his neck to see if anyone was nearby. Satisfied that there were no criminals in his vicinity, he opened the truck door and stepped out, looking around. People were running crazily down the other end of the street, screaming like animals. Sal didn't like the looks of it. He locked and set the alarm on his vehicle and hurried inside the pizzeria.

"Hey, look what the cat dragged in." Ben hollered to Sal from the kitchen.

"Yeah yeah, Lucy called me. The bridge is backed up. The boss is crashing the party, hope you don't mind."

"As long as you recognize that I'm the boss 'round here." Ben entered the parlor, chuckling. He furrowed his brow when he saw the concern etched into Sal's face. "That bad, huh?"

Sal nodded, "*Si,* make sure the back door is locked."

*

Lucy called her son over and over but was unable to get through; she broke every traffic law imaginable on her way to Pisano's. Her mind reeled as she replayed the horrific events she'd just witnessed. She was a pharmacist at a drug store in the center of the city, unfortunately close to the hospital. When rumors began to spread that the hospital would be shutting its doors to the public, people headed down the street for her store, hoping to get their hands on some miracle vaccine for the mysterious illness that was spreading through the city. She had cowered behind the shatterproof glass with her colleagues as the looters attempted to get through. She watched as the shelves of the store were cleared out and then as the people began to turn on one another.

Lucy screamed as blood sprayed onto the glass. People were being torn apart, eaten alive, right before her eyes. She grabbed her purse and headed for the emergency exit. The parking lot was no better. As soon as she was in the safety of her BMW, she made a grand exit, taking off the driver's side mirrors of three other cars as she went.

She shook the memories from her head and tried to concentrate on the road; Pisano's was just around the corner. She made a sharp left turn, tires screeching, and her BMW ran up on the curb. It smashed into a cluster of garbage cans, sending them clattering in different directions. She nervously fumbled with her things in the passenger's seat and got out. Lucy didn't even bother locking her 760Li.

The air was alive with noise and a strange man watched her from the corner. Lucy spotted him and whimpered, then sprinted across the street. The running sparked the man's attention. He snarled and rushed down the sidewalk toward her. She screamed and quickened her pace. The door to the pizzeria burst open and Ben ushered her inside and into Sal's arms. By the time Ben had bolted the heavy oak door shut, the man was already pounding on it.

The other employees inside began screaming, and Ben shouted for them all to *"shut the fuck up!"* He ran to the counter and pulled his Magnum from under the register, starting back toward the door. Ben knew the door wouldn't give, but what about the huge window when the crazy guy figured out he could just kick that in?

Ben pulled the door open and the man flew at him from the pavement, growling, teeth gnashing. Ben caught the man by the throat and threw him back out onto the sidewalk, warning him to stand down.

The man got back to his feet and Ben shot him in the leg, but the man remained standing and again lunged at Ben.

Once more he grabbed the man and threw him to the ground, but this time he noticed the glaze over his eyes and the strange wound he had on his scalp, almost like a bite mark. Ben had never been more shocked in his life, even after spending three years in the desert and nearly dying out there, he'd never seen a man take a bullet like that. The man attempted to get up again but Ben slammed his boot into his chest.

The man writhed and growled under Ben's weight, arms and legs flailing. Ben leaned in to get a closer look at the bite on the guy's scalp. A chunk of hair and flesh was missing, dried blood was crusted all around the wound, and the wound itself was black in color.

The smell was the smell of death; Ben was too familiar with it. He'd decided he'd seen enough. Without releasing the man from under his big, booted foot, he raised his gun and put a bullet in his head. He looked around, seeing if the noise had attracted any unwanted attention, but luckily for him there were fire trucks and sirens blaring on the next street over. He rushed back into the pizzeria after dragging the body around Sal's Lincoln, leaving it in the street.

Ben and Sal spoke in hushed voices near the door once it was secure. They agreed on covering the storefront window in newspaper and gathering everyone in the kitchen. Lucy switched a small television set on to the news, but the information was all emergency instructions to *stay inside and isolate yourself from those who exhibit signs of illness.*

Two of the female employees sat, huddled together and weeping near the freezer. A male employee paced behind Lucy, biting his nails. Sal's cell phone rang on the counter and startled everyone. Lucy ran to it and read the name across the screen.

Marco.

Sal and Lucy's boy, Marco, was the model son; perfect grades, an amazing athlete, and he helped out in the community during his free time. He was to graduate this year from Franklin High School and go to Florida State University on a full football scholarship. Both parents shared the dream of their son being in the NFL someday.

"Sal!" Her voice echoed through the pizzeria and Sal rushed into the kitchen followed by Ben.

Lucy put the cell phone on speaker mode. "*¡Mijo!*" Lucy squealed into the phone.

"Hey!" Sal couldn't help but be overjoyed and joined his wife on the phone.

"Ma? You guys?" Marco's voice crackled through the speaker, he sounded elated. *"You guys are alright?"*

"Yeah yeah, we are fine, where are you?" Sal asked his son.

"Look, I'm with some friends, I'm sorry you guys, we skipped school today, please don't be mad. I'm stuck on the bridge. It's crazy out here!"

The reception of the call was terrible and it felt like a miracle it had even gone through.

"Listen to me." Sal's voice became very stern. "I don't care what you did today, but you need to get home. Get off that bridge, Marco. I think you need to get out and walk."

Marco responded but his voice was too warbled to make out what he said.

Lucy began to cry and Sal hushed her quickly.

"Marco? You still there?"

"Yeah, I don't know if I want to walk. The radio is saying crazy things, I have no idea what's going on, people are just going nuts, dad."

"Marco you need to get off that highway, you need to get away from all those other people on the roads!"

Another voice was heard through the speaker, one of Marco's friends in the car.

"What...going...ahead." The voice was very broken up. *"Dad! Are you there? Something is wrong."*

"Marco? What is it baby?" Lucy was in full-on panic mode, her hands shaking, her lips quivering.

Marco's friends began yelling in the car. Lucy and Sal were screaming, demanding he tell them what was going on. Marco's voice was full of panic as he explained that people were getting out of their cars and running, some people were jumping off the bridge, others were attacking each other.

The call quality had dropped sharply. Marco began yelling and cursing, cutting in and out. Screams of horror, guttural growls, and dead silence immediately followed.

They never heard from their son again.

THE BREADWINNER

I

"Government Officials are asking everyone to please stay indoors during this time. A state of emergency has been declared for the following counties..."

The television blared from the living room in the small apartment that the Williams family shared in the heart of Columbia Beach City. James, the man of the house, sat on the couch with his bright eyes glued to the television set, attempting to make sense of the sudden sickness that seemed to be overtaking the world around him. Outbreaks of violence and looting were taking over the city; schools were closed, people were urged to stay home from work, and there were talks of a curfew being set country-wide. No matter what channel James stopped on, news anchors all had the same blank faces as they spoke. Their job was to give the people the news, not react to it, but it was becoming hard not to.

James' daughter Veronica was in her room down the hallway, chatting on the computer. The TV set was so loud; she could hear its muffled sound through the music she played on her laptop. With a sigh, she got up and slammed her bedroom door. She rummaged through the odds and ends strewn about her desk and found her bright pink headphones. Stuffing them into her ears, she flung herself onto her bed, plugged them in, and went back to Facebook messaging her friend Dee.

Deeeva95: *I can't believe how my mom is acting!! She won't even let me come over...I'm so bored I could kill myself.* ☹

Vr0n: *I know right? My dad has the TV on 24/7, it's gettin on my nerves like woah.*

Deeeva95: *Oh well, at least we don't have school again tomorrow!*

VrOn: *Yeah...but I'm totally pissed that track has been cancelled for like, what, almost a week now? This whole thing will blow over and all the crazies will disappear and then I'll lose my next three races.*

Deeeva95: *Quit bein dramatic, you sound like my mother.*

VrOn: *Lol, whatever, you know I gotta get my run on!*

Deeeva95: *Ugh, I gtg ☹ my mom wants me to be miserable with her and watch the news.*

VrOn: *Ahaha ok, text me later.*

Veronica sighed as she closed out the screen; nobody else seemed to be online from her friend's list. "Lame!" she shouted and threw her headphones down on the comforter. Nothing was on TV for days now, it was all the same emergency news casts on every channel, and unfortunately for her, they couldn't afford HBO or any of the other premiums. She wondered what Isaac was up to and got up to find out when she heard a loud crash from outside. She jumped and then laughed at herself for being startled so easily. Some idiot had crashed into the telephone pole right across the street from her building.

"Holy shit," she muttered, scanning the streets for any sign of panic, but nobody seemed too bothered by it. The few people out on the street were ignoring the car as if nothing happened, going about their business, but a lot faster than they normally would have. She let the curtain fall back into place and walked out of her room. Isaac's door across the hall was closed. She knocked and didn't get an answer. She shrugged and walked out to the living room. Her father and brother sat on the couch, eyes fixed on the television screen.

"Will y'all please quit watching that already?" she said as she walked to the tiny three point kitchen, grabbing a water from the fridge. "Somebody crashed their car right across the street but everybody's probably too busy watching the TV to care." She unscrewed the bottle top.

Her father James, noticing the beverage choice, quickly snapped, "Look, let the police worry about that kind of stuff and put the water back. Now. Drink a soda."

"Dad, you know I don't like—"

"I don't care, we need the water, V. Put it back, please." He turned back to the TV set. Isaac looked at her and pointed at the fridge, winking. She smiled as she opened the door and pretended to put the water back. Then she walked quietly into the living room and stood behind them.

"If you come into contact with any person who is exhibiting signs of violence or sickness,

it is extremely important that you isolate them and contact your local authorities. Help will be on the way shortly," the red haired news anchor announced.

Veronica narrowed her eyes, "Isn't violent and sick half the world's population already?" she remarked.

Her father turned to look at her and noticed the water bottle. "Damn it, V."

"What?" She giggled as she took another sip. "You can't stay mad at me, Pops!"

He shook his head and sighed. "I know darlin', but things are lookin' pretty bad out there. I just want to have enough supplies on hand for you and your brother in case it gets too dangerous and we can't leave."

"Dad." Veronica drew the word out, placing a hand on her small hip. She took another sip. "You watch too much television."

She walked over to the small window near the balcony door and pulled the blinds down a bit, trying to get another look at the crashed car. The driver's side door was open, but there was no driver to be seen. A few more people were out that she could see now, and Veronica thought they looked like a bunch of panicked rats, running around in the street with nowhere to go. She flipped the blinds back up and scowled at her brother and father. "I guess everybody out there watches too much television, too."

That night Veronica found it very hard to sleep. She kept getting up and peeking out her window, trying to see what was going on. Every so often she would hear people yelling, like they were fighting, and she almost got nervous enough to wake her father. She slept with her headphones in, her music playing, and dreamt of monsters in her closet.

II

"This shit is ridiculous," Isaac mumbled as he threw his smartphone to the table. "I haven't been able to get a text out all day." Veronica's older brother plopped down onto the dining room chair with a grunt and scrunched his nose up at her.

"Mine's no different," she responded without looking up from her laptop. Veronica had been trying to get a hold of Dee for over a day, but was getting no response. "Nobody's been getting online. And the people that have been on...I can't even get through to them." She furiously typed messages that never sent due to server errors or consistent time-outs.

Their father walked into the kitchen buckling his belt, eyes glued to the television in the living room as he did so. "I hate to break it to you kids," James said as he pulled his shoes on, "but it looks as if the Internet might be down for now." He motioned to the other room where a news anchor nervously announced that the government was "temporarily suspending cell phone and internet connections in certain parts of the country in order to maintain emergency lines."

"I don't understand dad! They just want to cut people off?" Veronica looked at him with pleading eyes. "What is even going on anyway? A couple people get a fever and beat each other up, and the rest of us have to suffer?"

"V, it's a little more complicated I'm afraid." He walked over and placed a large hand on his daughter's soft, dark hair. "It seems like things are getting a little scary out there, and it's time you two kids and I had a discussion about it."

Veronica thought back to the night before and remembered the screaming in the streets.

Isaac got up and walked over to the sliding door of their apartment that led to the balcony. He pulled back one of the blinds and stared. "I watched enough of the news with you dad, and I know that this is just like any of those hurricane warnings they send our way." He dropped the blind and turned toward his father. "It's a bunch of media hyped mumbo jumbo that they're cryin' wolf about so that they can scare people into spendin' a chunk of money they don't have in order to stimulate the economy." He stuck his hands in his pockets and rolled his eyes, looking at his sister. "Or some shit."

"There you go." Veronica smiled at her brother, closing her laptop. "Gettin' all smart on us." She giggled to herself and Isaac gave her the finger.

James, displeased with his children's vulgarity toward each another pulled the remaining dining room chair out and sat down in it, slamming his big fist down on the table. Not in anger, but as a warning. "You two need to quit it now." His deep voice filled the apartment only the way a father's concerned voice could. "You know I don't like you usin' that language around your sister, and I think you need to go ahead and sit back down with me. We are going to have this discussion."

"Yes, sir," Isaac mumbled as he returned to his seat at the small wooden table. The siblings, only two years apart, Veronica at sixteen and Isaac at eighteen, looked as though they could be twins, and neither of them looked as if they belonged to their father.

James was a shorter build, muscular, with sandy blonde hair and small green eyes. Veronica and Isaac were tall and lanky with catlike brown eyes, dark olive-skin, and chocolate brown hair. They were the spitting image of their departed mother.

James grabbed the remote off the table and lowered the volume on the flat-screen. The family had little by the means of nicer electronics, but James made sure his kids had the entertainment he thought they deserved. And by deserved, he made sure they had enough to keep the other kids from making fun of them when they came over. Times had been tough since Nina had given up the long battle to breast cancer three years earlier, but James had taken up a second job and tried to keep his children as comfortable as he possibly could since moving to into the small apartment in the city.

"Look, kids," he started, wringing his hands, unnerved by the conversation he was about to have. "I know it doesn't seem so serious to y'all right now, but whatever's hittin' this country," he said, glancing at Veronica to make sure she was listening, "it's hittin' us awfully hard, and it's happening right outside."

Veronica was the ace of the two children: fantastic grades, excelled in track and basketball, a nice group of friends. She was a natural-born leader with a good head on her shoulders. Isaac, on the other hand, had failed his sophomore year in high school and was kicked off the football team for poor test scores. His friends were into heavy drinking and experimenting with drugs, and James had to struggle to keep Isaac from following suit. Before the country's current crisis had even erupted, Isaac was enduring his second out-of-school suspension of his senior year.

One more, the principal had warned, *and he is out.*

"So there's a sickness. I get that." Veronica twisted a strand of her hair nervously, catching onto her father's uneasiness. "But isn't it just gonna pass? I mean, I know what they're sayin', they're sayin' people are attacking one another, eating one another. But who in the world just decides to start *eating* their neighbor?" She put an emphasis on eating as she continued talking. "But seriously, this just sounds like Isaac said, a bunch of hype they're tryin' to get us to buy into. I mean, I'm okay with them cancelling school and all, but there's been three accidents on our street in two days, and they're not even cleaning it up. Why are they tryin' to scare us like this?" She looked over at her brother, who was busy with his phone despite knowing it would not work. "If they're tryin' to scare us, it's working a little, but I don't see the point in shutting off our Internet." She rolled her eyes and sat back in the chair when she was done speaking.

"I know, I know, it seems crazy and pointless," James started with a soft smile, "but if this is as serious as they're making it out to be, then we need to just be patient and concentrate on the important stuff. Maybe right now, we need to take it seriously, just in case." He noticed his son wasn't paying attention and thought of Eliza, his son's girlfriend. "Look kiddo, I know you're worried about her."

Isaac looked up at his father with a scowl.

"I don't even know where she is," Isaac mumbled. "There's a bunch of crazy shit—sorry, stuff—happening out there, and she could be anywhere!" Isaac realized he was raising his voice and thought of his mother, she'd always taught them that when family discussion was in order, they never, under any circumstances, raise their voices at one another. "I'm just pissed is all dad, I wanna check in on her."

"I know, son, but you need to realize Eliza is more than likely with her mom and dad, and she's probably having a similar conversation with them, like we're having right now." He placed a reassuring hand on his son's from across the table. "What you two need to be concerned about right now though, is each other. Not your friends, or girlfriends or whoever, you need to worry about the people sitting next to you."

"Well, yeah dad, I know that. But are you ok?" Concern suddenly haunted Veronica's voice.

"I'm ok, V," James answered with a nod. "I'm not worried about me. I'm more worried about are the two of you being able to handle what we're supposed to be preparing for. James got up from the table, taking the remote in his hand. He motioned for the kids to follow him to the living room and have a seat on the couch. Isaac followed while Veronica paced behind the couch.

He turned to the local news, cutting off the recycled politically-correct garbage for a more honest channel and clicked the volume up a couple notches.

The local news anchor, an extremely slender and very beautiful black field reporter, filled the screen. She stood in the county college's baseball field and spoke about the current status of Oceana County affecting the local sport season, as if trying to take the edge off of what was soon to come. The way she spoke seemed serene, almost normal, as if she knew the whole thing was just a hoax to begin with. While she was speaking, a fight broke out behind her and was escalating quickly. The screen immediately cut to an in-studio anchorman announcing breaking news.

"*As we have been discussing,*" the pale-faced anchorman announced, "*we have breaking news from government officials. A curfew of six pm will be enforced in accordance with yesterday's declaration of a state of emergency. Any person on the street after the restricted hour will be taken into police custody. On a national level, the president has announced a nationwide school and work suspension. Any person outside of their homes between the hours of six pm and ten am will be detained by local authority. Even during authorized hours, we are urging you to remain in your homes regardless, unless absolutely necessary.*"

Veronica scrunched her nose up at the news report. "Are they serious? They can't be serious." She looked nervously at her brother who shook his head in response. He was obviously angrier about this than he was about his cell phone.

"*Government and CDC officials will be on-hand at local markets and pharmacies to monitor the distribution of goods to local residents. These scheduled supply handouts will be on a first come, first served basis between the hours of ten am and six pm. Again, we need to urge you to remain in your homes. We also remind you that any non-government official found on the streets between the hours of six and ten will be taken into police custody."*

The three family members watched and listened in awe as the news report continued. They saw the downtown of their own city transformed into some sort of militarized zone as the local news flashed footage of different sections of Columbia Beach City onto their television. Barricades were set up, the high school that Veronica and Isaac attended downtown had been turned into a temporary medical facility and people rallied around the edges, screaming and protesting the actions the government was taking, or rather, the lack thereof. The news reiterated the fact that officials were arresting rioters by showing people being pepper sprayed and put in handcuffs and zip ties.

The pale-faced news anchor returned to the screen. *"As we've previously stated, if you come into contact with anyone exhibiting signs of violence or infection, please isolate the victim and contact your local authorities. Do not leave your homes to go to the hospital for any reason. Local hospitals have been closed to the public. Please contact the authorities and medical personnel will come to you."*

"So they changed sick to *infected.*" Isaac stared absent mindedly at the screen, his eyes flat.

"And they closed the hospitals?" Veronica couldn't believe what she was hearing.

"What exactly are people being *infected* with?" Isaac looked at his father.

James had no answer for his son. He continued to watch the screen as an advertisement from the CDC on the importance of hand-washing came on.

"I don't understand." Isaac grabbed the remote from his father and began channel flipping. Veronica stood behind the two of them, chewing her fingernails. With every channel Isaac turned to, the same thing was repeated over and over, only in different words and by different people. He stopped briefly when he spotted an interview with a local attorney.

"This is your biggest case of the year. How do you feel the current crisis will affect the trial, Mr. Eckhart?" the pretty blonde reporter shouted over the crowd around the courthouse.

"So what, we've got a curfew and we've got a bunch of nuts running around. It's good for business," the cocky attorney responded. *"I've yet to see any government regulation predict my client's fate in court."* The lawyer quickly shuffled his client and assistants through the crowd, raising a hand and shooing off any other reporters with questions.

"See?" Isaac looked at his father. "That guy seems okay with everything."

James ignored his son's remark and took the remote from him, continuing to flip through the channels when Veronica yelled for him to stop.

To her dismay, the horror of the television screen displayed her friend Dee's entire subdivision engulfed in flames, just a few miles from where Veronica lived. Firemen ran about the streets, attempting to put out the massive blaze, and reporters shouted above the ruckus. It appeared as though every house was ablaze. Before the network had the chance to cut the broadcast, a resident of the community managed to grab the microphone.

"Get out! They don't have it under control!"

The reporter whose mic had been stolen fought with the crazed resident to gain it back.

"I'm telling you! Get out!" the man screamed and slammed his fist into the field reporter's jaw. *"They're killing everyone! Eating everyone! It's spreading! They don't know how to stop it! You need to get out of the city!"*

No matter how hard the mad-man of the burning subdivision tried to get his message out to the people of Columbia Beach City, the network cut the feed, and Channel 23 went offline for good.

III

It was as if the entire world had changed in a just a few hours. Nobody slept the night the local news networks cut their broadcasts. National channels stayed on, but were no longer reporting live. Generic messages were put up, replacing apprehensive news anchors' faces, messages instructing people to stay wherever they were and await the arrival of emergency and military personnel. Every radio station played the same emergency broadcast as the last. The message was the same, no matter where they checked.

Remain in your homes. Isolate yourselves from those who were exhibiting signs of bizarre or violent behavior.

Except the AM radio stations, that were full of crazies quoting Bible verses and begging sinners to repent. There was no useful information anywhere.

The day wore on, and Veronica watched the devastation unfold in the streets outside her bedroom window. People chased one another down the street, screaming and attacking whomever they could get their hands on. The violence and number of people in the streets doubled over night.

The residents of the city were tearing each other apart. Car wrecks littered the street and smoke hid the horizon. The mad man's words from the last news cast she would ever see echoed through her brain.

"Killing everyone. Eating everyone."

She felt the presence of someone behind her but couldn't seem to take her eyes off the scene.

"It's almost dinner time, pumpkin. Come on away from the window."

Veronica didn't turn to look at her father. She felt a swell of emotion come and go and thought for a split second that she would cry, but it was replaced once more with shock and emptiness. "Are they really eating each other, dad?" Her voice was barely a whisper.

James walked over to his daughter and placed an arm around her shoulder, gently pulling her away from the window. The curtain gracefully fell back into place and the horror from the outside world was gone from Veronica's view, but not from her mind. He hugged her tightly and kissed her forehead. "I don't know darlin', but you're gonna be just fine ok?" He stepped back to look at her face.

She met his gaze and mustered up a smile, she always felt like a little girl again in her father's arms. "Thanks, dad."

"Come on now, let's go bug your brother."

Veronica and her father entered the living room to find Isaac staring at the television set.

"Did you memorize that emergency message yet, son?" James walked to the kitchen and began to strain spaghetti in the sink. Isaac didn't respond.

Veronica walked toward the sliding glass door that led to the balcony but her father stopped her before she could resume the previous position from her bedroom window.

"No ma'am, I need you to go on ahead and set the table for me please."

That was one of the qualities she admired the most in her father. No matter what was going on, he was as cool as could be. She quietly removed plates and silverware from the cabinets and drawers while her father opened a can of pasta sauce and finished preparing the family's simple meal. She zoned out while cleaning a smudge off a fork and thought of her father's behavior when her mother had passed. Even then, he'd made sure he never fell apart in front of her or Isaac. If there was one person who could ever set an example, it was James.

Everyone jumped when a loud crash came from above. Isaac popped up off the couch and stared at the ceiling. James set the pot down and put a finger up to his lips. The trio was frozen in place; waiting, listening.

Another loud crash came moments later, followed by a loud yell and frantic footsteps. Isaac started to say something and his father motioned for him to keep quiet. A door slammed and an animalistic scream ripped through the walls, with more pounding footsteps and what sounded like someone slamming themselves into the doors and walls of the apartment above theirs.

Veronica took a deep breath and exhaled slowly, shaking her head. Tears had snuck their way into her eyes and she blinked them away as she set the fork she had been clutching down onto the napkin before her. The noise upstairs continued relentlessly.

"The people from the street," Isaac whispered, "did they get inside?"

Veronica placed the third and final fork down on its cloth napkin. "They aren't people." She turned to look at her brother's panicked face. "And they didn't get in from the street. Somebody upstairs just didn't follow instructions."

James nodded to himself, silently agreeing with his daughter, yet mildly disturbed at how unfazed she seemed by it all, at how hollow her voice suddenly sounded. How long had she sat at her window and watched the city destroy itself? He knew it was pointless to wonder what exactly was causing people to turn into savage monsters and attack the closest living thing to them, but he figured a teenage girl would at least be asking questions, not giving answers to her older brother.

He filled each plate with the contents of the pot and decided it was better for him to thank his lucky stars that his daughter was smart enough to assess and understand than panic and react to things foolishly. She'd always been that way, even when her mother had passed.

They ate dinner without speaking. The demonic screams from above were joined by a man yelling for his life at the sounds of a door cracking from its frame. His screams eventually stopped and the apartment was silent once more.

Veronica thought of Dee and her other friends, her teachers, and even the cute guy at the bagel shop down the street and hoped they were safe. Either safe or dead in the way that meant they wouldn't come back.

Earlier in the day she'd watched as a man who could have been a linebacker was taken down by two men half his size in the middle of the street. People ran right by him, chased by others or in search of safety. The gun he'd so desperately tried to fire into the faces of his attackers flew to the pavement as his arms were torn off by quick hands and hungry mouths. The large man's screams had fallen on deaf ears as he bled out on the street. What seemed like only a minute later, the man struggled to his feet, armless and disoriented.

Her mouth had fallen open at the sight. At first, she wanted to call out to her father or brother, to have someone help this man who had somehow survived this brutal attack, but she stopped herself as he roared like a wild animal at a family moving slowly along the cross street. She didn't look away. She couldn't look away, as he ferociously chased them out of sight.

IV

Samson had found himself in a bit of trouble; almost all the resources at his disposal had been exhausted, and he couldn't risk having his wife, Moira, leave the safety of their gated community.

The woman wouldn't even know what to do with herself out here.

As Samson made his way toward Paradise Bay in search of food and other survivors, he'd been enjoying the peace and quiet of the empty street when he heard the low moan behind him. He turned quickly in the tree-lined street, raising his 9mm. Samson hated guns, he loathed the men he'd defended in court who had used them in cold blood. Back then it was a paycheck, and now it meant defending his life.

Before him staggered the corpse of what once was a woman. Her soiled clothing hung from her emaciated frame, only one shoe on and half her right hand missing. The thing hissed and groaned, stumbling over its own pathetic feet, but never breaking eye contact. He lowered his gun, *She's a slow one.*

He pulled his titanium sport diving knife from its sheath, his hands shaking, but he knew what needed to be done. He walked over to an abandoned Chevy Cobalt, the only car on the road, and laid his pistol on the hood. Wiping the sweat from his brow he took in a deep breath. Despite the dead woman shambling toward him, the day was beautiful. Seventy-five degrees and sunny. The faint smell of honeysuckle met him on the breeze in front of the empty gas station, and the birds, busy in their trees, sounded lovely.

The woman groaned again and he snapped out of his daze, dropping his bag on the street beside the yellow car. As Samson drew nearer to the walking corpse, its eyes grew wide, its mouth agape. He raised the diving knife in his left hand and froze at the sound of another moan off to his left. The hair on his arms rose and he stepped back, turning in the direction of the sound. He scanned the woods; movement, but no need for panic. He raised the knife once more and brought it down in one strong fluid motion exhaling with a yell as the knife plunged deep into her skull. The woman collapsed in a heap, black blood dribbling from the wound as he yanked the knife from her head.

Samson only had a moment to gaze down at the now-still corpse below him, her gray, lifeless eyes forever fixed on the sky. In that moment, he imagined the state of consternation his wife would have been in, were she there. Moira would have run screaming from the sight of the thing, but had she witnessed Samson disposing of the creature, the woman would have soiled herself in the street. He smiled.

The moan he had previously heard to his left was soon joined by both a low growl and a high pitched wail. His smile became a scowl.

"Shit!"

Samson wiped the blood from the knife onto his pants and made a run for the Cobalt. The trees were alive with movement and the wails of the recently infected. The fast ones were the fresh ones, the ones he needed to worry about. He ran into a lot of them in the first few days, and they must have heard him shout as he was taking care of the woman on the street. Samson grabbed his gun and bag, crouching down on the side of the car, out of sight.

The first of the newly-dead emerged in lightning fast fury from the woods, growling and spitting as it looked around for prey. It had been a middle-aged man, wearing torn business attire, and it sported a gaping neck wound the size of Samson's fist. He looked around, dog-like noises escaping his ravenous and drooling mouth. Samson's heart was pounding in his chest so hard he was afraid the beast could hear it. He peeked through the Cobalt's backseat windows to the gas station, but ducked back down when another eater joined the business man. This one, a shrieking woman, barefoot in what was left of a blood-stained pin-striped suit.

Her lips were gone, exposing her teeth and turning her face into a permanent grimace. What was once the woman's chest was now a cavity of gore. The two eaters howled and frantically looked around the area, their movements jerky and quick. The business woman spotted the corpse Samson had just killed and moved toward it. The initial low moan Samson heard from the trees came once more as another eater joined the pair, but this one was like the woman he killed, slow and less oriented than the other two. It was almost comical, seeing the ferocity of the business couple in contrast to the lethargic thing that had joined them, but all just as deadly. They moved in a circle, seeming to sniff the air, thankfully too stupid and too hungry to realize just yet where he had run to.

Samson was trapped beside the Chevy with only two options: try for three perfect headshots, or run to the gas station with the high hopes that the safety of its walls was accessible. He mustered up the courage to steal another glance at the building. Having only been to a shooting range once before, and not fairing very well then, his luck with the gas station seemed to outweigh the headshot option. He opened his bag and grabbed a can of Pepsi from inside it, shaking the drink up.

Here we go, he thought as he reared his arm back and pitched the can over the car. The force of the can hitting the ground wasn't enough to make it explode as he'd planned, but the noise was enough to sow confusion amidst the trio and give him a decent opportunity to run for the gas station. With his bag on his shoulder and his gun in his hand, he sprinted toward the building and didn't look back.

The business woman noticed him first and let out a bloodcurdling scream, followed by the guttural growl of the business man. The two were after him and running almost as fast as he was by the time he reached the front doors of the gas station. He yanked on the door. Locked.

"Fuckin' figures."

Samson ran around the back of the building, passing a beat-up Ford truck, silently willing the back door to somehow be unlocked. He reached the rear, hearing the pounding footsteps of the business couple gaining on him. To his absolute shock, the back door of the gas station flew open and he was greeted by the barrel of a shotgun. The elderly man lowered his shotgun momentarily and squinted at Samson.

"Boy, you better be fuckin worth it." He pulled Samson inside and fired one magnificent round into the business woman's head before slamming the door shut and encasing them in safety.

V

Samson lay on the cement floor of the gas station's utility room, breathless. He stared with wild eyes at the man who had saved his life. He was an older man with a messy crop of white hair atop his head. The man pushed on the door with his foot, checking that it was secure. The eater outside frantically clawed and pounded on the door.

"Jesus Christ, I think I'm gonna puke." Samson got on all fours and spit on the cold floor beneath him. The room was filled with shelves of random automobile items and miscellaneous junk that no one had any use for any more. It smelled of stale cigarettes and piss.

"Well, son," the man said, turning to look down at Samson, "I'd appreciate you do so elsewhere." The man walked over to a door and swung it open, revealing a small room with a toilet and a basin sink. "No light, but you can borrow the camp torch." He motioned to the source of light on a table to his left. "Hell, you probably won't need much encouragement from your gut with a smell like that." The man chuckled to himself as he shut the door and walked to the small wooden table.

Samson coughed a few times. The smell that had emanated from the room was almost enough to make him go back outside. He sat back on his heels and brushed his hands on his thighs. The man had himself a seat on a metal folding chair, a Remington 870 resting in his lap, pointed straight at him. His face was covered in wrinkles, and a faded but still prominent scar ran across his neck. The man's right eye was ghostly, blind from either age or from incident or misadventure. Samson didn't want to know.

"Uh, nice gun you got there, sir." Samson eyed the weapon, and the man, cautiously. He looked like the criminal type. *But would this man have risked his own life just to take mine?* "Thank you." Samson cleared his throat and spoke again, his palms sweating. "For uh, saving me, you know."

The old man nodded, never taking his eye off Samson's hands. "You got anything useful in that there pack other than another soda can?" The man laughed wildly at his crack at Samson. "That was a good move out there though, I tell you what." His thick southern accent and jargon reminded Samson of his mother's father. He was a real good old boy, about as racist and country proud as you could find. Samson pegged him as either the hate crime type or a wife beater.

Samson slowly reached for his bag, opened it up and dumped its contents onto the ground. Three cans of Pepsi, four packs of crackers and cheese, and a bottle of ibuprofen. "I've got my knife on me, and as you can see, my gun is on the floor. I'll be no trouble sir, I can promise you that. But what I will ask is what the fuck do we do about the dead outside who keep knocking to come in?" Samson kept his voice low, but stern. He felt like a pussy for nearly losing his breakfast in front of the menacing stranger with the shotgun pointed at him.

"There ain't nothin' to be done about them out there." The old man quickly glanced toward the emergency exit door. "I'm not wasting my ammunition, and eventually they get bored. They're like wild dogs." The man reached into his right button down shirt pocket and pulled out a pack of Marlboro Reds. The left side of the shirt had the name AL embroidered on it. "Smoke?" He held the pack out to Samson.

"No, thanks." Samson declined; he'd quit six years before. End of the world or not, it had been one of his biggest accomplishments.

"Well like I was sayin', they're like dogs." The man spoke through a cigarette held between his lips as he pulled a lighter from the pack, never taking his left hand off the shotgun.

"How so?" Samson asked.

"They just wanna eat. And they only come near people cuz they wanna eat." He exhaled and tempting secondhand smoke filled the room. "When they see their food is gone and their beggin' ain't gettin' them nowhere, they move on."

Samson nodded. He hadn't really ever compared them to anything before, other than monsters he'd only ever seen in horror films. The two men sat in silence for a good while, and Samson's legs began to grow numb underneath him and he stretched them out before him. The persistent banging at the door had reduced to a scratching and a knock every now and then. Samson looked from the door to the man and back to the door again. He could hear a faint growl, almost the sound of frustration. "Looks like you're right, I guess." He shrugged his shoulders and rubbed his legs. "I'm assuming from the name on your shirt, that you would be Al. Am I right, sir?"

The old man scoffed, "What's with all the formalities? Ain't you seen the world's gone to shit? People are eatin' each other."

"Well, that's just who I am. Sir." Samson put more emphasis on the word, now that he knew it irked the old guy. "A lot might have changed. And I may have changed for the most part with it, but I'll hang onto the formalities for as long as I can, thank you very much." He smirked as he finished his sentence. For whatever reason, he could tell the old man didn't care for him at all. Maybe it was Samson's sudden arrogance in the face of his gun, maybe it was the $200 hiking boots that he wore in spite of the apocalypse, or maybe the guy could just tell he was a lawyer.

End of the world or not, nobody liked lawyers.

"Yep. Friends called me Al, family called me Al, everybody called me Al." Al dropped his cigarette to the floor and stepped on it. There were dozens of butts that Samson hadn't noticed until then. "And you can call me Al too."

"I'm pleased to meet you, Al. I'm Samson, but my wife calls me Sammy, and you can call me Sam. I'd get up and shake your hand," Samson said, stealing a glance at the gun, "but I'd hate for you to waste any shells." Samson smirked as Al narrowed his eyes and very slowly took the gun from his lap and placed it on the table. "Thank you, Al."

"Don't mention it." Al lit up another cigarette and held the pack out once more, offering what he had figured out to be his forbidden fruit. Samson shook his head, declining. "You travel pretty light there Sam."

"Cracker?" Samson asked as he collected the contents of his bag from the floor and put everything back in its place. Al didn't respond, so Samson took that as a no and zipped up the bag. "I live just a few miles from here. Franklin Woods."

"Oh!" Al clapped his hands once in delight. "Well fuck me, I knew it! You one of them rich folk!" Al had himself a good laugh followed by a coughing fit. When he was through, he wiped his eyes as if tears had filled them. "And tell me, Sam, your card get declined at the Franklin grocery store?"

Samson felt his face grow hot. Not out of embarrassment, but out of anger, and shame. The type of shame that a man felt for hating another man simply because he was poor white trash. He'd been correct in his assumptions about Al after all. "No sir, power's been out for some time now." He looked up at the lights and raised an eyebrow.

"Well, no shit there, bud."

"Unfortunate thing about the farmer's market, fresh food spoils quickly, and what kind of man would I be if I couldn't feed my family?" Samson worked each finger slowly, cracking his knuckles one by one as he spoke.

"Well, excuse me Sam, I didn't know you was tryin' to feed your family." Al's statement was hard to read. Samson couldn't tell if he was being remorseful or further pushing his boundaries.

"No worries, Al. I'm just trying to be a good father. But more importantly, I'm trying to be a good husband, because if those things out there don't kill me, my wife sure will."

Al had a genuine laugh at Samson's remark, enough so that Samson even had to laugh. "I don't think I could take another day of my Moira screaming. Telling me that I'm the breadwinner, I'm the one who is to provide for our family, and that if I were a real man, our children wouldn't be starving to death." No laughter followed Samson's last remark.

Al leaned forward, placing his elbows on his knees and rubbed his brow. He looked up at Samson, "This wife of yours, she a spoiled one huh?"

"She's provided for." Samson kept his face stern, knowing the old man was trying to test him.

"I bet she's a real looker. What are you, a doctor? Yeah, yeah!" Al sat back again, licking his lips and grinning. "Bet you one of them rich-ass doctors sittin' pretty at the end of the world, playin' ball with your kids in the yard and fuckin' that wife of yours at night while the rest of us rot out here."

"That's enough!" Samson snapped, seething with anger and disgust. He felt his stomach drop at the mention of any activity with his children from Al's lips. He was ready to jump on him and blow his head off but he kept himself calm, kept himself still. He thought of his wife, how absolutely bat-shit crazy she'd always been, but even more so now that the world had fallen apart. He didn't want to put Moira in any kind of danger, but he *did* want to put Al in a bad place.

"Hey bud," Al said, putting his hands up and batting his eyes, "I'm just tellin' it like it is."

"Yeah, I bet you fuckin' are." Samson moved to get up but Al had the shotgun back on him in no time.

"Hold on there, where ya think you're goin'?" Al's grin was disturbing.

"What exactly did you rescue me for, Al?" Samson glared at him.

"Well, Sam, just go on and calm down now. Have a seat back down."

Samson slowly lowered himself back to the concrete floor as Al continued.

"How exactly you think I been survivin' in here? People don't exactly drive up to this ol' piss hole to fill 'er up any more these days. So I do what I always done best: I trap 'em and I rob 'em, and then I go ahead and feed 'em to the dogs." Al wasn't grinning anymore.

Samson cursed himself for not being able to recognize exactly what kind of criminal the man was. He was a murderer and a thief, and Samson should have known better, but he did know exactly what Al would say next.

"But now that I know that you got yourself a pretty little wife back there in Franklin, I think I'll have you take me on up there to visit. Whaddya say?"

"Listen sir, you've done me the courtesy of providing me shelter when my life was in danger, and you haven't directly threatened me. So I'd be more than willing to do the courtesy of providing you with a home cooked meal and a bed in my family home. There's no need for things to get out of hand."

Al kept the shotgun on him. "You done?" Samson nodded, encouraging him to continue. "Well, I tell you what. You do as I say, no fancy shit, things are gonna be just fine. Your kids better not say a word, your wife better have some great tits on her, and you better be alright with me walkin' right on in and runnin' the show."

Samson nodded again, but this time more slowly.

Al packed a few things into a satchel before they left, and kept the gun trained on Samson as they moved toward the front of the station. The dead still lingered at the rear of the building and it would be a clean break out the front. They'd be more easily disposed of now that the odds were a little more even.

As Al unlocked the door, the shotgun still trained on Samson, he reminded him,

"Don't forget what I said back there, and things…in your words, won't get out of hand."

Samson narrowed his dark blue eyes at him and smiled. "You're gonna love my family."

VI

Nearly two weeks passed before they ran out of food, and the power had already gone out in the city. Hindsight 20/20, James shouldn't have procrastinated on the grocery shopping.

"I think it's absolutely insane and if you're going to leave, we should just all go together and leave the city," Veronica said.

James had decided to make a food run to the small grocer around the block and Veronica was not happy about it. She had protested and argued, begged him to get out of the city. Isaac sulked on the couch after being turned down three times when he told his father he was going to accompany him...and suggested maybe running by Eliza's.

"Now, you know what I already told you about Eliza. You need to sit tight and take care of your sister," James told his son. "I'll be back before you know it."

But James knew damn well that Isaac was the one that needed Veronica to take care of him, and he hated to admit it to himself, but his son would only slow him down. James knew what he needed, knew exactly where it was, and if all went according to plan, he could be there and back within ten minutes.

Veronica winced when she saw her father pull out his old Browning A-Bolt. "I don't suppose you'll be shooting any deer with that." She tried to smile to hide the fact that she wanted to throw up all over the room.

"I don't suppose so, V." Her father nodded at her and she nodded back.

Isaac had joined them near the door now, still disappointed in his father's decision to leave him behind, but dreading the moment his father walked out that door. "You promise me I get to be the one that totes the rifle next time, old man." He smiled at his father, wishing he wouldn't go.

"Only if you promise not to whine like a baby girl." His father smiled back at him and gripped his shoulder tightly. Veronica joined them at the door to embrace her father and soon thereafter closed it behind him.

*

The apartment building halls and stairwell were empty as James left. He considered himself lucky that the dead apparently could not turn doorknobs, considering all the noises he'd been hearing from his neighbors over the past few days. He swallowed the lump in his throat as he exited the dark stairwell on the ground floor and approached the front door of the building, wondering what might be waiting to greet him on the other side.

The street was littered with debris and the air was alive with alarms.

Car, fire, police, ambulance, you name it.

Any noise he made would be drowned out, and he was perfectly okay with this.

He moved faster than he ever had in his life, ignoring anyone running around him or the screams that carried on the wind. He didn't care who he was seen by because he didn't plan to be on the street for very long. A pang of guilt hit him hard when he saw out of the corner of his eye a woman being attacked across the street. He knew he didn't have the time to help her.

He kept going.

The grocer's door was a mere twenty feet down the block and he silently prayed that no one had had the sense to barricade themselves inside.

"Fuck," James said to himself as he noticed a man bent over an unmoving body on the curb up ahead. The man was savagely feeding on it; the body and face were so badly mangled from the thing's feast that James could not tell if it had once been a man or a woman.

He slowed his steps and quietly maneuvered around the gory scene. He had almost cleared the beast without being noticed when gunfire erupted from the streets up ahead. The eater on the curb snapped his blood soaked face up and growled.

His eyes locked with James' and a wail escaped his mouth, spitting chunks of flesh and blood at him. James raised his rifle but paused, thinking about the unwanted attention it could draw, and ran for the grocer's door instead. He charged inside, his heart fluttered and he couldn't help but feel relief and excitement that the entrance had been left unlocked. He spun around toward the door and the eater that was after him came charging through.

James swung the butt of his rifle up, cracking the thing's jaw. The eater fell to the floor and scrambled for its feet, but James was already on him. He struck again and again with the blunt end of his gun, smashing its face in until there was nothing left but a headless corpse in a bloodstained black and green track suit. James stood over the body, breathing heavily, his hands shaking.

"Holy shit."

He brought a hand up and rubbed his forehead. The mess on the floor might have been his doing, but he knew he did what had to be done. He assured himself that he had everything under control and continued on with his quest.

His adrenaline pumped at all-time highs, and he filled a bag with what little was left in the small corner store. He was back out the front door and out in the open in under five minutes. His feet were heavy and his heart was working hard as he turned back onto his street and nearly tripped over a woman crying on the sidewalk. It was the same woman James had ignored earlier.

"Please," the woman begged him. "Please, I haven't been bitten. I was stabbed, help me." She cried out in blind pain and fear. Her face was twisted in agony and her eyes burned holes into his soul. "Please help me, I've been stabbed." The woman clutched at her stomach and James felt the heavy burden of altruism in his heart.

He couldn't ignore her again.

VII

Veronica frantically twisted her hair and paced back and forth in the living room. It was all she could do to keep herself from standing out on the balcony and screaming for her father to come home. Isaac sat at the counter with his head in his hands, bouncing both legs up and down in a careless fashion.

"It feels like forever," Isaac kept repeating. "Something bad happened, I can feel it."

Veronica ignored him and kept pacing. She would glance at the sliding glass door every now and again, tempted to look, to go outside. "Just be patient," she told her brother. "He's coming back, I know it."

The two sat waiting for only a moment longer as Veronica heard the stairway door in the hallway fly open and slam back shut, filling the void of silence momentarily in the apartment building.

"V! Izzy!" Her father's voice rang down the hallway.

Something wasn't right. Both children ran out of the apartment door and recoiled at the sight of their father. Blood ran down James' body from a huge wound between his neck and left shoulder.

"No way!" Isaac grabbed the grocery bag his father was clutching and Veronica ushered him inside.

"What happened?" Veronica screamed at her father; his face was pale and he had lost a lot of blood.

The kids helped James to the couch and Isaac grabbed dish towels and napkins from the kitchen. Veronica squeezed her father's hand as her brother tried to stop the bleeding. James told them what happened during his trip to get food, of the eater he disposed of, and the two women who attacked him while he tried to help get another wounded woman inside.

"I shouldn't have come back, V." James shivered as he spoke to his daughter. "I shouldn't have come back, it's too dangerous."

A tear rolled down Veronica's face as she watched her brother grow more and more frustrated at the amount of blood their father was losing despite his efforts to stop it.

"I had to bring this to you or it would have meant nothing."

"It's gonna be okay, daddy." She didn't know what else to say and had given up on fighting back tears.

James slapped his son's hand away and held the dishtowel to his own body with his right hand; both his children held his left hand, kneeling on the floor next to the couch.

"Listen up you two, you're the whole reason I was ever put on this God-forsaken earth in the first place, and I'll be damned if I die thinking you can't take care of yourselves."

He stopped abruptly and winced in pain, gasping for air, and his eyes went wide before he regained composure.

"You take that food, and that water we got, and you get some shit together and you get to the bay. Just like V wanted, you go, get the hell out of this God-damn city and run."

James never liked to use foul language in front of his kids. Veronica knew he was serious. She knew her father was going to die and she knew what had to be done.

"I'm so sorry daddy." She sobbed and placed her head on her father's chest, despite the blood that covered it, she wanted to be able to hear her father's heart beating.

"Dad, please." Isaac's eyes welled up with tears and he wiped his nose on his shirt, clenching his father's and sister's hands in his own.

"Some of the best athletes I know, right kiddo?" James looked at his son, fully aware that his son had fucked up his chances of ever doing anything athletic in life because of his grades, but at that moment, had never been prouder and never knew a better football player in his life. "I love you two, okay?"

"We love you too, dad." Isaac nodded at James. Veronica sobbed on her father's chest.

"V, punkin, look at me will ya?"

Veronica sat up and stared with wild eyes at her dying father.

"I need you guys to take care of this."

"Take care of what?" Isaac asked, hurt and confused.

"I will try to hurt you and your sister." Neither child answered, the reality of the situation still settling in, numbing them both. Isaac's head was now buried in his hands but yet Veronica couldn't take her eyes off of her father. She continued to stare at James. At the discoloration in his eyes, the way his chest had stopped moving up and down regularly. How the blood had stopped flowing out of the wound. Her time to grieve had now passed as quickly as it had come, her father had died.

"Get back now!" Veronica shouted.

Isaac understood, and acted quickly. He ran to the door to grab the rifle, but before he could even reach it, he heard the growl come from what used to be his father. Veronica had run to the kitchen and her reanimated father was up, off the couch, and moving fast towards Isaac.

Isaac was too slow with the rifle and the eater shoved back into the wall, getting on top of him. The wind was knocked from Isaac's chest. He could feel the thing's spit on his skin, flying from its mouth as it hissed and growled, teeth gnashing and biting at the air an inch from his face. It struggled against the rifle that Isaac held out and across his body in an attempt to keep it back. He sucked air, trying to catch his back after being slammed into the wall.

"Hey!" Veronica screamed from behind the struggling pair, and the eater turned to face her. It didn't blink; it didn't hesitate in its attempt to attack her.

But neither did Veronica, and she plunged a nine-inch kitchen knife through its right temple and it fell to its knees. Its eyes rolled slightly upward and the head slumped over onto its left shoulder. Veronica took a step back as the eater finally fell to the floor, a marionette with cut strings.

Isaac slid down the wall and crouched; he cried out once in anger, in disbelief, staring at the twice-dead body of his father. The siblings didn't speak. They just stared.

But for the first time since her mother had died, Veronica was relieved she wasn't alive to see this.

VIII

They had packed two bags, one for each of them, for essentials. They had barely spoken, except to agree or not on what needed to be taken. There were no other discussions; they only had to follow their father's directions, get out of the city, run like hell. A flip had switched in Veronica and she felt as if she had suddenly aged ten years. She saw Isaac slip his phone into his pocket while packing up. She almost said something, but decided against it.

Who am I to take his hope away from him?

She zipped her backpack up, fighting back the urge to be angry at the world for taking hope away from her. But she came to the realization that things would be like this from now on. Bad things would happen and they would happen fast. She wanted so badly to be the optimistic girl she had been just that morning, but that morning felt like it was light years away.

There was a difference between being optimistic and being realistic, she knew that now. She could hope for the best all she wanted, but if she didn't think quickly and logically, she would end up like her dad. She briefly wondered if her father was somewhere up in the great beyond, rejoined with her mother, waiting for her and Isaac.

And then she remembered her life had never been, was not now, and would never be, a fairy tale.

For the first time in a week Veronica slid the balcony door open and let the outside world in. An opera of agony greeted her. Sirens, breaking glass, screams, alarms, screeching tires, and feral howls. Even up on the fourth floor, the smell of smoke, destruction, and death filled her nostrils.

Isaac stood in the doorway, "Are you sure you should you be standing out there like that?"

"They've got no reason to look up." She looked out into the city around her. Everywhere she looked there was smoke on the horizon. The streets were less dense but people still ran here and there, screaming as they went. Somewhere out there, people were shooting guns and driving cars. She looked off to the west, toward the bay. "You think if we can make it to the water we could get on a boat?"

"If the keys are there." Isaac reluctantly stepped out beside her. "And if they have fuel. Most marinas have fuel, but I don't know much about boats. I wouldn't know where to look for keys either. I'm sure them folks don't leave their keys hangin' around in the ignition."

"Yeah." She sighed as she answered him.

Veronica closed her eyes, but all she could see was the death of her father. She opened her eyes, and all she saw was the death of the world.

"Head east and that's just highway and more cities. Head west and we hit water, we can at least move along the water and stay along the beach towns. Everybody's back to school and work."

"What's that mean?"

It seemed as if though Isaac didn't want to look his sister in the eyes. Maybe it was because he wasn't ready to share the pain of their reality with her just yet, or maybe because he thought she would never be able to. Not after today.

"This time of year it slows down." She looked down over the rail at the pavement and spotted a single lifeless body directly below them. Judging from the way it looked, someone from one of the floors above them had jumped. Veronica nodded solemnly and twisted a strand of her long dark hair. "Kids go back to school, people use up their vacation time. Dad used to talk about it all the time."

"So, less people means less of them things." Isaac spotted the body on the pavement beneath their balcony and grimaced.

"Less people just means less people." She turned away from him and went back inside.

"Well shouldn't we at least wait until—"

"No." She stood by the door, staring at the lifeless body of their father. She had never wanted more to punch her brother right in the face.

She walked back into the house and crouched down; grasping the eater's head with her left hand, she pulled the kitchen knife from its skull with her right. She pretended to ignore the sickening sound as the knife pulled free and looked up at Isaac who was busy vomiting all over his sneakers.

"We leave now."

*

The apartment building was like a ghost town. Veronica imagined all the inhabitants dead, undead, or cowering inside until something forced them to leave or kill themselves. "Maybe nobody's home," she mumbled as she made her way toward the front entrance.

"What?" Isaac called out behind her.

"Nothing." She waved him off.

They stood before the door, neither one wanting to admit to the other that they were nervous about leaving the building. Veronica clutched the kitchen knife in her right hand. She looked at her brother with his solemn face, ten white knuckles around the rifle, and she knew he was scared shitless as she was. She just hoped he could, and would, use that rifle if he needed to.

She looked up from the rifle in Isaac's hands and felt like a light had turned on: Veronica remembered the gun the armless man had dropped...before he lost his arms. "There's a gun on the street, I need to get it."

"How do you know? Where do you see it?" Isaac strained to see where his sister was squinting.

"I can't see it from here, but I know it's there. I saw a man drop it."

Isaac's reply was shaky. "Is it even loaded? Is it worth looking for?"

"I don't know. But it will be worth more to us in our hands than to the ground, no?" She looked at her brother and swallowed hard, expecting him to argue with her about it.

"Okay. But let's be fast. Do you know exactly where he dropped it?"

She nodded quickly. "Yes."

He looked away from her and back out the frosted glass window of the door, "On three, then." He quietly whispered his count and they exited their apartment building for the last time.

The familiar sound and smell from the balcony was back but this time much stronger. Veronica was out and into the street before Isaac could clear the door. She swooped down, plucked something from the ground, and was running back toward him again.

She was saying something that he couldn't make out over all the noise. Something caught his eye a few yards behind her, and he realized by the time Veronica had nearly passed him at full speed that she was yelling at him to *run*.

Three figures noisily chased after them. His sister was in much better shape than he, considering she participated in sports, but he was barely capable of keeping up. They ran three blocks west of their home, and another four blocks north before they came to a bus lying on its side. The bus had been gutted by a fire, and bodies lie charred inside.

Isaac noticed some of them were not entirely dead and were trying desperately to get out of the bus to chase their next meal.

"Right!" Veronica yelled as she turned a sharp corner. Isaac glanced over his shoulder briefly and caught sight of the eaters chasing him. Two teenage boys about his age and a man who was old enough to have been his grandfather. One of the teenagers was missing an arm and the other's face was badly mauled. The older man had no shirt, and deep gashes decorated his chest.

"Fuck me, when do they give up?" Isaac called out to his sister. He felt the familiar burning in his chest from being winded, but he had no choice but to keep pushing.

"They don't!" Veronica called back. They ran up two more blocks and came across a whole other type of mess they hadn't seen before.

A crowd of about twenty eaters lined the street before them. A man in medical scrubs stood atop of a truck that had plowed into two other cars, firing a gun into the crowd that had gathered around him.

The man hadn't yet seen the siblings, and Veronica thought quickly. She sidestepped to the left, behind a line of parked delivery vans in front of a Florist's with busted-out windows. The vans gave them the cover to get by the man unnoticed.

At the last moment, Veronica threw herself to ground and rolled under the fifth and final van in the row. Isaac immediately followed suit and lie still on the ground beside his sister. His chest heaved and he was badly out of breath.

The three eaters that had been chasing them weren't fast enough to see where they had gone and turned their attention to the man standing on the truck. Isaac hadn't realized what Veronica had done until that very moment. His sister had saved their lives, lying under a van, out of breath, listening to a man scream at a crowd of hungry dead people.

"This can get very bad for us," Veronica said, completely unconcerned with the dead hearing her. "Roll back out the way we came, go back down past the vans and into the florist's. They've gotta have a back door, and we need to head back west."

"Sounds like a plan."

Isaac rolled out, somehow calmer, and looked around; no sign of danger on their side of the vans. Veronica came rolling out seconds after. They sprinted back toward the flower shop and carefully entered through the smashed storefront window.

"Careful, we don't know who's in here." he whispered, slowing his pace. He raised the rifle, hoping he wouldn't have to use it.

Veronica carefully scanned the darkened shop. Dusk was falling on them fast. They found the office of the shop that also contained the back door they had hoped for.

"I need something to drink before we leave." Isaac set his pack down on the desk.

Veronica closed and locked the office door. She didn't want to say anything to him for fear of jinxing themselves. So far their luck, if that's what she could even call it, was in order, and all they needed to do was keep running.

Isaac finished drinking from the bottle and offered it to Veronica. She took it from him and sipped delicately, handing it back. He tightened the cap and looked around the office for anything useful. "Do you think we should stay here tonight? None of those things saw us slip in here."

Veronica shook her head, "That man won't last long. Neither will his ammo. He'll either kill himself or they'll get him. We need to keep moving while they're distracted. Otherwise we'll have a lot more than bad memories to run from." She regretted sounding so cold, but it was the truth.

"Do you feel bad?" Isaac couldn't help but think about using the man as a decoy as he placed the water back into its place and closed up his pack.

"No. Him or us. That's what it was. I made a decision." She stared at the exit door. "Let's get going."

Isaac didn't respond. He just followed his sister silently through the exit.

The back door of the florist led to a very narrow and very empty alley. "Head back left, make a right when we get to the street."

He followed Veronica's direction just because he simply knew he would be lost without her. Geographically speaking, he would have been fine, but he very much so needed his sister right now. More so than he had ever needed another person.

When they got back onto the street, Veronica began running again. Isaac followed, glancing behind him and seeing no one in pursuit. He was relieved and knew they were running because she wanted to, not because they had to. Another sixteen blocks and the streets were almost pitch black. Their surroundings had grown quieter as they moved away from the city center.

Screams came every now and again, gun shots here and there, and the alarms were still going off, but he could now hear the sound of his own feet slamming down on the pavement, which made him a little nervous. They were moving at a comfortable jog and were much more alert at this pace. The pair had run a very strategic six miles from their front door.

They reached a pizza place they had frequented right on the edge of the city, a place that wasn't too far from the highway. Veronica decided it was as good a place as any to take a rest.

"No, not inside," Veronica had said when Isaac started toward the door. "I want to be able to see. We need to be able to run again if we have to." She sat down with her back against a Lincoln Navigator parked out front.

Isaac pulled on the door anyway. "It's locked."

He sat on the large window ledge and set his pack down. He took a couple of deep breaths; his calves burned and his feet ached. He knew he would feel like total shit the next day and wondered how long and how far they would have to keep running tonight.

Where are we even going?

He wanted to ask Veronica how she felt, but knew she wouldn't be honest with him. He was frustrated and upset. He was scared and he had no idea how he was supposed to be behaving. "What are we doing, V?" he finally asked her in a hushed voice.

"We're getting out of the city. That's the plan, I'm sticking with the plan." She studied their surroundings as she answered, craning her neck to peer down the street in the direction from which they came, he fingers twisting loose strands of dark hair.

"Actually, we don't have a plan." He rested his elbows on his knees and leaned forward, his remark getting his sister's attention. "Running isn't a plan. What do you want to do? Run all night? Run into the next day? Run until we're so exhausted that we have no energy left to protect ourselves? Just run, run, run?"

Veronica didn't want to admit that he was right, it wasn't in her nature to agree with her brother.

"No, Isaac. The plan is getting out of the city, at whatever cost." Her irritation made her snappish. "We stop when it's safe to stop, farther away from the city, in case we need to start running again." She could feel her face getting hot, embarrassed that she, in fact, did not have a plan. She simply wanted to put as much space between her and the apartment as possible. "And besides, protect ourselves? It's not like we've had to do much in the way of protecting ourselves so far. Running has worked out for us, wouldn't you agree?"

Isaac sat silent for a moment, staring at faint cracks in the sidewalk. They didn't always get along, he didn't expect them to all of a sudden bond over tragedy, but he didn't think it was the time to behave worse than they normally did. He rubbed the back of his neck and adjusted the collar on his faded green polo as he sat up. He knew his sister did not have a plan, that the two of them were just doing what they needed to get out of this hell hole, but his feet continued to throb and he had a plan for the remainder of the evening; and it did not include any more running. "Well so then things don't exactly change all that much, huh? If there are any other people out there, I guess they're all just probably runnin' from their problems, too. Just like any old day of the week."

"If that's how you want to see it, then good for you. I'm glad you've got it all figured out."

"Yeah, just be a bitch, V. It looks good on ya."

The volume of their voices had increased and the bitter air between them had temporarily lightened the seriousness of the situation. Veronica was about to fire back an insult at her brother before he could utter another sarcastic complaint, but she froze in horror and put her hand up to shut Isaac up.

She strained her ears and Isaac jumped up from the ledge, looking around. It was extremely hard to see, but they could both clearly hear it now: a frantic set of fast-moving steps and the familiar growl of an eater.

"Shit, shit, shit," Isaac chanted as he snatched up the rifle.

Before either of them could determine which direction the eater was coming from, it appeared faster than anything Veronica had ever seen. It was on her brother in an instant. The two went crashing through the pizzeria storefront, smashing the table that sat directly in front of the window.

"Isaac!"

She hadn't meant to yell out but couldn't help herself. She was responsible for this. She hadn't planned for this.

Veronica leapt through the window and was thrown off to the side like a ragdoll. Strong arms held her against the brick wall as she watched a man of at least six and a half feet tall grab the eater off Isaac's body. He brought its head down fast, impaling it onto one of the remaining panes of glass left in the window frame. Veronica's heart was caught in her throat and her thoughts raced.

Who is this man? Is Isaac alive? Who is grabbing me?

Nobody moved. Nobody said a word.

Isaac groaned on the floor and the large man offered a hand to help him up.

"I gotta warn ya, pal," the tall man said, "you make any sudden moves and I'll have a bullet in ya faster than you can cry mama."

Veronica felt the arms holding her ease up and she backed away from whoever it was. Isaac moved to his sister's side and saw that she was startled, but fine.

She promised herself she would apologize to him later, when she knew they were safe.

A third person with a lantern appeared and raised it, revealing the room. There, in the ruins of a former pizza parlor stood the tall man who saved Isaac, a very petite woman, and a second man who was at least a foot shorter than the other; all of them armed, all of them staring at Veronica and Isaac.

The woman's eyes grew wide and she took her hand off her weapon. "They're kids."

The tall man smiled and lit a cigarette. "Welcome to Pisano's Pizzeria," he said in a very bad Italian accent as he exhaled the smoke. "One of you better know how to fix that window you made your grand entrance through."

Veronica and Isaac looked at each other, not knowing how to respond, not knowing if they had just landed themselves in a bad situation.

The tall man snickered, "Ah, lighten up, I'm messin' with ya." He took another drag off his cigarette. "But I suggest we get a move on closin' her up before more of those assholes show up, lookin' for dinner."

IX

The newly assembled group forewent introductions in order to cover the gaping hole in the storefront. The stocky man disappeared into the back, reappearing with a stack of cardboard nearly as tall as he was.

"It's all we've got, they're too stupid to realize they can get through it."

The man spoke with a heavy Spanish accent and despite his size, moved around faster than any of them. It wasn't until Veronica had grabbed a piece of the large cardboard that she realized they were unassembled pizza boxes. She handed them to the tall man beside her and he attached them with duct tape. She couldn't help but smirk. Her father had always kept a roll around, he said it was the only tool a 'Southern Engineer' needed.

Everyone worked silently, and in a matter of minutes, the broken window was replaced by a wall of 'Pisano' pizza boxes.

"Let's go. They are stupid, but not deaf," the stocky man said, gathering the remaining cardboard and other bits and pieces of supplies he'd brought up front.

He led the way to the back of the pizzeria. It was a small parlor, and from the light the lantern cast around the room, it looked exactly as Veronica remembered... minus the broken glass and garbage.

Two red booth seats with white tables lined the walls on either side of the room and a large table, which had been in the middle, was lying on its side near the kitchen door. They were ushered past the counter and into the kitchen by the petite woman who stayed in the front parlor. Through the closed door Veronica heard the table being pushed up against it and saw the woman's head appear as she crawled through the drop-window over the counter to join the rest of them in the kitchen.

The smell hit Isaac first, and he began to cough and gag. Veronica's eyes watered and she brought her shirt up over her face and held it there. The woman shushed them, pushing them forward into the darkness of a small foyer. The tall man had already vanished up the stairs and the stocky man held the door open for the rest as the siblings crept up the stairs.

The petite woman closed and locked the first door and joined them on the steps while the stocky man secured the door he had been holding. The stairs led to a small living room with a large sectional sofa and La-Z-Boy off to the side. An unused flat screen television was mounted to the wall, and underneath it, a plethora of dead electronics.

The tall man was seated in the La-Z-Boy, feet propped up, gun in his lap. This room had two more lanterns, one in his corner, and another under the TV. The petite woman shut hers off and set it near the couch as she sat, ringing her hands, looking back and forth from the tall man to the stocky man, as if she was waiting either to speak.

"My name is Salvador Roja," the stocky man spoke first. He motioned to the small woman on the couch. "This is my wife, Lucy."

"You own the pizzeria." Isaac recognized the name instantly.

"That's right." Salvador nodded. "Did you used to come here?"

"Well, yeah, but, I know who your son his. He plays football for Franklin. My school's rival." He seemed pleased with himself but his face instantly went grim when a small squeak escaped Lucy's mouth and she pursed her lips.

Salvador placed a hand on his wife's shoulder.

"We have lost our son." He looked down at his wife, whose face rested on his hand.

"I'm, uh, really sorry. I wasn't thinking." Isaac turned his face down, embarrassed.

"You couldn't have known," Lucy spoke finally, wiping her eyes on her hands. She also had an accent, but slightly lighter than her husband's. "He was a good boy, I'm glad that you knew of him."

"My name is Isaac, this is my sister, Veronica."

Salvador gestured to the tall man. "This is—"

"I'm just Ben. Nothin' fancy." The tall man put his feet down and leaned forward, elbows on his knees. "I rent this apartment from Sal, I managed his kitchen, though now it's a bathroom."

Ben looked at Sal and they both shrugged. "Sorry buddy."

"Shit happens, yeah?" Sal responded, pleased with his quick wit.

Ben smiled, appreciating the humor, and gave him a thumbs up with one hand as he lit a cigarette with another. He got up from his recliner and retrieved an ashtray from the shelf under the wall-mounted TV set. He sat back down, silent for a moment, staring at Isaac as if trying to figure him out.

Isaac averted his eyes from the intimidating stare.

"Well, go on then. Let's get the story swapping out of the way. It's inevitable and I'd rather be depressed now than later," Ben said, looking at Veronica. He leaned back and propped his feet back up. Closing his eyes, he waited for someone to start telling their version of the same miserable tale that inevitably led them all to his apartment.

Sal spoke softly as he relived the painful moments of that first day. He hoped his son was dead, and not cursed to roam the earth, hungry for flesh. Lucy wept into his chest, memories of Marco swimming through her head.

"No one could have known how bad it was about to get," Sal had told the siblings as he finished explaining to them how they'd ended up stranded at Pisano's. He looked down at his wife, who was wiping tears from her eyes; he put his arms around her and everyone sat quietly by the lantern light.

Ben seemed to be in another world, staring at the ceiling, chain smoking in the recliner. His story was completely opposite everyone else's. It was short and to the point. He joined the military right out of high school and spent most of his time overseas. He was wounded in Afghanistan and honorably discharged.

"Pretty uneventful life until people started eatin' each other. Then again, I'd rather deal with this nightmare than ever spend another fucking night in that God-forsaken sand pit," he said. He rolled his cigarette around between his fingers before putting it out and sitting up to place the ashtray on the floor. "No family, not a whole lotta friends. Mostly everybody I cared about died in the fuckin' place so I'd say I don't have a whole lot to lose. Sal gave a good ol' boy a job and a place to live, and here we are." He cracked his knuckles and spread his arms, motioning to everyone. "Too bad we don't have any damn tea and biscuits to pass around."

Everyone remained where they were for some time; Ben on the recliner, Sal by his wife's side on the couch, Veronica and Isaac on the floor. Veronica had calmly explained that they'd lost their father, could no longer stay in their home, and were trying to make their way out of the city. Sal and Ben remained pleasantly distant while Lucy was very hospitable, offering them water and food, but neither sibling wanted for anything.

*

A few hours passed in silence, and Veronica figured everyone to be asleep. Ben had asked Lucy to get the kids something to sleep on and it was almost as if Isaac passed out before his head hit the pillow. Sal and Lucy lie motionless on the pullout couch and Ben had gone off to his bedroom. She crept around the apartment, trying to get a feel for everything. All the windows in the living room and kitchen had been covered in the same fashion as the downstairs storefront. If the eaters didn't recognize light, that was one thing, Lucy had told them earlier, but not all people out there would be as nice as the people her and her brother had so luckily stumbled upon.

There was not too much for Veronica to explore in the tiny apartment; there was only a small hallway off the kitchen with two closed doors. She assumed the one at the end of the hall was a bedroom and ignored it. She opened the other door slowly and stepped into a small bathroom with a square, uncovered window. Her breath caught in her throat as she gazed at the beauty of the full moon. It was as if someone had placed it there, in the middle of the window frame, just for her to see.

There was just enough light from it for her eyes to adjust to the small room. No one had been using the bathroom here, thankfully. She pressed her face up against the glass, it was cool. The only thing she could see clearly was the roof of the building across the small alley way. Finally alone, she felt herself wanting to cry, wanting to give in to the grief she felt for her father, her brother, Sal and Lucy and Marco. For anyone else who had lost someone or been lost, which at this point, she figured she should be grieving for the whole world. She asked herself how long they could really stay here, how safe creeping around like blind mice in an attic really was.

She felt movement behind her and went for the kitchen knife in her back pocket as she spun around.

"No need for that," Ben whispered. "Do you like sneakin' around people's houses at night?"

Veronica shook her head no, stepping away from the window nervously.

Ben pointed to the closed lid on the toilet, "Have a seat if you'd like." He closed the door behind him as she sat and he quietly inched the window open. She crinkled her nose at the smell of decay that had begun to creep in. "You'll get used to it," he told her as he sat down across from her on the ledge of the tub.

"Do you mind?" He held out an open palm with a rolled joint.

She shrugged and stared up at the moon again.

"Help isn't coming, you know?" He took a long drag off the joint. "I had a buddy I talked to right before the phones went out, still in the service. He said things were worse than a war zone in the bigger cities. He said not to expect help any time soon."

"I wasn't thinking there would be any help."

"Smart girl." He smiled to himself and offered her a hit of the joint.

"I don't like to." She remembered the sense of restriction she felt when she smoked a blunt with some friends from school last year, the feeling of unease it gave her. While everyone around her laughed and felt free, she felt trapped and anxious. Dee had told her to loosen up and it would get better, but it never did.

Ben laughed, coughing, trying to remain as quiet as possible. "Even smarter girl."

Veronica felt her face grow hot and was thankful there was no light in the bathroom for him to notice her blush.

"So, what makes you think it's okay to sneak around like this, anyway?"

"I wasn't," she answered, too quickly, and bit her lip sheepishly. "I just, um, wanted to be alone."

He nodded, looking up at the window. "Sorry for the intrusion."

They continued to talk casually in the tiny bathroom while Ben got his secret high. Veronica found herself wondering how old Ben was and then cursed herself, chasing the thoughts of a normal sixteen-year-old girl out of her head.

He asked what her and Isaac's plans were and where they were heading when Isaac was attacked.

"Well, like I told y'all earlier, we don't have much of a plan. But we really want to get to the water. You know, if we can't find safety there, like maybe with a boat or something, then maybe we can work our way along the coast." She twirled a strand of dark hair on her finger and stared down at her feet. "I promised my dad we'd head that way. There aren't a lot of people by the water."

Ben perked up at her last statement. "Well you must get your smarts from your old man."

She looked up at Ben, surprised by his approval.

"This time of year, the tourists don't bother us no more, and the Canadians haven't decided to migrate south just yet." He chuckled, "I can't believe I didn't ever think of that." He put out the joint and put it in his pocket. "I guess I'll admit that I just haven't really wanted to leave. We had a couple other people here with us just yesterday. Can you believe it? Couple of employees, but they didn't want to stay.

They wanted to try and make it home to their families. I mean, I get it. But after what we heard on the phone with Marco back when this all started, I wasn't too keen on goin' anywhere. They shouldn't have been, either."

"Do you know what happened to them?"

"Nah, I'd rather not think about it. Those two girls were dumb as bricks under normal circumstances so I can't imagine them keepin' their shit together out there in a time like this, cryin' over every damn thing. It was Roger's idea to leave, I just think he wanted to play the hero and get laid by Tweedle Dumb and Tweedle Dee, but ya know, it's just not my place to say."

Veronica couldn't help but giggle. Under different circumstances she might have been put off by his honesty, but right now it felt right.

Ben smiled, "So how about we sit down and have a discussion tomorrow about headin' to the bay?"

Veronica liked the idea of Ben coming, especially since it was probably safe to assume he could handle himself and keep them out of trouble. But she couldn't help but to be wary of going out there in a group like this. Would they be able to move fast enough, quietly enough? She knew that she could out run anything, and Isaac wasn't far behind her in that regard. But what about Sal and Lucy? Lucy seemed like the loose end of the group. Sure, she could hold it together with four walls surrounding her, but what happens when a group of eaters are biting at her heels?

Ben noticed Veronica had yet to respond and could just barely make out her facial expression enough to see she was worrying. "Listen," he got up from his seat on the tub and stretched. "Get some sleep, girl, and tomorrow, if you want to talk about your plan with everyone, you talk about it." He pretended to lock his mouth and throw away the key. She managed another smile as he closed the window back up and left her to her thoughts on the toilet.

XI

Isaac stirred the following morning, his body aching from sleeping on the floor. He thought of his bed, back in the place that used to be his home, followed quickly upon by thoughts of a girl he'd never again see.

Eliza.

He sighed and allowed her beautiful face to take up the space in his brain, but the thought of his father's body rotting in their apartment invaded his thoughts and a chill ran down his spine.

He blinked his eyes a couple of times and sat up. Everyone was awake and in the kitchen from what he could tell, except for him and his sister. Veronica was sound asleep on the couch. He went about tidying up his make shift bed and placed everything in the corner near the lantern.

"Good morning," Lucy greeted him as he walked into the kitchen. "I have some coffee here, it isn't very good though." Her smile was warm; she had nice soft features on a small face that was framed with thick black hair cut in a fashionable bob. Sal, on the other hand, had a thick dark beard, small sharp eyes and was balding.

"Thank you," Isaac nodded and took the cup. It was bitter and cold.

"More like instant shit than instant coffee, wouldn't you agree?" Ben said to him without looking up.

"It's just fine," Isaac lied and smiled at Lucy. "Thanks." There was a plate of something on the table next to some untoasted English muffins.

"Canned breakfast meat. It is also cold, I'm sorry," Lucy said, noticing him eyeing the plate. "Not much we can do since the power went out."

Isaac smiled at her again, "That's just fine, I understand." He took a seat in the empty chair and made himself a breakfast sandwich. The table didn't go with the chairs, and it seemed the whole kitchen was mismatched. Although Isaac didn't know him very well, Isaac figured it to be the appropriate kitchen for someone like Ben.

Sal sat silently across from Isaac, reading an out-of-date newspaper. He wondered if Sal had memorized it yet, imagining him sitting in the same spot each morning, reading the same headlines and articles over and over again. Ben stood smoking a cigarette over the sink, staring out an open window that had been covered up the night before.

"I thought you guys kept the windows covered up?" Isaac asked through a mouthful of tasteless food.

"This one overlooks the alley out back of the building, no light to be seen during the day." Ben put a cigarette out in the sink, never breaking his stare out the window.

"Anything interesting out there?"

"Interesting? Yeah, could be."

Ben's answer surprised him. "What do you mean?"

"Few days ago, we heard some screamin', but not the kind of screamin' we had been hearing from them things." He lit up another cigarette and looked at Isaac. "Like the kind you used to hear before all this. When it was just regular ol' people treatin' other people like shit. Ya know, robbin'...or maybe somethin' worse. But anyway, what I'm thinkin' is that if they found out we were in here, well, you know how that might go."

Isaac swallowed his food hard. "Yeah, I probably wouldn't wanna find out."

"So I'm just attempting to see them first."

Sal snorted behind his newspaper. "Paranoia. Stop smoking all that *mota* man."

Ben chuckled and flipped him off.

Another hour passed before Veronica finally woke up. She slept like the dead when she was exhausted. The rest of the group had made small talk, not really discussing anything of importance. Isaac felt awkward among the strangers; his sister was the one who made friends easily and she never had any trouble talking to people. He was relieved when she joined them in the kitchen. Lucy offered her some of the leftovers from the morning. She sat next to her brother at the table.

"What's been going on?" she asked him, hoping he hadn't pissed anyone off or told them too much about himself.

"Honestly, nothing. We've kind of just been sitting here. Nobody wanted to bother you."

"You needed the rest." Lucy smiled, sitting off to the side.

"Oh. Thank you." She broke off a piece of English muffin and chewed it slowly.

Sal was going through things in the pantry and Ben still stood beside the window over the sink, chain smoking. He met Veronica's eyes and nodded before returning to his quiet watch over the back alley. She remembered their conversation from the night before in Ben's tiny bathroom. No one said anything about leaving the city or heading for the coast, so Ben must have kept it to himself.

There was not much conversation over the next hour. Veronica left the kitchen after eating her stale breakfast and went over to her bag in the living room. The gun she had taken from the street was still there, along with the few things from the house. Everything looked fine. Isaac followed her in, doing the same with his bag, but only because he had seen her do it first.

"What are we doing, V?" He looked at her expectantly.

She didn't respond; she didn't know what to say.

"Well, I don't know what we're doing here, I'm just grateful they took us in like they did." He sat down on the linens he had folded earlier. "They didn't have to. You know that right?"

She sat down on the floor next to her bag and brought her knees into her chest. She didn't respond but she knew Isaac had a point. Maybe it was only right to try and make it to the bay with the group, stick together. They weren't by any means bad people.

"What do you think about asking them to come with us?" She stole a glance at the kitchen and made sure her voice was low.

Isaac shook his head, "I don't know. That's up to them. I mean, I wouldn't have left our house if we didn't have to. We might be safe here for a little while, if they let us stay. Don't you think? I mean, there's bad shit out there."

"There's bad shit everywhere, dude." She rested her forehead on her knees.

Since when did Isaac become such a pussy?

She hated that he kept asking her what they were doing or where they were going. Here was her older brother, looking to her for the answers when she felt like she might fall apart any minute.

Do I really seem that put together right now?

She immediately knew the answer was yes. She knew getting emotional would only hold them back and slow them down. It happened out on the street, almost got her brother killed, and all she had allowed herself was irritation. She was behaving as if the world outside didn't scare her a bit and she knew that was the way she needed to be. She lifted her head and looked at Isaac, his sad, dark eyes were fixed on the floor.

"I'm sorry, you know that?"

Isaac looked up at her.

"I'm sorry about last night and I'm sorry about dad. I'm sorry that the world sucks ass, and I'm sorry if there isn't any time to grieve." She paused, giving him a moment to say something but his words never came. She was disappointed. Her voice grew stern and she spoke slowly as she continued. "We have to do what we have to do, in order to keep going. Do you understand?"

She could tell her brother was getting emotional but she pressed harder.

"I might not have a solid plan or know exactly what I'm doing, I definitely don't know what the hell is going on with the world, but I can promise you I know one thing, and that is I will do whatever I need to do to keep myself alive. *Do you understand?*"

Isaac blinked back tears. His face grew hot and his mouth was dry. He wanted to tell her he was proud of her, that he always wanted to be the one to look out for her, but he knew how lucky he was to still have her here with him. He tried to open his mouth to thank her for saving his life and getting him out of that apartment, and to promise her he would put his big boy pants on from here on out, but Ben strolled in the room and sat down in his recliner.

"How's it goin' in here, you two?" He had a smirk on his face that made it obvious he had been eavesdropping.

"It's fine, dude." Isaac discreetly wiped tears from his cheeks, his face red.

"So, I can't help but hope that y'all know how to use those weapons you got on ya."

"Yes." Veronica was annoyed that he'd looked through her bag. "My dad loved to hunt and go to the range."

He scratched his messy blonde hair and laughed at her. "I figured so." He leaned back and put his feet up. Veronica imagined him watching football in that chair, once upon a time.

"Why do you ask?"

"Well, for one, you shouldn't just go carrying around rifles and pistols unless you know how to use them. I didn't want you to hurt yourself out there." He was still smiling to himself when Lucy and Sal joined them in the living room and sat on the couch. "What's the verdict?" Ben asked Sal.

"Well, there is not much. Not enough to supply five people." Sal realized his tone of voice might have been a little harsh. "I did not mean to be disrespectful, but it's the truth. We did not plan on two more. In fact, I hate to admit, but we were relieved when the other three left us."

"You're young, like my son was," Lucy chimed in. "We could not have turned you away."

Ben's face looked so serious; his lips formed a tight line and his eyes were narrow. "But the truth of the matter is that we would have had to eventually leave. Whether or not anyone else showed up." He said this without looking at anyone.

Sal rubbed his shiny bald head and sighed. "Yes. But we could look for food, maybe. See what's out there to bring back."

Ben laughed. "Sure, we could stay here, continue to shit in a pizzeria."

"We're going to the coast," Isaac chimed in. "If we're going to go as a group, we should all be on the same page and we should leave as soon as possible."

Veronica cringed at her brother's decision to volunteer information like that, but she was also pleasantly surprised that he'd made a decision on his own. She tried to hide her smile. It made her happy for the first time in days.

Ben, Lucy, and Sal decided they would leave with them in the morning. Things were packed, Ben cleaned his gun, Lucy made jam and peanut butter sandwiches on what remained of the English muffins for the morning, and the group ate canned tuna and green beans for dinner.

They quietly chatted and laughed as they ate, each of them thinking about leaving their semblance of safety and distracting themselves in daydreams of finding refuge somewhere on the gulf coast.

None of them slept very well that night.

XII

The crack of dawn came and the group gathered their things, readying themselves for the road. Veronica had overheard Sal and Lucy that morning, whispering to each other in Spanish. She couldn't understand what they were saying, but the conversation upset Lucy very much.

"We're gonna walk out the back door and take a left down the alley," Ben addressed them when they were all ready to go. "We stay together and keep it tight, don't talk unless it is absolutely necessary. When I go, you go. When I stop, you stop. Weapons always ready, but *do not* fire them unless you are saving someone's life."

Veronica held up her kitchen knife.

Ben laughed, "Yeah, you probably shouldn't let yourself get that close to one of them things, though." He continued laying out the plan on how they'd make it to the highway and out of the open as soon as possible. The farther they got from the city, the more trees there would be, and more trees meant more cover.

Veronica didn't like how nervous Lucy looked as she clutched the crucifix hanging around her neck. She prayed to herself in Spanish before they left and Sal made her assure him she was okay to do this. Before they left, Ben offered Veronica his own hunting knife in place of her kitchen knife.

"No, thanks," she said sheepishly. "My mom spent a lot of money a long time ago watching infomercials."

Ben chuckled as she shook it at him. "Lifetime guarantee."

The group, led by Ben, did exactly planned. They walked down the stairs and out the back door. Nobody wanted to reenter Pisano's kitchen again. Sal brought up the back as they took a left and made their way down the alley, slowing down as they neared the street. Ben put up a hand and the group stopped, he poked his head out to make sure the way was safe. The street was empty as he had wished. He motioned for them to follow and they took a right.

Two blocks up, they made a left and from there it was a two-mile stretch to the highway. They quickened their pace and were making excellent time.

Empty cars were everywhere, trash littered the streets and every now and then, they'd hear a wail or moan from somewhere. Embers glowed from dying fires in the hearts of ex-shops, and Veronica wondered if the lifeless bodies she passed on the streets had been lucky enough to lie dead where they'd dropped.

They heard Sal gasp at the back of the group and stopped.

Lucy screamed at the top of her lungs at the sight of a man with a knife to Sal's throat, who had his hands up in surrender. The man had long hair pulled back in a messy ponytail and his enormous arms held Sal in place.

Ben felt his chest tighten as he saw everything unfolding; he would have rather run into hungry dead than deal with maniacal living.

"Shut that bitch up," the man demanded, and another man appeared from the alley beside him. Lucy continued to scream as the man raised a gun to her face.

"Jesus Christ, Lucy, please," Sal pleaded with his wife. A scream even louder than Lucy's was heard in the distance, but this was a scream of the dead.

"Fuck this." The second man with the gun reared back and smashed his weapon into Lucy's forehead with a sickening crack. She dropped to the pavement.

Sal cried out and squirmed against the man with the knife, tears forming in his eyes as he watched Lucy's body twitching.

Ben, caught off guard by how fast everything was spiraling out of his control, finally had the chance to speak. "What do you want? Our bags? Take them. Now!" More howls and yells were heard, but this time closer than before.

"Look what that bitch went ahead and did," the second man yelled at his friend, still pointing the gun at Lucy's unmoving body. Everyone stared at the man with the knife, with Sal still in his arms. The man let go of Sal and threw him to the sidewalk.

"Drop all your shit! Weapons, bags, and fast."

Nobody moved but Sal, on the ground, holding his wife's head in his hands, frantically trying to find a pulse in her neck, praying to a God who wasn't listening.

The second man's gun was on Ben now.

"Seriously, take the shit and let us go. They're coming." Ben lowered his gun to the sidewalk while Isaac removed his bag from his back. Veronica heard the familiar sound of feet slapping against the asphalt behind her and turned around.

"Holy shit!" the man with the knife yelled as an eater slammed into Veronica, the two of them slamming down to the sidewalk beside Sal.

Isaac hurled himself at the eater, yanking it from her body. He didn't know he possessed that kind of strength.

"Isaac! No!" she screamed from the ground.

Her attacker turned on her brother and sunk its decaying teeth deep into his side.

Isaac let out a roar of pain as he grabbed the eater by its head and pulled it away from his ribcage, bringing a huge chunk of flesh with it. The eater hungrily gobbled it up.

Blood poured from his side and his knees grew weak. The eater thrust itself back on him, opening up another huge hole in his mid-section and began feasting on his flesh and innards.

The two looters watched on in horror at their robbery gone wrong. Sal, enraged by his wife's demise, brought himself up and head-butted the man with the knife, instantly shattering his nose. The knife buried itself into Sal's stomach and the man's face disappeared as Ben fired a shot into it.

Sal collapsed with his assailant's body still in his arms. He looked up at Ben, his face twisted in pain. Veronica threw herself onto the atrocity that was ravaging her brother and plunged the kitchen knife into the eater's head with a force so hard that the blade, along with its lifetime guarantee, snapped off in the eater's skull.

She cried out in anger, watching her brother bleed out.

"We need to go!" She attempted to get Isaac to his feet. "Please!" She looked back at Ben as he beat the ever-living shit out of the second man. "Ben!" she cried out to him, Isaac's blood covering her chest and arms.

He stopped, still holding the man by the throat, even though he had already stopped breathing. He stared into his lifeless eyes and wished he were still alive, so he could kill him one more time.

The desperate cries of the eaters were upon them as they turned a corner a few blocks away.

"Ben, you have to take her and leave me," Sal yelled to his friend. "Go, now!"

Ben cracked his neck and turned to the crowd of dead approaching them. He clutched his gun in one hand and picked up Sal's bat with the other. "Veronica, get out of here," he said sternly.

"Ben, what are you doing?" Sal winced in pain on the sidewalk, nearly passing out.

"Ben!" Veronica tried to hold her brother up with her shoulder; he was bleeding uncontrollably and had stopped making any noise. "I need your help!" Isaac became dead weight. She lowered him back to the sidewalk and shook him as she screamed. "Isaac!"

His eyes stared off at nothing. Her hands began to shake.

"Isaac?" Her voice cracked. Her brother had died, just as his father before him.

"*Amorcita,* you need to go."

Veronica looked at Sal as he closed his eyes for the last time.

Everything suddenly began moving as if in slow motion, and all the sound was sucked out of the world around her. She stared up at Ben, who started firing at the eaters running up the street, yet she heard no shots. She looked back at her brother's still unmoving eyes as they began to glaze over, a milky white, and knew what needed to be done.

She clawed at her gun from her bag. "I love you," she told him, yet she didn't hear herself say it, nor did she hear the shot she fired into his head. Without another thought, without another second to spare, she threw herself to her feet and tore off running in the direction of the highway as a tsunami of death advanced on her only friend left in the whole world.

She ran faster than anyone ever had, and had it been the right time, she would have entertained the thought of pretending to be the winner of a famous race. She hit the highway without a sound and kept running.

XIII

"These stupid assholes are going to get themselves killed!" Andrew cried out over his shoulder. His hulking frame took up almost the entire window as he watched the spectacle in the street below. Five people had silently made their way down his street only to be ambushed by the local creeps that had taken to lurking, robbing, and killing anybody they came across since the world "went ass up," as Andrew liked to say. One of the women in the group had begun screaming when the thugs revealed themselves.

A thin, pale hand found its way onto his dark skin, slowly caressing his arm. "Keep your voice down," Juliette said softly. "We don't want them to find us too."

Andrew turned to look at his girlfriend and shook his head.

"Are you bein' serious right now?" His brow creased as he shook her hand off his arm, "We need to do somethin' about this!"

Juliette folded her arms across her small chest. "We're not putting ourselves at risk for anyone else. I thought we agreed on that? No more playing hero."

"I'm not sayin' we do anything crazy, I'm sayin' we need to get rid of those fuckin' thieves *anyway*, send them other folks on their way and get back inside. I can't sit in here and watch anybody else get wasted out there."

Andrew's brother Clyde had joined them in front of the window. "And I sure as hell don't want all that hollerin' and shit outside bringin' those dead things to our front door. Drew's right, girl. I'm sorry, but we were gonna run into those crazy looters sooner or later, and I'd rather take them out now, while they're all distracted."

"Then you two do it. I'm not leaving, I'm not helping. I don't care about anyone outside of this apartment and I'm locking the door once—"

"Oh shit!" Clyde screamed out, smacking Andrew on his broad back and tapping against the glass. "Them fuckin' things are out there now!"

The other woman in the group on the street was knocked down to the ground by an eater. One of the group helped her and got bitten for it, another began fighting back against the attackers, and off in the distance, the screams of a certain kind of death could be heard.

"Things are not lookin' good." Andrew brought his big hands up and locked his fingers behind his head, closing his eyes, silently praying for a sign.

His brother squealed and squirmed, both in horror and intrigue at the scene unfolding on the sidewalk. He could feel Juliette's glare of disapproval. A loud shot rang out and Andrew's eyes popped open.

"Oh shit, they got guns!" Clyde clapped his hands and shot Juliette a sassy look. "I'm out." He flashed her a peace sign and smacked his brother on the shoulder, "Let's do this."

Andrew turned around to Juliette, she stood with her arms folded, an expression of anger painted across her face. Neither of them spoke as Andrew left his place at the window and joined his brother at the dining room table. The brothers were identical in their muscular physique and almost the same in height, Andrew at six foot four and Clyde just an inch shorter. Andrew had hard features and dark skin like his father, while Clyde was light-skinned and definitely took after his mother's femininity.

"How many you takin'?" Andrew asked his brother while he loaded his .357 and stashed extra ammo in his pockets.

"One for each hand and one for good luck," Clyde responded as he tied his long braids up in a tight ponytail. He had a .45 on each hip and a .40 S&W on the table.

Andrew had been a cop and had himself a fine collection of guns and ammunition. His brother was a gay black bartender in the south, so Andrew had made sure the man knew how to handle a weapon. Sometimes he thought his brother was a better shot. He stole a glance at Juliette who now paced near the large window.

"Hey."

She stopped moving when he spoke but did not look at him.

"We got this. You know that."

Andrew and Clyde moved down the stairs with a practiced grace; they knew silent footsteps were necessary but speed counted for everything. They exited the foyer that linked Clyde's apartment with the shop beneath it and moved quickly to the front, weapons ready.

The last man standing from the group awaited the onslaught of the dead and began firing into the vicious screaming crowd. Blood dripped from his knuckles with every blast.

The two brothers silently moved out and behind the man. Andrew climbed up on a nearby car while Clyde went out into the street to get a good angle on the eaters. The man didn't even flinch when he heard the other shots join his and the dead began dropping in higher numbers.

The eaters who got closest were met with a hard kick and a smash to the head from a Louisville Slugger. The twenty or so eaters were no match for the three of them.

Heads popped and exploded like firecrackers, and bodies dropped all around the men as they fought off the creatures.

Andrew dropped down to the street from the car. "I'm empty!" He pulled a golf club, his Lieutenant's favorite, from its place on his waistband. Joining the last man standing, he charged the remaining eaters, bludgeoning them to a second death while Clyde fired rounds into the ones that didn't stay down.

The street soon fell silent and the trio stood panting and listening, waiting to hear more screams. The city did not oblige.

The man with the bloody knuckles turned to face Andrew, his clothes stained and his skin streaked with gore. "Thanks." It was all he could manage to say as he turned away from the man who had helped save his life and crouched down. He checked the pulses of both the heavyset man lying motionless on the sidewalk and the small woman a few feet from him.

"I'm sorry about your friends. I wish we had been out here sooner," Andrew said solemnly as his brother came up beside him, watching the man prop up his friend against the brick wall of the building and drag the body of the woman over, placing her into his arms. He didn't need to check the pulse of the skinny teenager lying not far from them, half his face was gone and he wore an enormous hole in his torso, empty and red. The man dragged his body over, as well, and sat him next to the others. He remained on one knee for a moment, just looking at what was now gone; perhaps reminiscing, or perhaps not thinking of anything at all.

He stood and extended a hand. "Ben."

"Andrew, this is my brother, Clyde." They all shook hands.

"I appreciate the back up. I was goin' down with a fight, no matter what happened, but you saved my ass. I always wondered when somebody was gonna have to. Now I can safely say I'm not looking forward to the next time."

"Good, because there won't be a next time. Not from us anyway." They were all startled by Juliette's sudden appearance on the street.

"That would be Juliette. My brother's lack of better judgment." Clyde spit as he said it, giving Juliette a nasty look.

"Fuck you, Clyde. You can stay out here and leave with this asshole for all I care."

"Bitch, that's my apartment you're stayin' in."

"Enough with that shit!" Andrew yelled. "We already discussed this. If the two of you can't get along then don't talk at all. Ever."

He was so tired of their bickering, they never liked each other and always seemed to pick the worst times to show it. "Look, Ben, we gotta get off the street. I can spare some ammunition for you, but the three of us had a prior agreement about taking others in."

Ben chuckled to himself and thought of Pisano's. "Yeah, we did too." He motioned to the bodies of Sal and Lucy behind him. "This is why I couldn't stay even if you wanted me to. There's a girl running around out there and he," he said, pointing to Isaac's corpse, "was all she had left. When we were holed up in my place, we talked it over, we said we weren't taking our chances with anyone, and then these two kids literally come crashing through our window the other night." He lifted his shirt and wiped his brow. "They gave me a reason to leave this city, to leave that shithole apartment, and make me rethink my end of the world plans."

Andrew and Clyde listened as he spoke while Juliette stared angrily at her boyfriend, mouthing something to him that Andrew thought might have been *Don't even think about it.*

"The fact that everyone's dead and she's running around by herself is not their fault. It's not yours, it's not mine. It's these two pieces of shit." He grunted as he kicked the man he had beaten to death. "I really appreciate you goin' out on a limb for me, but I've gotta go find my friend." Ben gathered the bags and placed them on both broad shoulders. He nodded at the men and ignored Juliette behind him. He walked away, moving the bat as he went, as if practicing his swing.

"Hey man, why'd you tell us all that?" Clyde called out to him with his hands on his hips.

Ben stopped and turned, shrugging his shoulders.

"Because it looks to me like you're in the same situation I was in a few days ago, and everyone deserves an opportunity to get out while they can." He turned and continued walking.

Andrew couldn't help but stare at the bodies Ben had so tenderly placed next to each other. Everybody was somebody. He looked up at Juliette, her hardened expression still fixed on him.

When had she become so selfish?

He thought of all the others that she forced him to ignore. The helpless people on the highway that he ran from instead of staying and protecting. All of it to keep her safe. He was an officer of the law, his duty to serve and protect, and yet he'd been shut up in his brother's apartment, taking orders from his girlfriend because she didn't want to get her hands dirty.

"Andrew, goddamnit!" she yelled at him as he suddenly began jogging after Ben.

"Hey, man, hey! Wait up!"

Ben slowed and Andrew met up with him.

"Look, this girl, you sure she wasn't bitten?"

"No, I'm not. But I feel like I owe it to her brother to find out."

"Damn, man." He ran his hand over his sweating head. "Alright, look, where you headed?"

"Paradise Bay."

"Ok, I used to be a cop in Franklin Township. I know the area real well. I could come with you, I can handle myself coming back once you find her."

"I appreciate it, but that's not necessary."

"Look, man," Andrew said, holding a look of remorse in his eyes as he spoke. "I owe it to myself to help out. Since all this shit went down I've been pretty useless, and that's not who I was. That's not who I *am*."

Ben nodded. He understood. He hadn't had a lot of interactions with too many people since the world fell apart but he knew one thing was true: it was up to you to decide what you became in a world like this, and for some, that was a struggle.

XIV

Despite Juliette's protests, Ben came back with them into the apartment. Ben instantly disliked her. She was a tall, thin blonde with birdlike features. She paced a lot and was more than happy to inform Ben that she was a vegetarian and a personal trainer. She was the typical brat liberal type, and he was surprised she'd even made it past the initial outbreak.

Andrew decided that he wanted to take the day to pack up, and given the morning's events, that it might be a good idea for Ben to get himself cleaned up and rested. Ben didn't like the idea of wasting time, but he was pretty hungry and still in shock that Sal and Lucy, the people who had taken him in when he had nothing and treated him like family for so long, were gone.

Andrew showed Ben his enormous cache of weapons. "Holy hell, where did all this come from?"

"Well, some of it belongs to Clyde, I'm to blame for that hobby. I mean, he's a big guy and all, but he's actually a pretty big sissy."

"Fuck you, Drew!" Clyde yelled from the kitchen. Andrew chuckled.

"Anyway, I had a lot, obviously. But I took a lot of stuff from the station."

"If you were already out of the city, why would you come back? I know that things were bad everywhere, but didn't they want all the cops on the street to break up the so-called-rioting?" He made over-exaggerated air quotes and rolled his eyes.

"Yeah, well, I wasn't stupid. I knew it wasn't no rioting. Even my own LT told me that. Told me to grab my girl and get outta Dodge. Only, the getting back out part never happened. At least, not yet."

Clyde entered the bedroom and whistled at the weaponry that was spread out on the king size bed. He lit a set of candles on his dresser.

"Here ya go, we're probably 'bout the same size. Figure you need to get some clean clothes on you."

Ben took the bundle of clothes from him and thanked him. He removed a few things from his pockets and began changing.

"Oh, here, I got some of these too, get some of that nasty shit off of ya'," Clyde said from the bathroom, coming out with some baby wipes. He winked, handing them to Ben.

Andrew rolled his eyes. "Ignore him. Please."

The men laughed and Clyde spotted Ben's cigarettes. "Ooh, do you mind?" He picked up the pack.

"Nah, help yourself."

Clyde smoked in the bathroom while Andrew and Ben continued talking. Ben furiously scrubbed at his arms with the wipes to get the blood off his skin. He thought he'd never get the smell of the dead out of his nose, though. He remembered all the mayhem out on the street, he remembered the single eater he had put down, and then watching people literally get ripped apart right outside of Pisano's soon after that, but he had never been up close and personal with so many before. He was surprised he wasn't more shook up about it, but then again...not too many things conjured up any emotion in him these days.

"Me and my LT, we were pretty tight. Hank was one cool dude, we worked together for years. He was always up front with me about shit. I was with some other officers, trying to calm things down out at Franklin High School. A news reporter had been attacked, and we were trying to keep the situation under control. We were told to clear out the area, we couldn't believe our eyes. It was a mess."

Ben sat down in an oversized purple armchair in the corner of the room, allowing Andrew to tell the story that he didn't get to talk about because of Juliette. Clyde tossed Ben his Zippo and pack, pointing to a crystal bowl on the dresser next to him. "How did you navigate the highway? I heard...no, I know for a fact that it was bumper to bumper."

A clap of thunder startled all of them as rain began to pour down outside.

"Yeah, leaving, it was bad, but nobody wanted back in. Who the hell would? We were crazy for it, but we did what we had to do. The thing was, all these people that were runnin' away from the shit in the city, they had no idea that the same thing was comin' straight at them. I was able to finally get a phone call out to Juliette and she was freaking out, she was trapped at her place, couldn't get out, those things were practically beating down the doors to get into her house because she was makin' so much noise. I couldn't help it, I had to get to Juliette. All those people in their cars, I just ignored them. I left them there. I'll never forget those screams."

Andrew lowered his eyes to the carpet, they were full of remorse.

"When we got to Juliette's, her parents...they were already turned. Tryin' to get in the house to eat their own daughter alive." He shook his head. "Her father, he was never too keen on her datin' a black man, always hated me. But that didn't mean I ever wanted to put a bullet in his head."

"And that's how they ended up crashin' my party." Clyde quickly changed the subject. "Juliette's had us locked in here and callin' all the shots since day one, I can't stand it. This man is pussy-whipped like you wouldn't believe. And that bitch is crazy as hell too, she got all—"

"Hey," Andrew shot him a hurt look, "I keep tellin' you, man, ease up with the Juliette shit. She's scared, that's all. She don't wanna lose anyone else."

"Are you kidding me? You're smoking in the house now?" Juliette walked into the bedroom, the light from the candles dancing across her face. "Y'all make me sick. This guy is a bad influence, I can't believe you let him in here." She walked right back out almost as soon as she'd come in.

Clyde put a hand on his hip and flipped his long braids over his shoulder. "You see what I'm sayin'?"

Andrew shook his head and Ben put his cigarette out in the crystal bowl beside him.

This ought to be a blast, he thought as he lit another.

*

Veronica was too fast for any of the eaters she encountered as she ran, her light steps barely made a sound, and she was instantly forgotten to them. She began to feel cold drops on her skin and the sky erupted with what felt like the heaviest rain she had ever been caught in. The sounds of the world collided once again with her ears and she collapsed to the asphalt, panting, her tongue thick and dry in her mouth.

Veronica looked around, bewildered by her surroundings. She didn't even know she had made it this far.

How long have I been running? Where am I?

She looked around frantically; there were no eaters after her. She noticed a semi-truck about fifteen feet ahead of her. She got back onto her feet, looking around once more, and made it inside. It was a sleeper cab, and at that point, she didn't care if it was empty. She threw herself into the back and flopped onto the bed, slamming the small door behind her.

The space smelled awful, but she didn't care. She lie on her back, staring up at the ceiling, not even bothering to look around and take in the details. The rain slamming against the roof of the cab filled her ears and Veronica cried herself to sleep.

*

Clyde cleared the bed off and told Ben if he'd like some time to himself he should take advantage of it since the storm would be keeping them from leaving. Even through the closed door, Ben could hear Andrew and Juliette arguing, he was sure it was about him.

I didn't ask for this. He felt like getting up right now and taking off, but now that he had already wasted so much time here, it wouldn't make sense heading out at night when he had no idea where he would even begin to look for Veronica. He didn't know why he felt so obligated to find her, but that's all he could think about. Ever since she had told him about their plan to get out of the city and head for the water, he had felt the smallest spark of hope come alive.

When things got bad in the street, that spark tried to go out. But he had looked at Sal and Lucy, together on the sidewalk with Isaac, and that spark was brighter than ever, because he knew he wasn't ready to join them yet. And he knew Veronica wasn't either. In the short time he had spent with her, he knew that girl had more smarts and more balls than any of them. If anyone could make it out there on their own, it would be her.

XV

Drops of water fell from the gutters onto the air conditioning unit that took up the small window in the room. Ben thought of himself getting caught in the storm that had so quickly come on and was glad he'd decided to stick around. He got up from the armchair after having one last cigarette and practically collapsed onto the comforter.

The décor of the room was deep purple, everything matching, including the walls, which were lined with a gold trim. Lavender feather boas were draped on both bed posts and it made Ben laugh. He hated the color purple. Each room of Clyde's apartment was a different theme of colors ranging from violet to lilac. Ben noticed there was a large black and white painting of naked men's silhouettes hanging in the living room.

At least he didn't hang it in the bedroom.

Ben hadn't slept well at all the night before they decided to leave his apartment above Pisano's, and felt he deserved a nap. The storm was entrancing and he dozed off immediately.

Ben slept for about two hours before waking up to Juliette and Andrew bickering and Clyde singing in the background. Ben wondered if Clyde was singing on purpose; he seemed like the type to instigate things for his own entertainment. He stretched and got up, putting his cigarettes and Zippo back in his pocket. Although Clyde's jeans were a little tight on him, it was nice to wear clean pants. He threw on Clyde's red t-shirt and walked into the hall, cringing at Juliette's raised voice.

"We had a plan, you know how important it is for me to have a plan!"

"Baby, I understand, but just like before all this mess, plans fall through, plans change."

Ben could tell she was the neurotic type; definitely OCD. She was undoubtedly traumatized by her parents trying to eat her, and then that was made worse by Andrew having to kill them.

"This is good for us, this might be a blessing in disguise. We saved a man's life this morning, and we have the chance to help someone else."

"I'm not leaving."

"Nobody asked you to come with us."

Andrew looked at Clyde with a raised eyebrow. "Us? What you mean us?"

"Oh, you didn't think I was gonna sit back here and play house with blondie over there, did you?"

"Man, we can't leave her here by herself."

"No, you can't, so nobody is going to go anywhere." Juliette threw her arms in the air. "Give that man some of your stupid bullets for your stupid guns and send him packing!"

"No, I'm going. That's the bottom line. Clyde, you're staying with Juliette. End of story."

Andrew noticed Ben standing in the doorway and nodded a greeting. Ben stared at Juliette, and she walked over to Andrew.

"Excuse me if I'm a little too forward, I don't know any of you at all, but y'all like to argue pretty loudly, and it's not hard to hear what you're discussing."

Andrew started to apologize but Ben waved him off. "I understand, Juliette, that you have some sort of problem with all of this, but I just think you should keep in mind that one day you might not have a choice in leaving Clyde's apartment. And if it just so happens that you don't, then you never will, and that will be because you will die here. And that's the harsh truth for all three of you. I didn't want to think about it when we were all holed up in my place, but sooner or later we were going to run out of food, or run into those things, or hell, even better yet, get attacked by some thievin' pieces of trash, like them who end up killin' everyone in my group. But it's not the type of world where we get to sit around and wait for the sun to come out. Help ain't comin' and you gotta do things a little bit differently."

Clyde clapped his hands together, breaking the tension. "See? I like him. Tellin' it like it is. None of this pussy-footin' around waiting for all that mess out there to blow over."

"I like the idea of having somebody tag along that knows how to handle himself and a weapon. Two of you? Well that's even better. And no offense, I don't so much like the idea of having you out there with us, but it's a bad idea for you to stay here alone and rot. Do you think that sounds like a good plan? To sit here and rot if they can't or *don't* make it back?"

Andrew opened his mouth to say something but decided against it; he liked where Ben was going with this. Juliette looked sheepishly at the floor, avoiding eye contact with Ben.

"I'm gonna just let you go ahead and think about all that. What are y'all using for a bathroom?"

"The shop downstairs. It's nasty as hell too, just a warning." Clyde scrunched his nose up at the thought of the smell.

"Don't worry, I think I can handle it." Ben shared a laugh with himself. They at least had a bathroom in common. Between Pisano's, the shoe store under Clyde's apartment and who knows what other shops in the area, the dead wouldn't be the only overwhelming scent in the city after a while. He opened the shop's door and pulled his shirt up over his nose. The familiar smell of urine and feces greeted him and he did his business as fast as he could.

He returned upstairs and nobody was talking. Everyone seemed to be pretty deep in thought. Andrew packed a huge duffle bag full of weapons and ammunition while Clyde cooked some sort of stew on a camping stove.

"Yeah, it's not the best idea to use one of these things inside, but it's all we got," he said when Ben questioned him on the safety of it.

Juliette did yoga, or some kind of exercise Ben wasn't sure of, and he decided he would go back into the bedroom and stay out of everybody's way.

Andrew followed him into the bedroom and shut the door. "Listen, I normally wouldn't be okay with some crazy white boy comin' in here and talkin' to my girl like that, but what you said…it was true. And I think she needed to hear it. She's not that bad. She's got some problems." Andrew seemed hesitant to continue.

Ben held out his pack of smokes and Andrew shook his head no. "She was on some medication, ya know, those types of problems."

Ben raised his eyebrows as he lit a cigarette, "Well, sounds to me like she should probably still be on medication."

"She ran out of her house so fast that she didn't bring a single thing with her. It's taking its toll on her too. She hasn't been herself since all this happened."

"Yeah, it happens." He blew a puff of smoke up toward the ceiling. "So what then? Do we need to stop by a pharmacy on the way and steal a bunch of pills? I really don't care, I just want to get out of the city."

"Thank you." Andrew was relieved. "Yes. We need to try and find her some medication."

"Alright. Sounds like we're gettin' somewhere. When's dinner?"

"He's finishing it up now."

Clyde served everyone his very bland, very simple stew, but Ben thought it was better than canned meats and stale bread. Plus, he hadn't eaten hot food since the power went out. The rain had subsided for the time being, but thunder continued to rumble as the group ate their candle lit dinner in silence.

*

Veronica woke to silence. The musty aroma of the cab filled her nostrils. She sat up on the bed, which was surprisingly comfortable, and rubbed her eyes. The cab was pitch black. She rolled over and felt all around in the darkness until, as luck would have it, her hands fell upon a flash light.

She switched it on and squinted her eyes. A calendar full of naked women hung on the wall across from her, and other miscellaneous junk filled the room. A case of water sat untouched, as if waiting for her. She leapt toward it and tore into its plastic, chugging down almost a whole bottle instantly. She panted from her furious drinking and sat in silence for a moment, taking in her situation.

"Everyone I know is dead."

She looked around the sleeper, almost as if expecting a reply.

"Everyone I know is dead," she repeated to herself and her eyes dropped to the floor. She felt like she should cry, but couldn't muster up any more emotion. She was empty.

There was a small bag full of foul-smelling rags in the sleeper with her. She threw them to the floor and filled the bag with as many of the waters as she knew she could comfortably carry. She'd slept the entire day away but thought it wise to begin her trek to the bay under cover of night.

She crept into the front of the cab and carefully scanned the area around the truck. The coast was clear and she quietly opened the door. The rain had stopped for the time being, but she could still hear thunder every now and again.

Veronica looked around and found a comfortable spot to relieve herself, and as she squatted by a tree, her light shone upon a pile of discarded PVC pipe on the side of the highway. She made her way to it and picked out the perfect, most dangerous-looking piece she could wield.

She nodded at her find and adjusted the bag's strap around her shoulder. She smoothed out her filthy purple shirt and headed off for her destination.

Veronica wasn't sure how long it would take her to get there, she wasn't even sure how far she'd already come, but she was sure as hell not going to let anything stop her. She tried hard to busy her mind with song lyrics or anything at all to keep from thinking of the world around her, all the while straining her ears for the sound of a threat.

In the darkness, she didn't notice the big green sign off to her right:

Franklin Woods – 6 miles
Paradise Bay – 8 miles

*

The sky opened up at around 10:30 that night. The downpour of rain and a sky full of lightning lasted through the night and by morning it hadn't let up one bit.

"No way we're leavin' in this." Clyde was making breakfast by the window in the kitchen.

"Let's just wait it out, we're prepared to go anyway. As soon as it lets up, we'll head out."

Andrew looked at Ben who was at the window with Clyde. The guy was itching to go and Mother Nature decided she had other plans for them.

Ben watched the wind whip the rain around, sending it splattering into the window in a rhythmic spray. Trash flew around in the streets, and he found himself staring at the bodies lying motionless, rain washing away all the blood and gore, making them appear to be sleeping, not as the undead monsters he'd put down the day before.

He repeated Andrew's words to himself. "As soon as it lets up, we'll head out."

The entire day was wasted as the rain persisted. The winds howled and thunder boomed. Ben got antsy and felt trapped. Juliette took every opportunity to start a fight with Andrew, or find something to yell at Clyde about. Ben didn't know if he could take one more day of it.

As he went to bed that night on the floor of the living room, Clyde on the couch and the others in the bedroom, he couldn't help but worry about Veronica. He hoped she had found safety. The first bit of weather hadn't lasted long, but this second storm felt like forever. The only thing the rain was good for that night was helping him get to sleep.

Ben opened his eyes the next morning and Clyde was snoring so loudly he thought Darth Vader was in the room.

He jumped up and ran to the window. The streets were still wet, but there was no rain and the sky was a beautiful blue, without a cloud to be seen. The early morning sun was still rising and he thought he'd never seen anything so beautiful in such an ugly place.

He walked over to the couch and gave Clyde a shove. "Rise and shine, sleepin' beauty, we're already burnin' daylight."

Clyde yawned and waved a hand at him and rolled over.

Ben knocked loudly on the bedroom door. Andrew almost fell out of the bed trying to get up from the tangled sheets around his legs.

"What's the matter? Everything cool?" He swung the door open and was greeted by Ben's smiling face.

"Everything couldn't be cooler. Round up your lady friend, it's time to go."

Clyde had a hard time deciding between what *needed* to be take and what he didn't want to leave behind. He gave Ben one of his bed sheets at his odd request, but he didn't have any use for it. Juliette nervously packed her things. Andrew had let her know they were making a pit stop at a pharmacy and that she'd be back to feeling like her old self in no time. She still hadn't spoken directly to Ben since he'd arrived.

Ben had made a lot of sense, and she knew she couldn't help the way she was behaving, but he'd made her feel like a complete selfish waste of space.

Maybe I am, maybe we're all just kidding ourselves, it doesn't matter where we go, we're all rotting, and we're all just waiting to die. Her toxic thoughts raced around inside her head as she finished getting dressed.

Everyone had an enormous bag stuffed to the brim with supplies, food, or guns except for Juliette, who wore a simple small backpack with just a few of the things she wanted to bring.

They trudged down the stairs, and Clyde bid his apartment farewell as he closed the door. He thought about locking it, but figured if anybody ever needed a place to stay, his door would always be open.

They stepped out onto the street, looking up and down, listening for anything at all.

It was one of the quietest days in the city any of them could remember. Distant, random sounds were too far off to be of concern. Ben unfolded the sheet he'd been carrying and shook it out. He walked over to the decaying bodies of his friends and delicately draped it over them. The king-sized sheet was perfect for the three and he silently said his goodbyes, making a promise to Isaac that he would find his sister and keep her safe. He knew that's what the boy would have wanted to hear.

Clyde wiped a single tear from his eye before anyone could notice. Andrew bowed his head in a silent prayer for the dead, and Juliette piped in, ruining the moment. "Alright, any day now. I thought we were in a rush to tie up your loose ends, or whatever. I'm not very excited about standing out in the open like this."

Ben spit on the corpses of the street creeps who'd attacked them and never gave them another thought. He walked away without another word. He tried to give Juliette the benefit of the doubt, but still disliked her immensely. His benefit of the doubt reservoir was getting low. He wondered how long she would make it out here before someone else would have to start carrying her weight. At least that someone else would be Andrew. He didn't have time for coddled, spoiled women. Especially not coddled, spoiled women who should be on meds.

"So, where to, big guy?" He looked to Andrew.

Andrew thought for a moment before responding. "There's a CVS not too far from here. It won't back track us much from the highway. I don't even think it'll take us a mile out of the way."

"Wouldn't it be better to just get the hell out of here? Franklin's got pharmacies. Rich people *love* takin' pills. All sorts of pills." Clyde chewed his finger nails, spitting them out as he talked.

"Well, the only thing about that is Franklin's only got one pharmacy. What if we get there and it doesn't have anything that we need? At least this way we could hit up two of them once we get outta the city."

Ben nodded. "That's a good point. Let's hope one or both have something useful, or else we're just wasting time."

They followed Andrew closely, melee weapons ready, guns holstered. Using the guns on the street like they did two days ago was one thing; the eaters were already riled up and out in the open. This morning the streets were clear, and there was no use in sending the masses their way over one or two of them.

Most of the street-level windows in every building they passed were smashed to bits. Where there wasn't glass littering the streets, there were bloodstains, garbage, and body parts lying around. With each turn they took back east, it seemed as though the gore on the streets was thicker; the destruction of the city was more evident, and the smell of the dead grew stronger.

"I can't believe we're headed back here. You could have just gone and then come back for me on your way out," Juliette mumbled to Andrew as they walked.

Ben quickly shut her up as they continued down the street. "Ssh. There's no time for this right now." They made a right and came to an abrupt stop.

Andrew's hand shot up and he brought the golf club up slowly, motioning for Ben to follow his lead. Clyde stayed with Juliette, hand over her mouth, keeping her quiet once she noticed why they'd stopped. One eater was shuffling around by itself. It wore a long blue bathrobe and curlers in its hair. Its exposed body was gray and peppered with black, festering wounds. Almost her entire right breast had been ripped off and Ben couldn't stand to look at her half-eaten face.

The two moved very slowly around so that they could both take a swing if the other missed. A piece of glass crunched under Andrew's boot and the eater swung around in his directions. A low, lazy growl escaped its lips as the corpse shuffled toward him. With a loud crack, it dropped to its knees and onto its face. Ben wiped the bat off on her already-stained robe and nodded to Clyde.

"See? They got everything under control." Clyde said.

Juliette was shaking, but quiet. Clyde took his hand away and pushed her forward to catch up with the others. A few feet ahead, Ben heard the familiar hiss of an eater and readied his bat. When he finally saw where it was, he noticed it was in a red pickup truck with busted-out windows. The thing still had its seatbelt on. He couldn't imagine that being a just demise for anyone and put it out of its misery.

They continued, even more cautiously than before, up the block and stopped before making their final left onto the street where CVS stood.

"Okay, the drug store is right up there, gonna be on our left." Andrew spoke directly to Ben. "I don't know how well you know the city, but if we cross the street and go one more street up when we're done—"

"That's the road that leads to the highway. Yeah, I got ya. Straight shot back west and we're golden. None of this creepin' around corners shit."

"Alright. Clyde you good?"

"I'm just *fine*," he responded, still chewing his nails.

Juliette seemed like she was far off, somewhere else inside her head.

Andrew touched her face. "You good, baby girl?"

She nodded although she didn't look at him, staring off into nothing instead. Ben couldn't help but hope she would go catatonic.

They turned the corner one by one and made it to the front of the CVS.

"Shit! Just great. Only fucking place in the city with the gate down." Andrew exhaled and shook his head.

"Maybe there's a back entrance?" Ben looked around, making sure they didn't miss an alley.

"Nope, but everybody relax." Clyde pulled out his .45 and shot off the lock. The shot rang in everyone's ears, and Andrew almost punched his brother in the face. There was no time for freaking out, though. Everyone was too concerned with getting the gate up and getting inside. The door was also locked but Ben handled that one with the bat.

A ferocious scream came from close by and everyone rushed inside. Clyde pulled the gate down and shut the door quickly, but still saw two eaters tearing down the street in their direction.

"Are you stupid?! How stupid are you?!" Andrew had his brother by the shirt and was hollering at him.

"Andrew, stop, keep your voice down. It's over and done with." Ben peered over a make-up advertisement in the window, it hid his body so he wasn't worried about being spotted. "Please, let's just get this over with and take care of those two things we got out there now." The two eaters just stood there, looking around, not knowing where their prey had gone.

Then three more suddenly appeared.

Ben sighed, shaking his head. He figured they were safe for the moment, and they should take this opportunity with a fully stocked store that hadn't been looted.

Wonders abound.

Maybe it hadn't been ransacked because this *really was* one of the only places he'd seen so far in the city owned by someone with enough sense to pull down the gate before they left. Not everyone had Sal's forethought. Ben knew that even at Lucy's pharmacy, they'd all just ran out like scared animals.

They lucked out with this in a huge way. There was a ton of food and beverage options and first-aid supplies. It was like an oasis.

He met the others in the back where Andrew was speaking.

"We've gotta find keys. I'll go check the office, they locked the pharmacy up just as good as the rest of the place. But I know the office door won't have as good a lock on it." Andrew disappeared between the shelves and the rest just stood there, taking the store in.

There were rectangular windows near the ceiling in the corners of the room that allowed in natural light, and also allowed them to appreciate the luck they'd run into. As long as the eaters didn't know they were in there, they could take some extra time to evaluate the situation outside, examine their supplies, replenish and replace. Juliette could rummage through the pharmacy all she wanted.

Andrew returned a few moments later, keys jingling in his happy hands. He tossed them to Juliette, who went to work opening the pharmacy door.

Clyde grinned at him.

"See? Shootin' that lock off wasn't such a stupid move after all."

"No, you still did something stupid, but either way, I guess a thank you is in order." They embraced each other, sharing a brief unspoken apology.

"What do you think, Ben?"

"I hate to say it, but I think we need to wait out those things, and Juliette might need to chill out for a few. Let's stick around here for the time being and head out again when it's safe. If we're smart about it, we make it to Franklin by, what, tomorrow night?"

"You got it, man."

"And CVS got wine." Clyde wiggled his eyebrows. "Don't mind if I do." He hurried off to the non-working refrigerators on the other side of the store and helped himself to an unopened bottle of cheap Pinot Noir. He came back with a warm six pack of his brother's favorite beer, Yuengling.

Warm beer had never tasted so good.

XVI

The three men enjoyed their warm wine and beer; no matter how much better they might have had it in the past, it was the finest alcohol on the planet at that very moment. Juliette popped a few Xanax and stocked up her backpack with the antipsychotics for her mild-onset schizophrenia and bipolar disorder.

The diseases ran in her family, and although she was only twenty-three, if they were left untreated, the illnesses would definitely take their toll on her. Andrew had met Juliette a year before, when her mother had a nervous breakdown and needed to be Baker Acted. It was by no means a romantic situation but Juliette followed his police cruiser to the mental health center and proceeded to have a nervous breakdown herself.

Andrew and Clyde had a mentally-ill mother themselves, so Andrew knew how to handle that sort of thing. He didn't want Juliette to end up in the psych-ward like her mother, so he convinced her to calm down and have a cup of coffee with him. They'd been together ever since. Sure, it was an exhausting relationship, but Andrew was the type of helpful, caring person that only came around once in a lifetime for girls like Juliette.

He'd found no reason to give up on someone you loved, especially when that person wasn't always responsible for how they treated you.

The night came quickly, and their heads buzzed from the alcohol. They had eaten an unhealthy meal of snacks and spent almost the entire day drinking. Juliette softly snored in the corner near the pharmacy door, and Ben checked the front once more. It was too dark to tell if the eaters were still lurking around, but he didn't hear anything. They didn't dare use a flashlight or lantern for fear that the lights might be seen. The windows toward the ceiling were too high to reach without making a bunch of noise, and frankly, not worth covering up for only one night. They sat in the dark, chatting with one another until Clyde drifted off into a deep slumber. Andrew, somewhere in the dark, thanked Ben.

"For what?" Ben didn't feel like anything he'd done deserved a thank you. If anything, he still owed everything to Andrew and Clyde. They'd come out of nowhere and helped him fight off that horde.

"I don't know, man. Everything happens for a reason, so just, thanks. We might have never left. Juliette might have never left. I have a feeling this will be good for her."

No one said another word as they closed their eyes and let the booze take them away.

*

The sun cast a sliver of light into the room and across Ben's face through one of the windows. Everyone else seemed to be up and rummaging about the store. Clyde was figuring out how to fit snacks and wine into a bag already crammed with food and water, while Andrew went through first-aid supplies. Juliette packed up antibiotics and painkillers from the pharmacy.

Ben shrugged his shoulders and popped four Advil into his mouth, washing them down with water. He walked up behind the registers and grabbed as many cartons of cigarettes as he could, shoving them into one of his big bags. He looked around the counters for anything else that might be useful and decided to take a few bottles of lighter fluid, an extra Zippo, and a utility knife.

They all cleaned up with the plethora of personal hygiene supplies they had on hand and took some extra deodorants, cleansing wipes, and hand sanitizer. Juliette and Clyde both thought of taking extra personal hygiene supplies and argued over who got what, as if there wasn't enough for the both of them. Ben was at the front again, peering out the window.

"Is the coast clear?" Andrew had joined him in his watch.

"Looks like it, but who's to say they don't come a runnin' at the sound of that gate coming up? Or worse yet, some more of those looting thugs."

"Well...we're kind of, uh, lootin' now, don't you think?"

"Finders keepers, bro. That's how it goes."

Andrew and Ben snickered at the window while Clyde and Juliette finally decided to ignore one another and finish packing. They were all relatively close in age. Juliette and Clyde were both twenty-three, Ben was twenty-five, and Andrew was twenty-eight.

"So how long you been outta the service?" Andrew asked Ben while continuing to scan the street.

"How could you tell?"

"Oh you just *scream* military. That, and I can pick 'em out of a crowd. A lot of my family served, and a lot of the cops around here have been in."

"Ah, just over a year. Went in right out of high school."

"We're ready when you two are." Juliette came up behind them. Her bleach-blonde hair was pulled back tightly in a neat bun. For a personal trainer, she didn't have a very athletic build; she was very tall and thin, and with her hair like that, she reminded Ben of an anorexic ballerina. She waved her hand at the smoke from Ben's cigarette and coughed at him. Ben rolled his eyes and threw the cigarette to the tile, stepping on it. He eyed them all, a smirk on his face.

With everyone all packed up, we look like a group of gypsies.

"Let's give this a try."

Andrew very slowly removed the wedge he had placed under the front door and opened it. Everyone held their breath as he raised the security gate...the metal grated and clicked loudly, sending shivers down their spines.

They stood frozen in the doorway, awaiting the feral cries of the hungry dead which never came. They looked at one another and headed out.

Clyde stopped on the way out, ready to pull the gate down.

"Come on," Ben said. "It'll make too much noise, and there's no point in lockin' anything up anymore."

Clyde shrugged and they left it that way. As a group, they made their way across the street and Andrew ran ahead to peek around the corner. After a moment, he motioned for them to follow, and they fast-walked up the last block before reaching the road that would lead them to the highway.

Ben had already noticed that the streets were more congested with cars. Some had crashed into telephone poles, street lights, and other vehicles. Car doors yawned open, exposing blood-stained steering wheels. He swore he even heard an engine still running off in the distance.

Andrew ran ahead again to check out their final turn. Ben almost didn't notice him give the okay to continue. He was lost in his thoughts for a moment, hoping that he wasn't putting Veronica in any danger by taking his sweet time with this new group of people.

XVII

They slowly closed the gap between Columbia City and Franklin Township. The highway was a vast graveyard of vehicles, and they stuck to the east-bound lanes; less cars made it easier to walk without having to weave in and out so much. The shoulder even had cars in it, hindering their point A to point B.

The day was absolutely beautiful, despite all the death in the cars around them. And there was a lot. The highway and all its makeshift graves stood as a testament to the day the whole world went away. Bodies lie decaying in the road, birds picking at their skin. Every so often the group came across an eater either hopelessly wandering the highway, or crouched, greedily munching on something terrible. The group figured they were lucking out, but the way Andrew saw it was that the highway was still a highway, just a place for things to travel, living or dead.

"Nobody hung out on the highway when the world was normal. So why would these things be here now? Ya know? When Hank and I were headed back, the things were comin' up behind us, runnin' around in front of us, but the only reason they ever stopped was for people. When there weren't any more people out here, they moved on, either back to the city, or back to the woods."

Ben rubbed his hands together. "Yeah, they're pretty ADD, if you ask me. Sal used to watch them when they were still runnin' aimlessly up and down my street. They would literally run into each other, into cars, into walls. He said they were nothin' but stupid animals. They can't talk, don't care about anything but eating, and can't even figure out how to get to their food. He said even dogs were smarter;

at least dogs can figure out how to chew through a bag." Ben mimicked Sal's accent as he quoted him. He missed his friend and wished they were making the journey to Paradise Bay together.

They reached the bridge and Ben was reminded of Sal's son. "Do you mind if we stop for a few? I just want to look around."

"Look around for what? There ain't nothin' but dead people up here." Clyde dropped his bags and stretched. "I knew you was a freak."

Ben ignored that...he didn't know what exactly he was looking for. That last phone call between Marco and his parents echoed through his head and his skin crawled with goose bumps. He didn't know what kind of car Marco's friends were driving that day, or even if he would find some remnant of Marco or his friends. Maybe a part of him hoped Marco was hiding in one of these cars somewhere, but he knew it was highly unlikely. He hopped the guard rail to the west bound side and walked around, peering into cars, not knowing what he might find each time.

He looked out at the water that ran into the bay. It seemed to sparkle under the sun, a mirror that reflected everything around them. The trees, the sky, everything could be seen twice in its clear flowing beauty. He peered over the side and the mirror was shattered.

On the concrete of the foundation below were the splattered bodies of people who had jumped to escape the eaters. But he knew that they hadn't accidentally landed there; if they'd had any intention of living, they would have jumped out and into the water, hoping to be washed away somewhere with fewer nightmares.

Ben wondered if any of them were Marco. He wondered if they had been bitten and had enough sense to keep themselves from turning, contributing to the spread of the infection.

He wondered if any of them were Veronica.

Ben grew angry and came to the conclusion that he had seen enough. It was time to keep moving.

He rejoined the group back where they had stopped.

"Everything alright?" Andrew was sitting next to Juliette in the road, applying sunscreen to her fair-skinned face. She placed her oversized sunglasses back on once he was done.

"Yeah," he finally said. "Everything's fine. Break's over. We ready to keep moving?"

"Sure, just a few more miles of highway before we hit Franklin Woods. We can probably sneak in there and test drive one of those sweet-ass houses."

"Yeah, Sal and Lucy lived there. I'm sure they wouldn't mind us staying in their place for the night."

"Even better. No more breaking and entering for us today."

Clyde laughed at his brother's remark. "Whoever would have thought a cop would have raided CVS with us?"

Juliette smiled for the first time since Ben had met her; she was actually pretty. He wished she would smile more, and maybe then he'd try to make nice with her.

The group pressed on, their pace taking them the entire day to make it from the city to the other end of the highway. Nice and easy, cautious and quiet. Andrew didn't think there was a reason to waste energy or resources to make such a short trip.

As much as it pained him to go so slowly, Ben agreed and remembered his grandma's favorite saying: *haste makes waste.*

"I'm tired of walking," Juliette said softly to Andrew.

"You're in the best shape of all of us and you're tired of walking?" Clyde scoffed. "Gimme a cigarette, will you?" He threw his bags down and Ben lit two cigarettes, handing one to him.

Andrew rubbed Juliette's shoulders and kissed her forehead. "It's not that much farther. You heard Ben, he knows a place where we can stay."

"Oh...alright."

Clyde and Ben finished their smokes while they walked, looking around them constantly. The thick trees in the setting sun proved to be eerie for everyone.

"I'll take the city over this shit any day of the week. Imagine bein' lost out in that." Clyde flicked his cigarette out into the brush.

"Dude, what are you, a firebug?" Ben craned his neck to try and see where the butt landed.

"It just rained. And don't these new cigarettes go out by themselves? Annoyin' as hell."

Andrew and Ben shook their heads together. Ben couldn't help but look back to check if there was any smoke. Clyde was right, though, the new cigarettes were meant to go out, which was just as well. He didn't need anything else to worry about.

Within the next hour, twilight was taking the sky, and up ahead, they could see the enormous gates that held the community of Franklin Woods. Houses rose behind the gates like tombstones in a silent cemetery.

"I think it's an electric gate. How are we gonna get it open with the power being out?" Clyde turned to look at Ben.

"Well, I'm not an electrician, but I'm pretty sure those gates are made with fail safes for instances like this. Well, not exactly like this, but we do get a lot of hurricanes."

"Yeah, it's some legality, lawsuit, safety measure," Andrew chimed in as Ben walked past him and Juliette toward the gate. There was no guard in the shed, obviously, but he had looked out of habit. He gave the gate an easy pull but it only budged. He noticed someone had put a brass pin in place to keep it from opening and wondered if someone in there didn't want any visitors. He removed the pin and the gate opened with no problem.

"See? C'mon, it's getting darker every minute. We don't know what's in these woods."

Ben ushered everyone through the gate and closed the heavy thing behind him, replacing the pin. They walked quietly up the street, passing two badly mangled cars that were nearly in a driveway.

"Man, if I lived there, I'd be pissed as hell with this shit in front of my house." Clyde took a peek inside one of the cars and made a face.

"I'm pretty sure nobody lives there anymore. Keep moving." Andrew pushed his brother forward.

"I just saw a light in that house." Juliette stopped walking and pointed at the enormous home with the wrecked cars in front of it.

"C'mon, baby doll, there's nobody there. It's okay." Andrew put his arm around her.

The first street was a huge circle that led back to the front entrance and exit. One way in or out of Franklin Woods. Sal's house was on one of the roads off the main circle. Ben knew where they'd kept the key, and ran ahead to retrieve it before the others had even climbed the steps to the front door. He ran up and got both locks, the deadbolt and the knob, before sticking in his head and calling out.

Hopefully, there were no surprises waiting for them in there. After about ten seconds, he was satisfied that the house was empty and waved for the other three to join him inside.

They had plenty of food with them, but Sal always kept a stocked pantry. Everyone had their own bed to sleep in that night, and while Ben never prayed, he did thank Sal and Lucy, wherever they might be, for a place to stay.

XVIII

Franklin Woods was the most upscale community in Columbia Beach, Florida; so much so, it had its own zip code. Elegant mansions outfitted with the newest security technologies kept the minds of the residents at ease. The community housed the doctors, business men, trust fund babies and lawyers of the city, including criminal defense attorney Samson Eckhart, III and his stunning wife Moira. On weekends, the neighborhood buzzed with block parties and barbecues. The sounds of Franklin Woods—the children playing, the trophy wives comparing outfits, hairstyles and home furnishings and the husbands discussing work, golf and yachting—were always heard with welcome delight.

These days, Franklin Woods was not filled with the usual buzzing of the wealthy, but with an eerie silence that would unsettle even the deaf. An Escalade that had smashed into a BMW 7 Series, sat empty, the occupants of the BMW mangled in their luxury coffin in front of the Eckhart House on Damon Circle. Moira Eckhart stared at the crash every morning through the window of her second story bedroom before locking herself in the bathroom to begin her day. Moira didn't like that the crash had happened literally five feet from her driveway, but there was nothing anyone could do about it. Not anymore.

The world might have ended for everyone else, she thought, *but it hasn't ended for me.*

The most difficult part of Moira's day since everyone in the world began eating each other was still what shoes went with what blouse. She undressed in the morning and washed her body with the baby wipes that Samson would bring home when he went out looking for food. Since the water and the power went out, she had to use any means necessary to stay as close as possible to her routine from before everything went to shit. After cleaning up, she would cover her body in luxurious lotions from her collection. Anti-aging for the face, firming for the body, and softening for her feet and hands. Foundation came next, then the powder. Blush, eye shadow, mascara, and everything else came after. She examined the fine wrinkles in her brow and frowned. Her signature line was once "What's a girl to do without Botox?" But now that was something she'd have to figure out.

She would remove the curlers from her platinum blonde hair and brush it out, finally applying the finishing touch to her near perfect face, a deep red lip stain. Before leaving the room to dress, she would flash her water-bottle-brushed smile and wink, hands on her hips, and nod approvingly. *I'm just a twenty-year-old trapped in a thirty-eight-year-old's body* she would tell her friends, *except for these!* And by "these" Moira meant her 36DD breasts, the $12,000 gift from Samson on their fifteenth wedding anniversary.

Moira was as plastic as she could be while remaining human. She would dance through her closet, brushing furs across her face as she passed them. Pulling scarves from their hooks, she twirled and wrapped them around herself. Each morning was a different song, always classy, usually bluesy. Moira would serenade herself as she dressed and privately performed in front of the mirrors that lined the walls of the enormous walk-in.

Samson was downstairs by the time Moira finished her routine and slipped into her stilettos. She stepped out of the bedroom and quietly closed the door. "I hope you took care not to disturb the children, Sammy," she said without looking at him, passing by swiftly to the kitchen. Her heels clicked loudly on the hardwood floor, making his skin crawl. Samson continued lacing the boots he found while rummaging through one of their neighbor's houses and chose to ignore her. Samson had been a lawyer, an incredible one, but the once man of words found himself talking less and less these days. Samson saw that there was no more law, and without law, there were no lawyers. His once sought-after skills were meaningless. The only skill of importance that remained was to lie, and in the new world, he figured a good liar was a survivor.

Moira returned to the living room, her instant coffee in-hand. The woman was careless with their minimal resources. She would guzzle bottles of water and prepare lavish meals that wound up in the trash. It angered Samson to no end.

She stared at Samson expectantly. "Well?"

He ignored his wife, her bright blue eyes burning a hole into his skull. He stood up, his six-foot frame towering over her, even with her four-inch heels on. His back still to her, his gaze on the staircase before him, he thought back to the last conversation he'd had with anyone other than his wife.

Al.

"Sammy, goddamnit! I'm talking to you!"

Moira's shrill yell snapped him out of his daze. Samson's eyes remained on the staircase and he realized he had been holding his breath. He shook his head, and all thoughts of the redneck piece of shit he'd brought into his home disappeared.

Samson turned to his wife, her face beautiful even when she was scowling at him. "I'm sorry," he mumbled, "I lost myself."

Moira rolled her eyes as she took a sip of her instant coffee. "Lost yourself? Hmm, in where? There?" She reached up in an attempt to hit him in the head but her height betrayed her. "Well good for you. I'm glad you think you have the time to lose yourself while your family is shut away in this house." She slammed her mug down on the counter to her right and placed both hands on her hips. "If you pull the same shit you did last week, we're better off without you. You want to just bring home rapists? Murderers? You think that's funny?!" She was angry, angrier than he could stomach.

"Moira, sweetheart, I didn't mean for things to get out of hand, you know that." Samson wondered how many more times she would bring Al up. And how often. He took a step toward her and placed a hand on her shoulder. She shrugged him off and stepped back.

"Oh sweetheart, I didn't m-m-mean," she mocked him and pushed his heavy frame with both hands. "All you're good for is making sure this family doesn't fall apart." She stabbed a self-manicured finger into his chest. "And if you can't even do that without putting us in danger then you know what you'll be good for next."

Samson turned away from her as she continued to berate him in their living room. He stomped off toward the door, grabbing the Remington with his right hand. He stopped only to glance up the stairs as he opened the front door.

He thought back on when he had first met his wife. Samson came from a line of wealth. His father and grandfather and so on were all attorneys and the money had seemed endless. It was spring break seventeen years before and Samson had just turned twenty-one. He and his friends were armed to the teeth with money and flew down to Miami to have the week of their lives. The nights were long, full of young, beautiful women and expensive booze; during the day they slept in the sun and ate lavish lunches on the beach. It was the fourth night into their trip and they strolled up to the club entrance, flashing their million-dollar smiles at the bouncers, tipping heavily and saying their hellos. Samson found himself distracted by a fast-talking, big mouthed blonde being turned away at the door.

"No ID, no entry, shortstop." A heavily-tattooed guard smoking a cigar waved her away.

"This is totally ridiculous! My friends are already inside! I didn't see you ID any of them!" The small young woman was surely going to find herself escorted off the premises if she kept up the yelling. Samson smirked, watching the girl make a fool of herself. There was something about her Napoleon Syndrome he found both amusing and extremely attractive.

"Hey, Danny, this chick is holding up the line, man. Get her outta here." The tattooed guard called for one of the others to come over and take care of the situation.

"Hey! Hey! Get your fucking hands off me!" The small blonde kicked and hollered at the large man named Danny who had picked her up. Samson laughed and told his friends he'd be right in.

"Woah woah woah man, hold up!" He jogged over to Danny and the screaming girl. Danny turned to see the well-dressed rich kid who'd been at the club the last few nights.

"Oh, hey, my man, what's goin' on?"

"You've got my lady friend there. Mind if I have her back?" He pointed at the blonde who ceased her tantrum. She eyed Samson up and down and a small smile crept across her beautiful face.

"Well? You heard him!" She squirmed in the guard's grip as he set her down.

"You sure about her, man? She seems like trouble to me." Danny shook his head at her as she smoothed out her short white dress and fixed the straps back into place on her delicate shoulders.

Samson held out his hand, slipping Danny a hundred dollar bill. "Appreciate it dude, I got it from here." Danny shrugged, taking the money and patted Samson on the back as he walked back to the club entrance. He put his hand out, "Sam Eckhart."

"Moira Lewis." She shook his hand, still smiling at the dark-haired young man who towered over her.

"I think it's safe to say you're with me tonight?" He tilted his head back at the club and she rolled her eyes at his smug demeanor, but yet couldn't wipe the smile from her face.

"Whatever you say, big guy." She took his arm and they walked right into the night club she was just previously denied entry to. She winked at the guards who chuckled as she strutted by in her strappy gold stilettos.

The rest of the night Moira didn't dare leave Samson's side. She was only nineteen and had sneaked into clubs before, but never managed to get into one this nice. They danced the entire night, chatting and drinking and enjoying designer drugs. Samson and Moira made love until the sun came up and when she woke up, she slipped out of the suite without even a goodbye. Samson spent the rest of the trip wondering what happened to the sexy blonde, hoping he'd run into her again but when he returned to school, he soon forgot about her somewhere between classes and parties. He graduated that June with his bachelor's degree.

Two months later, he was packing up the remainder of his things; the following morning, he'd leave for his first year of law school. There was a knock at his bedroom door.

"Son," his father said before entering.

"Yeah, Pop, what's up?"

His father walked into the large, practically empty bedroom. Samson noticed his father's grim expression.

"What is it? What's the matter?"

His father, almost identical in stature to Samson, sighed and folded his arms across his wide chest. "I'm going to need you to explain to me why there is a pregnant girl asking for you downstairs."

Samson felt his stomach drop. His mind raced and he didn't know how to respond, because he wasn't sure who the girl downstairs might be. A dozen female faces rushed through his mind and he felt his face grow hot as a wave of nausea came over him.

"I thought we discussed this. You were to be more careful than this." His father spoke in a hushed but angry tone. "You need to get your ass down there now and figure this thing out."

Samson stood, frozen in place, dumbfounded.

"I said now!"

He rushed down the long hall in a panic and thought he might pass out when he reached the bottom of the staircase and immediately heard the girl's loud voice as he she talked to his housekeeper. He turned to look at his father coming down the stairs behind him, his face frozen in a stone cold expression. He swallowed the lump in his throat and walked slowly into the living room.

The room fell silent, and there before him sat a small-framed blonde with a swollen belly.

"Can you give us a minute?"

His father and housekeeper left the two alone.

Moira cried in his arms and he held her gently. She had nowhere else to go. She began showing and her drunken father threw her out. She had no job, no friends and no other family. "I'm sorry." She looked at him with her big blue eyes and didn't bother wiping the tears from them. Samson didn't know how else to respond other than to take responsibility for his drunken carelessness in Miami.

They were married in an expensively quiet ceremony without love or enthusiasm the following month on a weekend where he normally would have been out with his new law school buddies. His father paid for an apartment and a nanny off campus for Moira and Keira, when she was finally born. Samson had never seen himself as a family man, but he was ready for this life whether he liked it or not.

He finished law school and Moira relished in his family's money, becoming the woman he always knew he would grow to hate. Keira, of course, had nothing but the best, but so did Moira, and she had no shame in letting Samson know how much she adored his money. That's the way it started and that's the way it had stayed. A few years later they had their second child, also an accident, but also equally amazing for Samson and Moira. It brought them closer for a while, but eventually they fell out of whatever temporary love they had found themselves in and went through the appropriate motions of wealthy family life in a wealthy family town.

"Did you hear me?!" Moira yelled from behind him, snapping him out of yet another cruel daydream. Samson hadn't heard anything else and almost continued ignoring her but Moira's voice became soft. "We can't do this without you. Babe." She lingered condescendingly on the last word and he knew the face she was making without even having to see it. Big doe eyes and pouty lips. It was a daily routine with her. The madness that was his wife, almost like a game. Seeing how far she could push him. All for fun, all for her own benefit, all to make him feel like the man he had now come to be, and never letting him forget that in their status of society, no matter how crippled the world, he was the breadwinner. The staple of the family.

Family, he thought to himself before he answered. "I'll make sure things are right next time." Samson slammed the door behind him as he ventured out of their home in Franklin Woods.

XIX

They all slept in the next morning, embracing the comfort and sense of safety provided by the empty neighborhood. It was after eleven when Ben woke up. He had to relieve himself, *bad,* but he didn't want to use the indoor toilet. Opening the window and sticking his head out, he took a quick look around to make sure no one from the house had wandered into the yard before enjoying a nice, long morning piss. Sal would have gotten a kick out of it. Lucy, not so much.

He cleaned up and got dressed. Today they would look for Veronica. Ben thought about maybe staying in Sal's place for a little while. If it proved to be safe, then they just needed to get some supplies and board up the windows. *No unwanted visitors.* They could go from house to house and see what goodies might be left, and they might have just struck gold deciding to come here. He walked downstairs and Juliette was sitting at the breakfast bar, swigging a warm energy drink.

"I would have made coffee, but I'm not really sure how to do that without power."

"It's the thought that counts." Ben looked around the rest of the house now that there was daylight. Sal really had everything a man could need, and most of it, other than the food, was useless during a time like this. Too bad he didn't have a back-up generator.

Maybe we could find one and bring it back here.

After a while longer Andrew and Clyde joined them downstairs and they discussed the day's plan.

"We wasted the whole morning." Andrew was relaxed on the lush white sofa. "Franklin isn't very spread out once you get to town or the bay. It's just the couple miles between here and there that are pretty irritatin' without transportation. By the time we're done with town and heading back, I'm sure it'll be dark."

"This area seems a lot safer than the city. I know there are a lot of trees that those things can hide in, but that's also something to take into consideration. If we need to, we can use the woods to our advantage. Plus, it was pretty much dark when we got here last night, and there was no incident. I can't wait another day. She could be in trouble, she could be here, she could be gone, we don't know."

"Alright, man, I got you. Clyde? Any thoughts?"

His brother sat across from him, sprawled out on the matching white loveseat. He shook his head.

Ben clapped his hands. "Let's get our shit together and head out then. We don't have to bring much since we're coming back here. Let's spread it out in case any scavengers show up."

Andrew hopped up from the sofa, "Good idea. Juliette? Do you want to help?"

"Sure, I obviously don't have a choice on whether I'm going, so I might as well." She rolled her eyes and stormed out of the room.

It took a half hour to make sure that all of their things were hidden and spread about the house. It might have been an unnecessary precaution but none of them wanted to take any chances.

The sun was high in the sky when they left the house, and a soft breeze greeted them on the street. They passed the wreck house once more and Ben felt a sense of unease about the place. Juliette might have been a little crazy, but what if she really had seen a light?

They arrived at the gates, and Ben removed the pin, considering it. Who had put the pin there? It nagged at him.

*

Samson walked down the driveway and quickened his pace as he passed the wreck in the street. *If I could find a tow truck, I'd move this shit myself.* He hated that their house was one of the first in the development. "Too much noise and traffic" he had told Moira when they were first looking at houses several years before, but she had fallen in love with it the moment she stepped foot in the damned place. So in Samson's mind, the brutal accident that had become a permanent fixture on his property all came back to that miserable decision to purchase the third "Castle" (as Moira so tenderly referred to it) from the guard house in Franklin Woods.

As he strode by the empty houses toward the exit, he thought of all his neighbors, now dead. He'd taken care of some himself, and the others probably offed themselves before they could succumb to the travesty of the new world. He remembered the wild, angry look on Will's face when he had first spotted Samson in his yard during the first few days of the infection. Samson knew his longtime golf buddy had plenty of plywood in the shed next door that he needed for their windows. He hadn't seen Will or his wife Tracy since it had all started, so he figured they had gotten out of Dodge as quickly as they could.

Samson had entered the yard quietly that afternoon, making a beeline for the shed. He hadn't noticed Will in his haste, half standing, half leaning on the steps of his luxurious cedar deck. He wore two things: his sweatpants and an oversized and swollen bite mark on his left shoulder. Samson fiddled with the lock and tossed it aside. Will always left the key in the padlock. *What's the point of even locking the thing up?* Samson would wonder any time he had been over his friend's house for a cocktail or a barbecue.

He tossed the lock to the grass at his feet and swung the door open. *Bingo.* Samson entered the shed and grinned at the stack of boards in front of him. Picking up two pieces of plywood in each hand, he turned around to begin stacking them in the yard.

"Holy shit," Samson muttered to himself and dropped what was in his hands. Will had begun to shamble toward him. Lifeless, yet still moving, still growling. His eyes were vacant and cold, his mouth hung open with blood crusted onto the sides. Samson slowly lowered himself and picked up one of the pieces of thin wood, knowing what he had to do. Faster than he hoped Will could react, Samson ran to him and swung the plywood up, striking Will underneath his chin with the corner. The blow knocked Will back and down to the perfectly green grass. Samson rammed the corner of the plywood over and over again into Will's forehead, like a piston.

Blood splattered and stained Samson's clothes, the sickening crack after crack of his friend's skull filling his ears. Finally, on about the tenth blow to the head, Samson realized Will had stopped moving, stopped groaning. He angrily launched his makeshift weapon down onto the body of his dead friend, exhaling with a grunt.

He looked up and away from the bloody mess toward the open sliding door that led inside Will's house. He thought of his friend's wife and wondered if Tracy was still alive somewhere in that house. He climbed the porch steps and slammed the sliding door shut.

Every time he passed Will's house he thought of that day. Thought of his body, still rotting in his yard, and his wife, either dead or aimlessly shambling about with no purpose in one of their many rooms.

Just another house I can't steal food from, Samson thought as he passed the guard house and exited to the right out of Franklin Woods. Town was to the left, deeper into the community of Franklin, and the bay was to his right. Town was useless to him after his last few trips. The only building he felt like he hadn't carefully snuck around in was the high school, and he had no intention of checking it out. Since Al, he hadn't seen a soul, and he'd exhausted the small town's resources between Franklin Woods and Paradise Bay in just a short while.

The disadvantages of beach town living, nothing here in the off season.

The city, beyond the borders of their quaint area, ten miles away, was not an option. "What are you, stupid? You'll never come back! And then what would we do without you?" Moira would scream, always shrill, always wild, anytime he brought it up. Samson often wished he had the balls to go, just go to the city and never come back. What was the point anymore? But then he would remember the children, and he knew he couldn't leave them with Moira. It wasn't that Samson hated Moira, he just had always known what he was to her: a wallet. And now, in the wake of what the world had become, he was a grocery bag. The thought of it made him more bitter with each passing day. How she would admire not only herself, but all her material possessions and the house that she lived in and how she truly believed status or class still mattered. Every single time she would look in a mirror and smile at herself, Samson wished he could smash her pretty little face into it.

Trudging down the middle of the road he appreciated the peace and quiet of the end of the world. The lush greenery swaying in the breeze coming off the water, the soft whisper of tides touching the shores. Before he knew it, he stood on the docks. The empty boats rocked in the wake, and the closed doors of the abandoned Dockside Bar and Grill tempted him. *Looks like nobody's home.* He approached the building cautiously and tapped his wedding band against the metal of the dock's banister. He looked around and listened. Watching the windows closely, he tapped again. There was no response on the dock and no movement inside.

Opening the door, Samson took his knife out and poked his head inside. The place smelled of spoiled food so badly he thought he would vomit. Coughing, he removed his handkerchief from his pocket and held it up to his face. Tables and chairs were on their sides, strewn about the floor. Broken drinking glasses crunched under his feet with every step he took toward the bar. *I could use a drink. Or four.* Samson moved behind the bar and raised his eyebrows. He grabbed a bottle of American Honey whiskey and made a face at it. *Ought to help with the smell, at least.* Throwing the top behind him, he turned the bottle upside down and drank. He grimaced as the liquid warmed his insides and he exhaled loudly. Rotten fruit, jalapenos, and olives littered the bar counter. Moving toward the kitchen, he took another swig from his newly-acquired bottle.

Samson peeked through the grimy glass to make sure no surprises lurked in the depths of the rotting fish smell and set the whiskey down on the bar top. He brought the handkerchief back up to his mouth and walked into the kitchen. The place was filthy, filled with maggots and rotting fish. His stomach turned and he immediately regretted the American Honey. Hands on his knees and vomiting, Samson knew he just needed to check the stock shelves for dry goods.

"Pull it together big guy," he said as he spat. Holding the knife up, he listened for any response to all the noise he'd just made. Satisfied when no company came to greet him from the shadows, he moved on to the pantry. He thought about Moira and how funny it would be to see her in this kitchen right now, sobbing and retching, probably pissing herself with fear. He noticed an abundance of empty cans littering the floor and kicked one out of the way as he walked to the pantry.

"Yeah!" he shouted in glee as he discovered instant mashed potatoes, a few cases of soft drinks, and a bag of rice. "Probably full of fucking bugs, but I don't care." He talked in a baby voice to the bag of rice as he tied it up and set it by the pantry door. He shrugged his bag off his shoulders and put a few of the bottles of soda into it along with the four boxes of insta-mash. "Gotta get my carbs!" he cheerfully said to no one and zipped up the bag, placing it onto his back. He put his knife back in its place and grabbed the bag of rice. *Not a gold mine, but it'll do just fine by me.* He quickly exited the putrid kitchen and grabbed the American Honey on his way by the bar, *you'll taste better in open air.*

Samson figured he had lucked out and decided to use this peaceful time by himself to celebrate. Setting down the bag of rice outside the entrance, he strolled down the docks, admiring the luxury boats that were not his. They weren't anybody's anymore. "They're money pit, Sammy. We have plenty of friends with boats." Moira's voice echoed in his head as he remembered when he told her he had spent the day looking at potential purchases a few months back.

"I'll take this one, you bitch." Samson chuckled as he took a drink from the whiskey bottle. He placed his belongings down on the dock and boarded a gorgeous Viking Sport Cruiser.

The day was overcast but no rain. The breeze felt amazing on Samson's face as he sat down and put his feet up on his dream boat. He closed his eyes and pretended for just one moment that everything was right with the world on this early October afternoon and he was simply relaxing on his new boat. For the first time in a long time, Samson had a genuine smile on his face. He opened his eyes and looked out at the water. He wished he could just leave on this boat right then, set off into the sea through Paradise Bay and leave the crumbs for the birds. He remembered how much his son enjoyed swimming, how much his daughter loved fishing. The three of them would take trips without Moira; she wouldn't dare get her hands dirty or risk being seen while sweating. They would laugh for hours, Samson couldn't remember seeing joy like that on anyone else's faces but his children's. The time seemed to stand still on those days, and he frowned at the thought of never having another day like that.

The sudden sound of footsteps running on the dock toward the boat jolted him from his calm and he jumped to his feet. Samson's knife was already out when the small figure leapt onto the boat in a blur at him. He grabbed the figure in midair and threw it to the floor of the deck. A large piece of PVC pipe clattered off to the side and the figure yelped in pain as Samson forced a knee into its chest and raised the knife, ready to plunge it into its skull.

XX

"Please!" the small figure cried out.

"What the fuck..." Samson's eyes focused, his breath caught in his throat, his face red with rage. He lowered his knife as he realized the figure he had pinned down was a teenage girl. Her big brown eyes stared up at him wildly.

"Please!" she cried out again, breathing heavily, eyes wide.

"Why would you attack me?" Samson yelled. "You must have been watching me! You must have known I wasn't one of them!" His knee was still firmly placed on her chest, he didn't know if he could trust her.

"You stole my food," the girl responded, panting and angry. Samson was in awe. He had assumed she was an eater, and rightfully so. She smelled of rot, but only because she had probably been spending a lot of time in the restaurant. He leaned back and removed his weight from her body. With the knife still in hand, he backed away from her and kicked the pipe out of reach.

The girl scurried back and away from Samson, staring at her lost weapon. "You stole from me, I'm sorry. But you stole my food, and that's all I have. I haven't seen any other people, and I wasn't thinking. I didn't know what else to do." She wiped a tear from her face and locked eyes with Samson. Her long brown hair was matted to her head and face and she wore a tattered purple shirt over ripped blue jeans.

"How long have you been here? Are you alone?" Samson's voice was sterner than he had intended it to be. He couldn't believe his eyes. This young girl, who looked so much like his own daughter, had just tried to attack him with a piece of plumbing.

"I'm not sure, a few days I think." She eyed his knife. "I came from the city."

"By yourself?" He couldn't mask his shock. "I can't believe it. The highway's a mess, how did you get here?"

"On foot." She swallowed hard, "And yes, I am alone." She pulled and twisted on a string of her hair. Samson recognized this as a nervous tick. His daughter would twist her hair between her fingers when Moira scolded her. Then Moira would simply yell more about damaging her hair and causing split ends.

He lowered his knife. "How? How could you make it here from the city by yourself?"

The girl pulled her knees into her chest, her emaciated frame grew smaller as she hugged her legs. "I ran." Her gaze remained at her feet as she continued. "I lived in the city with my brother and father."

"Why did you leave?"

"I'm sure you know. It got bad real fast. My father wouldn't let us leave, but we needed to eat. So my father left for some food."

"Did he ever come back?" Samson's tone of voice had completely changed now. He thought of how he left every day, leaving his children alone with Moira.

"Yes." The girl's eyes moved from the deck to Samson and back again, almost as if checking on him, making sure he was listening. "He was attacked. Almost made it home perfectly fine, but he was attacked, on our street, right in front of our building. He had told us there was a woman who was hurt. She was bleeding a lot and crying, begging him for help. My father was a good man, I know he couldn't ignore her. He had tried to pull her off the street into the building but he said out of nowhere two other women came running at them." She didn't blink as she told her story; it was not the first time she was reliving it, and it would not be the last. But she would stop between sentences, swallowing lumps in her throat and widening her eyes so that the tough exterior she had built up did not crack in the slightest.

"You don't have to—"

"He said they were screaming, like animals." She glared as she continued. "They attacked the woman he was trying to help. They were clawing and biting, trying to eat her legs. My father had never hit a woman before. He said even though they weren't really even women anymore, he wished he hadn't hit them out there in the street anyway, they might not even have noticed him. But before he knew it he said they were on him like rabid dogs. One of them bit him. Tore a nasty chunk clean right out of him. The woman he had tried helping began screaming even louder, trying to get their attention. It worked enough for my father to grab his bag and shut himself inside of our building." Samson saw in the girl's eyes the smallest glimpse of grief. "I had never seen so much blood before. It was like watching a movie."

"I uh, I know what you mean."

She shrugged and continued, "The last thing my father said to me and my brother was to run. He said, 'You get out of this city and you run. You get to the water and you get out of the city,' and so that's what we did. We ran. I ran."

Samson was amazed as he listened to this girl tell a braver tale than his own.

"We ran past everyone and everything. There were fires and accidents, and sounds I never in my life want to hear again. We met up with some other people. Good people. And then things got a little more *complicated*. So that's when it was just me. Running. And when I got out of the city I was more careful and took a little more time, slept in abandoned cars and stuff. I did what I could to get here. I can kill the slow ones. But the fast ones, they're somethin' else."

"You've had to kill?"

"Yes." She looked up and met Samson's eyes. "I killed my own father and then my brother when the time came."

Samson suppressed a shudder at the blankness in her eyes when she said it.

"They weren't my family anymore. I think that was everyone's problem in all of this, nobody could let go of something that had already let go of them."

Samson briefly thought of Moira, of his children. He was angry again as he took in her last statement but tried not to let it show.

"If everyone had just listened." She laughed to herself as she looked down at the deck again, twirling her stringy hair. "I know it sounds stupid, but if people had followed directions, stayed inside, stayed away from the sick ones, well, I don't know. But, I think we were all just too damn stupid."

Samson sat silent, stewing in his rage, a teenage girl making more sense of the apocalypse than he ever could.

"But I know what I have to do. I don't know why I should keep trying. I know that there isn't anyone coming to save me. But I know I can save myself, save the people I love from a fate worse than death, and maybe..." She knocked her head back and stared up at the cloudy sky. "Maybe the next time I get the chance, I help save someone before it gets ugly."

Samson didn't know what she meant, but his anger subsided and he liked what she had said. He stared at this girl on the deck before him and smirked, he couldn't begin to understand what she might have gone through to get here, but here she was. Alive.

"What's your name?" the girl in the purple shirt calmly asked him, still staring up at the sky.

"Samson."

"Have you not had to defend yourself, Samson?"

"Of course."

"Did you know any of these things that you've defended yourself against?"

"Yes. Some." He joined her in looking at the sky. "A good friend. Some neighbors. A security guard. Not my family." He closed his eyes.

"I don't know where you draw the line Samson, but I am alive. And these things," the girl said, suddenly standing up and slowly moving toward him, her demeanor on the edge of threatening, "these things want me dead. I've had a lot of growing up to do in a very short time, and I can tell you what you've done is no different than what I've done. And for the same reason, I'm sure. To live. So if you don't mind, I'll be going. I can find other food for myself."

Samson was frozen in place as the girl grabbed the PVC pipe and shot him a glare before stepping off the boat onto the dock. He was overwhelmed by her frankness and strength. Her desire to continue even though she was alone was so glamorous in such a bleak landscape.

"Wait!" he called out to the girl that he so immensely wished was a child of his own, surviving in an upside-down world that didn't deserve her. The girl in the purple shirt turned around. "What's your name?"

"Veronica."

"Veronica, I can tell you're a better man than me." Veronica begrudgingly smiled in response to his unexpected remark. Samson's entire demeanor had changed suddenly. It was almost comforting to her.

"What do you say to some fishing?"

XXI

Having a teenage girl of his own, Samson knew how to deal with them; whether the world was normal or not. As luck would have it, when he had turned to stop Veronica from leaving he noticed the fishing poles underneath the seats toward the stern of the boat, and what better use for the dead rotting fish of the restaurant than for bait?

As the two fished off the docks of Paradise Bay, they bonded as only a dead man's daughter and a man consumed by obscurity could. The moments, like still frames in Samson's mind, burned a hole into his being. The bitterness of not being able to take his own daughter out to do the things she once enjoyed, the sadness of knowing his nine year old son would never grow to be a man in a normal world, welled up in his chest like a fire, and then temporarily subsided again.

In the remaining daylight hours that they spent together, they had come to know each other's stories, each other's lives from the world before and the world of now. Samson had told this girl more than he had told anyone about himself in his entire life. The man Samson had become was not the man he once was

"Or maybe," as Veronica had put it, "this is who you were meant to be."

He told her the story of Al. From the moment he threw himself onto the gas station's floor, he hated Al. Hated him maybe for saving him, but hated him more for turning out to be just like one of the scumbags he had once defended in court for a fat pay day. The rapists, the molesters, the simple country fucks who murdered one another for drugs or for fun. It was once a job that paid, but in their new world Samson knew Al embodied the perfect characteristics to bring home to Moira and the children. Only it wasn't just the need to fulfill Moira's requests that helped him decide what to do with Al, it was the fact that he knew Moira would be furious with him for bringing home a criminal.

"What did she expect?" he asked Veronica as he cast out another line into the bay. "That I would bring home an outstanding, upper-class citizen?" He scoffed. "For one, I don't think they exist anymore. And basically it boils down to I didn't think I had it in me to bring home someone that didn't deserve to die."

He continued the story of Al, vaguely discussing the details of how things got messy. Al had broken his promise to keep his cool, as Samson knew he would. He had pulled his shotgun out, slamming the weapon into Samson's chest and knocking him to the ground. He ordered Moira to undress, slowly, relishing in the misery that he for a split second believed he was inflicting upon the couple. His behavior had only fueled Samson's hatred for his kind. He remembered laughing at him, laughing so much while gasping for the air that had been knocked out of him.

Hysterically laughing on the floor because what Al didn't know is that Moira loved to put on a show. Moira was even crazier than Al. Between the laughter and the grinning, dancing woman in her underwear before him, Al had been confused and distracted long enough for Moira to smash her prized Tiffany's lamp over his head, knocking him out cold. Samson's laughter continued as Moira screamed at him uncontrollably to "shut the fuck up" and "clean up the fucking mess" he'd created.

He told Veronica of the long haul of dragging Al's heavy unconscious body up the staircase, how the nearer he grew to the closed door of his son's bedroom, his temporary insanity had deserted him, the noises from inside got louder, and the knot in his stomach grew tighter.

"How many?" Veronica asked without looking at him. She stared at her filthy hands, covered in the rotted guts of what someone might have eaten for dinner on a night that seemed so long ago.

"Two." He listened to the water sloshing beneath them. "The first one was the housekeeper. That's how I knew for sure Moira had snapped."

Samson continued his story.

*

His son, whose curiosity had gotten the better of him, snuck outside despite his father's wishes to find out what Samson had been doing in Will's yard on that fateful day. Moira had been entertaining herself, playing dress-up and Samson was freshening up in the back of the house. His son was completely free to explore. Before anyone had even noticed he was missing, Robbie burst into the house covered in blood.

Leti, their longtime housekeeper, began screaming as if she were being attacked. When Samson heard the commotion he practically flew across the vast expanse of the first level of their once-beautiful home. His daughter stood silent and unmoving, not watching the scene in the living room, but scanning the front yard nervously through the cracks in the freshly-boarded windows for any unwanted company. Moira leapt from the staircase and threw herself to the ground beside their son before Samson reached him.

"Towels!" Moira hollered, and Leti ran to the kitchen to get them. Robbie lay on the floor, bleeding out from a massive wound on his right forearm. It was so deep that bone showed through the chunks of flesh hanging from his arm. Nausea briefly overtook Samson before he dropped to his son's side. Leti thrust the towels into his hands and he applied pressure to the wound.

"Moira, I need you to calm down. I need you to get me a sheet." He stared down at his son's chubby, tear-streaked face as he barked orders at his wife. Moira sprang up from the floor, disappearing through the kitchen and down the hall. She returned a few moments later with a green, eight hundred thread-count Egyptian cotton bed sheet from the guest bedroom. Samson tied the sheet as tightly as he could around his son's arm and then wrapped and tied again until he was sure it was good enough to staunch the bleeding for the time being.

That was the first and last time Moira didn't get angry about someone ruining something in their home.

The eater that bit Robbie never showed up at the front door. Samson still didn't know how his son had gotten away and made it home unnoticed by the undead that attacked him. An hour had passed and his wife and daughter sat at his son's side as his fever grew worse. Samson stood by the door watching them with a grim look on his face, knowing what was coming.

When the world starting falling apart and all his cases were delayed "until further notice" he had been at the county jail, just finishing up with a client. On his way out he overheard a couple of the police officers discussing abandoning ship after seeing a few of the prisoners attack one another. They had realized the infection was spreading so fast because it was spreading through the bites. Samson then saw it for himself from the comfort of his own home as his friends and neighbors ripped each other apart outside in the street. The unlucky bastards that bled out too quickly got back up in just seconds and joined their attackers in chasing someone else.

"Moira, we need to talk."

She looked up at him, her make up running down her face, her hands and clothes covered in dried blood.

"I'll get fresh sheets for Robbie." She stood up and walked to the closet.

"Moira, please, we need to talk about this."

She scowled at him as he pleaded with her, sheets in hand she closed the closet door.

"What is it Sammy?" She placed a hand on her hip and waited for his response. Keira looked at her parents, fear in her round, brown eyes.

"I need to speak with you privately. Please." He shared a soft smile with Keira before he stepped into the hallway and motioned for his wife to follow him.

Moira placed the sheets at the end of the bed and left the room, closing Robbie's door behind her.

"Moira," he placed his hands gently on her shoulders. "Robbie is dying, he's been bitten."

"You don't know that!" She snapped back at him in hushed anger. "You don't know shit! You just need to get your ass out to a pharmacy and get something to help him!" She shook his hands from her body and pushed him away.

"He's been bitten! Obviously!" Samson argued back. "You know damn well what happens to—"

Moira slapped him hard across the face.

Leti, hearing the angry slap from all the way downstairs called out to them, "Is everything alright up there?"

"Stay out of this, Leti! You have work to do!" Moira shouted down to her. "And as for you," she said, shoving a finger into Samson's chest, "whatever it is you are suggesting I will have you know that I will kill you myself. That is my son you are talking about!"

Samson was stunned. "He's *our* son, Moira. That is *our* son in there, but he will not be for very much—"

A blood curdling scream erupted from their son's room, filling the house.

"Keira!" Samson yelled as he pushed past Moira and threw open Robbie's door.

He did not want to believe the nightmare happening before his eyes. Robbie was now on top of his sister, ripping out her throat like a savage beast.

He ran to his children and in one fierce movement tore Robbie off of Keira and threw him to the floor. Moira ran to her daughter, who lay sprawled out on the bed, choking on her own blood. Without hesitation, Samson grabbed the sheets from the end of the bed and wrapped them around his son's neck. Robbie growled and fought his father, but Samson had him pinned down. He pulled the sheet through the foot of the bed frame tightly, pulling Robbie back against it and tied the other end of the sheet around his wrists. Robbie hissed and howled, his face empty of all expression save sheer hunger. The same hunger Samson had seen on so many other dead faces.

"Oh my God! Oh my God!" Leti screamed from the doorway.

"Leti! Sheets! Now!" Samson yelled. He pushed Moira away from his daughter's dying body and placed a boot down on her chest.

"What the fuck are you doing?!"

Moira cried and yelled and punched him, throwing her small frame into his body. Leti ran into the room and threw Samson the sheets, running back out, escaping the horror of the bedroom.

"Get away, now!" Samson tied his daughter as he had tied his son, but to the headboard. Keira stopped choking and ceased all movement. "I'm so sorry, baby girl." He kissed her forehead and cried as his daughter's eyes clouded over with a milky white film.

Keira wheezed and her head jerked up at him. A ferocious growl escaped her mouth, and she struggled against her ties to no avail. Samson watched as Robbie did the same at the other end of the bed. It was as if his life was unraveling in slow motion. The monsters from children's nightmares had come and taken Robbie and Keira from him. He didn't know how his feet moved by themselves as he backed out the door, watching in absolute horror and amazement the two newly awakened eaters as they spit and screamed like demons.

Moira lay in a crumpled heap on the hardwood floor, reminding him of a pile of dirty clothes. He picked her up in his arms and cried. She continued to lay motionless and silent. Leti sobbed downstairs somewhere.

*

"That night I lay in bed listening to the howls of the children from down the hall. Moira hadn't spoken for hours."

Veronica was staring at him now as Samson spoke so solemnly. She understood his pain.

"She had gotten out of bed around 2 am, but I didn't think anything of it. After some time had passed I forced myself to get up and find her, thinking she might have needed me. But when I walked into the kitchen I found Moira standing over Leti's body with a bread knife in her hand. The only thing she said to me was, 'I need you to help me feed the children.' "

Veronica twisted a strand of hair between her fingers as she set her fishing pole down against the dock. She looked down at her feet. "But you're not going to feed me to your children."

Samson shook his head. "No, Veronica. But I do need you to help me free my children." He frowned as he spoke. "You asked how many, and two is a high enough answer for me. It isn't something I could ever, or would ever be able to do alone. You took care of your father and your brother when the time came. Something I couldn't do for Keira and Robbie."

He reiterated that he couldn't do it himself. He swallowed hard, saying it aloud solidified that he was a coward, reminding him all the more that he could have been a better father, and should have been a better man.

Veronica let go of her hair and looked up at him. "What about Moira?"

He put his face in his hands and squeezed at his skin. How had he allowed his wife to go mad? How had he allowed his children to meet a fate worse than any he could have ever imagined? He dropped his hands to the rail.

"Moira will handle Moira. She always does."

XXII

Not much longer than an hour passed before they arrived in town at their slow pace, but Andrew was right. The walk there was full of nothing but trees, making them feel as if time was standing still.

When it came time, they didn't want to split up, but figured they would cover more ground that way. Andrew and Juliette visited the local pharmacy, gathering what more supplies they could. It was nothing like the CVS in the city; this place had been ransacked, but they were able to at least scavenge a few things. Ben had requested more lighter fluid. He wanted to stock up so they would be able to make a fire for cooking or for heat if they needed to. Clyde and Ben scoped out the grocery store, but that too, had been cleared out. Except for a few shambling eaters, they hadn't run into many of the dead, so their work load was pretty light. After checking a few more small stores here and there, they met up at the police station.

"There isn't anything left here, but it's worth a check to see if your girl's hiding out," Andrew told Ben.

They were in and out within twenty minutes. Andrew and Hank had taken anything useful that was left when they'd taken off for the first time, and so the only thing left to do was to search the building for Veronica. They called out in hushed tones, trying not to attract unwanted attention. They did this in several more establishments, and finally the sun was getting ready to set. The only places left to search were a few small houses, an apartment complex, and the high school down the road.

Andrew sighed. "There's too many places left for today. We'll come back down here tomorrow."

Ben was frustrated, but then again she might not have even come here. She may have gone straight to the bay. He silently resented himself for not opting to go to the bay before checking the town. All she talked about was getting to the water.

"I really don't think she's in any of those houses. We check the high school, and then we check the bay. Tonight. We should have gone there first."

"I'm tired of walking," Juliette whined.

"Baby, it's gonna be fine. We're almost done." Andrew kissed her on her forehead and then turned to Ben." Look man, I don't think you want to go down to that high school. Last time I was there that place was crawlin' with those motherfuckers."

"You said they move on when there's no people. Sure, we see some stragglers here and there, but they're probably just too slow to keep up with the fast ones. I want to check the high school, we're already here, and we've already wasted too much time. Veronica was in high school, maybe she might have felt safe there or something. Maybe she'd try to find some kids her age. I don't know. But I'm not going to head back after searching all day and finding nothing."

"Ben, man, she's probably down by the bay already." Clyde joined in on an attempt to talk Ben out of going to the high school. He hadn't seen what Andrew had, but he had no intention of finding out for himself.

Ben had both hands clasped behind his head, his blonde hair drenched in sweat. He shook his head and his irritation showed.

Juliette slipped away from the group and walked down the road toward the high school off in the distance.

"Man, listen, there are a ton of boats down at the marina that she could have set up shop on. Oh, and a restaurant. Now that I think of it, the restaurant owners even got their own boat, maybe she found the keys and took off man. I mean, *I hope not.* But, we don't know anything. You said it yourself you weren't sure if you'd even find her." Clyde had taken his own pack of cigarettes from Ben's stash and lit two up as he spoke.

"I know." Ben took the cigarette Clyde offered him and exhaled loudly. "I know, I just don't want to lose anyone else. I feel like I should have found her already."

"Veronica! Veronica!"

The three men turned, stunned, Juliette screamed from down the street.

"Veronica! It's time to come out now, Veronica!"

"Holy fuckin' shit!" Andrew raced off in her direction followed by Clyde and Ben. "Stop it Jules, stop screamin'!" Andrew called out to her, but she didn't hear him. Her persistent yelling at the top of her lungs was met with a ferocious cry from up ahead.

Ben and Clyde stopped dead in their tracks. More wild cries echoed in response to the first.

"Oh no, oh shit no. Drew, let's go man! Grab that bitch and let's haul ass!" Clyde threw his cigarette to the asphalt and readied his weapon.

Andrew reached Juliette and shook her wildly. "What are you doing? Baby, stop yellin' like this, you're gonna get us all killed!"

Juliette laughed hysterically.

"I was just doing my part." She giggled.

"Yeah, you sure helped us out!" Clyde yelled at her. "I'm gone, man, I'm outta here."

The cries persisted in the distance and Ben's hair stood up on the back of his neck. "I'm not doin' this shit twice in one week. Let's go, head to the police station before they see us."

They ran for the station and got inside. Andrew bolted the door and they ran for one of the offices, crouched over and awkward.

Andrew gulped in a breath. "Stay in here, I'm gonna have a look."

Juliette still giggled to herself.

"Please, baby, please stop laughin', this shit ain't funny."

"Okay." She still had the smile on her face but her laughter stopped.

Clyde stared Juliette down. "You know I could kill you, right? You keep up your crazy-ass shit and you'll end up dead."

Ben came to her defense for the first time. "Clyde, I don't—"

"No! You keep out of this. This is between me and her." He pointed a finger at Juliette. "You hear me, you crazy bitch? You will end up dead, whether my brother likes it or not. Somebody or *some thing* is gonna kill your ass." Clyde stomped out of the room to look for Andrew.

Ben looked over at Juliette; she sat expressionless on the floor, like a lump of clay.

He joined the other two in the lobby; they crouched on the floor trying to get a good view over the desk in front of them. The dead's chilling screams drifted closer, and their feet slammed against pavement as they ran around the streets in front of the station, searching for the living.

"Too dumb to chew through a bag right?"

Ben wiped the sweat from his brow, "I can only hope I'm right, Andrew."

*

The walk back to Franklin Woods was a quick one. As the sky darkened and the shadows deepened around them, Samson and Veronica knew they had to move quickly and quietly. The area around Paradise Bay had been empty; but Franklin Woods was on the edge of town.

Samson quickened their pace when he heard movement in the trees on both sides of the road. The eaters were more active at night, like animals hunting.

"Just up here. Come on, now," Samson whispered to Veronica when he saw the guard house. Samson ushered her past it. "Third house in." He looked around to ensure they weren't followed and pulled the heavy gate, enclosing them in the community. Veronica waited for him a few feet ahead.

She eyed the house up and down as they approached. "I like your cars." She pointed to the wreck in front of Samson's house.

He rolled his eyes and started up the dark driveway. Veronica stood staring. "It's okay," he assured her. "We need to get inside, come on."

He unlocked the front door and placed the key back in his pocket. Quietly, he opened the door and the two stepped inside. Veronica stopped short at the door, appalled by the overpowering smell. Thirty different air-freshener scents fought for space in the room. Remnants of blood that no amount of cleaning could fix stained the hardwood floor in the living room. She looked over at the staircase, nervous about what she had just involved herself in.

She shrugged, *what else do I have to do?*

"Where the hell have you been all day?" a shrill voice called from the kitchen. "It's after dark already!" High heeled footsteps drew closer and a small, big breasted blonde woman emerged from the other room. "What the—" Moira stopped in her tracks with a doe in the headlights look. "We...we have a guest."

She brushed her hair behind her ears and wiped her hands on her pale blue skirt, glancing from Veronica to Samson and back again. Samson thought for a moment that she might have seen in the girl what he had: the marred innocence of the stranger who survived the world beyond their doors, the girl who might as well have been Keira's own sister.

But he knew she hadn't.

"Moira Eckhart, pleased to meet you darlin'. Excuse the mess, we don't have a housekeeper anymore." His wife grinned ear to ear as the façade of southern hospitality took over, and she strutted up to Veronica with an outstretched hand.

Veronica didn't speak, but instead stared at this unbelievably put-together woman in a ripped apart world. Samson took a step forward and stood between Moira and Veronica. He glanced at the handle of the bread knife sticking out from her waistband and shook his head in sadness. She stopped just short of Samson, confused.

"Moira." Samson's voice was low. He shook his head again. His wife crossed her arms in front of her and cocked her head in bewilderment.

"Oh, what the hell is this?" Her confusion changed to anger. "What are you doing?"

"I'm doing what I should have done from the beginning. Please understand, I can't do this anymore. I can't allow these things to—"

"What are you, stupid? These things? These things, Samson?! What *things*? These things are your children! Remember?! *Our* children!"

Her voice rose and she made wild gestures with her arms as she spoke. Her eyes were wide and crazed as she stood up straight, her tiny frame appearing larger with each word that came out of her mouth.

"What do you think you're going to do exactly? Why is this piece of white trash standing in my house?"

Samson removed his pistol and held it in his shaking hands.

Moira's face twisted with horror and rage as she screamed. "I have told you before and I will tell you again, I will fucking kill you in your sleep! I will slit this girl's throat and feed them myself!"

Moira ripped the knife from her waist and began slowly walking toward them, the knife pointed straight at Veronica. Veronica backed away and toward the staircase, ready to flee.

He answered her softly. "This is not my family anymore. I am not the breadwinner anymore." Moira's expression went from angry to blank. He pointed at the ceiling, "They are not my children. And you," he said, jabbing a finger into his wife's chest for a change. "You have *always* been crazy, but you are no longer my wife. I can't allow this world to determine what kind of person I become like you have."

Moira's anger returned. She slapped Samson's finger away and shoved him back against the couch, knocking the gun from his hand. She threw the knife at him and rushed to the stairs, shoving Veronica to the floor.

"Moira!" Samson called out as she disappeared up the stairs. He threw his bag to the floor and started after her.

Veronica watched as he too disappeared up the stairs. She heard a door slam open and loud growls and moans instantly filled the house. She crawled over to the gun, goose bumps traveling up her arms as grabbed the pistol and got to her feet. Her hands did not shake as she began climbing the stairs. She could hear Moira and Samson's muffled arguing but only faintly as the sound of her own heartbeat overpowered everything else in her head.

Maybe this was her chance to help someone, to help Samson, before things got ugly.

She turned the corner and the sounds of the undead were deafening as she entered the room. She slowly raised the pistol, ignoring both Moira's screaming and Samson's shouting. He tried to hold his wife back and away from the decaying monsters pulling on their restraints.

Just as Veronica squeezed the trigger, she locked eyes with the dead girl and felt a churning in her stomach, wondering if this is exactly how she would look should she ever meet this same fate. In the final fleeting second, Moira escaped her husband's grasp and leapt onto the bed. The bullet exploded out of the gun and into Keira's skull, her head slumping forward onto her shoulders.

Moira screamed as Robbie tore into the flesh of her exposed legs, she kicked as streams of blood sprayed from her calf and feet as her son continued to eat. Strips of skin and muscle ripped away from her leg and the bedroom was an instant bloodbath.

"Robbie, stop! Stop!"

Moira's screams and sobs seemed louder than both the gunshot for Keira, and louder than the one Veronica fired into Robbie.

Moira continued screaming, but now at Samson, who tried to aid her.

"Get away! Get out of here! You monsters! Get the fuck out and don't you come back!"

Veronica's ears were ringing; her mouth was desert dry and she felt like she was back in the city all over again. Moira punched and slapped and kicked at Samson. His face was frozen in horror as he backed away toward Veronica, who still had the pistol raised. Samson turned and placed a hand on the gun, taking it from her trembling hands.

Moira stepped off the bed but her legs gave out, spilling her to the floor.

"I will fucking kill you! Both of you!" she sobbed, dragging herself forward in their direction. The tendons in her legs were severed and useless, blood flowed in a glorious fashion from her lower extremities with every movement.

A single, perfectly filed fingernail broke off as she continued to drag herself into the hallway after Samson and Veronica.

"Do you hear me?! Get out of this house! And if you come back, I will kill you!"

Veronica thought that Moira might have screamed her words as a warning rather than a threat, aware of the lethal infection coursing through her veins. Veronica stumbled hastily down the stairs and into the living room. Samson grabbed another bag from the floor near the couch and ran to the kitchen, filling it with what he could. Veronica tried to read his face, but it was as if the man was suddenly made of stone. He gave the new bag to Veronica and placed his own bag on his back. He handed her the pistol and nodded, showing her Al's shotgun.

Samson hesitated at the door, listening to Moira's screaming from upstairs. He thought of his children, and the burden that had been lifted from his chest, their souls finally free of this wretched world. He thought of Leti, of Will, of Tracy. Of all the others that he once knew that were now gone. He couldn't allow himself to think of Moira.

"We need to go," he finally said to Veronica without turning to look at her.

The two left the house. Out of habit, Samson pulled the key from his pocket and locked the door. Moira had suddenly stopped screaming. He didn't stop to wonder why. They rushed down the driveway and Samson passed the wreck on the street for the last time. He looked over his shoulder for a brief second as they fled what was once his home.

He wondered if the man he once was had died in that house with the rest of his world.

They stopped briefly so Samson could lock up the gate to Franklin Woods. He pulled an industrial-strength chain from his bag along with the padlock from Will's shed. There was nothing left there for him. There was nothing left there for anyone.

Just another house Samson couldn't steal food from.

XXIII

The return trip to the Dockside Bar and Grill was silent, save for the demonic cries that escaped the trees surrounding them. Samson and Veronica quickened their pace to a slow jog from time to time but decided walking was much quieter and they'd have more time to make a life or death decision if it came down to it.

Veronica played the scene from Samson's house over and over like a bad dream in her head. She still heard Moira's vicious screams as if she were standing next to her. It was dark, but she could slightly make out Samson's facial expression.

Blank.

She worried that the man might have cracked. From Veronica's experience with the end of the world, she figured everyone went crazy and that there were two ways a person could crack. Like she did, or like Moira had.

When they arrived at the restaurant, Veronica thought Samson would have been a little more careful entering the building, but to her surprise, he walked right up to the door, threw it open and waltzed in, as if the place were still operating, business as usual. She looked around, listening to her surroundings. Water licked at the dock posts and the boats made their usual rocking noises. Somewhere off in the distance, the frogs croaked and she felt a pang of jealousy at how, for certain species on this planet, the world hadn't changed at all.

Behind the bar inside, Samson ignored the foul smell that repeatedly punched him in the nose. He rummaged noisily, and being a whiskey man, stopped when he found the bottle of Gentleman Jack that someone had so cleverly hidden behind the lesser-quality bottles. He looked up when Veronica walked in.

"I guess it doesn't matter," she said as she locked the door. "The glass isn't at all reinforced." She pressed her face up to the glass to peer outside one more time as she whispered her last sentence, "but it makes me feel better."

Samson couldn't tell if she was talking to him, and didn't really feel like he was up for any kind of conversation. He hastily opened the bottle and took a long drink. He clenched his teeth as the drink went down. Drinking probably wasn't the appropriate solution, especially since they weren't in the safest of places, but his apathy at the moment was strong.

He felt Veronica's eyes on him as he moved from behind the bar and started toward the back. He stopped, feeling as though he owed her an explanation.

"I need some time." His voice was low, monotone. He looked at her and raised the bottle up.

Veronica hadn't known Samson for very long, but she liked him. She understood him. Her father was the same way when her mother had died, and she understood now what she understood then: sometimes a man needs to be alone with his thoughts.

After a long pause she said, "Okay," and Samson disappeared into the darkness of the restaurant.

Veronica sat down in one of the booths, wiping the grime from the table before she laid her head on it. She squeezed her eyes shut and exhaled with a grunt. It seemed like every time she got the chance to stop thinking about how bad things were, it all came rushing back at once, knocking the wind out of her. She just wished she could grab her laptop, sling it down on her bed and post some quirky status update.

How important social networking once was to her had left her with a mind full of things to say, and no one to say them to. She wished she could pick up her phone and text one of her friends about the day she'd had, but which one of her friends were even alive? And how insane was the day they were probably having?

When she opened her eyes again they fell upon an overturned chair, and underneath it, a black server's book. She hadn't noticed it before; she thought she had scoured the whole place when she first came here nearly a week before. Her curiosity was stronger than her exhaustion and she got up to retrieve it.

It was dirty, from the floor, or from sitting there for who knows how long.

She didn't care which. She sat back down at her booth and opened the book. A few order tickets, not much cash and some notes. It was decorated with Sanrio stickers and a girl's name: Bethany. It was written in silver sharpie across the top. Veronica wondered how old Bethany was, if this was her part-time job while she went to school, or if she was a grown woman who really liked Hello Kitty.

She read over the notes which contained Bethany's schedule, random doodles of hearts and stars, and a flower here and there. She saw at the bottom of the paper a note in a different handwriting than Bethany's. It read, "Remember to smile!"

Veronica didn't smile, but she tore it from the server's book and stuffed it in her pocket. Her hand lingered over it a moment and she closed her eyes again. For whatever reason she felt a strong connection to Bethany at that moment, long lost and fate unknown. Stronger, than she did to herself and her own twisted reality.

"Remember to smile," she said to no one and lay her head back down on the dirty table, closing her eyes.

XXIV

Two hours passed, and the dead seemed to retreat back to wherever they'd left. Andrew was convinced they'd all come from the high school. He was more than sure that he'd seen the faces of the local kids on the creatures.

It was dark now, and they had left Juliette by herself. Not wanting her to hear them, they went into another office and shut the door.

"I'm not spending the night out here with her. No way. We go back to the house. You know, the one in the gated community, with all the walls and empty streets?"

"Clyde, it's not safe. Who knows if they're all gone?" Andrew pleaded with his brother.

"Nope. No fucking way. We could have been goddamn snacks out there today, and you want to camp out on a silver platter with the pale horse dinner bell in there? No fuckin' thank you."

"Ben, please help me talk some sense into him."

"I can't. I think Clyde's right." Ben had been thinking about the way Clyde had talked to her back at the apartment and how she would fire right back at him. He compared that with the way he talked to her today and how she didn't respond. "You said we would stop and get some medication for her and she would get her shit together. Well, dude, I don't know that she grabbed the right ones. Did you check them? She's gotten worse since we left, man."

"Thank you. See? White boy's got sense. Your girl is bat-shit insane and we are leavin' tonight. She tried to kill me, *she tried to kill all of us* with that screamin', so she don't get a vote. You're outnumbered, it's time to go."

"Oh my God, c'mon. You can't be serious?"

Ben leaned up against a desk in the dark room. "Andrew, it might not be such a bad idea. It's night. They wouldn't notice us if we were quiet. If you can keep her quiet, man, we can do this."

"I say we leave her here. Knock her ass out and come back for her in the morning."

"Clyde, that's takin' it a little too far don't you think?"

"Whatever, man." Clyde exhaled loudly, accepting his defeat. He turned to his brother. "Drew, I love you, you're blood. But I will take off and leave your ass in a second if she fucks up again. Go get her, let's go. Now." Clyde opened the door and left the office to go grab his bag.

*

Ben could hear Andrew talking softly to Juliette, coaxing her out of the room, making her promise she would be quiet. He asked her several times if she'd started taking the medication they had found at CVS. He couldn't get a straight answer out of her, but he was finally able to get her to leave the room.

Clyde glared at her, and Ben expected that at any moment he would snap.

Andrew unlocked the door and waited for a response to the sound. Nothing. "Ok, quick, and quiet. No talking, no guns, no nothing. Just walking. Back to Franklin Woods. Got it?"

Everyone nodded, including Juliette, which Ben thought was a good sign, or at least an improvement. They moved as quickly as they could without running; that would be too loud, and they needed silence.

They cleared the edge of town and made it to the main road leading back to Franklin Woods.

"Okay, just a couple miles, we got this," Andrew called out to the group.

They continued in silence, and after what seemed like an eternity to the weary foursome, they finally saw a clearing in the trees, the community appearing on their left.

Ben jogged up to the gate and stopped, gaping.

Andrew noticed and caught up with him. "What is it?"

Ben raised his hand and pointed.

Where the pin had held the gate closed, there was now a chain and a padlock. Andrew stood in disbelief. "What the fuck—"

Clyde joined them at the gate and his jaw dropped open, too. "Who the fuck did this?"

"I told you I saw a light in that house. I told you."

They all looked at Juliette.

Ben hated to admit she was right.

Did someone know we were in there? Did someone want to keep us out?

Ben stared at the impenetrable gates, "Of all the times for someone to pull this shit. Not only can we not get in, but all our stuff's in there. We're fucked."

"Goddamnit!" Clyde kicked the gate.

"There were people in there. I told you I saw a light in that house," Juliette repeated herself when no one acknowledged her.

"Yes, baby, you saw a light. I get it now. I get it." Andrew put his arm around her and rubbed her shoulder.

Suddenly from the direction of town came a long, low wail.

"Oh come *on*!" Ben couldn't help but yell.

"We should have never left." Juliette began shaking in Andrew's arms. "We should have never left the apartment. We should have never left the station. We should have never left. Now we're just sitting outside waiting to die."

Clyde turned to Juliette. "I am so sick of your—"

"Enough," Ben said. "We are not sitting out here, waiting to die. We can't do anything about the lock tonight. We shoot it, we die. It's not like the city. All of a sudden, this seems to me like this shit is worse than the city. But what we can do is keep moving. We need to get to the water."

"Oh, so that's the whole situation huh?" Clyde was fuming. "We get out of the station, all of a sudden there's a fuckin' lock on the gate and we're headed to the bay?"

"Clyde, it's not like that. You know this. It has nothing to do with Veronica right now. It's about getting the hell out of *here* and finding someplace safe." Another wail, this one sounding like it came from the highway.

Ben grimaced, *it's almost as if they're calling to each other in the darkness.*

Andrew clucked his tongue. "Let's get moving. Get your bags on tight, we need to be fast." He leaned in to his brother. "Get it together man."

The four of them started off at a fast pace toward the bay, like they had when they left the station, but it seemed like the wails and moans were coming from all over the woods now. They were echoing, making it harder to tell which direction they were coming from.

They picked up the pace to a jog, and off to the right, Andrew heard snapping twigs and the rustling of dead leaves. A low growl came from the tree line, followed immediately by an eater.

Juliette screamed and Andrew dodged out of its way. The eater fell over its own feet and skidded on the asphalt, but was back up in a flash. Andrew swung, and its face caved in with the force from the business end of the golf club. He brought it down onto its head one more time for good measure, but more howls came from the surrounding woods.

"Keep it movin' people, let's go." Andrew didn't stop to wipe the club off or attach it back to his waist band. They were running now, out of breath and panting, but *running* full speed ahead.

"Oh thank God! There it is, up ahead! There's the restaurant," Clyde yelled, shaking his fist over his head.

They gave it their all as they sped toward the Dockside Bar & Grill but stopped hard, piling into each other as eaters burst from the trees ahead of them.

"Shit, Drew, what do we do, man?" Clyde had pulled his gun, ready to fire into any of the undead that got too close.

"No guns! I don't think they've seen us yet. Head around to the back! Probably no windows there!" Andrew panted. "Go right, get into the woods, get past them and get to the back of the building!"

The group split up once they hit the woods, following Andrew's orders. The cries of the dead came from everywhere. Ben smashed the dirt beneath his feet as he ran; it was so loud he felt like bombs were exploding with each step.

His heart pounded so hard in his chest he couldn't help but think back to that night in Afghanistan. It seemed so long ago, but he remembered it like it was just yesterday. Running through the darkness, the sweat pouring down his face. The explosion behind him, the smell of copper in the air. The screams of his brothers in arms echoing all around him. His heart practically bursting from his chest. The bullet piercing his left shoulder...

But there was no bullet tonight.

Ben snapped out of it and with a loud cry, he charged forward. He was the first to clear the eaters in the road.

The dead could hear the group running through the trees but couldn't see them. They howled, and more joined them from the direction of Franklin Woods. Ben headed toward the back door of the restaurant. It was an emergency exit door, no way to open it from the outside. Andrew, followed by Juliette and Clyde, soon came frantically running and Ben heard Andrew yell out "Ladder."

Ben looked toward the roof and saw the metal ladder, he jumped up. "Fuck."

Juliette was coming straight toward him "Lift me up! I can grab it!"

Without waiting to see if he'd do it, she leapt into his arms and he pivoted, throwing her light frame at the bottom rung. She brought it down with a loud bang and fell to the ground. He pulled her back to her feet, and she was up the ladder in no time. Ben scrambled after her. Andrew pushed his brother forward to get up and Ben grabbed Clyde's hand, pulling him onto the roof with them. Andrew started up the ladder, and two eaters caught up, snatching at his feet as he hoisted himself up.

One of the undead grabbed Andrew's left foot and chomped down, but his boot was too thick. He cried out, and Ben and Clyde grabbed him tightly as he kicked with his other foot, smashing the eater's face. The dead man let go, falling back to earth, and Andrew pushed himself onto the roof. Ben pulled the ladder back up. They all collapsed in heaps, breathing heavily.

The eaters circled the building. Howling and hissing, growling and moaning. They could hear the heavy footsteps of the runners and the shuffling of the slow ones; like a pack of wolves, they were waiting. They could still hear the four of them breathing, could smell their sweat, and they would not be leaving them alone any time soon.

XXV

Samson sat on the floor of the dry food pantry in the rear of the restaurant. Every so often, he'd take another long swig from his whiskey bottle, attempting, and failing, to drown out his sick nightmare.

Everyone I know is dead, and everyone they know is dead.

He slammed his head back against the wall he leaned on but the alcohol dulled the pain he probably should have felt.

"Everyone who ever knew anyone is more than likely fuckin' dead!"

Samson chuckled slowly and softly. Once a successful attorney who was capable of getting any scumbag off the hook in front of the toughest judges, he was reduced to a mumbling mess, hidden in the back of a dark, abandoned restaurant, blanketed by the smelling rotting fish and spoiled food. He couldn't help but wonder if the universe was punishing him for something.

The pantry spun and he shook his head roughly, slamming it back against the wall one last time.

"Oh, I'm shitfaced," he said as he half-lay, half-fell onto the hard tile floor. The tile was cool on his face and he rubbed his forehead back and forth on it for a few moments.

He began laughing at the bizarre nature of his situation again, but the laughter soon turned into short sobs, which gave way to the sound of the cracking of his heart, exiting his mouth in a wail of raw emotion. It surprised him...he didn't think there was any left inside him.

His eyes squeezed shut, fist pounding at the floor beneath him, he cursed himself out loud for not being a better father, a better husband. He cursed Moira for not being a better wife or mother, or even a better person. And although he wasn't a religious man, he cursed God and all the other deities of the universe for abandoning him. For abandoning everyone.

Every time he lifted his fist and brought it back down in anger, in sorrow, more blood escaped him and smeared itself on the tile.

Across the kitchen and through the swinging doors, in the dining room, Veronica was already awake and on alert before Samson's emotional outburst.

She had dozed off quickly, her head filled with dreams of what Bethany the waitress might be doing right now. Maybe she hadn't been at work when everything fell apart; maybe she had been on one of the big beautiful boats outside in the marina, with coworkers and friends, and they simply sailed away, finding solace somewhere out to sea with the sun shining on all of their smiling faces.

A short time later, she couldn't be sure just how long, she was jolted awake by a feral scream from out in the parking lot. She jumped out of the booth and dropped to the floor, wincing at the broken shards of glass from who-knows-what. Slivers and knives embedded themselves into her hands.

She didn't know where the eater was or how many of them could be out there. She crawled toward the bar to get a better look out of a window with a lower risk of exposing herself. It didn't matter how dark it was, she would not be taking any chances.

She very carefully poked her head up, stopping at the bridge of her nose; she feared even the slightest fog of her breathe on the glass would be enough to attract them. Her heart felt like it was trying to escape her chest and she placed a hand over it, as if trying to placate the leaping muscle. She spotted the dead, and to her dismay, there were plenty. She could clearly see seven of them, all different heights and sizes. Each bore a unique wound, each telling a different story of the dead. But all these stories ended the same.

A few moved at a stunning pace, running in circles, slamming into one another, screaming, grunting, growling. Every few seconds one of them would act as if they'd picked up on some scent in the night breeze but then go back to running around. They were hungry, wild animals.

The rest shambled around as if following the faster ones, pathetically grunting and moaning.

They'll get bored, they'll move on, Veronica reassured herself. She would be fine if she stayed out of view. Samson had been asleep for probably longer than she had, and she would keep watch. She lowered her eyes from the window and squatted below it, trying to lower her heart rate. A few minutes passed; Veronica strained her ears and could still hear them hissing out front. She couldn't figure out what had attracted them here. They'd been very quiet.

Samson began screaming only as a drunken man could, from the dark, lonely pantry in the back. She cringed and chills ran up her spine. Veronica sprang from her spot beneath the window, racing toward the double doors of the kitchen. She knew better. She didn't hesitate; she didn't look back toward the glass doors or windows. She burst into the room and softened her steps as it got harder to see with no windows to let the moonlight in.

Swiftly and silently she entered the pantry and grabbed Samson's wrist, throwing herself on the floor beside him and wrapping her other arm around his big frame.

"Enough!" she hissed at him. "I understand, but it's time to stop now." She squeezed his wrist tightly and shook him with all her might until she could feel the tension in his body give way some.

The pantry was pitch black except for the beam from Samson's flashlight; Veronica grabbed it and turned it off.

"Ssh, please!" she pleaded with him, trying hard not to panic and still holding him as he attempted to push her off in his drunken stupor. Samson was so incoherent that she hoped he would just pass out; she briefly considered knocking him out with the heavy mag light.

He opened his mouth to yell, and she slapped her hand over it. "You get off me! Get out!" he shouted out at her through her fingers.

Although she could not focus on anything in such immense darkness, she kept her eyes wide open, fearing she might miss the minutest detail of her suddenly-hostile surroundings. She searched the depths of her brain for some sort of a plan that could get them out of here alive, but she could think of nothing. She couldn't get out of this one alone.

She needed this man to get his shit together.

"Samson," she whispered directly into his ear with the most sobering words she could have ever uttered. "They're here."

XXVI

It felt like an eternity passed as they each caught their breath and tried to calm down on the roof of the Dockside Bar & Grill.

"What do we do now?" Juliette seemed like she was back to normal again. Her eyes were focused and her expression was clear. Maybe the terror of the pursuit had snapped her out of her mania.

"I have no idea." Ben looked over at Andrew, still lying on the roof. "You said you knew the owners, that they had a boat at this marina?"

"Yeah, but let's hope they didn't take off in it when the world went ass-up."

"It's worth a shot, man. Where did they keep the keys?"

"I'd assume in the office. I've seen 'em before, got a stupid surfboard keychain on 'em." He then mumbled, "I have never understood surfboards in Northwest Florida."

"Is there access to the restaurant from the roof?" Ben looked around and spotted the large skylights. "What about these? Can I get down there through one of these?"

Andrew propped himself up on his elbows and looked over to where Ben was standing.

Clyde had also gotten up and went to scope it out. "Yeah. We could remove the cover if we had some tools."

Ben crouched down and inspected the large screws. Nodding to himself, he pulled the utility knife from his pocket. He popped the blade out, considering it. It might not have been a flathead, but the blade should work just fine. He pulled his hunting knife out and handed it to Clyde. "Here, you use this one."

The two of them went to work removing the top piece of the huge skylight.

"So what the hell do we do once we remove this big-ass thing? That glass ain't the regular shit, so what are we gonna use to break it?" Clyde grunted as they lifted the cover, then he and Ben carried it over to the far end of the roof.

"I'm gonna jump straight down and hope I make it to the floor," Ben said matter-of-factly.

Juliette shone her small flashlight down into the big opening now in the roof. A collection of dead bugs littered the surface of the grimy Plexiglas at the bottom.

"You sure that's such a good idea?" Andrew asked him, concern in his voice.

Ben shrugged. "Nope." He looked at each of their faces before dropping down. "Wish me luck."

*

Samson and Veronica remained on the floor of the pantry, as quiet as could be, in complete darkness. He could hear the eaters screaming outside as they circled the building.

"How many shells do you have for the shotgun?" Veronica asked.

"I think maybe seven or eight. They're in my bag."

She was afraid to turn the flashlight on, but had no choice; they needed to load his shotgun in case those things made it in.

Loud banging came from the roof, making them both jump.

"They're on the *roof*?!" Samson panicked, his drunken stupor getting the better of him. "When the *hell* did they learn to climb?"

"Ssh, shut up. Listen." Veronica heard voices. Real people, real words, not the moans of the dead. "There are people on the roof? No wonder those things won't go away."

"What kind of people are on the roof?" Samson shielded his eyes when she turned the big flashlight on. "How do we know these people won't just throw us to the dogs? Give me the bag, I need my shells."

She slid the bag over to him. "Be easy now, it could be help. They could be here to help us." She hated herself for saying it as soon as the words came out of her mouth. She remembered sitting in Ben's bathroom, telling him help would never come.

Her thoughts were interrupted as part of the ceiling collapsed. Glass smashed and pieces of the ceiling scattered as one of the huge skylights came crashing to the floor. Amidst the rubble was the body of a man struggling to get up. Samson raised the shotgun and Veronica shined the flashlight on the stranger.

"Identify yourself!" Samson called out. Still drunk, he almost laughed out loud despite the dire situation. He felt like he was in a movie.

The man on the floor groaned and cried out, startled by the voice behind him. "There are people in here?" He dusted himself off as he got up, wincing, and slowly turned around, his hands in the air.

Veronica's eyes went wide and her mouth dropped. She almost let go of the flashlight and let it fall to the floor but she kept it fixed on the man's face because she couldn't believe her eyes. "Ben?"

"Well, I'll be damned." Ben grinned from ear to ear as Veronica leapt from the floor and ran to him. She wrapped her arms around Ben and squeezed him in a hug. "Ah, ow! Okay! I just fell through the ceiling. It's good to see you, too." She eased up on him a bit as he returned her embrace.

"How are you alive?" She stepped back and shook her head. She was in disbelief. "How did you get here?"

"I had some help. Good help." He turned to the pantry, glaring at Samson who still sat on the floor. "Who's your friend?"

"Samson," he called out from the pantry, shotgun still trained on Ben.

"It's alright, Samson, he's my friend I told you about. From the city."

Samson slowly lowered the gun and tried to get up, his equilibrium betrayed him and he fell back down.

"Is he drunk?" Ben raised an eyebrow and cocked his head.

"Yes." Veronica nodded, biting her lip. "It's been a long day, to say the least."

Ben shrugged and looked up at the gaping hole in the ceiling as Clyde called down from the roof. "Hey! I don't know what the fuck you're doin' down there, but more of them fuckin' things are comin'."

The eaters began beating on the glass up front.

"Look, I've got some friends up there. One of them knew the owners of this place, says they had a boat. I'd love to sit and play catch-up but there's a huge problem outside and we need to go."

"Okay, tell them to come down." Veronica moved over to Samson and helped him off the floor.

Ben craned his neck back. "You guys need to get down here."

One by one the three of them dropped down into the filthy kitchen.

"There are other people here?" Juliette looked at Veronica with wide eyes.

"This your girl?" Clyde asked, crossing his arms over his chest. "Nice coincidence."

"No time for bullshit right now, where are the keys Andrew?"

"I'll get them." Andrew ran across the rank kitchen and broke down the office door with one kick. It sounded like he was tearing the place apart. The light from his flashlight bounced around the room as he searched. "Yes! They're still here! I got 'em!" he called out.

The eaters seemed entirely concentrated on the front of the restaurant now since everyone was off the roof and inside the restaurant. "Any ideas on how to get out of here in one piece?" Andrew asked as he rejoined the group in the kitchen.

"Whiskey," Samson said, holding his near-empty bottle up to the group.

"Is he drunk?" Andrew asked Ben.

"No, no." Samson waved a hand at Andrew. "Well, yes I am drunk. That I am. But I meant we set this place on fire. Sneak out the back. If we really have a boat, then let's burn this shit-hole to the ground, along with all those dead bastards outside."

Clyde nodded in excitement, "Now *that* sounds like a plan."

Samson shook the bottle of Jack around and motioned to the door leading to the bar, "There's plenty of booze out there. We can do this in no time."

Juliette removed her backpack and unzipped it. "Will this help?" She handed Ben the lighter fluid she'd stashed from the store visit earlier in the day.

"I knew this stuff would come in handy. Clyde, you still got my extra Zippo?"

"Right here." He held it up.

"Let's get to work, people!"

The six of them hurried around the bar, breaking bottles of rum and vodka all over. They sent whiskey bottles crashing to the floor and poured gin all over the tables, booths, and bar top. Ben finished everything off with a trail of lighter fluid leading right to the front door. The glass was not meant to hold the weight of that many ferocious bodies, but he couldn't help but stop at the door and look one of them right in the face.

It was once a girl, a little older than Veronica. She'd probably been very pretty, but now she pressed her face up against the door, snarling and spitting. She knocked out a tooth, too stupid to realize she couldn't bite Ben through the glass, but she was unfazed and kept snapping at him. Her light hair was stained with dirt and blood and who knew what else. Ben noticed her name tag said *Bethany.* He shook his head at her and thought of all the other Bethanys that were now a waste to the world.

"Goodnight, Bethany." Ben walked toward the back and he heard the glass cracking against the pounding fists and the pushing bodies. There must have been fifty of them out there.

"Let's put that fire exit to use." Clyde lit Ben's extra Zippo and set fire to the bar. It went up in a matter of seconds, and they didn't stick around to watch the place burn. As Veronica and Samson grabbed their bags, the glass finally shattered and screams filled the air.

Immediately, the smell of burning flesh and hair rolled back to them, carried by the fire's drafts; they had never smelled anything worse. Pisano's kitchen, The Dockside's kitchen...rotting fish and human waste were a better alternative to a burning body.

The group ran out the back, Samson slammed the door shut with all his weight as the first of the burning eaters reached the kitchen. Their violent screams rang in his ears and echoed through his mind.

"How do we know which boat is ours?" Veronica called out as they ran toward the marina, their feet pounding on the wooden dock.

"It says *Dockside* on it!" Andrew yelled back to her.

Samson couldn't help but wonder who had come up with such an unimaginative name.

EPILOGUE

The group made it to The Dockside in one piece. The boat, fortunately, was gassed up and ready to go. Its owners probably ready to take her out on a beautiful Autumn Florida day before the world fell apart and the luxuries in life were reduced to simple things...like breathing, sleeping, and eating. Samson and Clyde were able to take out the few straggling eaters that had noticed the group slip out the back. The rest of the group readied the boat for departure.

The building was now completely engulfed in the fire. It was an awful and indescribable sight to see the flaming eaters pouring out of the building as the boat started off. Their bodies burned and their howls continued. Juliette wept in Andrew's arms while Clyde lit cigarettes for Ben and himself. Veronica stood between Ben and Samson with a small smile on her lips. She couldn't help but feel lucky; it was as if by some miracle she had found some semblance of the family she'd lost through all this tragedy and ugliness.

They watched as the remaining eaters fell into the bay in a failed attempt to follow the boat. Their fires extinguished, and they bobbed to the surface, finally lifeless in the water.

"Where to now?" Samson asked Veronica.

She felt his eyes on her but never looked from the burning building. "We keep heading west."

HAVEN

BOOK II

PART I

HAVEN

I

The gentle rocking of the boat gave Samson little comfort. In fact, the drunken stupor he had put himself in the night before was showing its mean face with every movement *The Dockside* made in the gulf. He hung himself over the side and puked for what seemed like hours. His throat burned and his head felt like it would explode any minute. He slipped backward and landed on his ass with a grunt. Vomit trickled down the left side of his face and he casually wiped it away. Samson exhaled hard and propped himself up on his elbows, trying to steady himself and get rid of the spins. He cleaned his hand off on his black polo; no use in worrying what he looked like.

I'm already covered in blood, what does a little vomit hurt?

"You think you're finished yet?"

Samson saw dirty white sneakers appear out of the corner of his eye.

"I sure hope so." He looked up at Veronica who loomed over him, hands on her hips.

"You need to get some rest." She held out her hand. "We all need to get some rest."

Ben came up on the other side of Samson and helped Veronica get him off the deck. There was a small cabin on the boat with just enough space for the group of six.

Veronica had set up some linens and towels on the floor inside for Samson, and Ben helped him into the makeshift bed.

"Ya know, we might have had some medicine for all that pukin' you're doin'." Clyde stared down at Samson and spoke through a full mouth of potato chips. "But somebody locked us out." He raised an eyebrow at Samson, awaiting his response. Samson simply lifted his hand and waved it at Clyde.

"You can give him shit later, man, let him sleep the drunk off." Ben took a seat on a wobbly folding chair between Samson and the table Clyde sat at. "Got anymore chips?"

Clyde stole another handful of chips before handing them over to Ben.

Veronica stood in the doorway and watched Juliette sleep soundly on the small loveseat opposite the table. "How do you think she'll be when she wakes up?" Veronica spoke softly.

"I don't know." Clyde hesitated, as if he wanted to say more, but he didn't even have the energy to trash-talk Juliette at the moment.

The boat came to a stop and Andrew called out to them. Veronica stepped aside to let Clyde and Ben pass. She shut the cabin door behind her and followed them out.

"I figure this is as good a spot as any to drop anchor and let everybody get some sleep. Nobody gonna fuck with us out here unless they got a boat of their own." Andrew cracked his neck and gently massaged it with his left hand. "Shit, and the day those dead things learn to drive a boat will be the day that I die."

"Where are we?" Ben lit up a cigarette.

"Not really sure, to tell you the truth." Andrew looked around, but for all he knew, they could be halfway to Mexico and he wouldn't be able to tell. "Been headin' west now for almost three hours, and I'm not gonna tell you that we have a whole lot of gas left. I don't know shit about boats. So let's get some shut eye and make some plans in the morning."

"Got it." Ben nodded at the brothers as they disappeared into the cabin. "You should go in with them."

Veronica shook her head and joined Ben on one of the empty seats on the deck, pulling her legs up and hugging them to her chest. She leaned her head back and stared up at the black expanse of sky. She'd never seen that many stars in her life and it reminded her of how small she was, how insignificant they all were.

Ben dropped his finished cigarette to the deck and stepped on it. "So what's the grand plan for Veronica from here? You've gotten us this far." He smiled at her through the darkness.

She looked from the sky and squinted at him, trying to make out his facial expression, but Andrew had cut all the lights. "I don't know. I never really knew if I'd actually find a way out of the city, but I did. And then I never knew how I'd get out of the bay once I found the boats. So really, I haven't gotten us anywhere; everyone else has gotten me somewhere."

"Hey, hey. What is that attitude?" He lit up his last cigarette and tossed the empty pack to his feet. "If I recall, you are the reason we're even all on this boat, so don't get all emo teenager on me for Christ's sake."

She cracked a weak smile, but knew he couldn't see it. "Sorry. Guess I'm just still in shock. The last couple of weeks have been pretty intense." She swallowed hard. "The last couple of hours have been pretty intense."

"What happened back there in Franklin? Is this Samson an alright guy?"

"He's no better or worse than you or me. You'll like him. Everyone has been through their own stuff. Nobody's having a nice time." She rubbed her eyes.

He nodded, understanding. "Just wanted to make sure you didn't lose your spark."

She snickered somewhere in the darkness.

"I'm really glad we found you, kiddo."

"I'm really glad you found me too."

II

Andrew was the first to wake. The sun shone mercilessly on his face through one of the cabin windows and his body was drenched in sweat. He gently moved Juliette from off him and she groaned in her sleep. He stretched and every inch of his big frame ached. There was bottled water galore on the boat, and he grabbed one as he left the cabin to check out their surroundings in daylight.

The sun was out in full effect; he glanced at his watch, 11:45. They were all so exhausted, it didn't surprise him how long he'd been able to sleep in such cramped quarters. He squinted at the sun's reflection shining off the beautiful Gulf waters and climbed the steps to the captain's chair.

"Holy fuck."

Andrew didn't know what he was expecting to see, but he sure didn't expect to be this close to land, or that they'd be right in the middle of a vacationer's wet dream. He put the down bottle of water and fumbled for the binoculars that hung around the steering wheel, the ones which had kept knocking into his legs as he drove the boat the night before.

He recognized the resort immediately, with its tiki hut beach bars, an enormous indoor/outdoor swimming pool, and the algae-stained space straight down the middle of the towering building. It was once a breathtaking waterfall leading from the pool on the roof to the pool on the ground floor. Two smaller towers were to the right and left of the main one and an enormous green E sat at the very top of the center.

"That, my friend, is The Emerald City." Samson shielded his eyes with one hand and held a water bottle in the other.

Andrew hadn't even noticed Samson below him at the bow of the boat. "I know what it is," he called down. Samson continued to stare out at the resort as Andrew climbed down to join him up front.

Samson pointed at the binoculars and Andrew handed them over. "Stayed there a few times for some weekend getaways with the family." Samson stuttered over the word family as he scanned the beach with the binoculars. "Even thought about getting our own condominium, but I never got around to it." He lowered the binoculars and tucked the water bottle under his arm, extending his hand. "I don't think we were formally introduced. I'm Samson Eckhart."

"Yeah, I know who you are. Big-shot attorney that kept me nice and busy." He shook Samson's hand firmly. "Officer Andrew Hansen."

"Job's a job." Samson raised a hand toward the empty shore. "Or at least it *was* a job. The others, they're with you?"

"Yeah, my brother Clyde, my girlfriend Juliette, and the other one's Ben. Right place, right time, I guess. Just shitty circumstances."

Samson shook his head. "I can't imagine anyone meeting under pleasant circumstances anymore." He handed the binoculars back to Andrew and sipped from his water bottle, staring aimlessly, and was suddenly snapped from his daze by a flash of light from one of the towers. "Did you see that?" He squinted and snatched the binoculars back out of Andrew's hands.

"What's the deal, man?"

"I swear I just saw something." He adjusted the focus and searched floor by floor for any movement from the tower. As he was about to lower the binoculars again he saw the flash of light once more from the top floor. "Up there, somebody's signaling us."

Andrew grabbed the binoculars back from him and took a look for himself. Once more the light flashed. "Signal mirror or something." He mumbled, waiting for any more light. A figure appeared on the balcony. They waved one arm and then two, then back to one again. "Well, there sure is somebody up there, but who knows if that's them sayin' hello or tellin' us to go the fuck away."

Samson took a look again and the person added a little jump into their waving. "It looks to me like they might actually be a little excited to see us. We should wake the others." Andrew hurried to get the rest of the group while Samson remained at the bow. He decided to give whoever it was on the top floor a couple waves back. The figure stopped jumping and waving and quickly disappeared back inside the condo.

Samson frowned, not knowing how to take the sudden cease in communication.

A minute or so passed before everyone but Juliette joined Samson at the bow.

"How many people did you see?" Veronica held her hands out for the binoculars but Samson put them back up to his eyes again.

"Just the one, but they're gone now."

"Could you tell if he was armed?" Ben took a cigarette from Clyde and lit it up.

"Nah, can't even tell if it's a man or a woman from here." Andrew folded his arms across his chest, furrowing his brow. "If there are more people in there, maybe they went to go get them, same as us."

"Could be bad," Clyde exhaled his smoke and the soft breeze off the water quickly cleared the air again. "We're like sittin' ducks out here. What if this motherfucker went off to get a sniper rifle or some shit?"

"Relax." Samson gave him a sideways look. "They didn't look hostile to me. Besides, if they were looking to kill us I don't think they would have let us know anyone was home."

The group stood silently, studying the tower for any sign of activity. Veronica grabbed the binoculars and pointed at the beach excitedly. "Somebody's running down there." She followed the figure as it quickly moved on the sand toward a small hut. "How did y'all miss all the damn Jet Skis down there?" She looked from Samson to Andrew and back to Samson again, rolling her eyes. The stranger on the beach grabbed something from inside the hut and hopped onto one of the Jet Ski rentals, starting it up in no time. "We better hope this guy is friendly."

"He's going to ride a Jet Ski out here to us?" Clyde's hand instinctively went for his firearm but he'd left it inside. "Damn, I need my gun." He hurried back to the cabin, cussing the whole way.

"Grab 'em all," Andrew called out to him.

Veronica sighed, "Oh, great."

"What now? Give me those." Samson tried to take back the binoculars from her but she jerked away. Her mouth hung open at the dozen eaters shambling their way down the beach.

From what Veronica could see, the dead were not so graceful on the sand. They bumped into one another, knocking each other down and tripping over their own feet like undead Keystone Kops. They waddled and shuffled toward the water, arms flailing, almost moving as one.

The Jet Ski slowed as it grew closer to *The Dockside.* Clyde returned with what little weapons the group had, Juliette following behind with light footsteps.

The man on the Jet Ski came to a halt once he noticed the four guns pointed at him. He put his hands up immediately, revealing a shoulder holster. "Whoa whoa, I come in peace." He called out in a thick British accent. He looked from face to face across the boat, stopping at Veronica. He narrowed his eyes. "You've got children with you?"

"I'm not a child." She stepped forward, as if she had intended on doing something about his remark but Ben put his arm out.

"There are no children aboard," Ben responded, pistol still pointed at the man.

"Those things, behind you," Andrew nodded toward the shore, "do we need to be worried about them right now?"

The man turned around as the eaters tumbled into the water, getting knocked over by gentle waves, uneasy on their decaying feet in the crystal-clear waters. He sort of chuckled, "Nah, mate, lucky for us they don't swim. They get far enough out they sink and probably just stay there. To be honest, I don't care where they go once they're in the drink, as long as they don't bother me anymore." He wiped the sweat from his face on his forearm. "Listen, how about this, I throw my weapon aboard, you put yours down?" He spoke slowly and clearly.

No one in the group said anything to him.

"Look, I haven't got anything up my sleeve." He wore no shirt and shook his hands in the air, smiling at them.

Andrew looked to Ben and he responded with a nod. "Alright. Remove your weapon. Slowly." Andrew watched closely the man's every move. Once the man had the holster off, he brought his hands back up. "Toss it on up here, no sudden movements or I shoot."

The man nodded and with a light underhand throw, the gun gracefully flew up for Samson to fumble, but catch. The men looked at each other and dropped their guns to their sides.

"Alright then." The man rested his arms on the Jet Ski and leaned forward slightly, shifting his weight. "My name's Gary. I've been living up in the tower, where you first spotted me."

"How many of you are there?" Samson asked.

Gary looked at him and shook his head. "It's only me, now."

"You mean to tell me you've got the whole place to yourself?" Samson raised an eyebrow. "I don't buy it."

"Hey, look, I know, it sounds mad." He rubbed his eyes. Samson could see the familiar hurt in them. "There were more. I can promise you that. But we ran into a problem, quite a big one. The last few days I've just been sneaking around like a rat between buildings, trying not to get myself killed. I suppose the only advantage I've got over those things is I've still got my wits about me."

Samson took a few steps over to Andrew and leaned in close. "I want to know what happened. And if anyone here is gonna be able to call a liar on his bullshit, I'd like to think it'd be me."

Andrew thought about it for a second and nodded, "Alright, let's bring him up."

"Why don't you come on around back so we can talk this out." Samson walked to the back as Gary fired up the Jet Ski and brought it to the stern. The ladder dropped into the water with a light splash and Samson helped the stranger climb up.

"Welcome aboard *The Dockside.* I'm Samson."

III

Introductions went around as everyone found a place to settle on the deck. Andrew opened the boat's bright green canopy so the group could escape the sun without being cramped in the stuffy cabin. Andrew sat down next to Juliette and she latched onto his arm, childlike, hiding her face in his chest. He brushed a few blonde strands off her forehead and stroked her arm. Clyde passed some water bottles around and stopped at Gary, reluctant to share.

"If you haven't got it to spare, it's quite alright. I've got more than enough back at the resort." Gary informed Clyde.

He was a short man in his early forties with a small frame and tanned skin. He had a shiny bald head with a neat beard and didn't look his age. He wore no shirt or shoes, just a pair of light blue-and-white checkered board shorts. If he didn't open his mouth to speak, he looked like a typical Florida beach bum who'd grown up on the water.

Clyde's interest piqued at the mention of Gary's abundance of supplies and he shoved a bottle in his face. "Just take it before I change my mind." He sauntered away and wedged himself between Ben and Veronica, snatching up the pack of cigarettes from Ben's lap and making himself comfortable. Gary couldn't help but chuckle at Clyde's dramatic demeanor, and as his eyes met Veronica's, he could see that she, too, was amused.

"So let's hear it." Samson wiped the beads of sweat from his face with the front of his shirt. A breeze would find its way into the circle from time to time, easing the heat. It wasn't unusual for the random eighty-five degree day in October, but Samson wished he was laying in the ice-cold air conditioning on his Landeeca sectional with his feet up and a beer in his hand.

"I worked as a liaison at the port, not that far from here. International imports, blah blah blah." Gary used his hand as a puppet to mimic himself. "I'd be here in the States so often that the wife and I decided to buy a place over at the resort. Just so happens that we were here when everything got totally fucked." He looked at Veronica and Juliette and grimaced. "Sorry, loves."

Veronica shrugged and Juliette didn't respond. Gary took it as a sign that no one was bothered by the language and continued. "The main tower is for owners, mostly full, but a lot of people took off for home at the first signs of something being off. Naturally, all international flights had been cancelled, so Claire and I were stuck here in Haven. Not a bad place to be, I'd say. When things started getting really rough we brought what little guests were in the other wings into the main tower and blocked it off, bringing us up to about sixty. No one came in, no one went out." He stopped for a moment and his face went still. "Have you seen anyone turn yet?"

The entire group remained silent, their faces just as serious as Gary's. Each face told its own story of suffering and loss.

"Mind if I have one of those, mate?"

Ben tossed Gary the pack of smokes and his lighter. Gary lit a cigarette and went into a fit of coughing. He spat over the side of the boat. "My apologies, it's been a while." He returned the items to Ben and took another drag off his cigarette before continuing. "They don't all turn at the same rate, ya know? We didn't even realize we had locked ourselves in with the monsters." He rubbed his head, as if wishing the memories away. "So many of them. And they were so bloody fast. Two whole days had passed before we even knew that anyone had been bitten. Couldn't have come at a worse time either, middle of the night, pitch black. Oh, we thought we knew what we were doing. We thought we were prepared. But the problem was the fast ones go for your throat, they go for the good stuff. The faster you die, the more quickly you turn if you're not put out of your misery. Claire, myself, and three others..." he let the sentence trail as he took another drag. "Five fucking people out of sixty made it out of the main tower. Can you believe it? We made our way to the sky bridge that connects the buildings to one another; the plan was to lead them into the other building, trap them inside, and take care of what stragglers were left."

"How you gonna keep those things from breakin' through the glass?" Clyde interrupted. "That plan don't make any sense."

Samson chimed in, suddenly defending the stranger. "Seriously, Emerald City is no joke. A lot of money to build the place and a lot of money kept in the place. Trust me, the thing is like a fuckin' fortress. People with money don't stay at the Super 8, Clyde."

"Oh, well excuse me." Clyde rolled his eyes and looked away.

"He's right, though." Gary took a sip from his bottle of water and flicked the cigarette away. "Really, the plan we had, it *did* make sense. It would have worked. We just didn't have time. Running like scared animals through dark hallways and stairwells, the echoes of the dead ringing in your ears and bouncing off every wall, it's disorienting. We finally get down to the lobby and the goddamned place is crawling with them. We had no idea they'd already wandered in from the outside. Before I knew it, they were all over us. I don't even know what happened to the other three men. All I know is I heard Claire scream and I forgot they were even with us. I just remember dodging snapping mouths and clawing hands, I killed whatever came at me to try and find her in the dark lobby. And then I finally did."

Gary hesitated and cleared his throat.

"I spotted her beautiful face amidst that crowd of dead surrounding her and she... she just smiled at me." His voice was now barely a whisper. He put his face in his hands and exhaled with a sigh. Samson's chest tightened slightly as he replayed the final moments with his family in his mind. He knew Gary was telling the truth. He could not only hear it in the man's voice, but he could feel it deep inside of himself, an excruciating souvenir from the end of the world.

"What happened to her?" Juliette finally asked what everyone had been thinking. She wrung her hands as she sat under Andrew's large arm.

Gary wiped the tears from his cheeks and his olive green eyes burned a hole in Juliette's heart. "She shot herself in the head."

IV

Juliette squealed with every bump and jump as the Jet Ski made its way to the shore. She held on to Gary for dear life and kept her eyes squeezed shut. She was the last of the group to be taken to shore from *The Dockside.* Her companions were already waiting on the beach, smashing the heads of the undead as they stumbled their way through the sand. Gary had convinced them that joining him in Emerald City was the right choice and promised them a fair share of his supplies and a safe place to stay if they'd help him take care of a few of his own problems.

The Jet Ski came to an abrupt stop. "You ready then?" Gary called over his shoulder.

She nodded, watching as Andrew took a slow-moving eater out with his golf club. The hideous thing's jaw went flying off following the upswing. Samson cracked it over the head with his shotgun, bringing it to its knees. Putrid, black blood poured from the eater's face where its jaw had just vacated, painting the once-perfect white sand the color of death. Juliette flinched as Andrew brought the golf club down one more time for good measure.

"Come on now," Gary said, holding out his hand to her. "Before any more of them show up and we can't make it to the tower."

She sighed and grabbed his hand; she was light enough for him to hold up over his shoulders to ensure her clothes didn't get soaked, just as he had done with Veronica as he waded through the water. The rest of the group would have to worry about soggy pants and sand-caked shoes for now. As soon as Juliette's feet were on the ground, Gary returned to the watercraft and pushed it up alongside the other that Ben had used to help him bring everyone ashore.

"See? I told you everything was gonna be fine." Andrew beamed at his girlfriend as she ran to him, finding comfort in his arms. She didn't care that he was covered in blood.

"Right then. Looks like we've got more company." Gary pointed up the beach at a group of eaters that were making their way toward them. "Let's get a move on."

They trudged through the sand as quickly as they could, ignoring the stragglers. Veronica kicked a scrawny dead boy's legs out from under him when he got too close; Clyde was itching to pull the trigger but knew that it would bring the whole undead city down to the shoreline.

The group practically flew up the cement steps. Gary led the way up onto the pool deck through a large white gate. Juliette's eyes welled up with tears when they passed the pool. The water was a sick color, filled with bloated bodies. Everyone but Gary jumped once they got nearer to the buildings as eaters slammed themselves against the glass of the east wing doors.

"You get used to it, eventually." Gary ignored the savage beasts slamming their fists and heads into the doors.

Samson shivered at the sight of the eaters spitting and clawing, their muffled growls invading his ears. Their milky white eyes darting from human to human, obviously tortured behind the shatterproof glass, their meals standing just feet before them.

Gary motioned for them to continue. "Come on, this way." He ran up to a large potted plant that was slowly withering away and pulled out a large set of keys. He noisily unlocked the west building's heavy glass door and swung it open. "Inside, hurry now." One by one the survivors walked through the doors, marveling at the luxurious lobby.

"This place is huge!" Veronica didn't mean to speak her thoughts out loud and looked around sheepishly after the words left her mouth. The marble floors, even through their filth, sparkled up at her and the walls were covered in abstract art that she couldn't even begin to wrap her head around.

"That it is." Ben stood beside her, taking the emptiness of the building in and lighting a cigarette.

Samson scratched the back of his head with the barrel of the shotgun, turning in a small circle and remembering the vast expanse of the lobby filled with the bustling of families coming and going as they enjoyed their emerald coast vacations. Clyde threw himself into an oversized armchair and stared up at the ceiling, his eyes fixated on the enormous light fixtures that no longer served a purpose, while Andrew quietly consoled an anxiety-ridden Juliette nearby.

"Home sweet home," Gary said as he opened a door labeled "Laundry."

"Towels? Anyone?" The group nodded yes and he passed them out accordingly. They stood around and wiped themselves down as best they could.

"Any chance there's a set of spare clothes around here?" Ben asked as he wrung his socks out, trying to shake the sand from them.

"Well, I'm not sure what your style is, but with the amount of clothes I've found so far, something's bound to fit." Gary jingled the keys.

"So, what now?" Samson struggled to put his damp polo back on.

Gary smiled slightly at him. "Sorry to say that the elevator's out at the moment, but whenever you're ready, I'd love to give you the tour."

As they climbed the interior stairwell, Gary pointed out that aside from the eleventh floor, the twenty-three floors up from the lobby held eight condominiums each. The ground level was made up entirely of offices, shops, maintenance, and laundry. It was designed with state of the art security. The east and west wings were identical in layout, and the central building was for owners only, with extra amenities and coded security entrances on each floor.

"Of course, that's useless now, with the power being out and all. But that's why I've got this lovely set of keys here," Gary explained as they continued their ascent to the twenty-fourth floor, where he'd set up his living quarters. "Each plant at the pool deck, they've got a set of the security keys hidden in them. I keep the extra sets hidden...elsewhere. You never know when the shit's about to hit the fan. And as of right now," he said, stopping for a moment to face the group behind him, "the east wing is entirely off limits. I think you all saw for yourselves why."

Everyone was exhausted by the time they'd reached the tenth level, so when they finally arrived on floor twenty-four, they were ready to pass out, especially the men, their clothes both damp and sandy.

"The heat's a bit much with the stairs, I know," Gary carried on in an almost cheerful manner, completely unfazed by the climb. "But you will get used to it. You have to get used to it, unless you prefer jumping balcony to balcony, and I don't recommend that."

He opened the stairwell door to the top floor and a gust of wind greeted them, cooling their red faces. They stopped dead in their tracks, not expecting the sudden reminder of grim reality. None of them had been able to see this much of anything since the world had gone away, but now they were first-hand witnesses to the complete and utter loss of the world below them.

No cars moved on the streets, instead they sat empty and unmoving. There were no people walking or laughing or going about their day, just empty shells of who they used to be, milling about gruesomely with no purpose but to destroy any living thing they came into contact with. A few buildings in the distance still burned, and smoke was ever-present on the blue horizon. On the distant highway, nasty accidents that would never be cleared and bumpers kissing bumpers were all that was left of the once free-flowing system of highways and transit.

Ben lit another cigarette and Clyde followed suit. Veronica twisted a strand of hair and Samson stared blankly. Juliette cried and Andrew rubbed her shoulders.

Gary sighed. "I don't think I'll ever get used to that."

The distant call of seagulls snapped Veronica out of her trance. "The skies belong to the birds, the land belongs to the dead."

"Not if we take back what we can." Gary lightly patted her on the shoulder. "Let's get you to your rooms and find some fresh clothes. No offense, but you're all smelling a bit off."

"No argument there." Ben flicked his cigarette out and over the railing. The wind caught the butt and sent it off to land gracefully in an already trash-covered street where no one would ever clean it.

V

Each condominium was elegant and spacious, with its own balcony and breathtaking view of the emerald coast. The largest unit on the twenty-fourth floor was the stock room for all that Gary had scavenged from the building. One bedroom for food and water, another for shoes and clothing. The third was set up as a disorganized medical facility and Gary used the fourth for his own personal sleeping space. Samson wanted everyone to stay close together so they took the two units to the left. Each of them found clothes that would fit from Gary's homemade walk-in closet and took turns bathing in his endless supply of gulf water.

As Veronica dressed in her room, she felt like an alien. This was not her home, and after weeks of death, violence, running, and hiding, she didn't feel normal sleeping in a bed in some tower, pretending everything was alright. She walked to the huge sliding glass door and pulled hard on the handle. The door slid open, sunshine greeting her face and the sound of soft waves touching the sands filling her ears. Samson was already out on the balcony, staring out over the water.

"It's a lot to take in, isn't it?" He squinted at her over his shoulder as she stepped out of her room. The large balcony ran the length of the entire unit and each room had their own private access doors.

"Yeah." She stepped up next to him and leaned on the rail, the breeze flowing through her long dark hair.

"You okay?"

She thought about it. What it actually meant. Was he referring to what happened in Franklin Woods or what happened at The Dockside Bar & Grill? Or did he want to know how she was in general, in light of the world ending?

"I'm not okay with any of it. But I'm alive, so I guess I gotta be doin' pretty well."

Samson's mouth was a tight line. His eyes still squinted in the sun, staring off into the water. He watched as *The Dockside* bobbed in the gentle waves. "I'd say you're doin' alright by today's standards."

"Are *you* okay?" She looked at him but he didn't turn to look at her.

"Today's standards, Veronica." He tapped the railing with his wedding band and stopped immediately, looking down at it, the white gold shining in the light of the afternoon sun. Veronica cringed as Samson pulled the ring off his finger, showing off a tan line.

"We made it this far." Samson didn't throw the wedding ring from the balcony; that would have signified some sort of left over attachment to the inanimate object. He simply let it go.

"Just gotta keep reminding ourselves that we made it this far." He squeezed her shoulder as he passed her. "Gary's waiting for us, you coming?"

She nodded and followed him back inside, thinking. He hadn't even watched the ring fall.

*

Gary had arranged the furniture in his living room so the group could sit in a comfortable circle.

"Welcome, welcome!" he greeted Veronica and Samson cheerfully as they stepped through the front door. "Head to the kitchen before you sit, there's bottled water and fizzy drinks. Everything's warm, but I'm sure you're used to it. Some snacks and food, take a can. Help yourself to whatever you'd like."

Veronica's eyes lit up when she spotted the chocolate chip cookies sitting on the kitchen counter and took the whole bag with her to the couch.

Everyone giggled; it was surprisingly delightful to be able to watch a teenager stuff her face with cookies at a time like this.

"What?" she said through a full mouth. "He said help yourself."

"That I did." Gary smiled and clapped his hands together. "So, now that we're all here. Let's get some food in our bellies and get down to business." He leaned back in the light green armchair. "As one man, I can't possibly stake claim to this entire building. It wouldn't be right for me to sit here and tell you this is all mine, but I will say that I've been a busy little bee. I gathered every useful item from every single floor and I have spent hours upon hours trudging back and forth from the beach to stock up on sea water. I got bored sitting and waiting for someone to show up and so I scouted the area—not too far, I'm only one person. But with it just being me, it made it very easy for me to get around. So I explored and scavenged the other businesses and homes on this block." He scratched at his dark beard. "So like I said, I've been busy. But I wouldn't have invited you here to share this all with you if I didn't need you. I told you on the boat that I needed your help going out in the area for supplies, but I also need your help to clear out the central building."

"Clear out a building?" Andrew set his Coke can down on the coffee table. "Isn't that the building y'all got attacked in?"

Gary put his hands up, "Hold on, hold on. Don't get the wrong idea. Yes, we lost the building. I lost everyone. But I need the building back. *We* need the building back. You see this little guy I've got strapped to me here?" He patted his gun. "That's all I've got left, and I don't see you lot with an armory anywhere do I?"

"We had a lot more. A whole lot more. But some asshole ruined that for us," Clyde said, joining the conversation. He was clearly not ready to let go of the bitterness of finding the gates locked back at Franklin Woods.

Veronica caught Samson making a face from the corner of her eye.

"So you see? You need weapons. We had a ton of them stockpiled. Nothing fancy, mind you, but plenty of guns and ammunition. Knives and other weaponry, all useful in a time like this."

"And all this is in the building that happens to be filled with hungry-ass dead folk?" Clyde folded his arms across his chest.

"Well, I wouldn't say *filled.* That would be the east wing. But nothing could have wandered into that building and nothing would have been able to wander out. East wing is too high-risk, there's no way we'd be able just shoo them on from there. We need them dead and there's no better time like the present. I'm taking back what's mine." He looked at the faces in the group expectantly.

Ben cracked his knuckles and nodded at Gary. "If that's what we gotta do to stay, then that's what we gotta do."

"Alright, that's the spirit! What about the rest of you?"

"Yeah, yeah. Let's do this." Clyde put his hand out and Ben slapped him five.

Juliette looked nervous as Andrew also agreed to the plan. He reassured her with a kiss to her forehead. "This will be good for us. It's safe here."

"Samson?" Gary's pleasant demeanor was overwhelming.

He leaned forward on the couch and propped himself up, elbows on his knees, "I suppose I don't have a choice."

VI

"This is stupid and I'm pissed off." Veronica glared at Samson on the breezeway outside of Gary's condo.

"I know you are. I agree with Andrew though. Juliette can't be left alone and it would be best for you to stay up here with her."

"And so what if you all go in there like a bunch of over-confident jerks and end up getting killed? I'm stuck taking care of Mrs. Boohoo in there? That sounds perfect!" She threw her arms up and began shouting at him. "You know perfectly well I can handle myself and exactly what I'm capable of. I can't believe you!"

Samson sighed. He couldn't remember a moment in his life where he enjoyed temper tantrums. He looked up when Ben exited their unit and joined them.

"What's the matter with her?" He threw a thumb in Veronica's direction and smirked, exacerbating the situation. Samson shook his head.

"Are you kidding me?" She turned to him, hands on her hips.

"Chill out. We're gonna be gone for like, an hour. Juliette will probably sleep through the whole thing and you won't even know we're gone. What's the worst that could happen?"

"Great question." Samson walked off toward the stairwell door. "I'll meet you downstairs. Hurry up, we need to be done before it starts getting dark."

Ben coughed and spit over the railing. "Look, I know for a fact you're tougher than any of us. But Juliette's about as tough as a fluffy white bunny and needs taking care of."

Veronica stood silently, picking at her nails.

"This'll be good for ya. We got a good thing here, take advantage of it and relax for a change. Alright?"

She shrugged and looked up at his grin. "Whatever."

He tapped his baseball bat twice on the ground and nudged her chin before walking off. She watched him disappear and waited for the door to slam before going back inside.

Juliette sat on the couch with her knees pulled in to her chest. She didn't raise her head or speak when Veronica walked in. Veronica stood there for a moment, just staring at the skinny blonde, wondering what they could even talk about. Weeks before, the women were completely different people. Veronica would have sat down across from her and cheerfully babbled about running track and ask Juliette what kind of music she listened to. Juliette would have invited Veronica to the gym she worked at, offering a free fitness consultation and inquire which colleges Veronica was thinking about going to. But now Juliette was lost in her own mind, incapable of dealing with her situation and Veronica felt useless, holed up in the luxurious condo.

*

Ben exited the stairwell on the eleventh floor and joined the rest of the men on the sky bridge that connected their building with the central tower.

"Alright," Gary started, "the layout of Central is different than the other two buildings. The stairs run up the middle and everything is completely enclosed. No breezeways and no doors to the stairs so that means these bastards could be roaming anywhere. There's no need to check the rooms unless the doors are open, but there aren't a lot of windows in the halls so be extra careful. Make sure you don't lose these." He passed out LED flashlights to everyone. "Try to keep gunfire to a minimum; you don't want to end up cornered and you don't want to end up deaf." He motioned for the guys to follow him as he set a trash can aside and grabbed a hefty set of keys from under it. "Once I unlock this door, these keys go under the trash can on the other side and we lock ourselves in. Keep your wits about you and we meet back here.

"Wait, so we're splitting up?" Samson asked. "Isn't that what always gets everybody killed in the movies? I'm sure it is."

Gary chuckled. "Well it's unfortunate, but this isn't a movie and we've got ground to cover. We all know how to handle ourselves. Everybody ready?" They all looked at each other and nodded. Gary turned the key in the lock and it clicked loudly. He pulled open the heavy glass door and the putrid smell of rot crawled up their noses.

Gary turned and spat. "Ah, yeah, forgot to mention the smell. We should probably air the place out once we're done." He stepped aside and let everyone through and then locked the doors behind them. Everyone jumped as he put his hand up to his mouth and whistled loudly.

"What the fuck?" Clyde shoved Gary hard and pointed his gun down the hallway.

"Had to wake them up mate, get them moving. I don't know about you, but I'm not in the mood for a game of hide and seek."

Clyde grunted and moved forward slowly, stopping when he heard the faint wail of an eater on a floor below them. "I'm headin' upstairs, who's with me?"

Ben raised his bat in the air, volunteering.

"Alright, I'm going to need the other two then. Got the recreational rooms and lobby downstairs to deal with. My best guess is they're all congregating down there." Gary led the way to the steps, Clyde and Andrew clapped each other on the shoulders and the men silently parted ways.

Samson and Andrew followed Gary and repeated the same process on each floor. They were lucky that each level had no more than about three to four eaters at a time, a simple number for the three men to take on. Some floors had none at all.

The trio was more worried about being cornered than anything else. They finally made it down to the recreation level on the second floor. A fitness center and an indoor pool were off to the left and a small theatre and arcade were on the right.

Gary whistled again, trying to draw out the eaters. Low moans began to rise from the right and the men circled around, preparing themselves for the attack.

"I don't understand." Gary remained standing still while Samson and Andrew went to work on the eaters that had emerged from the theater.

"A little help would be nice!" Andrew shouted as he swung his club at one eater while dodging the attack of another.

Gary just stood staring at them, bewildered by something that the other two men didn't understand. Samson pulled his knife from the back of one eater's head and grabbed another eater trying to take a bite out of Andrew, slamming it to the ground. A once-chubby old lady, her glasses still somehow on her face, writhed underneath his weight, her jaws snapping relentlessly. Samson buried his knife in the center of her forehead and her eyes rolled off to one side, movement ceasing. Samson was back up on his feet and face to face with another eater for barely a second before Andrew caved in the side of its hideous face and the thing dropped like a pile of bricks.

"Last one, you take the honors." Andrew tossed the golf club to Samson, and in one fluid motion Samson took a bow followed by his best golf swing, one that the pros would have been proud of. He smashed the club so hard into the final eater's head that they heard its neck break.

The two men looked around, panting, astonished that Gary hadn't offered any help.

"What's the deal man?" Andrew stood directly in Gary's line of sight but Gary still didn't look at him. "Yo! I'm talkin' to you, what's your problem?"

Gary suddenly shoved him back. "*This* is my fucking problem!" He pointed to the minimal amount of eaters that they'd just put down. "Where are the rest of them?! You two weren't exactly quiet just then, were you? So that means there aren't any in the lobby. If there were, they would have been up here by now."

"Maybe they're just that damn slow, Gary." Samson cleaned his knife off as he spoke.

"Jesus Christ, don't you get what I'm saying? We've put down what, twenty of the bastards? Half the lower levels were empty. That means I was wrong. For whatever reason the majority of them went up, not down."

A string of muffled shots rang out somewhere above them.

"Ah shit! Clyde!" Andrew went running for the stairs in a panic. Samson and Gary followed close behind him, guns now drawn.

VII

"I've climbed more steps today than I have in my whole damn life." Clyde plodded up the stairwell from the eleventh floor, followed by Ben.

"Feels that way, don't it? Probably wouldn't be half as bad if it wasn't so dang hot." Ben wiped the sweat from his face with the oversized t-shirt he'd changed into earlier. The back of the gray shirt was already drenched in sweat. "Really glad Gary had some extra deodorant."

Clyde agreed as he adjusted his bandana around his thick braids. "Alright, let's wake these bitches up." Clyde tapped his gun loudly against a wall on the twelfth floor. "Come to daddy!" Down the hall to the left of them a lazy eater in a dirty dress struggled to pull itself up from the floor.

"I got her." Ben jogged up to the eater in the pink dress and swung his bat hard, smashing her head in. Gore splattered the wall and she fell forward with a thud, bloodstained blonde hair covering her hideous face. "Piece of cake."

Clyde was checking out the other end of the hallway. "All the doors are shut. We're clear on this floor."

They made their way up, the next two levels were empty, not even any lazy ones hanging around. They continued up one more level and found a single open door at the end of the hall.

"Yoo-hoo! Anybody home?" Ben called out. He looked at Clyde and shrugged, and they walked briskly toward the door. The light hurt their eyes as Ben pushed it open all the way. He covered his nose and mouth with his shirt and coughed. "Jesus

Christ." The half-eaten body of a woman lay sprawled out on the couch, sporting a bullet hole in her head. Ben guessed the rotted corpse on the floor with the back of its head blown off was the thing that had feasted on her. He kicked it over with his foot and a lump of decaying flesh fell from its mouth. Maggots and other bugs writhed about inside of the eater's half-missing skull and Ben gagged.

Clyde vomited in the corner of the room near the window onto the dead body of a man with a gun in his hand. "I've seen some nasty shit." He wiped his mouth and spat on the blood stained carpet. "But I will never get used to this fucked up business."

"Nice way to pay your respects to the dead there, pal."

Clyde looked down at the dead man who had eaten a bullet and cringed. "My bad, dude." He turned away and started for the door but then stopped. He crouched down, the crook of his arm covering his face, and pried the gun from the dead man's hand. He checked the chamber, "Empty." He shook his head and dropped the pistol in the man's lap. "Sad ass story."

Ben returned to the living room after checking the rest of the condo. "Let's get out of here, place is empty." They stepped back into the hall and although the building itself didn't smell very pleasant, it was like a breath of fresh air to leave the room of death behind.

Clyde spat on the floor again, looking at Ben. "I don't get it. Gary said this place needed to be cleared out. Where the hell are they all?"

"Probably downstairs, you heard how them things started hollerin' when he whistled. We lucked out, man." He pulled out his pack of cigarettes and held it out to Clyde.

He shook his head. "Nah man, my stomach couldn't take it right now."

Ben lit his cigarette and smirked. "Good, I'm runnin' low anyway. Let's get to it, I'm ready to get out of this oversized coffin."

The two men continued on to the next level. At the next landing a putrid smell, worse than the one they'd encountered in the condominium on the previous floor, hit them in the face.

"What the fuck?" Clyde rounded the corner and stepped into the hallway, his disgusted expression turned to horror when he was met by a huge group of eaters making their way to the steps. "Fuck! Get out of here, turn back!" he screamed back at Ben. Clyde scrambled to get back to the stairs.

Ben flew around the corner to make his way up the building but was blocked by an equally large group of eaters coming down the stairs. "Holy shit! Get back downstairs, now!" He slammed into Clyde on his way back around the stairwell and the two men went tumbling down the steps. Ben cracked his head against the bottom step of the floor below them and Clyde landed on top of him.

Clyde hurried to get up as the first of the many eaters made their way down the stairs. "Ben! Man, you alright? Get up!" He struggled to help Ben to his feet.

Ben groaned and put a hand up to his head, his fingertips coming back with a small amount of blood on them.

"Come on man, we'll patch you up later."

The surge of eaters from the back of the horde pushed the ones in front down the steps. They flowed down the stairs like lava, landing around Ben and Clyde's feet, snapping their jaws and grabbing at ankles. Clyde lifted a leg and smashed his foot down on one of the eater's heads. "Ben! Get a fuckin' move on!" He shoved him forward and into the hallway. Clyde tripped over the grabbing hands and rolled onto his back, kicking the moaning faces that clawed their way toward him. Ben grabbed Clyde under his arms and pulled him back and away. One single eater clung to Clyde's leg and was pulled along with him.

"Get her the fuck off of me, man!" Clyde tried desperately to kick her free but the dead woman tightened her grip on his flesh, breaking the skin. Clyde cried out as she buried her nails into his leg. Ben pulled his gun out and shot her in the head. His ears burned from the shot and added to the agony of the already-throbbing head pain.

He shot three more rounds into the closest eaters and pulled Clyde to his feet. They ran down the hallway toward the open door at the end. Clyde ignored the pain in his leg as he ran backwards, firing into the group of the dead and putting a few more down.

"Get in here, come on." Ben pulled him inside and slammed the door shut. He turned around and saw Clyde on the floor, his pant leg pulled up. "Are you bit?" Ben brought his gun up and pointed it at him.

"No! Fuck no! Get that fuckin' gun off me!" Clyde had his hands up. "Seriously, I'm not kidding. She didn't bite me!"

Ben hesitated but brought the gun back down to his side. He knelt down and inspected Clyde's leg. He could see the deep punctures, where the eater had grabbed him, but that was all, no bite marks. Blood ran down Clyde's leg from the wounds. "Go in the bathroom and see if there's anything in there to clean that up. Those things are full of disease and I'm not feelin' much like watching you die from an infection."

Clyde disappeared somewhere in the condo and Ben stood in the middle of the living room, staring at the door. The dead pounded and growled, trying to get in, but they never would, the doors were too strong.

And us? What about us getting out, then?

Ben kicked the dead eater on the floor angrily and threw himself onto the loveseat, staring at the dead woman on the couch across from him. "This is just great." He closed his eyes and put his head back, taking in the room he would die in.

*

Samson, Gary, and Andrew flew up the stairs in a panic, stopping at the fifteenth floor. The horde of hungry dead were gathered at the end of the hallway, trying their hardest to break through the reinforced door. The men went unnoticed by the distracted eaters, even as they panted loudly, trying to catch their breath.

Samson pointed at the horde and pointed at his shotgun, raising an eyebrow. Andrew had both handguns ready to go, he nodded and looked to Gary. Gary shook his head no and ran back into the stairwell. The other two followed him.

"What the fuck are you doin' man? My brother's in there!" Andrew whispered at the man, his voice full of anger.

"Be quiet. Do you really think we have enough ammo to put them all down?"

Andrew blankly stared back at him.

"We need to get to my stash now, while they're still interested in that door. Now come on, let's move it."

The tired men pressed on. They didn't stop to check any of the floors; there wasn't any time for that. They made it all the way up to the top floor and Gary pulled out his keys. Fumbling on the large ring for the right key, he finally slipped it into the heavy door and pushed it open. "Grab some shit and let's go. I've got to find something."

Andrew looked around in disbelief at the number of weapons in the living room before him. "Where did you get all of this?" His mouth hung open at the boxes of ammo, the stacks of guns, the bladed weapons piled on the couch.

"That doesn't matter right now," Gary snapped at him and fished around in a cabinet under the dead television set.

"Kind of does," Andrew muttered, then holstered one of his own handguns for a .357 Magnum sitting alone on the coffee table. "Shit, it's as if you were waiting for me." He turned the gun over in his hand, admiring it and smiling.

Samson shook his head and smirked as he loaded up a second shotgun. "Gotta love a cop and his guns."

"Better than a lawyer with a gun."

"I'll second that," Gary called out from the floor, pulling out three pipe bombs.

"You've gotta be shittin' me." Andrew had seen and confiscated many a homemade explosive device before. "Let me guess, doesn't matter where you got those from either?"

"You're catching on. Now let's hope our friends downstairs haven't lost interest in what's on the other side of that door."

They raced back downstairs and crouched in the stairwell. Gary poked his head out, pulling a lighter from his pocket. The eaters were still pointlessly beating on the condo door, a few of them just stood around growling at one another, growing bored with the task at hand. Gary pulled his head back and held one of the pipe bombs up in front of his face. "The good man that put his skills to work on this fantastic explosive right here is probably standing over in that group over there. So, it's a little ironic if you ask me, but, never-the-less, I am grateful for it." He looked at Samson and Andrew, "This is going to be very loud and quite jarring, but as soon as the dust has cleared, we go in guns a-blazing. Alright?" The other men nodded and sat back on the steps. Samson covered his ears as Gary lit the short fuse.

Gary ran down the hall to get closer to the horde. "Fire in the hole, you sorry sack of twats!" He reared his arm back and tossed the pipe bomb into the group of eaters, backtracking quickly and jumping into the stairwell. He covered his ears and looked at the other men with a smile.

"Cheers."

VIII

The three men huddled together in the stairwell with their hands over their ears, waiting for the explosion that would give them the upper hand against the eaters.

Samson furrowed his brow, unsure why nothing had happened yet. He was about to open his mouth and say something when it did.

He heard the explosion and the doors popping free of their frames. The group of eaters roared once and then ceased. Pieces of ceiling crashed to the floor and sheetrock crumbled and caved. The trio barely felt any shockwave on the staircase; the building was solid, and Samson had never been more pleased with quality structural integrity.

As quickly as the eruption had occurred it was over, followed by silence. Andrew pinched his nose and popped his ears. Gary crawled over to peek his head out. Bodies lay unmoving on the floor surrounded by arms and legs. Only a handful of badly maimed eaters remained and were beginning to pick themselves up.

"Drew, if that ain't you out there, I'm gonna kill whoever just pulled that shit!" Andrew heard his brother scolding him from the unit down the hall and breathed a sigh of relief, chuckling to himself.

"Let's take care of the rest of these chumps and get the hell outta here." Andrew leapt from his spot on the stairs, Magnum out, and began taking care of the dead.

"Jesus Christ, can we *not* fire guns inside?" Samson cringed with each shot fired, the ringing in his head unbearable.

Gary joined Andrew in the long hall and the two quickly disposed of what was left of their previous obstacle. Heads popped and bodies dropped to the floor, never to be a nuisance again.

"Boy, am I glad to see you." Clyde emerged from the room, putting a bullet in the last eater's head that stood between him and his brother. The two brothers embraced, laughing at their luck and circumstance, never so elated to see one another in their lives.

"A little warning would have been nice." Ben joined the rest of the group in the hall. "I'd be pretty pissed if after everything we've been through I was killed by a flying door."

Gary led the way back upstairs so that the five of them could gather as much ammo, guns, and other things as they were able to carry in one trip. "Not looking forward to coming back here anytime soon." Gary locked the room up and followed the men back down to the eleventh floor.

On the way back to the double doors on the sky bridge, Gary noticed Clyde's limp.

"What's the matter there?" He pointed at Clyde's blood soaked pant leg.

"That's nothin', just got scratched up." He waved a hand at Gary and continued toward the door.

Gary stopped walking and raised his weapon. "Show me. Now."

"What the fuck is with people wantin' to point guns in my face today? God damn, chill out." He bent over and rolled up his pant leg. "Satisfied? You think Ben would have let me walk out of that room if he knew I was bitten?" He stared at Gary, hands on his hips.

"How'd that happen?" Andrew crouched down to take a closer look at his brother's leg, concern in his voice. "This looks pretty bad."

"One of them dead things got a little too excited. She scratched me up somethin' nasty, wouldn't let go. I cleaned it, it'll be fine."

Andrew inspected the wounds closely; they were deep and starting to ooze pus.

"Well it needs to be cleaned again. This looks infected, with no doctors, we need to be extra careful. Who knows the diseases these things carry." He stood up and looked at Gary. "You mind takin' that weapon off my brother now?"

Gary didn't move. "You just said a very interesting word, Andrew. *Disease.* These things carry the disease that ended the fucking world, in case you don't remember."

"Hey! Hold up, I didn't get bit!" Clyde started moving toward Gary, but Andrew put an arm up, blocking him.

"I'm sorry, I can't risk it. I've been through it before. I can't lose everything again." Gary slowly put his finger on the trigger. "I'm sorry."

The men all began yelling at one another and the tension was thick. Finally Ben stepped in front of the gun and put his hand on the barrel. "We give it a day. If he doesn't show signs of turning then we know that it's only the bite. You said it yourself: when it happened before, you didn't know the person in the building had been infected. Now you know. You're aware of it. You can keep an eye on it. We're not puttin' him down like this."

The two men glared at one another, Ben's stern eyes bore into Gary's, and after what felt like a silent eternity, Gary finally dropped the gun to his side.

Gary brushed passed him and didn't speak as he retrieved the hidden set of keys and let everyone out of the building. "Don't make me regret this," he said quietly to Ben as he exited the central tower. Ben nodded and kept following the others.

*

Veronica sat nervous on the couch, the loud sound she'd heard couldn't have been anything other than an explosion. The lock clicked in the door and she grabbed her PVC pipe, jumping up.

The group of men walked solemnly through the door.

"What the hell happened?" She couldn't help but show her concern; she dropped her pipe back onto the couch.

"Nothing, where's Juliette?" Andrew dumped the pile of weapons he was holding onto the recliner and left in the direction Veronica pointed.

"You guys sure made a hell of a racket." She walked toward the stuff they were unloading in the living room and marveled at the guns, knives, and other weapons that were before her. "Wow, Gary, you sure weren't kidding when you said you had an armory."

He feigned a smile and began sorting through the contents on the recliner. She looked at Samson who paced in the kitchen, tossing a water bottle back and forth between his hands. Ben had made a beeline for the back balcony. "What's everybody's problem?" She leaned against the silent refrigerator.

"It really is nothing, Veronica. We're all just a little tense." Samson finally opened the bottle and took a sip. "Things got a little hairy but everything's fine."

"Yeah, I can tell you what happened." Clyde joined them in the kitchen. "Trigger happy Gary over there is what happened."

"Excuse me, but I saved your life, remember?" Gary stood in the entrance, hands propped up on the entry way.

"Oh yeah, I remember, and then you tried to take it."

"Tried to take it? Will someone please tell me what's going on?" Veronica raised her voice a bit, hoping they would explain.

"Clyde, go clean your leg up, will ya?" Samson tried to hand him a water bottle but Clyde shrugged it off, disappearing into the room with the medical supplies, intentionally bumping into Gary in the process.

"Gary thought Clyde had been bitten. He's nervous about the scratches he got when they had a close call, but seriously, that's it. Nothin' to be concerned about alright? We're gonna keep an eye on him and make sure he doesn't get sick. It will be fine." Samson started toward the front door. "I'm going to get cleaned up."

"Why was that so hard to explain when y'all first walked in?"

"Sorry, little love, everyone's had a long day. We're just tense. The sun's starting to go down. Let's take it easy the rest of the night." Gary walked off into his bedroom to wash up, leaving Veronica to her thoughts. She heard the sliding glass door open and shut. Ben stopped in the entranceway on his way toward the front door.

"I need a bath." He looked down at his filthy hands. "How was Juliette while we were gone?"

"The most boring person ever. I thought she might have overdosed on Xanax at one point."

"Figured as much. I'll meet you back in here when I'm done. I'm starving." He paused before leaving. "Do you mind checking in on Clyde?" And he closed the door behind him.

*

The fact that it was just so easy for Gary to accept Clyde's undetermined fate sat uneasy with Ben. Someone he had just met that day had stepped into their already-damaged comfort zone and almost killed a member of their group at what *might* be a threat of infection. Maybe somebody somewhere in the world had figured out just exactly what this disease was that caused this sudden apocalypse, but Ben knew for a fact it wasn't anybody in this tower.

"Trial and error," he said under his breath as he let himself into the unit he shared with Samson and Veronica. The door to Samson's room was closed, and Ben thought it best to leave him be. He hadn't quite figured the man out yet.

He drew himself a saltwater bath and scrubbed his skin until he thought it might bleed. Once he was rinsed, he dressed in fresh clothing and dug through his bag. He retrieved a small joint and internally rejoiced that it hadn't been left back in Franklin Woods. He grabbed an oversized decorative conch shell from off the bedside table to serve as his ashtray and sprawled out on the king sized bed.

Lighting his joint he tried not to think about his journey and how he'd ended up here. He chalked it up to servitude; leading Andrew, Clyde, and Juliette out of the city, his main focus was on ensuring Veronica's safety. But somehow, he had found a way to fail Sal and Lucy. Ben lay back on the comforter, letting the bed pull him in and encase him in its warmth. His entire body ached, if felt like every muscle in his body screamed at him. He closed his eyes. Had he failed Veronica too when her brother died in the street?

When Ben opened his eyes again, the glaring sun was invading his room. A light film of sweat covered his body and he groaned, propping himself up. He checked his watch; it was a little after 8 am the next morning. "Holy shit." He washed his face in the bathroom and brushed his teeth, thanks to Gary's overabundance of hygiene products.

The condo was empty and he was correct in assuming that everyone was over at Gary's. When he arrived, they were all seated in the living room. The unit smelled delicious and Ben's stomach growled.

"There he is!" Gary cheerfully greeted him. "Come on in then, have a bite to eat. Samson's cooked us up some spam and powdered eggs on the balcony this morning."

Ben grabbed a plate and helped himself to what was left in the kitchen before sitting at the breakfast bar.

Gary got up from the recliner and grabbed a seat next to Ben. The others chatted away in the living room, scraping their plates clean. "Listen, mate, the others and

I, we've put what happened yesterday behind us, alright? I'm hoping you and I can do the same."

Ben chewed a piece of meat with his mouth open and stared at Gary for a moment. "Sure. Sounds great."

IX

The group of seven stood on the roof of the west tower and looked out over the city of Haven. Gary had brought the rest of them up there that afternoon to sell them on his second task: scavenging and rescue.

"I'm not asking you to explore the whole world here, I'm just showing you how simple it will be to get out there and get what we need." Gary put a hand on Andrew's shoulder and pointed toward a large cluster of close buildings. "You see that there? That's Emerald Park."

Andrew brought the binoculars down from his eyes and handed them over to Samson. He turned to Gary. "Yeah I see it, but what is it?"

"Emerald Park was the shopping mecca of Haven! The only place worth going to around here...outside of the pubs and restaurants."

"A mall? You kiddin' me? The world ended. No way in hell I'm goin' to the mall."

"Well, no, technically not a mall. It's an outdoor shopping park. Hence the name? Hear me out, please. There will be food there, tools we need, clothing that never belonged to the deceased." The excitement grew in his voice as he spoke. "Water, fine wine, medicine, entertainment, and best of all, more people." His eyes were wide, resembling a child's.

"You don't know that there are people there, and if there are," Samson paused, glancing over his shoulder at Gary, "how do you know they're the sharing type?"

"I *do* know there are people there." Gary was practically shouting. "At least there were. At one point. Back toward the beginning of this all, before the incident here, a few of us were up on the roof of the central tower. There was a car I spotted speeding in the direction of Emerald Park and it crashed. I thought they were goners but they proved me wrong and jumped out. It made sense to me then, the crash, someone had turned. It was obvious from the way they disposed of the bodies."

"Yeah but how do you know they weren't just some maniacs killin' for fun?" Ben interrupted. "Or better yet, how do you know they weren't infected themselves, and attacking the ones that were just fine?"

Gary smiled. "Because they got back in the car and drove away. I just have a feeling they're alive out there. And not just them! There must be others, there *has* to be!"

The thought of the seven of them being the last people alive in the city weighed heavily on their chests. They'd all had the same collective thought in passing; that this might be it, that they were all just waiting to die. Yet something in Gary's voice sparked a sense of panic in all of them. What if they were the last remaining human beings in Haven? What if they were the last remaining alive on the coast? The state? It couldn't be possible and suddenly they all refused to believe they were it, and their panic turned into hope. Gary had sparked hope in them.

"If there are people out there, what do we do when we find them? What if they're hostiles?" Ben scratched at his blonde hair as he spoke.

"We take care of that, if need be. We plead our case to them, that we should band together and rebuild what we can here. If they don't accept or join, then we leave; hopefully, it won't come to violence. We just have to take our chances out there. This is our city, the city doesn't belong to the dead."

Veronica finally joined the conversation. "I'm not staying behind this time." Samson opened his mouth up to protest but she cut him off quickly. "You don't know who it is that we might be approaching. Whether they're friendly or not, it will still look threatening when a group of armed men come marchin' up to their doors. And I hate to say it, but I'm a teenage girl, and you need to use that to your advantage."

"She's got such a brain on her." Ben cracked a smile. "Veronica can carry her own weight. Let's do this before I change my mind."

"Yeah," Andrew agreed, "I like the sound of you comin' along, you used to run right?"

She looked up at Andrew. "I still do."

"Touché. We could use a scout though, and if you know how to handle a weapon, even better."

"This is coming together perfectly. I say we leave as soon as tomorrow? We make our way to the park and—"

"Here's a million dollar question for you," Samson interrupted Gary's enthusiasm. "How do you suppose we get not only these so-called *'other survivors'* back here, but all these supplies you're talking about?" He made big quotation marks in the air with his fingers.

"Had you let me finish, Sam, I would have gone on to tell you that there's a rather large banking complex across the street from where we're headed and they happen to have an armored car park there. So, all of the necessities we'd be bringing back, along with the *'so-called survivors'*, would fit just right into a couple of those." Gary mocked Samson's air quotes with a set of his own. "We then keep the trucks locked up in the tower's garage, and assuming things go smoothly, we can come and go as we see fit."

Samson and Gary had a staring contest. Veronica couldn't figure out what had irritated Samson so much, but she could see it in his face. She could hear the sudden arrogance in his voice and the defense in Gary's. She glanced at Ben as he lit a cigarette and passed the pack back to Clyde.

"If you two are done, we should get packed up so we're ready to leave first thing in the morning." She looked at Samson expectantly but he said nothing.

Gary clapped his hands excitedly and startled Juliette.

"Drew," she said to her boyfriend, "are you staying here with me this time?"

Andrew shook his head, "Nah baby doll, Clyde's sittin' this one out. He's gotta take care of that leg."

Clyde rolled his eyes and shrugged. "Yeah, I could use the beauty rest."

The group left the roof to begin preparing for their journey to Emerald Park. All except for Samson. Veronica had called out to him, asked him if he was coming, but he ignored her. He still held the binoculars in his hands, standing in the same place as he had the entire time they'd all been on the roof.

It was one thing to him to go out and forage for supplies to bring back to his bizarre excuse for a family in Franklin Woods. It was a completely different thing to leave the comforting walls of The Emerald City to search for strangers in a dead city. Whether it was a false sense of security or not, it didn't matter to him. He felt small and useless in a group of hardened survivors.

He was barely over the fact that he had manipulated a young girl into killing his already-dead children. He couldn't even find it in himself to leave Moira as she took over his life for almost two decades, nor as she was plunging into the depths of madness in a broken world. No, he left his wife as she was dying, after he brought a stranger into their home that shot her children in front of her.

"Yo!"

Samson, startled by Ben's voice from the rooftop door hadn't realized he'd been holding his breath. He gasped and turned to the tall young man peering out at him.

"Yeah! I'll be right in!" Samson looked out over the empty city one last time before heading inside. It pained him that he couldn't stay back at the resort and daydream of being on vacation. It pained him even more that the world was what it was and he wouldn't ever take an expensive vacation again. Samson shrugged as he walked. He was a coward. And he no longer cared.

X

The group parted ways on the twenty-fourth floor the following morning. Juliette remained with Clyde, assured by Andrew that he wouldn't turn while they were away. She was then reassured by Clyde who proceeded to cuss her and tell her, in typical Clyde fashion, how lucky she was to even have him there to keep her company.

The rest of the group followed Gary down to the lobby and reluctantly back outside. They agreed on minimal-to-no gun use in order to keep their presence unknown to the dead as they snuck around Haven to reach Emerald Park along the route Gary had mapped out.

"The absolute quickest way possible," he had told them. He led the way back out into the pool area, stopping momentarily to remove a padlock from a large white gate off to the side of their building. Even the outer walkways on the ground floor were secure. Floor to ceiling bars temporarily encased them in safety as they made their way to the front of the building. Veronica wrapped her hand around one of the bars as she passed and attempted to shake it. The white painted steel didn't budge and she found herself once more admiring the luxury of The Emerald City.

They passed closed office doors, utility rooms, various shops, and eateries along the gated path. The resort's amenities really were exclusive to its guests. It seemed as if even back before the world went crazy that they wanted to keep everything out that they possibly could, somehow preserving an elite and untainted paradise of tourism.

"Stay here, I'm going to check the grounds around the exit," Gary whispered to them before disappearing around the final corner. He quickly returned and pulled his enormous key ring from his pocket. "This is just a precautionary measure. We don't know what could happen out there." He walked over to a large, fake potted plant and placed the keys amidst the white rocks. "The other precautions are the padlocks. There's only one key." He held up the padlock key which he kept separate from the others. A colorful plastic keychain dangled from the key that read *'Haven Is Home.'*

"Where's that one going?" Samson asked him.

"In the dirt. Now let's get a move on before we all decide this is a terrible idea."

They all followed Gary around the corner except for Samson. The day wasn't anywhere near as hot as it had been the last few days but he was soaked with sweat.

Veronica poked her head around the corner and motioned for him to follow. "Come on, we gotta go." Samson nodded and willed his feet to move forward.

Gary held the heavy gate open and ushered everyone through. He closed it gently and snapped the padlock back into place. He held the key up and jiggled it for everyone to see and made sure they watched as he pulled up a fistful of bright green grass and pushed a mound of dirt aside. He patted the area down once he was finished and cocked his head to the left as he stood, "Follow me."

The once-pristine streets of Haven were littered with trash and grime. Local business storefronts were smashed and signs of uncontrollable looting were present everywhere. Samson wondered why Gary thought Emerald Park would be any different from the raided stores in the surrounding neighborhood. A gas station nearby had a car sticking out of its storefront, black char running up the sides of the building, the remnants of a fire caused by the crash.

Veronica took in all the emptiness and destruction; she hadn't had the chance to do so back when she was in Columbia City. Maybe it was because she didn't allow herself to accept that her home had been reduced to nothingness, or maybe it was just because she was too busy running for her life.

Under normal circumstances, the five-mile walk would have only taken them just short of two hours, but the world no longer offered any of its remaining inhabitants such banality. The group had to backtrack several times in order to avoid eaters. About at the halfway point Ben suggested that they duck into one of the houses on a side street and take a break. The five of them jogged down the empty street in the direction of a row of multicolored townhouses and Ben chose at random the blue and green one. They padded up the driveway and Ben put a finger up, telling them to hold on as he smashed his elbow through the glass panel that ran alongside the door.

Andrew shook his head, laughing as Ben cleared the glass from the pane and he reached forward, turning the knob with ease. "Did you even check to see if it was locked?"

Ben looked at Andrew with a smile and shrugged. "Nope, but thanks." He made sure they weren't spotted by anything before closing the door and locking it behind him. The townhouse had most likely been a beach rental. The place was fully furnished with uncomfortable wicker furniture. An overabundance of seashells decorated the living room and tacky palm tree wallpaper covered everything.

The cabinets in the kitchen were bare, but luckily Gary had made sure they brought nourishment with them for the short trip to Emerald Park. Veronica pulled a bottle of water from her bag and decided to check out the rooms upstairs. The brilliant sunlight illuminated the entire house so she left her flashlight in the bag. She climbed the stairs slowly, running her fingers along the smooth surface of the walls. The place had been scrubbed clean very recently, the front door probably left unlocked by the housekeepers. She poked her head into the first bedroom on the second floor, two double beds in a room painted bright blue. She thought of the last time she had stood in someone's doorway like this. The growls of Samson's dead children crept back into her mind. The absolutely vacant look in his daughter's eyes as she put a bullet in her head haunted Veronica. Moira's screaming suddenly filled the house. Veronica covered her ears and slammed her eyes shut, desperately trying to push the moment out of her mind again.

She gasped as a hand came to rest on her right shoulder.

"What's goin' on up here?" Veronica spun around and wrapped her arms around Samson, burying her face in his chest. He was taken off guard by the flood of emotion that had suddenly taken over Veronica. He slowly put his arms around the girl. "Hey, it's alright," he comforted her, thoughts of his daughter bringing moisture to his eyes. "What happened? What's wrong?"

"I never apologized." She was slowly regaining her composure as she whispered into his shirt, her eyes still closed. "I never apologized for what happened at your house." She pulled away from him and looked up, tears streaking her face.

He shook his head, pangs of guilt stabbing him. "Nobody needs to apologize for anything." He took his hands off her shoulders and ran them over his unshaven face, as if wiping his cowardice away. "Don't you remember what I told you?"

She shook her head. "You're a bigger man than me, Veronica. Don't you ever forget that." Her face remained expressionless. Samson sighed. "Let's just say I owe you. Big time."

She smirked and then laughed, rolling her eyes at him. A small part of her wanted to smack him, another part of her wanted so badly to call him *Dad.*

He smiled back at her and in that moment, once again, Veronica and Samson bonded like only a fatherless daughter and a man lost in obscurity could. "Break time is over. You gonna be alright?"

She nodded and closed the bedroom door behind her as she followed him. The rest of the house would be left undiscovered. Andrew, Ben, and Gary were already ready to go. Veronica threw her water bottle back in her bag and zipped up, nodding at Ben who then led the way out.

The group made better time once they had taken a break and harnessed their anxieties of being in an unfamiliar city that was crawling with the dead. Gary was the only one who seemed to be enjoying the beautiful day. The closer they got to Emerald Park, the more eaters they were seeing. Most of the eaters stood around by themselves, looking as though they were simply lost patrons of the abandoned outdoor mall. The clusters here and there were what worried the group of survivors. As they entered Emerald Park's streets, the small yet dangerous groups of undead were getting harder to avoid. Yelps and growls could be heard as the eaters bumped into one another and became agitated. Gary motioned for them to get off the streets of the store fronts and move through the empty parking lots around the back. They all crouched together by the side of an abandoned blue Tacoma.

"Alright," Gary whispered, "that's the back of the building we want to get around to. We move around there and make our way very carefully to the front."

"Why don't we just bust our way in through the back?" Ben wiped the beads of sweat from his forehead.

"Yes, let's break down fire and freight doors. How remarkably simple and quiet."

"Guys?" Veronica pointed in the direction from which they'd just come. A lone eater had spotted them and let out a wail.

"Fuck," Ben cursed under his breath.

The very slow moving eater started shuffling in their direction, moving its head around wildly, gasping and grunting as it moved, attracting unwanted attention from a nearby cluster.

"We need to move." Gary tightened his backpack's straps.

A piercing screech erupted from one of the eaters in a group off to their right, alerting the rest of the undead in the area.

"Now! Follow me!"

Gary sprinted off toward the large cream-colored building in front of them. There was a loading bay area with a breezeway through to the other side. Veronica headed straight for the loading bay, passing the rest of the group, her speed unmatched. She leapt up onto the elevated platform and stopped when she reached the end of the long breezeway. She tried to remain as silent as possible, breathing through her nose. She scanned the street before her; the eaters here were milling around, the presence of humans still unbeknownst to them. She spotted the half-open sliding doors of Target almost immediately. She heard the slapping of pavement as the rest of the group caught up to her.

"Over there! You see?" She pointed at the bright-red framed outer doors to the department store.

Gary looked past the others and grimaced; the quick of the dead were almost upon them. "I don't see any other options. Let's get out of here." He was gone almost as soon as he'd arrived.

Andrew and Ben were right behind him; Samson was hot on their heels. Veronica knew she was the fastest, so she made sure everyone was clear of the breezeway before she took off. She followed Samson just as the pursuing pack of eaters made their way into the hall. She made it across the street and into an adjacent lot, making the grave mistake of looking back at her pursuers as she ran.

She lost her footing on a cement parking block and went down hard. Her chin struck the surface of the pavement and ripped open. Pain shot through Veronica's face and she cried out, blood running down her neck from the fresh wound.

Gary and Andrew hadn't heard her when she fell and kept running. Ben stopped to go back for her.

"I've got her! Get inside!" Samson called out and rushed to Veronica's side. The girl was almost in tears, a flap of skin hung from her chin and she was covered in her own blood.

"Jesus Christ." He couldn't help but cringe at the state she was in. Samson pulled the Remington from his shoulder and blasted an eater as it ran up on Veronica. He threw his bag to the ground and ripped his button-up shirt from his torso. He balled it up and shoved it into her trembling hands. "Hold that against your face and go."

She immediately took off toward Target. Ben was waiting at the door, firing rounds into the dead around her as she made her way to him.

Samson met an eater with a kick to the chest, launching it away. It growled angrily as it landed on its back. Samson brought his boot down hard onto its head, caving it in and then taking off after Veronica. He knew there was no way he could use the shotgun and run at the same time. He swung the gun up and knocked over an eater when it got too close for comfort.

Veronica was almost to the door when Samson heard Gary screaming and cussing. The interior doors of the department store were locked and they couldn't get them open.

"Pile up the carts!" Samson yelled through exhausted breaths. "Use the carts! Move the fucking carts!" He hoped to whatever Gods still existed that Gary and Andrew had heard him, that they would listen to him.

An eater plowed into him, taking him to the ground. He cried out, struggling with the undead beast. With a surge of adrenaline, he shoved the decomposing eater off and scrambled to his feet. Its head exploded, the remains splattering out the back of its head in a red mist as Samson pulled the trigger on the shotgun at the last second.

Ben grabbed Veronica's arm and tossed her into the vestibule. Andrew began pulling the red shopping carts from their place and tossing them aside; he shouted at Gary to help him. Ben called out to Samson and an expression of complete confusion took over his face as Samson stopped running just a few feet short of the door.

"Dude! What are you doing? Get your ass in here!" Andrew pushed Ben to the side, placing a cart where he stood. Gary followed up by strategically placing another on top of it.

"Samson!" Veronica screamed his name repeatedly. Samson raised his weapon and shot another approaching eater. Ben fired out at the undead from inside the vestibule.

It was only when she stopped screaming that Veronica noticed what Andrew had already seen and Ben had not. It was only when she stopped screaming in fear and started yelling in anger that Ben then realized what happened to Samson.

Samson winced in pain from the bite on his left shoulder.

When the carts were in place and he knew Veronica would have enough time to get out of danger, he walked up to Andrew's barricade and pushed the shotgun through. He screamed out in pain as the surrounding eaters latched onto him and tore into his flesh.

Veronica slapped the shotgun out of his hand and to the floor, crying out for him. She grabbed onto his arm and pulled it through the space between the carts, her tears mixed with her own blood, stinging her wound as they flowed down her face and onto her neck.

Samson's blood sprayed in every direction; the dead feasted upon him, his screams of agony seemed endless. Veronica didn't realize her companions had crawled through the shopping cart opening, and she didn't hear the interior doors suddenly open behind her. She fought and kicked with all her might against Ben as he wrapped his arms around her waist and dragged her inside. She elbowed him in the face and ran back out toward the barricade.

Samson's cries no longer filled the air; only the horrific slurping and chewing of the eaters. Samson's arm lay limp, still in the same place it was when she last held it. She reached out to grab his hand one last time but Ben once more wrapped himself around her. She cried out for Samson, the tip of her middle finger grazing the tip of his only for a brief moment before she was thrown to the department store's tile floor, the interior doors slamming shut.

XI

Andrew's head was spinning. He knew there were always risks involved with venturing out into the land of the dead, but to have one of their own ripped to shreds by the eaters was almost unbearable. So far, their trip to Emerald Park to find survivors and supplies had proven to be nothing but a catastrophe. Veronica lay on the floor to his left, sobbing in Ben's arms. Ben and Andrew locked eyes for a moment and both their faces told the other man the same thing: *"I wasn't ready for that."*

The eaters had ceased pounding on the shopping cart barricade outside and the vestibule remained empty, momentarily filling Andrew with relief. Gary remained mute, rubbing his temples with both hands, simply gazing in awe through the grime of the interior doors. The dead feasted upon what was left of their fallen companion.

Gary barely knew Samson. Ben and Andrew barely knew Samson. Veronica barely knew Samson... but in the world's state of disarray, the two seemed to have found in each other what they had lost. No one else in that room had been so lucky as to find such a treasure. No one else in that room could even begin to describe the new meaning of the phrase *getting to know someone.*

"We should move away from the doors," Gary spoke, eyes still fixated on the gore feast outside.

Andrew nodded. He walked over to Ben and Veronica, crouching down beside them. He reached his hand out to take a look at the wound on her chin but she slapped his hand away. Andrew recoiled and locked eyes with Ben again. Ben cradled her, shaking his head at Andrew.

"Hey man," he said, putting his hand on Ben's shoulder, "we need to get away from the doors. She hurt herself somethin' nasty, we need to do somethin' about it."

Ben's eyes were red from crying and every time he blinked they burned. He ran a hand through Veronica's long hair, kissing her gently on the forehead. For the first time since he'd met her he actually felt sorry for her. He didn't know whether it was because he wasn't there to experience the loss of her father with her, or because she wouldn't talk about what happened to Isaac. All he knew is that she didn't deserve this loss anymore. She didn't deserve the abrupt end of her adolescence in the way that it had happened.

None of them should be going through this, but it hurt him the most that this young woman—the girl whose fearlessness had once given him a reason to leave the death trap he'd been holed up in—was falling apart in his arms.

Ben scooped up Veronica and stood. She seemed to be devoured by his hulking frame, appearing childlike and lost. He understood the father she'd so desperately sought in Samson, and the daughter he'd needed her to be. He would make sure Samson didn't die in vain.

Gary pulled a flashlight from his bag and reloaded his handgun. Andrew followed suit. The group made their way back toward the pharmacy. Cautiously passing empty aisles, Andrew felt like a cop again. He ran his light up and down the pitch-black, looted rows of no goods, making every silent footstep count. He imagined that he was simply searching for an armed robbery suspect and not eluding the dead.

He stopped short and held up a hand. "Wait a minute." He craned his neck and listened, there was movement somewhere off behind them. "We ain't alone." He spun on his heels and swept the area with his flashlight, the reality of the apocalypse seeping back in. Gary was down on one knee, ready to fire into whatever came at him from the darkness.

Andrew heard movement again, this time closer. He could make out the sound of footsteps, delicate in their approach. He crept forward, motioning for Gary to do the same.

A flash of movement off to his left. "Over there!" Andrew pointed the flashlight toward the greeting card aisle. Gary panicked and shot blindly.

"Goddamnit Gary! Hold your fire!" Andrew hadn't expected the Brit to be so overzealous. He put a hand up and motioned for Gary to stay put as he darted over to the aisle their visitor had run down. He stood with his back against a stack of shelves lined with party favors. "If you have a weapon, throw it out to me," he called out into the darkness and got no answer.

He raised his voice. "Now."

A homemade weapon crafted from a duct-taped sets of knives and a broken broom handle rolled out of the dark toward Andrew.

"Thank you." He paused and kicked the weapon back toward Gary. "Now, I want you to make your way very slowly out to me. You understand what slow means? Do it slow, do it now."

The stranger moved and Andrew backed away from the aisle, weapon pointed and ready.

A small, thin woman with short red hair appeared in their line of sight. She squinted at the flashlight beam, arms raised, and fully emerged into the open space of the main walkway. "My name is Dr. Catherine Booker. I'm here to help." She was stunningly calm.

"Alright, Catherine, I'm Officer Andrew Hansen. You got any other weapons on you?"

Catherine shook her head.

"Are you alone?"

"Right now, yes. I'm with a group in another building." She put her hands out toward Andrew, "Please, I mean you no harm. I saw what happened out there. What can I do to help?"

Andrew hesitated, but finally dropped his weapon. He put an arm up and nodded at Gary who slowly lowered his gun.

"We have someone who's injured," Ben spoke up from the back.

"Were they bitten?" Concern played across Catherine's face.

"No. She fell, split open her face." Ben shifted Veronica's weight in his arms and lowered her.

Veronica looked up at Catherine. Catherine recognized the girl's age immediately, saw the blood-soaked shirt that she held against her face and lowered her arms. "Like I said, I'm a doctor. Please." She motioned for Veronica to move toward her.

Andrew looked at Ben and Ben looked at Veronica. Veronica slowly began walking to Catherine who lowered her bag to the floor and held her arms out. She took Veronica by the shoulder and guided her to the cool tile floor. "What's your name, sweetheart?"

"Veronica."

"I need some light here," Catherine called out to Andrew. She unzipped her pack and began pulling supplies out, completely elated to have the opportunity to help. "Veronica, I'm Dr. Booker, but please call me Catherine." She went to pull the shirt from Veronica's face but Veronica grabbed her wrist. "It's okay, it's okay."

"Don't touch the shirt." Veronica removed it herself and exposed the gaping wound to Catherine. A chunk of skin hung loosely from the bottom of her face; most of the bleeding had already subsided, but the trauma still remained.

"I'm going to touch your face, okay?" Catherine examined the wound, poking at the exposed meat. Veronica didn't make a sound. "Does it feel alright?"

"Hurts like a bitch."

Catherine smirked. "Strong girl. That's good." She cleaned Veronica's injury thoroughly and placed a gauze pad and bandage over it while Gary, Andrew, and Ben looked on cautiously. "She's going to need stitches. I have everything we need in the building across the street. Come with me, please."

"How many of you are over there?" Gary asked her.

"There are five of us total, three are out on a run."

"How do we know you're friendly?"

She smiled softly at him, looking at Veronica's chin and back.

Gary had a soft spot in his heart for redheads. His heart ached for his wife, Claire. "What do you say, then?" He turned to the other two men.

"I'm not a doctor and even I know I need stitches." Veronica picked herself up from the floor. "Y'all do what you want. We came here looking for people anyway. Right, Gary?"

Gary said nothing in response.

They filed back toward the exit, Veronica following closely behind Catherine, Ben following closely behind Veronica. Gary and Andrew covered the rear. They all followed Catherine back through the fire corridor that connected Target with a teenage clothing store.

The store was thick with dust but was a breath of fresh air from the previous darkness they had been wandering around in. Sunlight poured in from every possible direction; the brightly colored autumn collection of clothing suddenly adding life to the abandoned building. Catherine dug in her bag. "You're going to want to stay away from the windows," she said, and began to snap photos of nothing, the flash reflecting off of every metallic object in front of her.

"What in the hell are you doing?" Andrew asked, turning to eye the roaming dead just outside the windows.

She hushed him with a finger. "Just wait."

Faint music drifted from across the street and the eaters began to move toward the source. Everyone's eyes lit up. No one had heard music in over a month.

Andrew cocked his head. "How in the hell..." He trailed off as he approached Catherine and joined her at the enormous storefront.

She grinned at him, "We've got it down to an art."

PART II

AND NOW WE'RE HERE

I

The woman's eyes fluttered open and she groaned at the warmth of a body next to her. She cringed and very carefully rolled out of bed. She wiped the sleep from her eyes as she crouched down on the floor, searching for her clothes. She pulled her panties up and figured she'd make a mad dash for the bathroom and find a shirt on the floor somewhere in there.

"Good morning, Michelle," the man in her bed mumbled as he propped his head up on his hand and looked at her.

She quickly covered her breasts with her arms. "Hey." She looked down at the ground and noticed her bra peeking out from underneath the bed. She scooped it up and turned around, pulling it around her body and fastening the clasps. "So, yeah, I'm gonna let you get dressed."

She decided she'd use the hall bathroom and let the man in bed use hers. She ducked into the bathroom and slammed the door shut, hoping she wouldn't wake her roommate, Lulu, whose long purple robe hung on the back of the door. Michelle pulled that around herself and washed her face in the sink, swishing water around in her mouth and spitting, watching the water circle in the drain before disappearing.

A light knock at the door was followed by a high pitched and comical hello. Michelle yanked the door open and pulled Lulu inside. Her jet-black hair was pulled back in a tight pony-tail and her face looked fresh; she'd obviously been up longer than Michelle.

"Ssh! I don't want him to hear us."

The two women giggled like little girls.

"Oh, ya big slut!" Lulu couldn't help but crack up at her roommate.

"Jesus," Michelle's hands went up to her head as she looked at herself in the mirror, her long curly hair looked wild. "I don't even remember his name. Holy shit, Lu, what is his name?"

Lulu opened a drawer and handed her a hair tie, shaking her head and sighing. "Geeze, Michelle, he's my cousin." She opened the bathroom door; the man from the bed had just walked into the hall from Michelle's room. "Good morning, Zach." She gave Michelle a look and winked before leaving the bathroom, giggling again. "I've got coffee made, why don't you grab a cup with me?" The two wandered down the hall toward the kitchen and Michelle put the lid down on the toilet and sat, pulling back her wild mess of hair and shaking her head in disapproval.

"I can't believe myself sometimes," she said to no one and went back to her room to shower.

Lulu poured Zach a cup of coffee at the breakfast bar. "I don't know how you like it. Milk is in the fridge and sugar and stuff is next to the coffee pot." She handed him the steaming cup.

"I take it black, thanks." He raised the cup to her in cheers and sipped it lightly. He looked at the television in the living room and noticed it was on mute. "Do you mind?" She looked up at the remote in his hands.

"Oh, nah, go ahead, I just got sick of hearing about the same thing over and over again. The nut jobs are out in full effect today, apparently." She moved a strand of pin-straight hair from her face and tucked it behind her ear as she stirred her coffee. Zach stood behind the couch facing the TV and listened to the news explain in great detail the dramatic increase in rioting and violence over the last twenty-four hours.

"We are urging people to stay in their homes as a state of emergency is being declared in the following counties." The news anchorman went down his list and gave details of what steps government officials were taking to ensure the safety of its citizens.

"I can't believe they don't have this shit under control yet. It's pretty unnerving." Lulu stared at the screen. Random acts of violence and rioting had started popping up around the country over the last few days, and nothing seemed to be getting better. The once-busy city of Haven had become a ghost town over the last week as tourists cut their September vacations short and the peaceful upper-class community had turned to bedlam.

Zach stared down at his cell phone; no signal. "Hey, do you have Wi-Fi?"

"Yeah, the password is on the back of the modem over there." She pointed to the edge of the counter and walked over to the couch, plopping down on the soft blue cushions. She grabbed the remote. "God, it's the same thing on literally every channel."

"I think your Internet is out." Zach picked up the modem and hit the reset button. "Did you pay your bill, Lu? I'm not getting any connection." He gave up on the modem and pulled his phone out again. He punched in a number and hit send, only getting three short beeps. He looked down at his phone.

Call Failed, Try Again?

He frowned and hit send again only to get the same response. Lulu continued flipping through channels and finally stopped when she hit HBO. A fuzzy screen with no sound greeted her.

"What the fuck? We don't pay for premium to not work." She threw the remote onto the coffee table and grabbed her phone.

Zach looked at his cousin, "Is your phone working?"

"No." She saw the worry in Zach's face. "Did you try restarting yours?"

He nodded in response.

She picked up the remote again and searched the channels for something other than the *'stay in your house'* speech. Michelle entered the room and avoided eye contact with Zach, making a beeline for the coffee pot. She rolled her eyes at the TV, she was so sick of the news already.

Lulu stopped on a channel with a field reporter downtown saying citizens were not happy about the government's decision to cut all cell phone and Internet services.

"Emergency officials are encouraging those of you with landlines to please only use your phone to notify authorities if you come into contact with anyone showing signs of sickness or violence. Please do not leave your homes at this time, local hospitals are filled to capacity. If you or anyone you know are exhibiting signs of dangerous or abnormal behavior, please notify emergency personnel and do not leave your place of residence."

Michelle made a face of disgust, "No cell phones? Sickness? What the hell? I thought this was all a bunch of political protesting or some shit." She rinsed a coffee mug and began pouring slowly, eyes glued to the TV.

Screams erupted off camera and the field reporter yelled, *"Get this on tape!"*

The camera swung in the direction of the screams as a large group of people poured out of a nearby office building and began savaging anything near them. One of the women in the group looked directly at the camera. The reporter said, *"We should get out of here."* The camera came back to the reporter but he was already running for the news truck. The view panned back in the direction of the attacks just in time to catch the crazed woman filling the screen. The camera went down but did not shut off. Violent screams and growls filled the airwaves, yelps of pain and prayers to God went unanswered as the woman ripped out the cameraman's throat.

II

Michelle couldn't peel her eyes away from the insanity on the news. Coffee flowed up and over the rim of the mug and onto the counter. The hot brown liquid spread out and over the edge, dripping onto her feet. "Shit!" She slammed the pot down and jumped back. Lulu and Zach were startled by her outburst and Zach rushed to the paper towels, spreading them all over the counter in an attempt to sop up the coffee.

Lulu remained on the couch, her eyes filled with tears. "What the hell just happened?" The feed had gone dead on the station and the words *'Please Stand By'* took its place.

Michelle couldn't find her voice. She knew something out of the ordinary had been going on the last few days, but she hadn't realized how serious the situation was. Just last night, their big group of coworkers was out drinking and partying, and then this morning people were murdering each other in the streets.

The horrific scene on the news was only a few miles from their apartment complex. Zach and Michelle locked eyes but she looked away toward Lulu.

No one could have guessed that Michelle, the loud-mouthed Italian, had only known Lulu, the soft-spoken Japanese girl, just shy of seven months. They both worked as stylists at a swanky salon and became fast friends from the moment they met. They shared all the same interests and liked partying, probably a little too much. When Michelle broke things off with her ex three months ago it just so happened that Lulu was looking for a new roommate. Ever since then they were practically inseparable. Lulu's cousin Zach joined them and their other coworkers for a night out on the town the previous evening and one thing led to another, the end result a familiar outcome for Michelle: a complete stranger in her bed.

"I need a cigarette." Michelle opened up one of the cabinets and reached in behind a stack of spices.

Lulu wiped tears from her face. "I thought you quit?"

"So did I." Michelle bumped into Zach as she walked by, she couldn't help but give him a dirty look. *Just what I need, stuck in this goddamn apartment with this guy*, she thought as she unlocked the door to their back porch.

"Are you sure you should go outside right now?" Zach pushed his glasses up on his face.

"We're on the second floor, I'm sure it's fine." She stepped outside, pulling the door closed behind her. The wail of sirens greeted her. She scanned the parking lot below her but it seemed as if everything in their neck of the woods was fine. She couldn't find anything out of the ordinary other than the fact that not a single person was outside on such a beautiful day. No one walked their dogs, no kids rode bikes or played on the swing set across the lot.

She fished her cell phone from the pocket of her pink cropped sweatpants and lit a cigarette. No missed calls, no texts, no notifications. The phone had zero bars. She angrily slammed it down on the railing, shattering the screen. It fell to her feet and she kicked it across the porch, the $400 device meaning nothing to her at that moment. She ran her fingers through her still-damp hair as she smoked, pulling a long lock in front of her face and scowling. The highlights were fading and she had planned on touching them up at work whenever the salon reopened. She let the pink strand fall back into place and jumped at the sound of a window shattering in the building next to hers. She leaned out and looked over to her right, seeing nothing, but recoiled as she heard screaming and three loud gunshots.

"Fuck this." Michelle threw the cigarette out over the balcony ledge and hurried back inside. "Did you hear that?"

Zach was on the couch with his arm around his cousin, consoling her. "Hear what?"

"Jesus, are you not paying attention to anything? The building next door, somebody is shooting."

"Oh god, I can't deal with this," Lulu sobbed into her hands.

"Come on Lu, it's gonna be alright," Zach soothed.

She shrugged him off. "Dude, they're talking about some kind of infection." Lulu looked up at Michelle through wet eyes.

"What are you talking about?"

"I don't know, it's all bullshit now on the news. Scrolling messages, prerecorded emergency warnings from earlier. I don't know what's going on."

"How safe is this building?" Zach wiped his glasses clean with his gray t-shirt.

"Safe from *what*?" Michelle asked, her hands on her hips.

"I don't know, like, from the psychopaths we saw on the TV? Or the people apparently shooting guns next door?"

"I don't know. If somebody wanted to get in here badly enough they could find a way. We're upstairs, so I guess that makes it a little safer." She rubbed her temples. "Look, I don't like hearing the sound of gunshots in my apartment complex, okay? That's not very fucking comforting."

"What are we gonna do, Michelle? We don't have a landline, we can't call the police." Lulu's voice was muffled by her knees she spoke. She was curled up on the couch, her small stature made her look like a child.

"Should we go check on your neighbors?" Zach got up from the couch and walked toward the front door.

"Fuck no! What are you, stupid?" Michelle ran to the door and stood in front of it. "This isn't really one of those situations I want to be the good guy in. That kind of shit is gonna get you killed. Did you not hear me say I heard gunshots?" She was raising her voice now, with every word she was angrier with him. She didn't understand the situation, she had no control over it.

"Well what do we do, then? Do we just stay here? Do you even have anything in this place other than coffee and beer?" Zach folded his arms across his chest.

The trio was startled by a blood-curdling scream from outside, followed by gunshots that Lulu and Zach heard for themselves this time. Lulu jumped up and rushed to the window, pulling a shade to the side. A low moan escaped her lips followed by more crying. The other two joined her at the window and looked out into the courtyard. A woman carrying a child was running toward the parking lot, three psychos chasing after her. Michelle and Lulu recognized the woman from the building next door.

"It's Janice! We need to do something!" Lulu cried out.

"Shut up!" Michelle put a hand over Lulu's mouth and held her still.

The child in Janice's arms was screaming at the top of his lungs. Janice kept frantically looking behind her and didn't notice the two that had come running up in front. She collided with the first of the attackers and they bounced off one another, falling to the ground.

The child went flying.

"Oh my God," Michelle whispered, watching with horrified eyes as the first three attackers ripped the child apart. His screaming ceased as blood shot up into the air and onto the assailants. Janice wailed and kicked at the two men who were biting chunks of flesh from her body. She tried desperately to get to her son until all movement ceased.

Lulu dropped to the floor and vomited between sobs. Zach backed away from the window, shaking, his hands on both sides of his head. Michelle stayed at the window, the shade drawn, her eyes fixated on the courtyard.

III

No one spoke. Lulu curled up on the couch and stared at the television, awaiting an anchorman to appear on the screen and say that the situation was under control. Zach, after cleaning up Lulu's vomit, joined her on the couch.

Michelle had retired to her room and sat in her computer chair by the open window. She was serenaded by the sounds of chaos. A Diet Coke can sat on the windowsill, her makeshift ashtray. She thought of her mom, her sister, all of her other family members and friends. She couldn't help but wonder if they were safe, but decided that worrying about it was useless. She was in Florida, they were back home in Chicago. If the rest of the country was in any sort of similar situation as Haven, there would be no way she could get to them safely.

She spent quite some time by herself in her room, smoking by the window, staring at nothing. She racked her brain for a plan, trying to figure out what they should do, where they should go. She wondered what the roads were like, whether they should even attempt to leave town. There was no way that they could stay; she hated to admit it, but Zach was right. They had no sustenance in the apartment. A few cans of soda, beer, and a couple snacks.

Her stomach rumbled at the thought of food, she hadn't eaten anything since the day before. She dropped her cigarette into the can and headed for the kitchen. Lulu was still staring at the TV, a blank set of eyes on a blank screen. Zach sat with his head back and his eyes closed. He opened them when Michelle entered the living room and watched as she ignored him.

She opened the pantry and set a box of Oreos down on the counter, pulling two out. Zach joined her at the breakfast bar and she pushed the box toward him.

"Thanks." He pulled a few cookies out for himself and opened the fridge.

"Can you grab me a soda?" Michelle asked, her mouth full of cookies.

He pulled three cans out and handed one to her.

Walking back to the living room, he set a can in front of his cousin. Lulu's eyes didn't move from the television. He grabbed her face gently by her chin and her eyes met his. He motioned toward the soda.

"Drink something. Please?"

Lulu nodded and he popped open the can for her before returning to the kitchen.

Michelle slowly chewed the last of her cookie. Zach stood beside her and put his hand on the small of her back, "How are you doing?"

She flinched and shoved his arm away from her. "Don't touch me."

He looked confused, maybe even hurt, but she didn't care.

"What's your problem?"

She laughed at that. A genuine, hearty laugh. "Is that a serious question?"

He shrugged his shoulders, awaiting her answer.

"Everything is my problem." She stormed off and stopped at the couch, looking down at her friend. "You need to get your shit together." Lulu watched as she disappeared down the hall.

Michelle locked her bedroom door and started up the shower. She sat on the floor of the tub and cried until the water ran cold. When she was done dressing and drying her hair it was completely dark outside. She smoked another cigarette and returned to the kitchen. Zach had put a DVD in after giving up on getting anything useful from the dead networks. Lulu was in the kitchen, heating up Ramen noodles.

Michelle grabbed a packet and waited her turn. Lulu hugged Michelle tightly without saying a word. Michelle held her stiffly in her arms; she was no good at comforting others. Lulu silently left the kitchen and joined her cousin on the couch, eating her noodles and watching the overrated comedy he'd chosen.

Michelle brought her food with her to her room, closing and locking the door again. She ate in silence and thought about packing up and leaving in the middle of the night. She thought about trying for Chicago, how easy it could be just going it solo and not having to worry about anyone else, but she couldn't convince herself to leave Lulu here. A soft tap at her door derailed her train of thought. She got up and opened it a crack.

"Can I come in?" Lulu looked even smaller than she normally did as she leaned against the wall outside Michelle's room. It was almost as if she'd been reading Michelle's mind.

Michelle waved her in and closed the door again.

Lulu scrunched her nose up at the bed in disgust, thinking of Michelle and her cousin together, and chose to sit in the computer chair. Michelle crossed her legs on her bed and leaned back against the wall, closing her eyes. Lulu studied her for a moment, trying to figure out how she was so relaxed. "Is the world ending?"

Michelle chuckled and looked at her roommate. "The Internet is gone, so it might as well be."

Lulu pulled her feet up onto the chair and rested her arms over her knees. "What are we going to do?"

"Beats the shit out of me." Michelle closed her eyes again. "You got any bright ideas?"

"Maybe." Lulu shrugged her shoulders and looked down at floor, embarrassed of the plan she'd been rolling around in her head.

"Well let's hear it, Lu."

"We go to work. Like, literally go to work. The salon."

Michelle opened her eyes and made a face. "Why the hell would we do that?"

"Because the building is perfect!" Lulu suddenly sounded excited. "Think of the other stores that share the building with us! A jewelry store, a vitamin shop." Her excitement grew with every word as she continued explaining her idea. "And there's a restaurant and a cell phone store. Do I need to keep going?"

Michelle snickered, "I hate to break it to you, but cell phone service is non-existent and diamonds aren't going to help you, no matter how much you like them." She reached across the bed and grabbed her cigarettes.

Lulu handed the can of ashes to her. "No, you're not thinking." She tapped at her head and dropped her feet back to the floor. "The glass is shatterproof in both of those stores, and what do you think they have? Secure inventory rooms. Hellooo? Safety? Ringing any bells?"

Michelle nodded her head, a line forming in her brow. Lulu had definitely piqued her interest. "Target is across the street. And there's roof access, too." She was starting to work out the details of Lulu's strange plan in her head when a long howl was heard outside followed by a series of growls and screams.

"Shut the lights off, now!"

Lulu jumped up to obey, rushing out of the bedroom, flipping the light switch as she went.

Michelle heard her calling to Zach to turn everything off. She peeked out the window into the parking lot. There were a few people milling about, looking disoriented. All the other apartments she could see were dark.

We must have been the only assholes with our lights on, she thought, shaking her head.

Lulu returned to the room and stood at the window with Michelle, watching the strange behavior of the people in the lot below. They seemed to sniff at the air, wildly waving their arms and heads around.

"What do you think they're doing?" Lulu whispered.

"You wanna go ask them?"

She looked at Michelle, her eyes full of fright. "Leaving suddenly seems like a really bad idea."

"Well," Michelle took one last drag off her cigarette, "at some point we aren't gonna have a choice."

IV

Michelle, Lulu, and Zach spent the rest of the evening in the dark, working out their plan in the living room. Zach brought up the fact that they'd have to make sure they had supplies once they got to the gigantic outdoor mall where Michelle and Lulu worked.

"We're gonna need to make sure we're prepared. Once we get in, we may have to stay for a while. Or, I mean, something could happen along the way, we get stuck or we have to hide or something. I don't know how any of this shit works, but we should probably stop somewhere and stock up." Zach spoke quickly, wearing his nerves on his sleeves.

It drove Michelle crazy.

"Yeah. We don't have much here," Michelle said, throwing Zach a dirty look he couldn't see in the darkness. "You already pointed that out. So we'll hit the gas station up on the corner on our way to Emerald Park."

"What do we do about the crazy people out there?" Lulu's voice was shaky.

"Keep the hell away from them. You saw what they did to a child out there. They're obviously out of their minds." Zach replied, he reached a hand out and squeezed his cousin's shoulder reassuringly. "If the psychopaths out there are out for blood, then we do what we need to do to defend ourselves. I'm assuming you don't have any weapons here?"

"I have a broken pool stick. I keep it under my bed in case anyone breaks in."

Michelle rolled her eyes at her roommate. "No Zach, we don't have any weapons."

"Now hold on, I liked Lulu's answer a little better. You have to get creative. Let me ask a better question. What do you have in the apartment that can be used as a weapon?"

"Like Lulu's pool stick?" Michelle tried to hide her amusement.

"Yes, like Lulu's pool stick," Zach replied, clearly not amused.

"Let's see. We've got a toolbox on the porch. That's probably got some useful stuff in it. We have a bunch of knives in the kitchen but they can barely cut steak." She lit a cigarette as she mentally inventoried. "We have a couple of tennis rackets in the closet and I have a big ass Maglite in my car, but other than that I think we're fresh out of ideas."

"Alright. Well that's gonna have to work until we find something better. Let's try to get some sleep, we're gonna need our wits about us when we leave in the morning." Zach went to get up but Lulu grabbed his hand.

"Will you sleep in my room? Please?" She sounded like a child as she asked. "I'm really scared."

"Of course."

Michelle left the living room with a sigh. She felt like she was trapped in the apartment with a bunch of babies. She locked her bedroom door and brushed her teeth in the dark. When she was finished, she curled up in her bed and out of habit, reached for her cell phone. She remembered that it was still outside on the porch with a shattered screen. She mumbled cusswords at herself and rolled over, falling almost immediately to sleep.

She woke the next morning to knocking at her door. "Are you planning on getting up anytime soon?" Zach's muffled voice travelled through the crack in the door's frame.

"I hate him so much," Michelle said as she stretched in bed and tossed her blanket to the side. He repeated the same knock and call and Michelle snapped, "Yeah! Alright!"

She stomped into the bathroom and turned on the light. She washed her face and threw her thick curly hair back in a ponytail. She put some mascara on and brushed her teeth, faking a smile in the mirror before turning out the light and getting dressed.

Lulu and Zach were waiting for her in the living room with a mound of luggage piled around the coffee table. Michelle made a beeline for the coffee pot. "Are we going camping?" She smirked at Lulu as she poured herself a cup of breakfast blend.

"Did you even pack anything?" Zach fiddled with his glasses as he spoke. "You already overslept, we need to get a move on."

"As a matter of fact I did put a bag together. I don't know where you think we're going but it ain't on vacation." She gulped down the hot coffee. "We don't know what to expect out there, or how long it will be until help comes along and clears this mess up." She thought of the words that just left her mouth and wondered if there would even be any help coming. She pushed the fear from her mind and finished off her liquid breakfast. "I'm just not too worried about my carry-on luggage at the moment."

Lulu looked at all of her bags, suddenly embarrassed. "I just wanted to make sure I have clean clothes."

"Yeah, and I don't even have any other clothes." Zach stood up and pointed at the coffee table. "Take the hammer, Michelle, and grab your bag. I'm ready to get out of here."

Michelle retrieved her overnight bag from her bedroom and looked around one last time before shutting her door. She didn't know if she'd ever set foot in her own bedroom again, but for the most part she just didn't care. Back in the living room she noticed that Lulu had set all but two bags to the side, one that she carried and one that Zach had shouldered. "Are you driving?" Lulu looked at her, broken pool stick in hand.

Michelle grabbed her keys and the hammer from the coffee table. She looked from Zach to Lulu and back to Zach again. "Here goes nothin'." She unlocked the front door and pulled it toward her.

An assortment of sounds hung on the air and an awful odor greeted them on the second floor landing. Michelle cautiously descended to the first floor and looked around, not a soul to be seen. She avoided the remains of Janice and her son in the courtyard and she hoped Lulu would choose to do the same; she didn't want her holding them up by vomiting again. The trio walked in silence down the sidewalk around the building, not knowing what to expect around the corner in the parking lot.

Michelle's red Camry hybrid sat crookedly in its space, the result of a night of drinking. The majority of their neighbors' cars were still in the lot, none of them brave enough to leave after what happened to Janice, or perhaps none of them lucky enough. Michelle played with her car keys as she walked, unknowingly pressing the alert button. The car's alarm went off, startling all three of them.

"Oh shit! Sorry!" Michelle dropped the keys and bent down to pick them up. She fumbled with them and finally got the alarm turned off. Violent cries erupted all around.

"Oh, Jesus Christ, no." Lulu grabbed her cousin's arm and began weeping. The maniacal screams grew closer and the three companions could now hear the sound of feet slamming against the pavement, headed rapidly their way from all directions.

"Get to the car! Hurry!" Michelle broke away from the others and ran for her car, the hammer clattering to the ground behind her, ignored. Her heart raced as she finally saw what was after them. Vicious, mangled creatures that looked like something out of a horror film raced toward her, growling and hissing all the way. She yanked her car door open and threw her bag inside, slamming the door and screaming for Lulu and Zach to hurry up.

The first of the eaters slammed its body into the driver's side door just as Zach and Lulu made it safely inside. The dead thing pounded its fists against the window, leaving smears behind. Lulu screamed and continued to cry in the passenger's seat.

"Shut *up!*" Michelle yelled at her and threw the car in reverse. She put her foot on the gas and smashed into the body of another eater. One of her front tires ran over it and Lulu screamed again.

Michelle put the car in drive and took off toward the exit. She checked the rearview and was not surprised to see the group of dead still chasing. Some of them were dismembered, some of them half naked, but all of them equally terrifying.

Every corner she turned in the complex brought more and more of the crazies out of hiding. "There's so many of them," she whispered. She sat with her mouth hanging open, dumbfounded.

"Michelle!" Lulu cried out and Michelle brought her eyes back to the road just in time to see the disfigured, half-eaten teenage girl charging the car head-on.

"Fuck you!" Michelle pushed down on the accelerator and the Camry plowed into the girl at fifty miles per hour. The girl's body smashed into the windshield and rolled up and over the car.

Lulu's screams were endless, Zach was yelling for her to stop. Michelle's adrenaline was pumping full force. She checked the rearview mirror and couldn't believe her eyes.

The girl she'd just run down with her car was getting back up. "You've got to be shitting me." Michelle slowed the car to navigate the final turn for the exit and sped away, making a left out of the complex and heading toward Emerald Park.

Zach turned around in his seat to see what Michelle was talking about but she'd taken the turn too fast. "What happened? Is the girl dead? Are they still back there?"

Michelle ignored his questions and kept driving. She passed the gas station.

"Hey, what are you doing? I thought we were going to stop there?" Zach was clearly in panic mode.

"I'm not stopping anywhere until I know those freaks aren't following us anymore." She took a series of turns.

Zach was glad she knew where she was going and that Lulu had finally stopped screaming. As they sped through the streets of Haven, Michelle dodged scattered groups of people as they ran. People were running, hiding, or dying right before their eyes.

Michelle took one last right turn that took them the wrong way on a one-way street. She scanned the area and pulled the car off to the side of the road, right in front of a corner store about two miles from their home. She was still breathing hard and her hands were shaking. She had a sinking feeling that nobody would be coming to help them.

"This is where we stop. Get in there, get whatever we feel like we're gonna need and get the fuck out." She turned around and faced Zach, her face flushed and her palms sweaty. "I hit that crazy chick doing *fifty* and watched her ass bounce on that pavement. That would have killed anyone."

"Yes! We're all aware of this!" Zach shouted at her.

"Yeah, well, what you're not aware of is the fact that she got right back up and started chasing us again."

V

The corner store had already been cleared of anything of real value by the neighborhood inhabitants. Michelle grabbed several plastic bags and began filling them with whatever was left that could be useful to the small group. Zach cleaned his glasses on his shirt and kept watch at the door. Every so often he would duck down as a person would run by screaming. Sirens wailed in the streets and breaking glass and screeching tires were nonstop. Lulu followed Michelle around the tiny store like a puppy, whimpering and trembling. There was almost nothing of actual nutritional value left in the store but Michelle kept searching. She grabbed packs of batteries and shoved them into the bag regardless of type. Matchbooks and lighters, candy and gum, cigarettes and Tylenol; whatever she could get her hands on, she took from the shelves.

"Hey," Lulu quietly called out to Michelle as they made their way through the last corner of the store. "Look at all this spray paint."

Michelle turned to her and made a face. "What do we need spray paint for?"

"Windows." Lulu picked up a can with each hand and shook them gently. "We can paint all the windows. Those psychos won't be able to see inside."

A smile crept across Michelle's face. She couldn't help but feel a sense of overwhelming joy that Lulu had proven herself useful after her bout of hysteria. "That's my girl." She winked at Lulu and tossed her some plastic bags. "Fill 'em up and let's get the hell outta here."

The two women grabbed their corner store treasures and headed for the door.

Zach, crouched beside the entrance, put a hand up, motioning for them to stop and get down. Lulu and Michelle ducked into the aisles opposite from one another.

Zach peered out the door to watch a man who looked as if he had been almost beaten to death staring curiously at Michelle's red Toyota. Blood ran down his face and chest, staining his white t-shirt. His hands were mangled horribly, as if someone or something had been chewing on them. Wheezing grunts floated on the air from him; he cocked his head a few times left and right like he was trying to understand a puzzle. From somewhere in the distance came horrendous screams and the man by the car shot up straight and took off that way at full speed.

Zach let his breath out in a *whoosh*; he'd been holding it the entire time. He looked over at his cousin and her roommate and nodded toward the car. "We're clear."

Michelle gathered up her bags and stood, noticing now what she did not see before. On a shelf in front of her were packs of solar-powered garden lights of various sizes, but all had the same solid metal stakes on the ends. She grabbed as many as she could fit into her already overflowing shopping bags.

Outside, Lulu scanned the area, trembling in fear of being noticed by an eater as Zach packed up the trunk. Michelle jogged over to the car, arms outstretched and he took the rest of the bags from her. She pulled a pack of garden lights out and opened them up as he slammed the trunk. She threw the trash behind her and admired the heavy, shiny object she held in her hand. The end of the stake wasn't sharp enough to cut, but would be useful to her in other ways. "Perfect," she said.

They piled into the Camry and drove off toward Emerald Park.

Michelle tried avoiding main roads, sticking to the narrow side streets lined with vacation homes and small shops as they got closer to the shoreline of the tourist mecca of Haven. She thanked her lucky stars that the city was already in its off season, otherwise their nightmare would have been unimaginably worse. She pulled onto the last cluster of side streets she'd be able to navigate before being forced to take the main strip that lined the Gulf Coast.

She nearly choked as Lulu screamed and Zach yelled out for her to stop. Michelle slammed her foot down hard on the brakes, everyone rocked forward as the car came to a halt just inches before plowing into a pregnant woman who had run out into the street.

"Holy shit," Michelle panted as she stared at the disheveled woman. Her big belly jutted out from her small frame, like she was ready to pop. The woman had one arm outstretched toward them, the other held her stomach tightly. She was sobbing and covered from head to toe in blood and a dozen other substances.

"We have to help her." Zach adjusted his glasses and pushed his matted black hair back from his forehead; the day had proven unfortunately humid and he was drenched in sweat. The pregnant woman lost her balance and braced herself on the hood of the car with a thump. Zach threw open the car door and ran to her side. Lulu said nothing, her eyes filled with tears and her hands were over her mouth. She looked back and forth from Michelle to the woman on the hood.

"Goddamnit. Fine." Michelle unbuckled her seatbelt and exited the car to help Zach. She narrowed her eyes in disgust once she got a better look at the pregnant woman. Blood dripped down her legs from an obvious miscarriage, and several wounds ran all down her side, showing through the holes of her blue nightgown.

"Were you attacked?" Zach put his arm under the woman and held her up. He tried to get a better look at the woman's wounds. "I think she's been stabbed." He looked at Michelle but she shook her head.

"Those aren't stab wounds, Zach."

He examined them more closely and realized she was right. They were bite marks, and they were deep. Chunks of her flesh were missing and she was bleeding badly. He noticed another gaping wound nearer to her protruding belly and his heart quietly broke for her.

"We need to get her into the car. Come on, let's get out of here." Michelle helped the two of them along, putting her arm under the woman on the side opposite Zach. They stumbled as her feet gave out from underneath her. She had stopped sobbing now and was quietly moaning in pain. "You got her?" Michelle asked Zach. He nodded and she opened the door to the backseat before running around to the driver's side. Zach gently placed the woman into the car.

Lulu unbuckled herself and turned around to take a look at their new passenger. "Oh my God." She was crying now. "Is she dying?" She looked at Michelle with terrified eyes. "Do you think her baby is okay?"

Michelle said nothing and put the car in drive as soon as Zach's door slammed shut. *I know I'm going to fucking regret this,* Michelle thought as she sped down the empty streets.

"Do you think we'll be able to find her a doctor?" Lulu asked Zach, who was trying to keep the woman upright in the backseat.

He shook his head solemnly at his cousin. The woman's limp body kept falling over onto him, and he was covered in her blood and whoever else's was all over her.

Michelle kept glancing in the rearview mirror at the near dead woman in her back seat. She tucked a stray curl back behind her ear and watched as the woman's eyes rolled into the back of her head. Michelle's grip tightened on the wheel as the woman began gurgling and going into convulsions.

"Shit, we're losing her!" Zach tried his best to hold her still but her body rocked in his arms.

Lulu whipped back around and buckled herself back in, covering her ears and squeezing her eyes shut. As quickly as the convulsions had started, the woman fell still once more. Zach's chest heaved up and down as he stared down at the dead woman in the backseat with him.

Flecks of blood smeared across his glasses and he squinted through them at her lifeless face. He bent down and put his ear to her mouth but felt no air and heard no sound. He lingered there for a moment, devastated that someone had just died in his arms.

He looked up to Lulu and Michelle and said, quietly, "She's gone."

Her eyes had already glazed over and reopened anew. It was too late for him as the once-dead pregnant woman tore Zach's ear off. Zach began screaming and Lulu joined in as she realized what was happening to her cousin.

Michelle swerved as one of Zach's flailing arms hit her in the head. The pregnant woman had a death grip on his head and her teeth tore into his face. Blood sprayed out and splattered onto the windows, the seats, Michelle, Lulu, and even as far as the windshield.

"She's killing him! Michelle, stop the car! She's killing him!" Lulu pleaded and screamed.

Michelle unintentionally pushed her foot down on the accelerator and lost control of the car as Lulu grabbed one of her arms. At the last second Michelle yanked free and hit the brakes, but smashed into an abandoned vehicle.

Zach's body was thrown into the front seat, slamming up against the dash and he lay dying and choking on his own blood. Lulu continued to scream as the dead woman in the backseat continued to devour Zach's flesh.

Michelle's head had hit her window hard, there was a ringing in her ears that seemed to drown out everything else. Her eyes worked just fine though. Zach's dying eyes locked with hers and she realized in that very moment exactly what had happened and what needed to be done. One of his hands gripped the garden light in her lap and thrust it toward her.

Michelle jumped out of the car and, in one swift motion opened the door to the backseat, dragging the flailing, screaming body of the undead pregnant woman out of the car. The dead woman's head bounced off the asphalt, and Michelle beat her face in with the heavy garden light until all movement ceased. She kicked the body to the side and slammed the door shut on her way to Lulu's side of the car.

Michelle felt like a robot. Lulu protested as Michelle grabbed for Zach's body. Michelle slapped Lulu across the face in response and hoisted Zach's half-eaten body out of the car, slamming it onto the asphalt.

She straddled his body and raised the garden light with both arms. Zach's eyes shot open and locked with hers once more, but they were not the same eyes she had just looked into moments before. His half-eaten face and neck made her stomach turn but she swallowed her bile. He growled demonically and his torso squirmed under her as she plunged the metal garden stake straight through the middle of his forehead. No more sound or movement came from Zach. No more sound or movement would ever come from Zach.

In a matter of two minutes there was only Michelle and a catatonic Lulu left in a blood-soaked hybrid. The pair silently backed up and continued on their way to Emerald Park. The front end of Michelle's car scraped against the pavement loudly before finally falling off and leaving them in silence once more.

VI

Lulu's eyes stung from crying. Her head pounded and her skin felt tight. She wished she would wake up from this nightmare. A week before, if anyone asked her how she was doing, she would have responded, "YOLO."

Lulu was the carefree, airheaded type who broke the traditional Asian stereotype by never having studied a day in her life and barely making a C in any class she took. She immersed herself in girly things and ballet classes, cosmetology, and pop music. If it weren't for her familial wealth, she'd never have a dime to her name. She was the type of girl who had been sheltered from the ugliness of the world, always getting her way and never having a real responsibility or worry thrust upon her. That's more than likely what had attracted her to Michelle in the first place.

Lulu didn't usually hang around with the strong-willed or intimidating type, but Michelle was like her in the ways that mattered: absolutely gorgeous, always got what she wanted, and never turned down a party. But no matter how hard Lulu tried to silently hope and pray that she could turn back the clock, open her eyes and be in her oversized, comfy bed, it just wasn't possible. This mayhem was real. Her white tank top was stained with blood, her denim capris would never be untainted, her hair was a mess, and for the first time she didn't care how she looked. She was alone with Michelle and no one else in the world and she was terrified. A complete stranger had just murdered her cousin in the backseat and then her roommate had done it again.

She understood. She desperately tried to convince herself that the pregnant woman did not come back to life and eat Zach's face. She replayed the events over and over a million times in her mind and still couldn't believe Michelle had stuck a garden stake through Zach's forehead.

Lulu suddenly felt a wave of heat rush through her, the world spun and she felt like she was going to pass out. "Michelle, stop the car." The words barely came out and Michelle didn't respond. "Stop the car!" Michelle looked around and pulled into a driveway. Lulu hyperventilated, clawing her way out of the car. On her knees in the stranger's driveway she dry heaved and spat.

Michelle rushed around to her side, crouching down and gently rubbing her back.

"You're gonna be fine," Michelle whispered. She didn't like just stopping like this. She felt exposed. Lulu was making too much noise and she had to get her back in the car. "Come on, we need to go." She reached out and took Lulu's arm.

Lulu shrugged Michelle off as she vomited. "I'm not done," she gurgled, then spit. And then the tears began again.

"Okay, I know that, but my car is pretty fucking disgusting right now, so it's probably safer for you to be getting sick in there." She grabbed her arm again but this time with more force. "Let's go. Now."

Lulu pulled the bottom of her shirt up and wiped her mouth off, hurrying back into Michelle's car. She looked at Michelle curiously. "Do you know what's going on?"

Michelle laughed, "Yes. We're going to Emerald Park to lock ourselves the fuck inside. I am trying to keep us alive. Does that make sense of things?"

"That's not what I meant!" Lulu shouted.

Michelle's sarcastic smile disappeared and she looked solemn as she backed the car out of the driveway.

"Zach is dead. That lady, she was alive and then she was dead and then she killed Zach. But then, you killed Zach! I don't know what the fuck is going on!"

"Alright, please." Michelle winced. "Stop yelling at me. Okay? I have no idea why this is happening, but I can say it's probably a good idea to stop wondering about it. You'll drive yourself insane, and that's no good to me. To either of us."

She cracked her neck and scanned the road, reminding Lulu of a machine.

"I'm sorry about Zach."

"Are you?"

"Yes."

The women didn't speak again until they got closer to the shopping center. Michelle was forced back onto the main road, bobbing and weaving between abandoned and wrecked cars before finally driving on the wrong side of the road. It was easier to avoid a head-on collision than it was to make it through the tangled mess of cars on the westbound lane.

"I'm a little worried that all of these cars are heading in the same direction as us," Michelle mumbled.

"Most of them are empty." Lulu stared out the window.

"Yeah, but why? Where did they all go?"

Her question went unanswered as they continued driving toward their destination.

They passed a bike shop on their right and Lulu perked up. "Hey, why don't we stop there?" She pointed at the store and looked at Michelle. "It would be easier to get around and we would be less noisy. Nobody cares about cyclists, ya know?"

Michelle appreciated the thought. "Yeah. I can't ride a bike."

"Who doesn't know how to ride a bike?" Lulu looked perplexed, but Michelle just shook her head. Lulu sat back in her seat again and went back to staring at the chaos they were passing at a mere twenty miles per hour.

There was so much debris and garbage in the road it was too dangerous to go any faster. Michelle didn't want to risk breaking down in her already mangled vehicle or getting a flat tire and being stuck with the bike option.

Lulu couldn't believe the amount of blood and gore she saw on practically everything they passed. Bodies lie in the road, half-devoured and twitching. The several eaters they drove by ignored the car because they were too busy...feasting.

Michelle's grip on the steering wheel grew tighter as they approached Emerald Park from the highway. She slowed the car almost to a stop and felt her heart speed up. An enormous crowd of the dead stumbled aimlessly about, some of them running in circles, slamming into one another and then resuming their pointless actions, others stood around staring off into nothing. The bodies were wounded in different ways, some of them actually appearing normal.

Michelle crept the car along and turned off onto the delivery road so they wouldn't be spotted. She pulled off to the side and put the car in park. "Fuck," she whispered.

"What are we going to do?" Lulu's hands shook and she folded in on herself, shrinking in the seat. The delivery road was empty and lined with thick foliage on both sides, but she was so terrified of being spotted.

Michelle shook her head from side to side, racking her brain for a plan of action. She put the car in drive and Lulu panicked, grabbing her hand, eyes wide.

"I need to know what the back lot of our building looks like, Lu. We can't stay here."

Lulu pulled her hand back and crossed her arms, hugging herself tightly.

Michelle made it down the road and slowly turned the corner into one of the back parking lots of Emerald Park. The lot was fairly empty, except for three or four cars here or there; it looked as if the eaters were sticking to the main entrance near the highway.

She kept inching the car forward and then stopping, waiting for a sign that they'd been noticed, but all stayed well. She pulled up as close as she was going to get. They were diagonal from the back entrance to their building, right in front of a Target and across from a shoe store. Another row of buildings sat behind them, leading to the other side of the enormous shopping center that was closer to the beach.

The lot and road in front of them was thick with eaters. Michelle counted the few blessings she figured she had left that they'd gotten this far. She had no idea how she was going to get them, along with their belongings, safely into the building. Her head was out of room for positive thought.

And Lulu…Lulu already seemed somewhere far off in her own mind.

Michelle sighed and rested her pounding head on the steering wheel, closing her eyes and listening to the soft hum of the hybrid's engine. Her mind began to fill with songs and lyrics and she wished she hadn't destroyed her phone so carelessly; she'd at least like to die with some music.

She opened her eyes and saw that Lulu rested her bloodstained shoes up on the dashboard and curled herself up in a ball. The car was trashed, Michelle didn't even care. She absentmindedly counted the laces on Lulu's shoes and hummed a song to herself.

She shot up, back to reality. "We're getting into that building."

Lulu slowly rolled her head to the side and looked at Michelle, tears in her eyes.

"Wipe those tears away darlin'," Michelle said, removing her store keys from the ring still in the ignition. She placed the salon's key ring on her middle finger so she didn't lose it and put her hands on Lulu's shoulders, facing her body towards hers. "I am gonna need you to listen to me very carefully. I really need you to get it together and give me a hundred percent right now Lu, can you do that? Do you trust me?"

Lulu nodded. "What are we doing?"

"Take your shoes off." Michelle began removing her own shoes and pulling the laces out. Lulu followed suit. "Do you have your phone on you?"

"No, I have Zach's."

"That'll work. Pull up his music player." Michelle fished her auxiliary cable out of the center console.

"Michelle, at least tell me what we're doing."

A smile danced across Michelle's face that made Lulu a little uneasy. "We're going to crash my car into the shoe store."

VII

Michelle eased the car up beside another and the two women climbed out quietly. They carefully took their belongings out of the trunk and quietly, furtively loaded up as much as they could from the plastic bags into their duffle bags. They'd be easier to carry.

"You seriously didn't need to bring this much stuff," Michelle said, rolling her eyes as Lulu reluctantly parted ways with half of the clothing and cosmetics in her duffle bag, filling the empty space with the things they'd scavenged from the corner store.

They both were down to their socks and Michelle rigged the steering wheel with their shoelaces. Lulu handed Michelle Zach's phone and she plugged in the auxiliary cable. She grabbed the remaining garden light from the already-opened package and smirked at it.

Who knew how useful these things really were, she thought as she wrestled it into position over the accelerator.

"Oh my God," Lulu whispered, tapping Michelle on the shoulder.

Michelle froze, expecting the worst. She slowly turned on the balls of her feet, still crouched behind the car door, in the direction Lulu was pointing. Two people were hiding beside a truck on the opposite end of the parking lot. The woman was peering over the bed of the truck, scoping out the position of the eaters and the man was waving at them.

"No way."

Lulu scowled at Michelle.

"I said no way, Lu. Have you already forgotten? I can drive back to where we left Zach."

"Of course not! But we can't just abandon them!"

"Goddamnit, keep your voice down." Michelle poked her head up to check for danger but they remained unnoticed. "We *can* abandon them. And we *will.* I'm not fucking this up for strangers."

"I won't go with you, then." Lulu's eyes began to get watery again and Michelle clenched her fists.

"Un-fucking-believable. You are unbelievable. You know that?" Michelle shoved her over in the direction of the other car. "Get over there and stay there. I'll handle this."

Michelle crab-walked over so she was in plain sight of the couple. They were both looking at her now, she put a hand up, signaling them to wait. She laid her body down flat and pointed to the ground, imitating a crawling motion, hoping they understood.

They both got down and waited for her signal. She popped back up and had another look at the group of eaters milling about in the road up ahead. She motioned for the couple to head toward her. The man began crawling quickly, but the woman got up and took off in a sprint.

Michelle panicked and put both hands up, hoping the idiot could see. The man lunged for the woman's leg, saying something to her, and she dropped to her belly.

Michelle glanced back at the dead, who were somehow still oblivious to the shenanigans in the parking lot.

It took five more minutes for the couple to finally make their way across the parking lot. They had to keep stopping and laying still when Michelle would notice eaters randomly turning in their direction. To Michelle, those five minutes felt like an eternity.

When they were safely behind the abandoned car with Lulu, the man opened his mouth to speak.

Michelle shook her head. "We don't talk now. You follow me and that's that. Understand?"

The man and woman both nodded. Lulu and Michelle gathered their duffle bags and strapped them to their bodies. Michelle pointed at the few remaining plastic bags and then pointed at the woman who wasn't carrying anything; Michelle decided she needed to make herself useful.

Once everyone was in a ready position and away from her car, Michelle went back to the driver's side and picked up Zach's phone. She turned the volume all the way up, then pressed play as shoved the garden light into place on the accelerator. The hybrid's engine whined to life in time to the sound of the music.

"I fucking hate the Smashing Pumpkins!"

She punched the steering wheel twice, the second time letting her fist linger and allowing the horn to blare. The attention of the dead was definitely aroused and their ravenous wails filled the air. She slammed the gear shift into drive and rolled away, the car taking off across the parking lot as planned, but it didn't make it to the shoe store.

Michelle willed the car to keep moving as it plowed into the wall of undead at full speed. Bodies crunched and flew over the Camry as it drove off down the road. She didn't care where it went, as long as it kept them chasing it.

"Let's go!"

The group jumped up and ran full speed toward their destination. A loud crash of broken glass and twisting metal came up the street, and the music played on.

The dead roared and howled, causing a raucous unlike any the living had ever heard. It sent a rush of chills down Michelle's spine as she silently said goodbye to her beloved red car and pulled the set of keys off her finger. They had just made it by the set of dumpsters and a small delivery dock for the restaurant, when they heard an extra pair of footsteps behind them.

Lulu screamed when she saw the eater in pursuit, and to Michelle's surprise, the woman who had joined them grabbed her and covered her mouth, talking softly to her and trying to calm her down.

"Get that door open!" the man called to Michelle and he dropped his bag, pulling a hand hoe out of his cargo shorts. He plunged the small tool into the side of the eater's head. He quickly pulled it back out with a grunt and the hideous thing collapsed to the ground.

"I love garden tools so much right now," Michelle said excitedly as she turned the key and pulled open the back door to the building. "Everybody in!"

The eaters finally lost interest in the Toyota and were swiftly making their way to the group's location. They savagely beat on the fire door as it closed, their screams resembling the howls of demons.

Lulu whimpered and the woman held her tightly, stroking her hair. She was short, like Lulu, but Michelle could tell she was in her forties. Her nails were dirty but nicely manicured, and she wore her red hair in a short bob. The man was probably the same age, with a farmer's tan and long brown hair pulled back in a low pony tail.

He wiped his hand on his already-dirty brown shorts and held it out to Michelle. "I'm Desmond. This is my wife, Catherine." Michelle shook his hand and waved at Catherine.

"That's Lulu, I'm Michelle."

"Thank you for helping us out there." He placed the garden hoe back into his pocket. "You ladies have a plan?"

"This is it." Michelle shrugged and looked around the bright white hallway. The power was still on, but she knew that would be a short-lived commodity.

"How did you get here? You look like you've been through hell." He narrowed his eyes at her, examining her state of disarray. Desmond and Catherine didn't look nearly as rough as Michelle and Lulu did. Michelle's multicolored curly hair was all over the place, Lulu's face was swollen from crying and both of them were coated with the mark of the apocalypse: blood, sweat, and grime.

"That was my car out there." She pulled her hair tie out and tried to get her hair under control when she noticed that Desmond made a face at it.

Lulu let out another scream when the jewelry store's door burst open at the end of the hallway, and they all turned. An overweight security guard stood with a gun rattling in his shaky hands. He lowered it when he recognized the girls.

"Francis!" Lulu pulled away from Catherine and sprinted down the corridor, throwing her arms around his neck. She sobbed into his chest, happy to see someone she knew alive, and in misery for the loss they'd all endured.

"Great," Michelle muttered under her breath.

"Oh my God, are y'all alright?" The chunky guard holstered his weapon and hugged Lulu tightly. "Where did you come from?"

"Our apartment. We didn't know where else to go," Lulu answered, her voice muffled in his chest.

Michelle folded her arms. She disliked Francis in every way possible. "And now we're here."

Francis introduced himself to Desmond and Catherine, ushering everyone into the back room of the jewelry store. He'd obviously been camping out there; food wrappers littered the floor along with empty water and soda bottles. The toilets still worked and the four newcomers took turns relieving themselves. Francis was running low on his supplies and handed out the last of his beverages. It felt good to just sit and not feel the sense of urgency to flee anything.

Michelle had washed her face and sat in a desk chair rubbing her temples. She hadn't counted on running into any other people. She hadn't counted on having to take in to account any other person's wellbeing. She wasn't that type of person. She felt she was lucky enough to be able to get Lulu this far with her. She sighed and sat up straight, staring into the weary faces around her. Those she knew, those she didn't. Regardless of how she might have felt in that moment about anyone, she knew she had to get the gears moving.

She clapped her hands together and got everyone's attention. "Break time's over."

VIII

The group got busy scouring the remaining stores in the building. Michelle and Lulu went to work cleaning then filling all the sinks in the salon and spa. Francis unlocked the door to the vitamin shop so Catherine could get busy organizing what would stay and what would go to make room. Desmond wanted to get into the cell phone store to make sure as much technology was charged up as possible before the power went out, and Francis went to work in the breakfast café, salvaging the perishable food. Michelle reminded everyone to keep as quiet as possible and stay low near the windows to remain unseen.

Once it was dusk, Francis killed the lights and they set upon the tedious task of spray painting the jewelry store's windows. They kept having to stop and duck down as eaters shambled by the store-front. Some would pass immediately, easily fixated on something in the distance and others would linger, either staring up at the sky or turning mindlessly in slow circles before moving on.

The fumes were getting to everyone and they decided the jewelry store would be enough for one night. They sat quietly in the kitchen of the café as Francis and Lulu utilized the still-working stoves, cooking up a lavish meal of eggs, grits, hash browns, biscuits, and a variety of breakfast meats. They stuffed their faces and ate as if they were on death row and this was to be their last meal. Soon, everyone became sleepy and drifted one by one to the spa section of the salon, using massage and waxing tables as beds.

Before joining his wife, Desmond stopped by the cell phone shop. One by one, he unplugged the phones, charging cases, back up batteries, and music accessories. He was in the middle of turning them all off when he heard someone behind him in the dark. He turned quickly and recognized Michelle's tall silhouette and that long, curly hair.

"Why are you doing all this?" she asked him quietly.

He continued to power down the plethora of electronic devices. "The way I figure it, we don't have many days left with power. This stuff is more useful than you think, even without working cell towers."

She shrugged and sat down on the floor with him. "Is this what you did for a living or something?" She began helping him power everything down.

Desmond chuckled. "Nah, more like a hobby. Once upon a time I wanted to work with technology. Build tech, fix tech, the whole nine. But then I met a pretty little red head who stole my heart and I decided to become a doctor so I could get to know her better. Over a hundred grand in debt between the two of us, but it was worth every penny."

"A doctor?" Michelle ignored the love story and raised her eyebrows. "Wait, so, you and Catherine are both doctors?"

"That's right. Ain't y'all a lucky bunch, huh?" He smiled.

"Yeah, I guess we are."

The two finished up in the cell phone store and let the back door close behind them. Desmond followed Michelle down the brightly-lit fire corridor toward the salon. The lights went dim and flickered for a few seconds before coming back on in full. Michelle exhaled loudly and shook her head.

She took the deluxe spa room in the very back of the salon. She valued her privacy, and all the other sleeping arrangements had already been made. Her mind was busy, running a mile a minute, but her body was exhausted and she soon fell fast asleep. The rest of the group was high on the elaborate meal they'd just consumed and slipped off soundly into food comas, with the exception of Lulu, who sobbed silently to herself.

She mourned for Zach, and for the rest of the lives lost in whatever this sickness was that had consumed the world. *How many people are dead? What are other parts of the country like right now? What is causing this? Is help going to ever come?* A million questions more drifted through her mind. She said a silent prayer for the world and finally drifted off, snoring softly.

*

"Good morning, sunshine," Michelle gently tapped at her best friend's arm, she paused and pretended to look at a watch on her naked wrist. "Or should I say afternoon?"

It seemed as if only a few minutes had passed when Lulu was woken up by Michelle.

"Afternoon?" Lulu rubbed her eyes and sat up, stretching and yawning. "Jesus, I feel like I didn't sleep at all. Sorry." She lowered her stockinged feet to the floor and stood up, stretching once more.

"I wouldn't sweat it, it's barely past noon. Come up to the roof, Desmond had a great idea to help us get around from building to building." She glanced down at both her and Lulu's feet. "Plus, we need to figure out the shoe situation. Can't be runnin' around in socks during the *asockalypse.*"

Lulu made a face.

Michelle laughed at her joke. "Get it? Socks? Apocalypse?" She frowned, "Too soon?"

Lulu cringed, "Ugh, don't say that word." She rubbed her eyes once more and followed Michelle out of the salon toward the roof access door.

Up on the roof, Francis and Desmond were fussing with something on the far north end of the building. Lulu winced at the gravel digging into her feet, *Definitely need shoes.*

She stopped a few feet away from the men and smiled at Francis. The chubby man grinned back, a slight blush on his cheeks, and gave her a wave. Lulu peered over the side and immediately pulled back; there were about a dozen eaters directly below them milling about. They hissed and groaned, desperately looking for the source of the survivors' sounds and unable to locate them.

"Don't worry about them down there, check this out," Francis called her over.

Michelle watched as Lulu gracefully made her way toward Francis and knelt on the gravel beside him. She rested a hand on his shoulder and Francis blushed again. Michelle rolled her eyes...there was no way Lulu could have a thing for him. Francis was a high school dropout who got his GED at twenty-three and became a security guard at a high-end shopping mall. He lived in a trailer park about a half hour from Emerald Park and could barely even claim the city of Haven as his hometown.

He was the stereotypical overweight hillbilly Michelle hated about the south. Not to mention he had written her about a hundred parking tickets since she'd started working at The Luxe Salon & Spa. Yet Lulu had always been so sweet to him whenever he'd come in and ask Michelle to move her car. She'd always make sure her lip gloss was on just right when she'd see him ride up on his Segway. She'd flash him her perfect smile and even give him a hug on occasion. Michelle secretly seethed as she listened to Francis explain Desmond's plan. She didn't even hear Catherine come up next to her.

"I'm happy to say we've got enough supplements to last us about a year!" Catherine said excitedly.

Michelle jumped slightly, startled by Catherine's presence and enthusiasm. "Don't vitamins expire?"

Catherine chuckled, "It's all a money game. As long as you consume them within a safe period of time after expiration, there's nothing to be scared of." Catherine's green eyes sparkled as she spoke.

"Whatever," Michelle mumbled. "Are we ready to get this show on the road?" She looked at the others expectantly, hands on her hips. "Mama needs a new pair of shoes."

Desmond looked up at Michelle, blue eyes squinting in the afternoon sun, "I'm pretty sure there are more important things than shoes in these stores, but let's get to it." He smiled at her, a genuine smile, and stood up. "Somebody's gonna have to stay put. We're gonna need to be let out, locked out, and then let back in."

"I vote Francis. I can't imagine he's very fast." Michelle looked directly at him as she poked fun, a smirk on her face.

"Yeah, and who's got the gun?" Francis shot back.

"I'll stay." Catherine put a hand up. "I don't have a weapon, and frankly, I don't know if I'm quite ready to be back out there." Her eyes suddenly looked sad. Desmond walked over to his wife and kissed her gently on the forehead. He held her close and rubbed her back with both of his hands.

"Alright then, we goin'?" Michelle began walking back to the roof access door.

"You know the plan, babe?" Desmond asked his wife. Catherine nodded and they embraced once more. "I'll give the signal, we should be ready in about twenty."

Lulu caught up with Michelle at the door. "I don't know if I'm ready to go back out there, either."

Michelle kept walking, but called back to Lulu, "Doesn't matter. The world isn't waiting around for you to be ready."

Michelle disappeared through the door and Lulu felt Francis put his arm around her shoulder. "Don't worry, we'll split into teams. I got ya." He winked at her and she smiled, but on the inside she was terrified.

Back down in the jewelry store, the group gathered whatever empty bags they found in the building and readied themselves to venture back out into eater territory. Desmond and Michelle would head to Target, and Francis and Lulu would check out the building directly across from the one they were in. When Desmond gave Catherine the signal, she turned on two different cell phones Desmond had taken from the shop and synced them with the Bluetooth speakers on the roof. She set them on the ledge and put her fingers to her mouth, whistling loudly. She whooped and hollered, getting the attention of the majority of the eaters aimlessly wandering in the parking lot. She pressed play simultaneously on both phones and preloaded pop music blared from the speakers. Leaning over the side, she nervously watched as the door opened and her group slipped out. She pulled the key Francis gave her from her pocket and patiently waited for the four of them to creep silently to their separate destinations. She spat out over the roof onto the eaters and cursed the dead.

Desmond's plan was working.

Catherine ran across the roof and slid down the ladder into the hallway below. She got to the exit door and slipped the key in, turning it and locking herself inside. Her hands shook as she climbed the ladder back up and made her way back toward the speakers. A much larger group had formed below the north corner of the roof now. She followed Desmond's instructions; she was to turn all the electronics off and await his signal once they were finished scavenging the selected buildings.

With the music off, the eaters' screams were a hundred times louder. Her skin crawled and shivers ran down her spine. She backed away from the ledge and crossed her arms, humming softly to herself in hopes it would take her mind off the howls of the dead.

Next time, she thought, *headphones.*

IX

The eaters at the north end grew bored of their futile attempts at clawing against the stucco walls soon after Catherine had stepped out of sight. The minutes grew into mind-numbing hours as she nervously paced on the roof, waiting for a sign from her comrades that they were ready to return. She could feel her fair skin starting to burn under the intense afternoon sun and despite the warmth, she wrapped her pale green sweater around herself to block out the rays. A flash of light off to her right caught her attention and she jogged over to get a better look at the source. Inside the Jos A. Bank across the street, she saw the flash again, and hoped to God that it was Desmond and the rest of the group.

She put up a hand and signaled to whomever was in the store that she was ready. Catherine quickly returned to the music set-up, yelling the whole way, trying to cause as much a commotion as she could, drawing the attention of the dead once again. She hastily turned everything back on and hit play, and the crowd formed once more below her corner. The dead hands in the air, the screams, and the gut wrenching smells reminded Catherine of a concert at which she was the main event. She broke her stare away from the empty, deformed faces glaring up at her and scanned the rest of the surrounding lots. There were a few stragglers scattered about here and there, slowly but surely making their way over to see what the fuss was about, but they would simply have to be dealt with accordingly.

Catherine almost lost her footing on the way down the ladder. Her heart pounded as she regained her composure running for the fire exit door. She heard two back to back gunshots from outside and cursed herself as she fumbled with the key in her sweater pocket.

She threw the door open and was face to face with Michelle who shoved her out of the way. Lulu came crashing through the door, arms lined with overflowing shopping bags. Outside, Desmond shoved an overstuffed, red shopping cart in the direction of the door and turned around to thrust his leg forward at an attacking eater. His boot met the thing's chest with a crack and it flew backward, growling and hissing as it hit the ground. Francis slammed the dead thing back to the ground as it tried to recover from Desmond's kick and put a round in its head.

Michelle grabbed the shopping cart as it rolled toward her and guided it through the door. "Come on! Our cover's blown!" she hollered to the two men outside. The eaters seemed to no longer be drawn to the music with the smell of perspiring flesh so close by. Francis came flying through the door, bulging back packs on both shoulders, followed by Desmond, just in time for Michelle to slam the fire door safely back into place.

They all collapsed to the ground, panting heavily, unfazed by the sound of pounding fists and blood curdling screams. Desmond kissed his wife hard as she kneeled before him, checking him for bites.

"We're safe babe," he said, wiping tears of joy from Catherine's eyes. "Go kill the music, we're safe."

Catherine nodded and returned to the roof. The remaining four survivors on the floor caught their breath and looked at each other. Francis was the first to break the silence as he slapped one of his overstuffed backpacks and let out a cry of joy. They fell into a fit of hysterical laughter, completely taken aback by how well Desmond's plan had worked. They marveled at the bounty they brought back with them, all in the face of death beyond their building's safe walls.

Michelle fished the red digital camera she grabbed at Target from her back pocket and it made a soft chirp as she turned it on. "Say cheese!" She snapped a photo of her three companions and they all erupted in laughter once more. "Told you this thing would come in handy." She went back through the photos she'd snapped through the windows of Jos A Bank. "Catherine's pretty photogenic."

"That she is." Desmond laughed as he agreed.

"Great work out there. I mean it." Michelle looked from smiling face to smiling face. She didn't ever think they'd be all sitting around sharing a laugh like this in a million years, but here they were, having every right to celebrate their small victory. "I don't know about y'all, but I'm ready to see what we got!" Her excitement brought another round of hoots and hollers out of everyone; the dead wailing from beyond the fire door had nothing on their cries of triumph.

The group took their belongings to the back of the jewelry store and began sorting through everything. Cans upon cans of food, mountains of clothing, pounds of dried goods, a plethora of batteries and other gadgets, and all the bottles and jugs of water they would need for the next few weeks until they made another run. When Catherine joined them from the roof they started taking their stockpiles to the different locations where they would be stored within the building.

Lulu was excited to start up the "Paint Party," now that they had enough spray paint to finish covering up the remaining windows. Michelle went to work touching up her hair in the salon, now that they had more water she didn't see a problem with using one of the sinks for her own benefit.

Francis went up to the roof to relax and watch the sunset while the others busied themselves in their own interests. He lugged the rolling computer chair up the ladder behind him and made himself comfortable. He pulled a half smoked cigar from the front pocket of his stained white uniform. Puffs of smoke escaped him as he lit the strong-smelling Ashton, savoring the bold flavor and closing his eyes. He couldn't help but think of the current state they were in. The scavenging, the unimaginable amount of death surrounding them all. Here they were, five adults, locked inside of a building as the world they once knew had just suddenly come to an end. Yet they all seemed okay with it.

"Why?" he found himself asking aloud. He opened his eyes, aware that he'd brought himself out of his quality time on the roof. He answered himself back, "We're okay with it because we're alive."

If this is what you call living, the heavyset man thought as he slowly exhaled, making Os in the smoke.

Shots rang out from the main road to the north, startling Francis and making him choke. He coughed hard and jumped up, knocking the black desk chair over behind him. He stumbled, still coughing, over to the ledge to get a better look. A huge Dodge Ram, raised with a lift kit, was barreling down the highway, weaving in and out of abandoned cars. Six people were in the truck bed, shooting at the dead as they passed.

"Holy shit." Francis bounded over to the roof hatch and threw himself on his belly, he stuck his head down into the hole and called out, "Y'all get up here! Now!"

He returned to the ledge and watched as two extremely fast eaters ran into the truck's path. The driver plowed into one of them but the second leapt onto the hood, howling and punching the windshield.

"What the hell's going on?" Michelle jogged up behind Francis, her hair in foils atop her head. Lulu, Desmond, and Catherine followed closely behind her.

Francis pointed out at the swerving truck, the driver attempting to get the eater off his windshield. One of the passengers, a man, let out a cry as he was thrown from the truck bed. The cluster of eaters in pursuit were soon upon him, ripping him apart, feasting on him. One of the women in the truck screamed out, another woman struggled with her as she tried to jump from the moving vehicle.

"Oh my God! We have to do something!" Lulu's eyes were wet with tears, her hands covered her mouth as she watched the scene unfold.

"We can't, Lu." Michelle shook her head and winced as the driver finally lost control of the enormous redneck truck and flipped it. The eater on the windshield went flying off into the ditch on the side of the road. A man in the truck bed was able to escape the vehicle as it rolled, but the remaining passengers were crushed.

The survivors on the roof looked on in awe; even from their distance they were able to see blood as it splattered in all directions and limbs as they were torn from the passengers' bodies. The eaters nearest to the wrecked vehicle were upon it in no time, like vultures on road kill. They picked apart the remains, squawking and screeching. The dead seemed to almost fight with one another over the best parts.

The man who had jumped from the tumbling Dodge had clearly suffered an injury to his left leg. He attempted to shoot at the eaters who were quickly gaining on him but kept falling to his knees, missing shots he probably would have hit dead-on if he'd been in better condition. The eaters had fenced him in; with nowhere to go and realizing this was it for him, the last remaining survivor from the Dodge Ram with the lift kit raised his gun to his head and blew his brains out.

That final shot cracked through the air and Lulu felt as if it had gone straight through her heart. Desmond caught her as her legs turned to jelly. She collapsed in his arms, mumbling incomprehensibly. "Lulu? Lulu, can you hear me?" He laid her down flat on the roof and she stared up blankly at the sky. "Lulu, it's very important you answer me, okay?"

"I- I can't breathe," she stammered, gasping for air. "We...let them die."

Catherine dropped down beside her, shooing her husband away, "She's fine, Des." Catherine pulled Lulu up and draped her sweater over her shoulders. "Lulu, look at me, sweetie, look at me, you're having a panic attack. I need you to look at me and take big, deep breaths." Lulu's dark eyes finally focused on Catherine's. Catherine squeezed Lulu's shoulders, "There was nothing we could do, honey. Nothing."

Lulu broke down into hysterical sobbing.

"Get her inside, now! Before she draws those things back over here!" Michelle barked at Catherine. Her blood boiled.

Just when I thought Lulu was finally getting it together, she has another breakdown.

She pulled the foils from her hair and threw them over the ledge, the breeze carrying them off. The sun was barely in the sky and she watched as things that were once people fed on the recently deceased. Their small victory from this afternoon was nothing but a distraction from the hell they were living in. She stared at the wrecked truck for a moment more before turning to Francis. She studied him, how he kept looking from the wreck to the hatch and back to the wreck again. He began to walk toward the roof's exit but she stopped him. "That gun you have, was it yours?"

"What?" He spun around and faced her. The question didn't register right away. "Oh, yeah. Yeah, that's mine. Why?"

"You got any more?"

"Nah. Not here." He scratched his scalp through his shortly cropped hair, looking down at his feet. "Sounds stupid, but, I didn't think this thing, whatever it is, was gonna be so serious. Only brought the one with me."

She slowly nodded and waved him away, remaining on the roof by herself, the lone member in the audience of a horrific production. She stayed there until she could no longer make out the feasting figures in the dark. Once they got their hands on you, one of two things happened: you join them, unless you were fortunate enough to have someone put a bullet in your head...or you were nothing, ever again, but an unrecognizable corpse that nobody ever gave another thought to. Michelle promised herself she would never succumb to either fate, that no matter what, she came first. She felt a small flutter in her stomach as she realized she liked very much the thought of a world that revolved around her.

X

A few short weeks passed before Michelle woke up one morning and couldn't take the cabin fever anymore. The power had gone out, the water stopped running, they'd done all they could to fortify the building. All the windows had been painted with a double coat of multicolored spray paint, and the front doors to all the stores were reinforced with bike locks. One way in, one way out. Desmond and Francis had been on another run, pretty much emptying Target's pharmacy and anything else useful in the store. The group even made their own weapons.

Lulu went through intense therapy sessions with Catherine, who they all found out had a strong background in psychiatry before she moved on to internal medicine. Michelle spent the majority of her time alone, either in the deluxe spa room or on the roof, soaking in the apocalypse.

Since the Dodge Ram incident, Michelle stood by idly as she watched more clusters of other survivors meet their demise. She never alerted the others, wanting the catastrophe all to herself. She studied their actions, where they went wrong, and learned from it all. She found herself silently cursing the few groups that managed to make it past Emerald Park unscathed.

The ones that dare venture into Emerald Park, though, those were her favorite. This was not their shopping center, they had no right to be here. She'd made sure Francis locked every door to every store in their vicinity on his last run. She watched with excitement as people ran frantically from shop to shop, trying to find a way in, certain death snapping at their heels. A few times (though she'd never admit it to anyone if they asked) she even aided the eaters, throwing handfuls of small rocks from the roof in the direction of the panicked stragglers.

The particular morning that Michelle decided she needed more, was an absolutely beautiful day. She brushed her teeth and washed her face before exiting the salon to find the others. They chatted loudly in the vitamin shop, they'd taken to eating meals there since the café was reduced to a bathroom.

"Hey!" Lulu cheerfully greeted Michelle and tossed her an unopened pack of Pop Tarts. Michelle nodded her thanks and grabbed a bottle of water from a shelf.

"What's up, Michelle? How'd you sleep?" Francis sloppily chomped on a bowl of cereal and water. It made her stomach turn.

"Oh, it was great, just like The Ritz Carlton. Amazing." She smirked as she spoke, her words dripping with sarcasm.

They had a good laugh and continued breakfast, Desmond helping his wife clean up afterward. Michelle sat quietly, waiting for Lulu to retreat to one of the other stores to do her morning workout routine before she brought up the subject of leaving again.

"I thought we decided on that last run so we didn't have to go out again so soon," Francis said.

"Yes. We did. But I've been doing a lot of thinking." She leaned forward in the desk chair she sat on. "Trust me, a lot of thinking."

"And?"

"And it's inevitable. We have to go back out. There's that gun shop you were telling me about that's not too far from here. We need weapons."

"We have weapons, Michelle. Why put ourselves at risk for guns?" Catherine crossed her arms over her chest.

"Are you serious right now?" She looked at Desmond. "Come on, help me out here. Fatty's out of bullets and this whole thing is fucked if someone were to try to take it from us."

"Hey, enough with the fat shit," Francis snapped at her.

Michelle put a hand up and made a face.

"Michelle has a point." Desmond looked at his wife and then at Francis, who was visibly angry. "We haven't been thinking about other people. Real people, who are living and breathing. Actually dangerous. All this would be for nothing if we ran into a bunch of bad apples. Let the wrong one in, ya know?"

Michelle looked pleased, nodding at him in approval.

Catherine uncrossed her arms and rubbed her sweating palms on her pants. "Well, once you get the gears rolling, there's no stopping you." She planted a sweet kiss on her husband's cheek. "I'm not going. I'm assuming there's a reason Lulu isn't here for this conversation, so I'll hang back here with her."

Michelle and Desmond looked at Francis expectantly. He exhaled loudly and shrugged.

"Come on," Michelle encouraged him. "Lighten up, Francis."

"What am I gonna say, no? We'll take my truck. It's full of gas."

Michelle jumped up and clapped him on the back. "Yes!"

The three of them were prepared for the quick trip in no time. Catherine went to her usual spot on the roof to ready a distraction. The group downstairs heard the music begin to blare and Lulu reluctantly inched the door open, peeking outside.

Michelle gently pushed her aside and shot her a look. "Don't be bitter about this."

Lulu said nothing in response as Michelle exited the building, followed by Desmond. Francis gave her a quick hug and a planted a tender kiss on her cheek before he left. It managed to make her smile despite the situation, and she quietly pulled the door closed.

The trio snaked around the back of the building and reached the corner beside the vitamin store. Francis pointed out his truck parked across the street, a mere fifteen feet from where Michelle's car had gone crashing through the storefronts. They sprinted for the truck, footsteps echoing painfully all around them. They had only seconds to make it. For once, Michelle had trusted Francis. Even though he was overweight by about a good forty pounds, the guy could run when he needed to. He was the first to make it to the truck and it made a chirping sound as he unlocked the four-door cab. Michelle and Desmond made it in just as the dead grew dangerously close.

Francis turned the key in the ignition and it clicked in response. "Come on, beautiful," Francis spoke gently to his Chevy, turning the key once more. The engine roared to life and he threw the truck in reverse, slamming into an eater approaching from behind.

Francis felt his back left tire roll over the body and gave it no extra thought. They hit six more eaters as they exited Emerald Park at an alarming speed. Michelle's heart was racing, adrenaline searing through her body. She turned around in the backseat and watched the eaters fade in the distance as Francis drove west in the eastbound lane. She cried out enthusiastically, grabbing both men in the front seat by their shoulders. They grinned, excited by her intensity.

The seven miles to the gun shop were talkative ones. Francis was obviously educated on his firearms and yammered incessantly. Michelle listened in and out, distracted by the outside world. Desmond joined the conversation, reminiscing about hunting trips. Francis pulled off the main road and took them down a deserted side street.

"Back roads are the best," he said casually. He turned the black Chevy again and bounced down a dirt road, finally coming to a stop amidst the underbrush and tall pines. "We'll leave the truck here. Seems like we didn't attract any attention, so we'll keep it that way." Francis nodded at the windshield, "We're on the road behind the old strip mall. It ain't even a quarter mile from here."

Desmond nodded and gathered his bags from the floorboards. "Good thinking, man."

Michelle silently agreed.

They made their way up the dirt road, not hastily, but it wasn't a stroll in the park either. Francis couldn't help but keep thinking what a nice day it was. The temperature was perfect for this time of year. It was so quiet, quieter than he'd ever heard it. He could hear the emerald Gulf waves slapping the shore from where he was walking. He smiled to himself, even under their circumstances. He imagined being able to walk on those beaches safely again one day; toes digging into the soft white sand, listening to the gentle tide roll in and toasting a glass of champagne to the sunset. To everyone else, Francis was a dumb hillbilly, but on the inside, he liked to pride himself on being hopelessly in love with nature.

The tiny strip mall housed a gun shop, a deli, and a liquor store. They approached the rear of the small building and scanned the area. Not a soul, dead or alive, to be seen. "How are we going to get in?" Michelle asked in a hushed voice. "These are all fire doors, same as at Emerald Park."

"Not quite. Look a little closer." Francis pointed.

Michelle could see the surface-mounted deadbolt from where they were crouched.

"Who the hell wants to break into a gun store in the south? They'd be stupid as hell to try, I tell you what," Francis snickered as he and Desmond went to work breaking the lock off the door. Michelle wandered off around the side of the building, keeping her wits about her, making sure there was never anything lurking nearby. She tried her luck on the first door of the liquor store. She chuckled as the door opened toward her. She ignored the middle storefront, having no use for the deli. She gave a slight tug on the gun shop's door and stepped inside. The place had definitely been torn apart, which was a disappointment, but there was definitely plenty left to go around.

She smelled nor heard any signs of the dead in the store and quickly ran to the back door before Francis and Desmond made any more noise and got themselves killed. She startled the two men when she unlocked the deadbolt and pushed the door out. They both shook their heads and followed her in.

"I'm gonna check out the liquor store boys. Any requests?"

"Tequila!" Desmond called out, buried in some box.

"I'm good," Francis hollered.

Michelle headed to the liquor store, a bounce in her step, almost skipping. As she pulled the door open, she paused and looked back at the center shop, the deli. She listened intently…she had sworn she heard the clicking of a lock. After a minute of no surprises, she shrugged it off and stepped inside.

To her dismay the liquor store had been trashed. Broken bottles of alcohol lie strewn about and glass crunched underfoot as she stepped into the darkness. A few remaining bottles were left on their shelves and she stuffed them into her backpack, not caring what they were.

Michelle worked her way through the narrow aisles. She stopped at the front register and grabbed a pack of cigarettes, pulling one out and lighting it up. She coughed and laughed at herself; she had been trying so hard, even in the apocalypse, to not smoke.

She heard the click first, immediately followed by the hard barrel of a gun pressed against the back of her head. Her heart skipped a beat and she froze, the cigarette falling from her lips to the filthy floor. Her hands flew up on either side of her in surrender. She felt the gun come off her and heard a man instruct her to turn around.

Very slowly, she did as she was told, all the while forcing crocodile tears from her eyes. She locked eyes with the man. He was filthy and she was surprised she hadn't smelled him. He wore camouflage hunting apparel with a red bandana tied around his right bicep.

"Please, I mean you no harm," she told him, her voice shaking.

"What are you doing here?" the man asked her, his gun still trained on her face.

"I'm thirsty, and I'm hungry," she lied.

"You alone?" He glanced quickly out the storefront windows to the right of him.

"Yes." A single tear rolled down her cheek. "Please, I'm scared, and alone. I got separated from my group." She allowed a forced sob to escape her lips. "Please don't do this to me."

It felt like an eternity before the man spoke again, his face remaining expressionless until he finally dropped the gun and set it down on the small counter that separated him from Michelle.

He took a deep breath and scratched at his dirty hair with even dirtier fingernails. "Mind if I have one of those?" He eyed the cigarettes and she kindly smiled at him, offering him one. He took it from her. "Do you have any supplies with you?" She shook her head. He rolled the cigarette around between his fingers. "I tell you what, I got a small camp just north of here. There aren't many of us, we don't have much. But I'm not gonna just leave you here."

Michelle feigned happiness and wiped the fake tears from her face. "Oh, thank God, thank you so much. Did you come here by yourself? To find others? Like me?"

He picked up the lighter from the counter and nodded his head. "Not exactly to find others, but we pick up who we can along the way. You know how to use a gun?" He placed the cigarette in his mouth and sparked the lighter, bowing his head for a split second to touch it to the flame.

Michelle scooped the gun up from the counter and pointed it at the man. Shocked, it was his turn to drop the cigarette from his lips. Without a further wasted second, without another thought in her mind, she pulled the trigger and shot the stranger in the center of his forehead. In a spray of blood and brains, the man dropped to the floor with a thud. Michelle put the gun back down on the counter and pulled out another cigarette. She rounded the counter and pulled the lighter out of his dead hand. She stared into his wide-open, lifeless eyes.

"Of course I know how to use a gun."

XI

Michelle savored the cigarette smoke, holding it in and exhaling slowly through her nose. She gazed down at the corpse of the stranger she'd just shot in the head, fascinated with the way his body had crumpled to the dingy floor of the liquor store, marveling at the deep crimson pool of blood as it slowly formed around his head. She stared deeply into his cold, empty eyes. Michelle had never killed another human being, but her skin was covered in gooseflesh and the tiny hairs on the back of her neck stood straight up; every part of her body was white hot with it. The corners of her mouth began to twitch and she fought the urge to smile out of simple respect for the situation.

Desmond had watched the events unfold through the dirty window of the storefront. He initially had a weapon drawn, ready to spring inside at any moment, fearing for Michelle's life. His jaw hung open as he watched her smoke and stare. There had been no motive, there had been no rhyme or reason for her actions. Desmond had heard everything. Michelle baited the stranger and then took his life.

Michelle suddenly felt eyes on her and turned to the window. She glared at Desmond and flicked the cigarette at him. The butt bounced off the glass and dropped to the floor. She crossed her arms over her chest and locked eyes with him. "Well? Are you going to come in?"

Desmond hesitated, unsure of what to do. She continued to stare at him, her eyes full of disdain. He reluctantly pulled the door open and stepped inside the musty store; the smell of copper and gunpowder in the air. He opened his mouth to speak but no words came out.

She hopped up and had herself a seat on the counter, lighting up another cigarette and cocking her head at him, as if trying to read his mind.

"Why did you do this?" Desmond finally found his words.

Michelle gently shrugged. "He could have followed us, stolen from us, killed us. Any number of things."

Desmond's face flushed. "You know that's bullshit. You didn't have to kill him!"

She took a long drag off of her cigarette. "Are we going to have a problem?"

Before Desmond could answer, Francis burst through the double doors, a rifle in hand. "Holy hell." He eyed the body of the man on the floor. "Jesus Christ, what happened?" He looked back and forth between Desmond and Michelle, who just stared at one another. "Hey! I asked y'all what in the hell happened here?" Francis loosened his grip on the rifle and knelt down beside the dead body. "He sure as hell don't look like one of them dead things. Will one of you please tell me what the fuck just went down?" His agitation showed in his deep southern drawl and finally Michelle lowered herself down from the counter and dropped her cigarette, putting it out with her shoe.

"He tried to rob me. Problem solved." She looked Francis in the eye as she lied, speaking calmly.

Francis wiped the sweat from his brow and sighed, "Well damn, are you alright?"

"I said, problem solved." She grabbed her bag and placed it on her back. "Are we good here? I'd like to grab our loot from the gun shop and head back." Her attention was fully focused on Desmond now.

"What do we do about him?" Francis pointed down at the body.

"Leave him. Let's get out of here, in case there are more of them."

Francis nodded in reply and started out the door. She grabbed the stranger's gun off the countertop and walked toward Desmond. He tightened his hand around his own gun and swallowed hard. "You never answered my question." She stopped in front of him, close enough to feel his breath on her face. "Are we going to have a problem?"

The thick tension in the room was cut by Francis tapping at the glass. "We got company!" he called in to them. Michelle craned her neck and spotted two badly maimed eaters stumbling through the brush across the street toward the strip mall.

Desmond avoided her question. He pushed past Michelle and stormed out the door. She watched as he walked right up to the first of the eaters, placed the barrel of his gun directly against its head and pulled the trigger. The second eater wobbled over to him, a low growl escaping its blood-caked lips. Desmond reared his arm back and pistol-whipped it in the face. The eater tumbled to the ground and screeched at him. Desmond hit it again and again, black fluids spraying his clothing, bits of flesh flying from the dead thing's face. He beat the eater to a pulp; he beat the eater until it no longer groaned or moaned or made a single move. Francis looked on, horrified that Desmond would put himself so close to one of the undead like that.

"Ah, testosterone," Michelle chuckled, joining Francis on the sidewalk.

Desmond stomped off toward the gun shop to gather the rest of their things. He called to Francis, "I'll meet you back at the truck."

Francis scratched his head, confused by the situation at hand, bewildered by Desmond's behavior. "You sure, man?"

Desmond ignored him and disappeared inside the store.

"He's sure." Michelle cocked her head in the direction of the truck. "Let's go big guy. I'm driving this time."

"Nobody drives my truck but me," Francis protested as he followed her back around the building.

"I said I'm driving!" she snapped back at him and stopped short, hand outstretched and open, waiting for the keys.

Francis's confusion mounted, he fished the keys from his pocket and shoved them into her hand. "Whatever, man."

The two of them sat silently in the idling truck. Michelle didn't like that Desmond was taking his sweet time. She chain smoked in the driver's seat, much to Francis's dismay. He decided against arguing with her, he didn't understand her or Desmond's recent change in attitude. Michelle had always been a royal bitch to him, but something was different about the way she suddenly seemed to carry herself. He chalked it up to the fact that she could be pretty shaken up by the attempted robbery and kept to himself in the passenger seat.

Desmond finally appeared on the road. Michelle tossed the cigarette out the window and gave Francis a push on the shoulder. "Get in the back," she ordered.

"What the hell for?"

"Just get in the back!" She pushed him again, much harder this time.

Francis threw the car door open, "You've got a serious fuckin' attitude problem."

He waited on Desmond and took the overstuffed black duffle bag from him, tossing it into the bed of the truck before climbing in the backseat.

Michelle stroked the gun in her lap, nervously biting the insides of her cheeks as Desmond took a seat beside her in the front. He still hadn't said anything directly to her; he avoided eye contact as he buckled himself in and instructed her to drive. She made a U-turn and proceeded back toward Emerald Park. The silence in the car was awkward, deafening.

Michelle's mind raced with a million possibilities of how the scenario would play out back at the shopping center. A furious knot began to form in her stomach and she felt herself growing angrier with each passing second of silence. She kept glancing over at Desmond, hoping to see some sort of sign in his face, hoping to catch his eye and get a reassuring nod that their little secret would remain so. Francis remained oblivious as he stared out the window in the backseat.

"Desmond—" she began.

"You killed a man in cold blood. I have nothing to say to you."

Michelle slammed both feet down on the brakes. The tires screeched and the truck came to an abrupt stop. Francis yelped as he was thrown forward, hitting his head on the back of the seat before him. He rubbed his head and second guessed the words he'd heard come out of Desmond's mouth.

Michelle clenched her left hand on the steering wheel, grinding her teeth. "Let me ask you a question." She turned her head toward Desmond, his face still full of surprise from the sudden halt on the abandoned highway. "Who's the better doctor? You? Or your wife?" Her nostrils flared as she awaited his answer.

"What?" Desmond's hands began to tremble as he unbuckled his seat belt. He didn't like the way she was looking at him, he needed to get out of the truck.

Michelle raised her voice as she repeated the question, screaming at him now. "Who is the better doctor? You?! Or your wife?!"

Desmond slammed his hand down on the dashboard, not ready to accept what he knew Michelle would do next. "My wife!" He screamed back at her, slamming his hand once more down onto the dash.

"Good." Michelle snatched the gun from her lap and shot Desmond through the temple. Blood, hair, and bits of brain exploded onto the window on the other side of his head. The sound of the gunfire smashed through the silence of the car, pounding through both Francis and Michelle's ears. Francis screamed in the backseat while Michelle sat and watched pieces of Desmond roll sloppily down what was left of the passenger side window. She turned and pointed the gun at Francis only when he attempted to get out of the vehicle. "Sit the fuck down!"

Francis was crying now. He flung the door open and foolishly grabbed for the rifle on the floor of the backseat. Michelle quickly put a bullet in his neck and another in his face. Francis slumped forward, half in the truck, half out. Michelle's chest heaved as she threw the gun at Francis' dead body.

"You stupid asshole!" she screamed at his lifeless corpse. "You just had to sit back down." She lowered her head, disappointed, but not surprised by the security guard's inability to follow directions.

She jumped out of the truck and hurried to the other side, dragging Francis's heavy frame out of the vehicle. She opened the door to pull Desmond out, but his body fell to the pavement on its own. She stared quietly for moment at the two bodies, not a racing thought in her mind, but simply peace.

Michelle climbed back into the driver's seat and buckled herself in. She put the car in drive and continued on her way back to Emerald Park. She glanced in the rearview mirror only once.

XII

Lulu and Catherine watched from the roof of their building as Francis's black truck sped out of Emerald Park. They stood staring for a few moments before Lulu began suggesting some activities to pass the day while they waited for the safe return of their friends. The two women grabbed a small table from the festering depths of the café-turned-bathroom and lugged it up to the rooftop. It was too beautiful of a day to spend trapped inside the building, hiding like scared animals; they were perfectly safe up on the roof.

"Bust!" Catherine shouted in glee, throwing both arms up in the air and raising the roof. "The house always wins!"

Lulu smacked her cards down onto the table. "Really? That's like ten in a row." She sighed and crossed her arms over her small chest. "I'm over this game. No more cards; evidently I am terrible at everything."

Catherine chuckled. "Nah, just poker and blackjack." She sipped from a warm bottle of water. "It's just a learning process, we've got all the time in the world."

"Yeah, I guess." Lulu sat back in the uncomfortable black desk chair and squinted through her sunglasses up at the cloudless sky. "What a gorgeous beach day."

"Oh please," Catherine said, putting a hand up, "I'm surprised I haven't already turned into a lobster." She checked her watch. "In fact, I think it's about time I put more sunscreen on." She got up and rifled through the small bag under the table, searching for her sunblock.

"You just put some on before we came up here."

Catherine peered over the table at her, "I know I did, and that was over two hours ago. I think I must have left it downstairs. I'll be right back."

"Two hours playing cards?" Lulu called after her. "What a waste! We're doing something else next!"

Catherine smiled and headed down the hatch.

With the sudden *nothing* to preoccupy her, the ambient sounds of the dead infiltrated Lulu's consciousness and the familiar smell of rot and ruin tiptoed its way back to the attention of her senses. She crinkled her nose and stood, giving her small frame a nice, long, well-needed stretch. She rubbed the palms of her hands over her butt and laughed at herself, she couldn't remember the last time her ass had fallen asleep. She made her way over to the south end of the building, curious to see what had the eaters so riled up today. They were making much more noise than usual.

"I swear if I see a poor dog down there I'm just gonna lose it," she mumbled to herself as she strolled over to the ledge.

Lulu's hand went up to her mouth and her eyes widened. Out of habit, she ducked down and cautiously surveyed the lot across from her. "My God."

There were people scattered around the parking lot, running for their lives.

She scrambled on her hands and knees to the hatch. "Catherine!" she called out for her comrade in a hushed voice. Lulu heard yelling now, frantic, but couldn't quite tell what was going on or make out what they were saying. "Goddamnit, Catherine!" she shouted down the hatch, hoping desperately none of the strangers in the parking lot could hear her.

"What's the matter?" Catherine appeared at the base of the ladder.

"People!" Lulu quickly crawled back over to the ledge, satisfied that Catherine had already started back up.

"No way." Catherine shook her head at the sight waiting for her below. "How did they know we left the gate for the carts open?" The women watched as the strangers piled into the vestibule of the Target department store across from them. Carts were taken from the opening between the vestibule and the store and piled up strategically in the exterior doorway to block out the eaters.

"I don't think they knew." Gunshots rang out as the survivors defended themselves against the onslaught of the dead. Lulu straightened. "Jesus Christ, we have to help them." The eaters were beginning to close in around the entryway and a man just stood there. "He's going to get himself killed! Catherine!" She grabbed her friend by the shoulders, pleading. "Please, we have to help!"

Catherine's face remained blank as she continued to watch on. "He's doing it on purpose."

The screams of agony that emanated from the man's sacrifice tore through the air and ripped Lulu's heart to shreds.

Catherine turned to her, "You're right, we need to do something." Catherine pulled the building key from her pocket. "Francis's key ring is downstairs. You take this and you lock me out, I can't let those people die."

Tears welled up in Catherine's eyes as she thought back to the beginning of all this mayhem, all this loss from a world torn apart. Her mind drifted back to abandoned patients back at the hospital, of how she'd panicked and found no other choice but to escape the crowded and maddening halls of Haven Coastal Medical Center. She had never put her own life before that of a patient's, but she was one of the only remaining doctors left on staff that day. She would never abandon the memory of the people in agony who she passed by in order to reach the safety of her husband's arms.

Her colleagues had begged and pleaded with her to leave with them in the beginning, attempting to convince her of the futility of trying to aid these disease-ridden people. She didn't want to believe them, and she couldn't understand how they jumped ship like that.

She would never forget the patient that died in her arms that day. The pale young man, trembling and bleeding to death. She'd never forget the way he gazed up at her and thanked her for being there with him so he wouldn't have to die alone.

She would never forget how his pupils dilated and how the light in his eyes went out.

How those eyes glazed over.

How he woke from the dead and tried to rip out her throat.

"Catherine, please, we can go together. Let's go together." Lulu stood up, shaking her head. The screaming had stopped across the lot. Lulu's stomach fluttered at the sudden silence.

"No. You need to stay here. Not just for me, but if Desmond comes back before I do."

Catherine stood and started for the hatch. She was a doctor; it was her job to save lives, and she would redeem herself on this day. She gathered a small bag from the jewelry store and stuffed necessary items inside, speeding to the exit. "Lock me out. Let's go, hurry."

Lulu was hesitant to unlock the door. She stared at the key, more nervous than she had been in weeks.

Catherine clutched Francis's key ring in one hand and a makeshift hatchet in the other. The two women hugged one another tightly. "No music, the dead are distracted enough. You'll know when I need to get back. Be on the lookout, don't leave the roof until it's time."

Lulu swallowed the lump in her throat. "Alright. What do I do if Michelle and everyone gets back first?"

"Then that means I'll have more help, if I need it. You've got this. I know you do." She nodded at Lulu, her bright eyes full of determination.

Lulu double-checked the small medicine bag strapped to Catherine through eyes blurred with tears. Catherine held up her makeshift weapon and nodded reassuringly.

"Okay." Lulu counted to three and exhaled with a grunt, shoving open the door, relieved to see no stragglers in their neck of the woods. Catherine bolted out the door and was gone.

In a flash, Lulu had the door locked and was back up on the roof, frantically scanning the parking lot. She finally spotted the doctor at the side entrance to the building directly across from her. She breathed a sigh of relief as Catherine disappeared inside the dark confines of the store. Her pulse began to slow and she grabbed one of the black office chairs. Her previous thoughts on the beautiful day soon transformed into how humid and overwhelmingly hot it had become. There was nothing left to do but fight the mounting anxiety and await the return of her fellow survivors.

PART III

THIS PLACE IS DEATH

I

Veronica, Ben, Andrew, Gary, and Catherine bolted from the clothing store as the dead, distracted by the music on the roof, cleared the area. As the group neared the rear of the building, the fire door cracked and Lulu's nervous eyes peeked out. When she spotted the running survivors, she threw it open the rest of the way and waved them in.

They piled inside and Lulu secured the door. She threw her arms around Catherine, "You did it!"

Catherine returned the embrace and nodded, smiling. "Yeah, they're alive." She took a deep breath, "Everyone, this is Lulu. She'll show you around while I patch up Veronica."

The group expressed their gratitude at being taken in and introductions went around. Catherine took Veronica by the arm and led her down the hall. Ben followed behind; he didn't want Veronica out of his sight.

"Have a seat anywhere you'd like, I'll be right in," Catherine told Veronica as they arrived at the vitamin shop. She turned to Ben, saying, "I know you're worried about her, but I know what I'm doing." She smiled at him, admiring his big-brother attitude and placed a hand on his arm. "No offense, but you'll only get in the way."

Ben sighed as Gary rounded the corner, joining him at the door.

"She'll be alright, mate. We'll wait here, I'll keep you company." Gary clapped him on the back as Catherine shut the door.

*

Veronica stared blankly ahead as Catherine sewed up her chin in the stock room of Vitamin World. Every once in a while she would wince, but Catherine had done a good job of making sure the area was comfortably numb. Veronica marveled at the set-up the doctor had here, as if the entire pharmaceuticals section had magically transported itself across the street. It was a Grade A stopgap walk-in clinic.

She wondered where Gary was, knowing he'd be jealous that it far surpassed his medical area back in the tower. But then again, Catherine was a doctor; Gary did what he could with what he had. She shrugged and Catherine smiled.

"What are you shrugging about?"

"Did I?" Veronica's voice was flat and congested, barely recognizable as her own. She couldn't tell what had made her face swell more; the crying or the splitting wound Catherine was patching up.

Catherine nodded. "You've been deep in thought, pretty girl."

Veronica liked Catherine's voice from the moment the woman spoke in the dark department store. It had a soothing effect to it.

"Do you want to talk about how this happened? Your friends inside said you fell. Sometimes it helps to talk about it." Catherine pulled her needle through flesh and stole a peek at Veronica's bloodshot eyes.

There is a stone cold woman inside there.

She tried to imagine the madness of the new world that had broken this girl, forcing her to grow far beyond her years.

"I made a stupid mistake." Veronica grimaced in pain again as she spoke. "I made a lot of stupid mistakes." She glanced down at Catherine, trying to gauge her response, but the doctor remained professional and courteous, eyes flicking back and forth between her work and Veronica's eyes.

"We've all made stupid mistakes. It's hard not to when you have to live like this." She gave a soft smile, urging Veronica to continue.

"I've been running track since I could remember. One of the first things I was taught was to never run like you're being chased, only run like you've got somewhere to go. That way, you don't ever need to look back. But I looked back, and I fell flat on my face. And Samson..." Her voice trailed off as she said his name. Her other mistake. "I lost my father and my brother when this all started."

"Me too. Or, at least, I have to assume I did. They live in Texas. My brother's an asshole and my father's in a wheelchair. I doubt either of them were lucky enough to get to safety. So I just pray to God that neither one of them ended up like those things out there. I try not to think about it. That's all I can do." Catherine's expression was solemn.

Veronica thought about how it would be nice to not know what had happened to her father and brother. In fact, she found it downright enviable compared to being cursed with the memories of killing her undead father and putting a bullet in Isaac's skull.

She kept that to herself.

"I met a man named Samson and ended up pretending that he could be my new father. I know he saw me as a daughter. I didn't mind. I liked it, it made me feel better. And that was my second mistake."

Catherine finished up the stitching and began to clean up the excess blood. "What exactly was the second mistake?"

"Hope, I guess."

Catherine placed some gauze over her handy work and taped it up. "Twenty-seven stitches, my dear." She pulled her gloves off and threw them into the trash along with the rest of the blood-soaked items and used medical supplies. She pulled a chair up and sat down across from Veronica. "I want you to do something for me."

Veronica nodded.

"I want you to take everything that you just said and I want you to pretend you never said it. We are living in hell. A real-life nightmare. Something plucked from the sickest minds imaginable, except it is reality. There is nothing we can do to explain it. There is nothing we can do to change it. The only thing we do is stay alive."

"Why don't you listen to what you're saying then?" Veronica felt her face grow hot. "What's the point of doing any of this?"

"We're human because we hope. When you let hope die, that's when it's over for you. You'll belong to this dead world. You succumb to this nightmare. I have hope that I will wake up tomorrow, and I will look into my husband's eyes, I will hold his hand and I will be alive. When you have nothing else, you still have hope, and you can still give that to others."

Veronica didn't realize that she had begun to cry again until Catherine gently wrapped her arms around her shoulders.

"You are hope, Veronica. And I think your friend Samson saw that in you. Just don't let that hope die with him. Okay? You with me?" She pulled back and held Veronica's shoulders in her hands.

Veronica hesitated, hating to admit that Catherine was right. She just wanted to wallow in her misery, let it swallow her up and consume her…but then where would that leave everyone else? She wasn't alone.

She had Ben, who fought his way out of a dead city to find her. She had Andrew and Clyde, who saved Ben's life and were with him every step of the way. Juliette, who so desperately needed others. And Gary, the cheerful man who lost everything, except for his hope.

She finally answered Catherine. "Yes. Okay. I'm with you." The two smiled at one another. Through the blood and gore soaked exterior of the upside-down world, they were the smiling women in the stock room of a vitamin shop with renewed hope on their side.

"I'm going to give you something to sleep, okay? You need rest, desperately." Catherine gave Veronica a sedative cocktail and led her to the salon.

Ben and Gary had waited outside the back door of Vitamin World and fell in step close behind.

"Michelle, she's out on a run with my husband and Francis," Catherine said, turning to Veronica. "She normally sleeps back here, but I'm sure she wouldn't mind. It will give you some privacy and some much-needed rest." She opened the door to the private spa room Michelle had claimed as her own.

"When are the others coming back?" Gary asked.

"Soon. I'm sure of it. It'll be getting dark soon and Desmond wouldn't risk it," Catherine said, watching as Ben gave Veronica water to swallow the pills with.

"I'll be right outside this door," Ben told her, his hands on her shoulders. "If you need anything, I will be right there."

"I don't need anything but sleep." Veronica looked at Ben through drowsy eyes.

"Come on, Ben. She's alright." Catherine motioned for him to follow.

He exited the room and closed the door softly behind him.

"We should get up to the roof. Andrew and Lu will want to know how Veronica is. Come on."

Ben crossed his arms. "I told her I was stayin' right outside this door."

"With what I just gave her, she's probably already asleep. You'll be sitting here an awfully long time with nothing to do." She grinned. "Come on, I take good care of my patients."

He couldn't help but feel a little more at ease. He knew Veronica was safe and they'd all lucked out today. Ben smiled back at Catherine. She was a modest-looking woman, but there was a refined beauty about her that he admired.

"I heard what you said in there, to Veronica," Gary mentioned to the redheaded doctor as they walked side by side down the hall. "Thank you, it was lovely."

"It was just the truth." She patted the Brit on the back.

The sun had begun to slide down the western end of the sky, ready to end its workday. Twilight was fast approaching and the group of five waited patiently for the return of the others. Lulu had already shown Andrew how the music set-up worked as their distraction lifeline. She was full of excitement as she explained it to the others while they waited.

Gary heard the approach of a vehicle in the distance and Catherine spotted the black truck as it slowly approached the entrance to Emerald Park.

"Hey! Pigs!" Lulu shouted at the eaters. "Suck on some Adult Contemporary!" She pressed play on one of the cell phones and Andrew did the same with another. They giggled and the rest of them on the roof began to yell, quickly gaining the desired attention of the roaming eaters in the parking lot.

"Lu, you have the keys, get downstairs and get ready to let them in," Catherine instructed.

"I'll help." Gary followed after her and they dropped down into the building.

Francis's truck stopped at a safe distance and sat for a moment. Catherine narrowed her eyes at it; she couldn't see into the cab from this distance, but she felt it in her gut that something was awry.

The driver's side door snapped open and Michelle hopped out. She snuck around to the bed of the truck and hoisted a large bag onto her shoulders. Catherine's heart began to pound uncontrollably. "Where's Des?"

Ben furrowed his brow, picking up on the concern in Catherine's voice.

Michelle strategically advanced to the building, keeping herself hidden behind other vehicles. A few of the eaters began losing interest in the building and Michelle cursed under her breath, ducking behind a Ford Taurus.

"Who the fuck is that on the roof?" she grumbled, spotting the two men standing with Catherine. She checked the safety on both guns she carried and repositioned the overstuffed bag of firearms around her backpack. She was going to have to make a run for it.

Catherine's eyes filled with tears. "Where the fuck is my husband?!" she began to scream, leaning her body out over the ledge. "Where is Desmond?! Where is my fucking husband?!"

Andrew pulled her back from the ledge, squirming and screaming. The eaters who had previously lost interest were most definitely interested in the roof again. Their decrepit arms reaching up, rotten fingers clawing at the stucco.

Michelle saw this as her chance and bolted out from behind the sedan toward the back of the building. She cleared the group of eaters, but they howled as she flew by. She turned and began firing at them, completely missing and falling on her ass. She heard Lulu call out to her as the fire door opened. Michelle raised her weapon and pulled the trigger, the body of an undead elderly woman toppling over onto her.

She scrambled out from under the corpse and made it to the door, a complete stranger pulling her into the building, firing a round into the brain of the closest eater. Its skull shattered and it dropped.

Gary spit onto its lifeless body and slammed the door shut, Lulu locking it.

On the roof, Andrew could barely keep Catherine contained; she writhed and screamed in his oversized arms.

"Let her go!" Ben hollered over the music.

Andrew loosened his grip and she collapsed to the gravel, free to move, but lacking the desire to do so. She quietly moaned to herself. The tears subsided. She willed her body to go, to seek out Michelle and utter from her lips the question that burned a hole in her brain. But she knew it in her heart: her husband was gone.

II

Michelle shoved the heavy duffle bag forward with her foot and it rolled over on its side. She panted and pulled her thick curly hair from its ponytail, shaking it out and exhaling loudly.

"Michelle, where are Francis and Desmond?" Lulu's voice trembled, because she feared what Michelle was going to say. The blood on her best friend's clothing told the story.

"Who the fuck is this guy?" Michelle asked, pointing to Gary and ignoring Lulu. Her brows drew together, lower jaw jutting.

"I'm Gary," he introduced himself to the tall woman with the multicolored hair.

"What are you doing here?"

The two stared at one another, with Lulu standing off to the side, hugging her arms into her chest, her hands over her mouth. She held back the tears but her efforts failed once Catherine began down the ladder from the roof. The tears streamed down her face silently as she pushed herself past Michelle and Gary. She opened her arms to Catherine but the doctor moved her gently to the side.

"Catherine." Michelle turned to her, holstering one of her guns and opening her mouth to speak but it was shut for her as Catherine marched forward and grabbed Michelle by her shoulders, throwing her up against the wall. For a small woman, Catherine was strong, and Michelle knew she was in full aggression mode.

After all, she did return to safety without the woman's husband.

Neither woman spoke, Michelle could feel the heat of Catherine's breath on her face, her green eyes full of anguish.

"Catherine," Michelle spoke her name again. This time more sweetly, with a pain in her face, and a tear in her eye. "I'm sorry."

Catherine let go of Michelle and backed away. She looked Michelle up and down.

Whose blood is that? Is that Desmond's blood? What happened to Francis? How did you make it back by yourself? Why are you alive and why is my husband dead? What happened out there?

All these questions ran through Catherine's brain and yet she couldn't find the strength to bring them out of her mouth. Michelle's face showed Catherine what she wanted to see. A woman haunted by fresh loss.

But her posture...all wrong. It wasn't that of a defeated warrior; she had an inexplicable intensity in her stance, one that stunk of arrogance and sickened Catherine to her core. Michelle stepped forward and put a hand out toward her.

"I'm sorry, there wasn't anything I could do."

Catherine batted the hand away. "I need to be alone." She stormed off down the hall, silent as she waited for Ben and Andrew to clear the ladder.

"Jesus, how many more of you are there?" Michelle dropped her backpack to the floor, glass bottles lightly clinking together as it settled on its side. Gun still in hand, she awaited a response.

"Those two brutes would be Andrew and Ben," Gary said, his voice light and accent extra thick. "We've got one more, a girl, she was injured. She's asleep in the spa."

Michelle enjoyed the way Gary spoke to her. He was respectful that this was not his home, they were guests, and he didn't yet know if they were truly welcome.

"She wasn't bitten, I know that'll be your next question. We were pretty shit out of luck though. Your friend, the doctor, she helped us to safety and patched up Veronica. We owe her, big time."

"What are your intentions here?" Michelle asked, a hand on her hip.

"It was my idea to come. I wanted to further explore the area, gather as many supplies as we could. Perhaps find others, bring them back with us, to safety."

"You mean, you have some place else?" Lulu chimed in, suddenly interested. Andrew hadn't mentioned anything to her on the roof about where they'd come from.

"Indeed. A few kilometers from here, quite the place." Andrew shot Gary a look. He didn't want him to give up their location. His brother and girlfriend were there, and he didn't want any trouble for them. Gary winked at him.

"Well you sure picked the right place at the right time." Michelle finally holstered her other weapon, one now on each hip. "I'm sure we can work something out with the supplies. Looks like you're already nice and cozy. Michelle." She held out a hand and Gary returned the gesture.

She approached Ben and Andrew and did the same, exchanging names and handshakes. She allowed her hand to linger on Ben's for a moment as she sized him up before returning her attention to Gary.

"There was an unexpected turn of events today. I'm sure you can piece it together for yourselves." Her eyes wandered to Lulu. She could see the hurt in her friend's face. "I'm sorry about Francis, sweetie." She pulled her in and hugged her tightly, feigning grief. "If y'all don't mind, I'm gonna go ahead and get cleaned up. Then I'd suggest you take turns doing the same."

Michelle snatched her backpack up from the floor and grabbed the strap of the duffle bag, dragging it behind her and into the Luxe Salon.

Lulu scratched at her scalp. "I'm gonna go with Michelle. You three can hang out in one of the other stores for now. I'd leave Catherine be if I were you."

The three men nodded and filed into the cell phone store, shutting the door behind them.

*

Michelle lit candles and placed them around the washing sink. The thick coating of paint on the windows was a blessing and a curse; it kept them from being noticed by the eaters, but it also completely blocked out any natural light. Not that it would have mattered with nightfall upon them, but she found the roof was her favorite place. The stores in the building felt too much like prison cells. Michelle poured some water into the sink and began to undress.

"What happened out there today?" Lulu asked as she entered the salon.

"I don't think we should talk about it." Michelle kicked away her dirty clothes and began scrubbing at her skin. Between the candles and the bath soap, the salon smelled of delicate lavender. "One day. But not today."

"I understand." Lulu approached her friend and dipped her hands into the clean water, splashing them on her face. "Did they feel pain?"

"No," Michelle said flatly. She gave her friend a look that told her the conversation was over and finished cleaning up. She redressed and tiptoed to the back of the spa. Michelle put her ear up to the door of her private quarters and listened. She was satisfied that the girl inside wasn't awake and cracked the door open. A flashlight in the corner of the room was left on and pointed toward the ceiling, Michelle could barely make out the girl's form in the poorly-lit room. Soft snoring drifted to the door; she was definitely asleep.

"What do you think of these people?" Michelle whispered, turning to Lulu.

"I like them."

"You like everyone."

"I know, but, I mean it. They're good people and we finally helped somebody besides ourselves today. As shitty as it is out there, we're not alone anymore. We're not the only people left out there."

Michelle thought of the stranger in the liquor store from earlier that day. She wondered if anyone would go looking for him when he didn't return to his camp. She thought of Francis and Desmond, lifeless on the highway.

If anyone did go looking for the man in the liquor store, would they end up coming this far? Would they find Francis and Desmond, clearly not turned, with bullet holes in their heads?

"Michelle?" Lulu reached out and lightly brushed her face. "Are you alright?"

Michelle's hand shot up, grabbing Lulu's wrist as she was snapped from her thoughts. "I'm fine." She let go and shook her head. "Sorry."

She walked back toward the front of the salon and returned with both the duffle bag and the backpack. She placed them onto one of the massage tables and opened them.

"That's a lot of guns," Lulu said, reaching out for one of the weapons.

Michelle slapped at her hand. "No. You don't need one of these yet."

Lulu looked hurt.

"You need to learn how to handle one first. We keep this between you and I, we don't need our visitors to know what I brought back with me just yet. Got it?"

Lulu nodded. "What's in the other bag?"

Her question elicited a smile from Michelle. She proudly produced four bottles of top-shelf liquor from the backpack. "Only the best. Glad this was even left. The place was in pretty bad shape."

Lulu pointed at one of the bottles and Michelle grinned again.

"Yes, these are for sharing."

III

Ben, Andrew, and Gary sat around in some office chairs in the break room of the cell phone store. Gary spun around like a child, out of harm's way, finally feeling like his mission had been accomplished.

"What do you make of all this?" Andrew asked Ben.

"They've obviously been thriving. This place is set up well." Ben fiddled with the lantern on the desk as he spoke. "I think that, just like us, they've seen their share of bad luck. Especially today, for all of us. Seems like the shit's hit the fan."

"Don't I know it." Andrew rested his forehead on the top of the backrest of his chair.

Gary stopped spinning and planted his feet. "I've got to say, I'm sorry about Samson." They both looked up at him. "I didn't know him quite as well as you lot, but that doesn't mean I'm any less sorry for the loss."

"We didn't know him all that well, either," Ben replied. "Veronica got hit the hardest on this one. I think he was a good dude, though."

"I don't think it's about how long you've known someone anymore. I think we should all be glad to know anyone at all these days." Gary's perpetual positivity shone through, once again at the right moment.

There was a light knock at the back door and Lulu stepped into the break room. "The salon is free, if y'all are ready to get cleaned up."

"Thank you, love." Gary nodded at her. "How are your friends?"

"I don't know." She smoothed her black hair over the top of her head and adjusted her ponytail. "Um, we're going to eat some dinner. We'd like you to join us. So, whenever you're ready, just come find us in the jewelry store." She left the room.

"Alright, let's get to it," Ben was the first to rise, heading straight for the salon. He checked on Veronica to make sure she was still asleep and sat on the floor beside her makeshift bed while Andrew and Gary cleaned themselves up.

Andrew whistled from outside, and Ben quietly left the room. He scrubbed himself and reluctantly put his dirty clothes back on.

I am so tired of being covered in apocalyptic filth.

He couldn't wait to get back to the Emerald City and just stay put for once. He heard the door to the salon open and looked up. It was Michelle, who looked remarkably good for the day she'd reportedly had. She padded up to him in bare feet, and smelling of sweet flowers. She held something out to him.

"A little bird told me you were out."

He looked down and saw a pack of cigarettes in her hand.

"Go on, I've got more than enough for everyone here and then some." She appeared delighted when he accepted her offer and put them in his pocket. She watched him carefully as he pulled a gore-stained white t-shirt over his head. She said, "That used to be white, huh? We have extra clothes. You should probably change before we eat. I'll take you to our stash."

Her brilliant curls framed her face as she leaned on the sink and tilted her head at him. This woman was gorgeous, but Ben was unimpressed by her straightforward flirtation. He'd known plenty of easy chicks just like Michelle in his life; he wasn't the type of man that usually went for easy.

"I appreciate it." He forced a smile at her and put his hand out. "After you." She walked slowly toward the door, purposely swaying her hips. Her short white skirt barely left anything to the imagination and she wore a pale yellow halter top that complimented her warm skin tone.

Ben chuckled to himself and shook his head. *Way too easy,* he thought as he followed her out the door on a quest to find clean clothes.

Michelle had the capability of making even Ben feel slight discomfort. She watched him every second she could, making as much eye contact as possible and flashing her perfect white smile at him. Despite the day's events, she seemed completely recovered and ready to socialize.

Everyone had finally settled in to the dining area that the jewelry store's oversized vault had become and gorged themselves on food. The women of Emerald Park clearly had an abundance of it and were more than happy to share. Once Lulu had downed her first drink she began to smile more, less hesitant to speak, and she didn't seem so overshadowed by Michelle's bold personality. The two women created a certain chemistry when in each other's presence. It was suddenly easy for anyone on the outside looking in to see the charismatic bond that they shared.

Ben's mind kept wandering to Catherine, who remained alone on the roof. He tried to enjoy himself, but between Veronica sleeping alone and Catherine mourning above them, he found it hard to concentrate. The Patrón Gold wasn't helping either.

Andrew began to open up a little bit to the new female acquaintances, letting them know that he had a brother and a girlfriend back at their safe house. Gary babbled on drunkenly about how he knew he'd find other survivors, the importance of positive mental attitude, and learning to trust.

Ben could tell what he was doing; he was trying to recruit these girls to join up with their group while simultaneously attempting to get into bed with one of them tonight. He smirked, *sly dog.*

Everyone exchanged stories, both of the new world and the old. The stories of their lives from before the end of the world took center stage. No one wanted to think about the atrocities that lie beyond the comfort of the building anymore. At least not at that moment.

Ben was the only one drinking tequila, so rather than pouring himself another drink, he grabbed the bottle and tucked it under his arm. "Did anyone take any food to Catherine?"

"I did, last time I went to the little girl's room. I don't think she's eating it though." Lulu was starting to slur.

"Cool. I'm gonna take a walk, check on Veronica, check in on Catherine."

"What?" Gary hollered at him, three sheets to the wind. "We're just getting this party started!"

"Man, you're a mess." Ben laughed and patted Gary on the back.

"Yes, but aren't I a fuckin' lovely one?" Gary cracked himself up and Andrew clapped and guffawed at the man. Lulu giggled uncontrollably.

Michelle eyed Ben as he wandered out of the vault.

He checked in on Veronica, still sound asleep. It was a quarter past midnight, and whatever Catherine had given her, he wished he had some for himself. He was glad she could get as much peace as she could. He hoped her sleep was deep and dreamless. He turned to leave the spa and was startled by Michelle, who had snuck up behind him.

"Jesus Christ," he murmured as he backed away from her. "Nearly scared me half to death." He started toward the exit.

"Wait a second there, soldier. I came in here to find you and that bottle of tequila." She seductively took his arm but he pulled back.

"I'm not a soldier anymore." He thrust the bottle toward her, "Here, take it if you want."

"That's not what I want." She leaned in toward him, letting her long hair fall over her shoulders. "You know what I want."

He gently pushed her away from him. "Well I'm sorry, that's all you're gonna get." He held out the bottle toward her again and she rolled her eyes at him.

"Oh, come on, you don't have to be shy with me." She put her hands on her hips. The first available, but more importantly, attractive man she meets since the world ended was playing hard to get.

"Lady, I ain't shy. No offense, but you could probably take a lesson or two in modesty."

Her jaw dropped open at the sudden kick to her ego and he nodded at her, smiling. "Have a good night."

"Faggot!" she screamed at him, infuriated at his rejection. Michelle threw a fit in the salon. Her face was red with embarrassment and fury as she stared at Ben's retreating shape.

IV

Ben poked his head out through the roof access and squinted in the darkness, trying to find Catherine. The dead were riled up tonight; he could hear them screeching in the streets below, crying out in what sounded like frustration. He quickly discovered why, as the faint melody of music drifted toward him from the opposite end of the roof.

Catherine sat alone in the north corner, surrounded by wireless music speakers playing a cacophony of different songs all at once. Ben grimaced as he grew nearer; there could be no way she was enjoying that. He gave a slight wave but she didn't notice. Her head stayed down.

He cleared his throat and yet she still didn't look up. He sat down across from her, the gravel digging into the palms of his hands as he lowered himself. He undid the top from the bottle of tequila and took a small swig.

She finally looked up at him and put her hand out.

"Be my guest," he said, offering the bottle up to her. She lifted it to her mouth and tilted her head back, gulping the hot liquor down.

"Hey, hey, go easy." He leaned forward and eased the bottle away from her.

She coughed harshly, gasping for air. "Thank you," she croaked. She caught her breath and, with the sleeve of her sweater, wiped her eyes. "Tequila was always Desmond's drink."

Ben nodded, pulling the pack of cigarettes Michelle had given him from his pocket and lighting one up. He held the pack out to Catherine.

"No, thank you."

"Mind if we turn the music down a bit?" He cocked his head toward the roof ledge, "You're causin' quite the commotion down there."

She leaned forward and went about turning the phones off.

"Couldn't decide on a song?"

She shook her head, "No, I just didn't want to focus on anything."

They sat quietly together on the roof, listening to the raucous all around them. The putrid stench was something that his senses had eventually gotten used to; it was always in everything: the air, your clothes, your hair. It was the sound of them he couldn't wrap his mind around.

They never grew silent, they never grew tired. No matter where he went, it followed, because it was the sound he'd grown to know so well that he heard their moans even when they weren't around.

It was a never-ending orchestra of death that had become the soundtrack to all of their lives.

Catherine sighed, grabbing the bottle from between Ben's booted feet and sipping. "I knew this day would come," she finally spoke, her voice monotone. "I've been sitting up here forever, overthinking, overanalyzing. That's what I do."

Ben wasn't sure how to respond, he had just met these people a few hours before. He opted for a silent nod, which seemed to work.

"I used to feel this emptiness. We never had children. I couldn't have children. But, I have never been more thankful in my life than I am right now for my infertility." She took another drink before asking, "Do you have children?"

Ben shook his head.

"Good. This is not the world for them. Hell, I'm not even sure if it was a world for children before people started eating each other."

"You're probably right. I don't like to think about it, but, I saw more dead kids when I was overseas than I have since this whole thing started." He flicked his cigarette butt over the roof ledge and hoped it would somehow catch the horde of eaters on fire.

"I had no control over losing my husband today. I don't like to think about trying to keep a *child* safe."

Veronica's face flashed through both their minds. They were silent for a few more moments.

"Des was such a careful man. I've already accepted it, I accepted it the moment I saw her get out of that car without him and Francis. I will just never understand it because I don't want to hear about what happened from *her*."

Ben raised an eyebrow at her last sentence, but decided against exploring the subject matter of Michelle. "Gary lost his wife. You should try talkin' to him about Desmond."

"I'm not in the mood to bond with anyone over a shared tragedy."

"Isn't that what we're all doing?"

"I suppose you're right," she said, chuckling in discomfort, "so I'll just keep talking to you, if it's all the same."

"That's why I came up here."

"I thought we were going to be okay here. I don't know if I'll ever be okay anywhere, to be honest, but I just..." She paused and her entire tone of voice changed. "Will you take me with you back to wherever it is you came from? This place is death."

Ben thought about what she said. He couldn't help but want to respond that *everywhere was death,* but he knew that it wasn't what she needed to hear.

"I feel like if we didn't, our whole trip down to this shopping center from hell would have been for nothing. Of course we'll take you with us." He thought about Samson being eaten alive, the pain it caused Veronica, the loss it caused their group, because of Gary's quest. But then he thought about how if it weren't for Gary, they would have never come to this place, they would have never found other people, they would have remained alone, locked in a tower. In fact, if it weren't for Gary they would probably still be on that boat, out of gas somewhere in the Gulf...

Ben shook his head rapidly; he was the one overthinking and overanalyzing now.

They continued to talk in the humid darkness on the gravel-covered roof, inadvertently bonding over shared tragedies. A cloud-covered sky blocked out the stars and the air was thick with ozone, the scent of an impending thunderstorm.

On the other side of the roof, Michelle glared out at Ben and Catherine. An inexplicable anger brewed inside her. Perhaps it had been Ben's rejection or maybe it was because she wasn't the center of attention she'd hoped she would have been when she returned today. She stumbled down from the roof, half drunk, and stomped off toward the salon, slamming into Gary as she turned the corner.

"Jesus Christ!" she yelled at him, falling onto her ass on the hard tile.

"Oh, sorry love, let me help you up." Gary couldn't help but giggle, feeling the full effects of the alcohol he'd consumed.

Michelle shoved his hand away and got up from the floor on her own, smoothing out her skirt.

"I was just trying to find some place quiet to have a piss." He slurred his words and seemed preoccupied with her breasts.

"Come with me." She snatched his hand and yanked him along behind her.

"Whatever you say!" Gary cackled and followed behind her like a puppy.

*

Veronica groggily stared up at the ceiling of the deluxe spa room. She still felt the effects of the sedatives, but couldn't seem to drift back off to sleep. She'd been startled awake by a woman yelling and cussing earlier, but had neither the energy nor the curiosity to get up and find out what was going on. If it had been serious, someone would have come and gotten her.

Her eyes drifted to the corner of the room with the flashlight aimed up which intermittently flickered.

The batteries are dying.

She wondered how long she'd been asleep; she felt like she was in a different universe in this room. Visions of Samson's demise crept into her mind and she would force them back out again, only to be replaced by her father's death, and then Isaac's. It was a vicious cycle in her mind that she could only block out by counting to ten over and over again.

Mindless counting.

She imagined that this was what hell was like, lying in a dark room with nothing but your own hideous mind. She wished she had any other thoughts but her own.

Veronica jerked, startled by a slamming door somewhere in the spa beyond her private quarters. She heard a man laughing hysterically and a woman talking. She strained her ears, trying to make out what they were saying. All she could hear was mumbling and laughing; she urged her body to roll over and get up, and nearly collapsed to the floor for her troubles. But she held on to the edge of the massage table tightly. She silently forced herself to move toward the door, her lethargic movements resembling the shuffling of the dead. She stopped short when she recognized the man's voice.

"But what about Veronica?" Gary said with a laugh. "We'll wake the poor girl."

"Catherine's got her so doped up she probably won't even remember her name when she wakes up," Michelle replied, hastily unbuckling Gary's belt and unzipping his trousers. He sloppily kissed at her neck and his drunk hands fumbled around on her body. Frustrated, she shoved him back onto one of the tables. "Hands off."

Gary grinned ear to ear and winked, "Yes ma'am." He placed his hands behind his head and cackled again.

Michelle rolled her eyes as she pulled her panties down her long legs and kicked them off to the side. She crawled up onto the table seductively and Gary let out a low whistle.

"Shut up. Not another word." She mounted the Brit and let out a hushed sigh.

"Oh, gross." Veronica cringed in disgust as she realized what was going on in the other room.

Their moans of excitement and pleasure filled the air and grew louder with each second. She collapsed back onto the massage bed and pulled her pillow over her face, drowning out the mid-coitus moans.

She preferred the moans of the dead any day.

She realized that the phrase '*Be careful what you wish for*' rang true as she tried to force memories of her father and Isaac back into her mind. She tried to concentrate on the day she'd spent with Samson on the bay, fishing and laughing, but every time she seemed to finally block out the animalistic sex, one of them would express their satisfaction with an overzealous grunt.

I really am in hell, Veronica thought as she tugged the pillow down harder onto her face and pressed it up against her ears.

V

The best part about waking up each morning for Veronica were the few seconds that she forgot about the end of the world. The moments she shared with herself as her eyes fluttered open and the calm she felt before anything current in her life had the chance to register were the best. No matter where it was she found herself waking up, whether it be a floor, a stranger's borrowed bed in an abandoned home, or a massage table, she always imagined that she was at home in Columbia City in her own bed and her father James would enter her room at any moment to wake her for school. But that moment when James would tap at the door lightly and sing her name, announcing that it was time for breakfast would never come. Just as soon as the waking seconds were there, they were gone, and the horrors and tragedies of reality came rushing back in, taking their accustomed place once more in the forefront of her consciousness.

That was the worst part about waking up each morning for Veronica.

She stretched and felt the pull of her aching muscles from being still for far too long. Feeling the urgency of her bladder, she found her shoes in the dark and crept out of the private spa as quietly as a mouse. She didn't know this building, but she remembered where Doctor Catherine had told her their bathrooms were. She braced herself for the onslaught of foul stench and pulled open the café door.

The ripe, sickening stench barreled into her nostrils and she tried her hardest to ignore it. Holding her breath, she finished up her business as quickly as she could and found her way back out to the fire corridor. She slammed the door behind her and took a deep breath of the stuffy yet refreshing air which greeted her. A door down the hall opened and she took a defensive stance, relaxing when Ben turned the corner.

"I thought that was you, how's the face?" He smiled when he saw her and she grinned back, her face still swollen where the stitches were, but she looked much better. Her long dark hair was pulled back into a messy ponytail and her clothes looked a size too big.

"It hurts, but it'll be fine. I can't believe I slept that long. What have y'all been doing? Did the rest of Dr. Catherine's group get back yet? How are they? Are these people good? Will they be coming back with us?"

Her rapid questioning was too much for his head to handle all at once. Ben put a hand up and chuckled. "Alright, alright, slow it down. Let's get you something to eat and we'll go over everything."

The door to the salon opened and closed again and Andrew joined them in the corridor. "Hey there darlin', how ya feelin'?" He rubbed the sleep from his eyes.

"I'm feeling fine, thanks. What about you?"

"Hungover, but it's nothin' I can't kick." The big man stretched his massive arms above his head and followed Ben and Veronica in search of some breakfast.

The three chatted while they ate. Ben explained the unfortunate circumstances of only Michelle returning yesterday afternoon, and Veronica put two and two together, guessing that's who Gary was with last night. She shuddered at the memory as it emerged in her mind and she shook it off. She felt terrible for Catherine; no one got the chance to say goodbye anymore, and she knew what that felt like. They all did.

"I say we leave as soon as we can. I know Juliette's safe with Clyde, but I don't wanna be away from her for much longer." Andrew chewed his food loudly between words. "Gary kept rambling on about that bank across the street with all the money trucks last night. I'm thinkin' that's our best bet."

Ben nodded, "Yeah, there are enough of us, we just need to figure out a game plan and get on the move. I don't want to be out here much longer, either."

As the trio finished breakfast, the remaining survivors woke up and joined them one by one. Veronica avoided eye contact with Gary and expressed her condolences to Catherine silently with a simple nod.

The woman understood; she gave Veronica a soft but weak smile and nodded in return. The last of the group to join was Michelle.

"You must be the youngin'." She smirked, grabbing a paper plate and fixing herself something to eat.

"Veronica."

Michelle walked over and held out her hand, "Welcome Veronica, I'm Michelle."

As Veronica shook her hand, there was something about the woman she instantly disliked. Although she couldn't quite put her finger on it, she didn't feel the sense of trust she'd felt when she met Catherine or Lulu. Something seemed a little off.

Gary looked pleased that Michelle had finally joined them, smiling at her as she took a seat beside Lulu. Michelle expertly ignored him, and his smile pulled a disappearing act.

"Well, now that we're all here in one room, let's take this opportunity to discuss what we plan to do." Gary looked at everyone as he spoke, awaiting a response.

"Ben and I already talked about getting out of here today, as soon as we can." Andrew was the first to speak; Ben nodded in agreement.

"What you were talking about last night," Lulu chimed in, "the armored trucks? I think that's a good idea."

Catherine looked a little confused and Gary quickly filled her in. They would ready the supplies that her group had already stockpiled in the building, making them easily accessible to the truck so they could be loaded as quickly as possible. At least three people would have to go get the trucks; two drivers and one to cover their backs and keep the eaters at bay. They would back one of the trucks up to the building and load their supplies, the other truck would come pick everyone up. The easiest and least risky way to get everyone inside would be from the roof.

The emergency hatch on the top of the armored truck would serve its purpose, as their situation was definitely an emergency. The gated parking garage across the street from Emerald City was their destination, and the gates were up, which meant the dead had probably already wandered inside.

"But we'll worry about that after both trucks are in and the gates are down and locked. And then, we'll carry everything across the sky bridge that connects with the central building. It'll be tedious at best, but it will get done. Weapons and ammunition weren't the only reasons I had you two help me clear the central building." Gary beamed at Ben and Andrew, his crazy little plans all coming together and making perfect sense.

"Yeah, that worked out perfectly. Almost got Clyde killed," Ben remarked, lighting a cigarette.

"Hey hey, thought we put that behind us? It did work out perfectly. Clyde is fine." Gary's smile hadn't decreased in wattage.

"So let me get this straight," Michelle said finally, speaking in an aggressive tone and lighting a cigarette of her own. "We march into the bank while avoiding hordes of dead cannibals, swing back and pick up the supplies along with the rest of these misfits, plow through a city of the undead and assume the throne in the fortified rich-bitch condominiums that are The Emerald City?" She blew a puff of smoke out, staring directly at Gary, an amused look playing across her face.

"Yeah, that about sums it up."

She took another drag off her cigarette and exhaled. "Alright, I'm in."

VI

Andrew and Ben were the best shots by far, both expertly trained in firearms. They argued back and forth over who would stay and cover from the roof and who would accompany the truck group.

"I'm the fastest. *And* the most agile," Veronica said.

Ben sighed. "How's your driving, cupcake?" She fell silent and he nodded. "Right. You're staying here."

"I'm going," Michelle interrupted. "Ben stays here to cover from the roof; he was military, so he's probably a better long-range shot than the cop. It's Gary's plan, so he'll come with me and Andrew. The rest of you, just be ready."

There was no further argument, she'd made her point rationally and was ready to do business. Ben breathed another sigh, this one of relief. Veronica was always eager to help, and while she was capable of holding her own, he was more interested in keeping her safe than anything else.

The group worked quickly, piling up the food, water, medicine, and other supplies they'd gathered during the last several weeks at Emerald Park. Just as Gary had instructed, their spoils were stacked neatly and organized, easily accessible from the truck once the fire door was opened and the clock was ticking.

Andrew slipped away momentarily into jewelry store's showroom. The place had an eerie feel, a dusty coldness that gave him chills. The multicolored paint on the large windows reminded him of the abundance of stained glass in the churches he attended once upon a time. The faint sounds of the undead didn't help as they shuffled about pointlessly just beyond the glass. He silently thanked God that they were unaware of his presence as he scanned the glass cases of engagement rings.

He slipped behind the counter and slid the back open, reaching in and pulling out a white gold ring with a breathtaking solitaire diamond, which sparkled even in the dim showroom. The ring would need no resizing for Juliette's delicate finger. He grinned and slipped it into his pocket, patting it and turning to leave. Ben stood in the doorway and smiled, clapping Andrew on the back as he passed. "Congrats dude."

"Don't be congratulatin' me yet. Might be the end of the world but she could still turn me down," Andrew said with a laugh.

The men met the rest of the group on the roof once all the supplies were stacked and ready. They could hear Michelle screaming before they even made it all the way up.

"I don't care what kind of day you had! Get over it!" Michelle had her finger in Catherine's face. "This is all fucked!"

Ben and Andrew jogged over to the women huddled around the speaker setup.

"What's going on?" Ben asked.

Michelle rounded on them, pointing. Her hair was a wild mess and her eyes full of anger. "Dr. Idiot left everything uncovered last night. Take a look around, see how it's all nice and wet? That's called rain."

"I'm so sorry. I, I just didn't even think about it," Catherine stammered, raising a hand to her forehead.

"Look, Michelle, I was up here too last night. It's as much as my fault."

"Doesn't matter," Michelle said, shaking her head at Ben, "it wasn't *your* responsibility."

"There's a whole cell phone store down there full of phones and speakers. It's not a big deal, we'll just swap everything out. All this did was just cost us a little extra time."

Michelle laughed hysterically. "How many weeks do you think we've been here? This is the last of the charged phones. All that extra shit downstairs is dead! All of it!"

Gary was busy fiddling with the phones on the ground, pulling the batteries out and attempting to dry out the insides. Michelle kicked one of the speakers beside him and he jumped as it went flying, water splashing out of it as it bounced across the roof.

"Like I said, this is fucked." She pulled a cigarette out and let out an exasperated sigh, "Can somebody please give me a light?"

Ben tossed his lighter to her and walked over to the ledge where Catherine and Lulu were standing, quietly talking. The eaters below were in a frenzy, attracted to all the yelling and excitement on the roof. They'd nearly doubled in their numbers overnight. Ben looked down into the crowd full of snapping mouths and glazed eyes gazing up at him, blood-soaked hands hungrily reaching upwards, clawing at the building, clawing at one another.

"If one person can cause all this," Lulu said, pointing down at the dead, "there's no reason that a whole group of us wouldn't be able to bring the whole damn parking lot over here." She looked out on the lot as she spoke, eyeing the clusters that had formed throughout the shopping center. She couldn't imagine what an aerial view would reveal; she shuddered to think how many hundreds more there were lurking around Emerald Park that she couldn't see.

"It's our only option. The whole building is surrounded, our only saving grace being they have no idea how to get inside." Catherine's eyes were red, her face paler than the usual. Large black bags hung under her eyes, the furrows around her lips deeper than before.

Veronica joined them near the ledge, arms folded. She wore Lulu's clothes, a much better fit than her oversized findings from Gary's collection. Samson's blood-stained button-down was tied tightly around her waist, and despite the bandaged face, she was looking much more like her fierce self. She looked to the entrance to Target. Amidst the dead shuffling by the entryway lie a grisly pile of human remains that the dead had neglected to devour.

Samson's blood still streaked the glass in such a manner that even the rain couldn't wash it away. She felt her face grow hot and her nostrils flare. Ben watched her as without a word she retrieved the speaker Michelle had kicked away. With a powerful scream she reared her arm back and launched the useless gadget into a group of eaters that seemed to be ignoring the building. The group below them, as if attending a show, roared in response, soon joined by more roaming eaters interested in the food on the roof. Catherine picked up the other speaker and followed suit. Soon enough, everyone on the roof was hollering and throwing things, causing such a ruckus that if they hadn't already been up and walking, the dead would have been awakened.

"Where are the keys for the bike chains you keep on the doors downstairs?" Andrew asked Michelle.

"In the salon, why?"

"Doesn't look like we're gonna be going out the fire door. There's way too many of 'em." He turned to yell, "Now would be as good a time as any to get our asses movin' Gary!"

Andrew and Michelle were already running toward the roof hatch.

"Somebody needs to lock us out! Lu, come on!" Michelle called out before heading downstairs.

Lulu grabbed Gary's arm and sprinted for the hatch.

"Ben, you've got us covered, yeah?" Gary shouted back as he ran.

"Don't you worry your bald British head, my friend. Be careful out there!"

Michelle moved swiftly and gracefully through the building, grabbing a backpack and Francis's set of keys in one swoop. She gave the room one last look around before leaving for good. She tossed the keys to Lulu and began tying her hair back tightly.

"Ya gotta be fast, Lu. You can do this, I know you."

For once Lulu appeared confident, and even though these weren't the best of circumstances, Michelle was never more proud to have such a friend in the woman. She pulled her in and hugged her tightly before stepping into place behind Gary.

"Everybody armed?" Michelle and Gary nodded as Andrew put his hand on the café's door handle. "Alright, brace yourselves…let's go."

The four of them ran through the café's putrid stench straight for the front doors, holding their breath as best they could as Lulu removed the bike lock and turned the deadbolt. Gary, Andrew, and Michelle jammed through the entrance and Lulu quickly pulled the door shut, sliding the bolt and replacing the bike lock. Her hands shook and her heart pounded as she slammed the café door behind her for good and dry heaved in the fire corridor.

The wet ground proved to be bad news for the trio headed toward the banking complex. Their shoes noisily slapped the pavement and splashed puddles as they ran. But the sky was overcast; this was not the day they needed the blinding Florida sun in their eyes.

The rest of the group on the roof continued to yell and scream, attempting to create as much of a distraction as possible. Shots rang out as Ben fired into the dead that surrounded them.

"Incoming!" Gary cried out.

Andrew raised his pistol and fired at the two eaters who'd come up on their left. They lunged at Gary who was able to dodge the first but went to the ground under the deadweight of the second just as Andrew put a bullet in its head. Michelle sprinted passed them and Andrew grabbed Gary's arm and pulled him along, barely stopping to give him enough time to regain his footing.

"Gotta keep movin' man!"

They bobbed and weaved through cars once they made it to the highway with the dead still in pursuit. Gary turned to see an eater as it crawled its way across the hood of a vehicle at an alarming rate. Its clothes were falling off its emaciated frame, chunks of flesh missing from its neck and arms, and was almost right on top of Michelle when Gary finally got off a shot. The bullet pushed a sickening black cloud of gore and rot out the other side of the dead man's head.

Michelle barely flinched.

They made it up to the abandoned finance building and headed for the back. Industrial fencing and barbed wire at least twelve feet high ran the perimeter of the armored truck lot.

"Keep 'em off me!" Michelle yelled as she dropped the backpack and removed one of the bike locks she'd stuffed inside. Gary and Andrew fought off the dead with blasts of gunfire while she readjusted the bag on her back and shot at the fence.

"Fuck!" She missed. "Concentrate, concentrate," she coached herself as she took one more careful shot at the lock on the fence and the gate popped open. "Let's go! Let's go!"

The three of them scurried behind the temporary safety of the fence and Michelle snapped the bike lock into place, pulling back her hand as a bloated clerk waddled up to the fence and chomped his teeth down. The eater's teeth cracked and broke off against the metal, and Michelle's look of horror turned to relief as she checked and rechecked her fingers for any break in the skin.

She grinned at the eater, at the black blood and pus oozing from its rotten mouth. "Fuck you, fatty. No lunch for you today." She hurried to catch up with Gary and Andrew.

Andrew hammered the glass on the bank's doors but just as he figured, his gun butt just bounced off. He shrugged and fired three rounds into the lock on the door and pulled it open, ushering the others inside.

The large bank lobby smelled fresh and clean. The office furniture, minus the settled dust, was immaculate and the carpet felt plush and new. Michelle peered through the blinds and saw the growing crowd at the fence. "Hey, I don't know how long that's gonna hold. We need to find these keys and get going."

"I'll check the offices. You two, get movin'." Andrew began tearing the place apart.

Gary jumped over the teller's counter and disappeared around the corner while Michelle ran upstairs to search the second floor. After what seemed like an eternity of precious wasted time, Gary emerged from the back with a handful of truck keys.

"I'm superstitious. They've got to be the right numbers." He laid out a few sets of keys on a desk.

Andrew rolled his eyes. "You kiddin' me?"

"No. I am not." Gary carefully thought about which truck he would choose, walking his fingers from one set of keys to the next, and Andrew called out to Michelle, grabbing a set off the desk.

A crash came from outside and Andrew made it to the window in time to see the dead pouring like lava through the vulnerable gate. "We gotta move! Now!"

Michelle heard the crash and the urgency in Andrew's voice and put two and two together, rushing down the stairs and back into the lobby.

Gary calmly lifted a set of keys and dangled them in front of his face. "Okay, we can go."

The three of them plowed out the side entrance as the horde of undead burst through the back. The trio raced to the trucks that matched the numbers on the keys and separated, Andrew to his truck, Michelle and Gary to theirs.

"Get in the back, you'll be more useful at lifting all that shit into the truck," Michelle ordered.

Gary nodded and they heard the roar of an engine somewhere off in the lot. "Andrew's ready, let's get this thing started."

Michelle hesitated for a moment before turning the key in the ignition. She thought of all those awful parts in horror movies where the car wouldn't start just as the killer crashed through the window. An eater's face suddenly appeared in the driver's side window, pounding on the armored truck and screaming. She jumped and a yelp escaped her lips.

"What is it?" Gary hollered from the back of the truck.

Michelle shook her head and with a laugh, started the truck. She eyed the dead thing pushing its face against the window, smearing its disgusting fluids all over the glass like a snail.

"Everything's fine." She put the oversized truck into gear and floored it, checking the side mirror to see that Andrew was following. "Hang onto your ass, Limey!"

The truck smashed through the gate, plowing through the dead and bouncing onto the road with barely a scratch. She eased the truck through the backed-up traffic and car accidents and onto the other side of the highway, sliding into Emerald Park and toward the building. She could see as everyone began to run for the hatch, eager to load up the approaching truck.

Michelle smiled; for once, in a world like this, things were going as planned.

"Alright Gary, get ready. This isn't going to be easy." Michelle swung the truck around, the enormous tires rolling over and crushing bodies that should have already been dead. Skulls and body parts crunched under the truck's weight, howls filled the air and the truck, as massive as it was, shook from the dead repeatedly slamming into it. Fortunately for Gary, he was on the back end where they were not so interested. He crouched at the back doors, watching through the small window, for his chance.

Michelle slowly rolled backward toward the fire door. It flew open and Lulu's terrified face appeared, screaming and recoiling back into the building as she saw the horrific carnage.

"Back it up faster! Go!" Gary held on to the metal grating on either side of him and braced himself, kicking forward and sending the back doors flying open. The truck's momentum shifted and was brought to an abrupt halt just shy of crashing into the building.

Lulu peeked out at him.

His chest heaved and his heart pounded. "That was a close one, eh?" He laughed once.

Ben appeared in the doorway and thrust out a hand, helping him from the truck and into the corridor. "Let's get to work."

As the group in the building worked on stocking the truck, Andrew drove in circles, attempting to create a distraction while his comrades did their business. The dead followed after him in almost a comical fashion as he did figure eights and donuts. The eaters were torn by their options but soon figured out that they couldn't catch up to Andrew. They began stumbling back to the building in order to join the teeming crowd.

Andrew noticed and frowned, "Shit." His attention turned to the windshield as rain began to fall. "Double shit." He stopped the truck and fumbled with the wipers.

"That about does it. I'll barely be able to squeeze myself up to the front." Gary patted Ben's shoulders with both hands. "I'll see you back at Emerald City; safe travels, my friend. You too ladies, especially you." He flashed Veronica a grin and climbed back inside the rocking truck.

"You too, Gary." Veronica turned and headed for the roof.

"Michelle!" Lulu called out. "I'll see you soon!" Lulu couldn't see her or make out what Michelle said in response but knew she'd heard her, and that was enough.

Lulu and Catherine went up after Veronica, and Ben pulled the fire door closed after the truck was clear. The door stopped short as an eater shoved its arm inside after Ben.

Ben cried out and attempted opening and closing the door back onto the dead arm to shake it off, but it wouldn't work. The thing's arm moved around furiously, trying to get a hold of Ben as the mouth outside screeched and squawked, drawing more of the undead to the door.

There was nothing left for Ben to do, there was no way he was getting that door closed. He gave the door one last pull and sprinted down the hall, the deafening wails of the eaters filling the corridor and sending shivers down his spine. He pounced on the ladder and shouted up to the roof, pulling himself up and looking back down only once to see the eaters piling up below him. He scrambled across the roof and saw the horrified faces of his companions on the roof.

"They're inside. They got inside."

Catherine jumped up and down, waving her arms wildly at Andrew and screaming for him. The truck turned back toward the building as the rain pounded down from the cloud strewn sky. Andrew pulled up to the side of the building with a screech of tires, metal scraping the stucco, the passenger side mirror flying off.

The emergency hatch on the truck's roof flew open and Andrew's head popped out. "Come on, y'all! Careful now, this roof is slick!"

Catherine was the first over the ledge with no hesitation, dropping the five feet down onto the roof with a thud and a yelp, scurrying down into the hatch with Andrew's help.

"Veronica, go," Ben ordered.

"No, you first." She bit her lip and crossed her arms over her chest. "I'm not leaving you like I did Samson."

Ben respected her statement and nodded. He pulled himself over and dropped gracefully to the roof of the truck, holding up his arms. "Come on, now!"

The eaters' screams from inside the building were getting louder; Lulu began to breathe heavily, panic setting in.

"You go ahead, Lulu, they can't get up here, don't worry," Veronica said, comforting her.

She tried to help Lulu over the ledge, but Lulu panicked and slipped, falling onto Ben. Ben tried to catch her but slipped when she tumbled onto him. She cried out as she lost her footing, eaters running full-speed into the truck.

Lulu slid off the roof, screaming.

Ben hollered out for her and lunged, missing her by mere inches. She hit the pavement with a crack and howled in pain. Lulu didn't even have time to register what had happened as in a matter of seconds the eaters were on her, ripping into her and tearing her insides out. She screamed in agony and Ben turned away.

Veronica had already dropped down from the ledge and grabbed Ben's arm. "We need to go!" she yelled. Between the hammering of the rain, the sloppy sounds of the eaters feasting, and Lulu's shrieks, she could barely hear herself think.

Ben nodded and scooted over to the hatch, waiting for Veronica. She peered down at Lulu's twisted grimace as she was eaten alive. Ben's eyes widened as Veronica pulled the 9mm Gary had given her from her waistband, putting Lulu out of her misery.

"We need to go," she said once more to Ben as she waited for him to drop down into the truck before doing so herself.

VII

"I never did like plans," Michelle said as she exhaled cigarette smoke. She gazed out through the foggy glass on the sky bridge that connected the parking garage with the central tower of Emerald City. "End of the world or not, nothing ever goes as planned." The words came stillborn out of an expressionless face.

Veronica stood beside her, staring down at the mindless dead who milled about the dirty streets, wondering how else Michelle would react to Lulu's death. She had been the one to put her down; she figured it was only appropriate that she tell Michelle about it.

But Michelle already knew. She had seen her friend disappear off the side of the truck, out of her view, and she knew that was it. Lulu was gone, just like everyone else, and there was nothing she could do about it. Gary's plan had been simple enough, but it hadn't included Lulu's death.

Michelle's plans had been simple as well: eliminate all threats, take control of Emerald Park, take control of her own life for once. She saw this new world as one for the taking, but maybe she had been wrong. She hadn't planned on more survivors, she hadn't planned on leaving the building she had called her own, she hadn't planned on Lulu's death. Michelle simply hadn't planned on the end of the world.

She dropped the cigarette to the carpeted floor and stomped it out. "Let's grab a luggage cart and get this shit upstairs."

Veronica watched her walk off.

The group remained quiet the rest of the day and evening, even while making countless trips back and forth from the parking garage to the twenty-fourth floor, lugging box after box of supplies. It was dusk by the time they'd finished.

They reunited with Clyde and Juliette, introducing the two remaining people from Emerald Park. No one discussed the lives lost. Juliette and Clyde silently accepted the fact that Samson did not return with them, and neither Catherine nor Michelle brought up that anyone else in their group had ever existed. Everyone ate separately and silently that night, taking the time to mourn the last two days in their own way, and taking the time to be thankful for the few things they had left.

Veronica switched rooms, compiling her belongings with Samson's and washing the blood from his button-down shirt as best she could; she would wear it every day. Andrew asked Juliette to marry him at sunrise and for the first time in as long as he could remember, she smiled from ear to ear, crying tears of joy instead of fear or misery. Clyde's ankle wound was already starting to heal. Catherine had tended to it properly and everyone was relieved to see that the spread of the deadly infection did not include fingernail scratches.

Over the next two months, it was almost as if a sense of normalcy had crept back into their lives; cooking, cleaning, recreation, exercise. They were so far above the pandemonium that they found a way to almost block it out completely. They took turns on the roof, not to watch for signs of trouble or make distractions for the dead, but for target practice with hunting rifles, and occasionally finding out if they could hit a golf ball into the Gulf of Mexico. They had dinner parties and bonded over common interests of the Old World.

Catherine made progress with Juliette with the surplus of medications that they had in their possession and ensuring she filled her time with busy work and healthy activities. Even Veronica began to like Juliette. Every morning they would run the full span of all twenty-four floors and nearly collapse with exhaustion and laughter when they were finished.

Clyde and Ben had found the mother lode of marijuana stashes on one of their cleaning expeditions in the central building and decided if they kept it between the two of them, it could last them at least a year. Catherine taught Gary as much as she possibly could about the basics of first aid, medical care, and simple emergency procedures. Everyone, even Juliette, learned how to properly handle a firearm.

Michelle was the only exception. She only hung around when there was alcohol involved or guns being fired. She casually slept with Gary, ignoring him unless there was something she needed. She spent the majority of her time wandering the buildings on her own and occasionally spying on her fellow survivors. She studied their movements, the things they said about one another when no one else was around, and even made a secret discovery of her own: a major stash of liquor in one of the units in the central tower that everyone else had somehow missed.

She wished Lulu was there to share.

She would drink alone and find herself wandering to the doors of the forbidden building. She'd run her fingers over the lock and imagine what it would be like to bust open those heavy doors and let the dead into their safe haven. She'd lose track of time staring into the filmy, cold eyes of the eaters on the other side…mesmerized by their haunting cries, by their clumsy fingers attempting to grab her through the glass.

They'd gnash their teeth at her, their infected mouths opening and closing endlessly, putrid fluids dripping from those open jaws and smearing across the glass. She would mimic their sounds and movements, laughing at them, laughing at herself. Sometimes she would hold one-sided conversations with them, ask them why they were stuck in there in the first place and if they were ready to leave; one time she even swore one of them nodded at her.

One morning Michelle woke from a hangover with the glaring light of the sun in her face. It was probably past noon. She groaned and stretched, yawning loudly, and headed for the balcony. The air was heavy and cool this time of year, but on the top floor she felt zero humidity. She breathed in deep and exhaled. The beautiful white sands were speckled with random eaters with nowhere to go. The dead knew there was food somewhere near, but couldn't figure out where, so they never strayed far from Emerald City. On the surface, the crystal green waters of the Gulf seemed serene and immaculate, but from her elevated point, Michelle could see the dark figures looming under the surface, doomed to wander the seabed and taint its beauty forever.

She was briefly startled when the door to the balcony one unit over opened. Clyde and Ben emerged with cigarettes in hand. She flashed Ben a smile. "Mornin'."

He lit his smoke and passed the lighter to Clyde. "More like afternoon." He smiled, squinting in the sun.

Clyde flipped his braids over his left shoulder and scrunched his nose up at Michelle. "Where you gonna disappear to today, Hermit the frog?" He laughed and Ben snickered.

"Nice, one of the many reasons I'd rather not spend my time around you." She leaned her left side onto the balcony and placed a hand on her hip, staring at him.

"Go tie your hair up, bitch, you look a hot mess." He waved his hand at her, shooing her away. Michelle rolled her eyes and looked at Ben, he shrugged and she disappeared back inside of her condo.

"She's definitely one of the weird ones, but you don't need to be so rude, man," Ben said, chuckling at his friend.

"Well, since Juliette got her shit together, I gotta give *somebody* a hard time. Besides, I don't like her, just somethin' about her don't sit right with me."

Ben laughed again and flicked his cigarette off the balcony. "Drama, drama."

*

Michelle bathed and brushed her teeth.

Why couldn't Ben have just come onto the balcony by himself?

She hated Clyde and all his feminine glory. She found new reasons every day to dislike the people in the group more and more.

Juliette was a stuck-up nut job. Catherine thought she was everybody's therapist. Gary was too damn happy. Everybody fawned all over Veronica. Andrew really didn't bother her, but that was because he was too far up Juliette's ass all the time, and Ben didn't pay her any attention. She examined herself in the mirror.

She was still more beautiful than she could ever hope to be, but there was no catching his eye.

She kept to herself when she finally left her condo to grab some food, barely murmuring a greeting to Gary in the kitchen. She returned to her living room momentarily to grab a lantern before heading for the eleventh floor. The doors to central were always unlocked since it had been cleared out. She retrieved one of her liquor bottles from its hiding place and headed for the locked double doors on the other side of the building to hang with the dead.

VIII

Michelle's favorite eater had probably been a very handsome man when he was alive. He'd obviously been wealthy, being in a place like Emerald City. Even in death, he had ridiculously great hair and dressed to impress. She loved how she 100% controlled his attention as she'd move from one side of the door frame to the other, his cold eyes following her every move as she slowly walked and drank from the bottle of vodka. Full of stone-cold desire. Ben didn't look at her like that.

No one did.

She passed the remainder of her time that day sketching in a used art book she'd found in the same condominium as the old liquor bottles. She drew cityscapes and forests on fire, freehand portraits of the survivors in her group and what she imagined they'd look like as eaters. A profile of Ben's face. Several beautiful silhouettes of Lulu dancing ballet. Her heart ached for her friend. Any friend.

Feeling lonely for the first time that day, she forced herself from the floor, the near-empty bottle almost dropping from her hands. She stumbled back to the twenty-fourth floor of the west tower, polishing off the bottle of vodka and snacking on stale potato chips as she went. She had no concept of time as she entered Gary's condo, where everyone normally gathered at night. No candles were lit, no lanterns on...the place was quiet.

She walked slowly to his bedroom and listened at the door, his soft snoring greeted her ears. She sighed and walked back out onto the breezeway. A clap of thunder erupted and it began to drizzle. She leaned forward and looked down into the darkness below her. A flash of lightning lit up the streets and she saw a glimpse of the eaters, like cockroaches, roaming below their palace in the sky in alarming numbers.

The rain began to fall more heavily with louder and more constant thunder. She drunkenly wandered into the wrong condominium and closed the door behind her. She sighed again, rubbing her eyes and grabbed a half empty bottle of water from the coffee table and chugged. She looked down and noticed a pack of cigarettes, still not realizing she was in the wrong unit, and slipped outside for a smoke.

Her head was swimming. The cigarette made her lightheaded, and the hammer of rain all around was hypnotizing. She turned and leaned her forehead on the cold, wet glass of the balcony's sliding glass door that lead to the bedroom and closed her eyes. Holding the cigarette up to her lips with one hand, she scratched her head through her thick, curly hair with the other, opening her eyes. She dropped the cigarette when she realized she wasn't looking into her own empty bedroom, but she was staring directly at Ben as he slept.

Instinctively she jumped off to the side and hid, feeling like a drunken fool and nearly sobering up from her mistake. She peered in from the side and to her delight he remained asleep, unaware of her presence. She couldn't help but smile at him, undoubtedly high as a kite and sleeping peacefully. She placed her cheek against the glass and watched him as he slept. The wind began to pick up, the rain getting stronger and the thunder only getting louder.

The door to Ben's bedroom suddenly opened and Michelle stepped aside again, shocked to find that Catherine had entered. Ben stirred in the bed and propped himself up, their conversation inaudible over the sounds of the wild storm. Catherine untied the belt from her robe and dropped the plush, white material to the floor. She was completely nude, her pale skin almost glowing every time the lightning flashed across the sky. She knelt on the bed and kissed Ben softly, smiling tenderly at him. He took her in his arms and the soft kiss transformed into a passionate embrace.

Michelle clenched her hands into tight fists, seething with sudden anger and jealousy, completely unaware that any sort of love affair had been occurring.

She made herself sick thinking about how Ben rejected her that first time as he watched his hands roam Catherine's body, not in the way that Gary touched her, but in the way that a man touches a woman when he *truly* wants her. Had she ever been truly wanted by anything but the hungry dread, or had she always manipulated her way into everything she'd ever had?

She felt her teeth grinding against one another. How many times had they made love like this? How many times had she spent drinking alone and loathing these people? All but him. And now she loathed him, too. She was right to despise him the moment he rejected her, but she never wanted to, until now.

"What the hell are you doing out here?" Juliette asked with her hands on her hips, the wind blowing her blonde hair around wildly. "Are you drunk?"

Michelle was startled by the blonde. She hadn't even heard her open the door on the other side of the balcony. The knot in Michelle's stomach was suddenly a ball of fiery rage. "Wrong place, wrong time."

"What the fuck is wrong with you?" Juliette shot her a confused look as she watched Michelle slowly turn toward her, breathing heavily, her fists clenched. Juliette backed away nervously.

Without any implication, Michelle charged toward Juliette in one swift motion, diving for and grabbing her legs. Juliette's scream was masked by the raging storm as she was lifted up and tossed over the side of the balcony like a ragdoll.

She screamed the entire way down from the twenty-fourth floor, but it was a scream that would never be heard by anyone other than the dead that roamed the beach.

EPILOGUE

Veronica stirred in her sleep, rolling over in the massive king sized bed. As flashes of lightning filled the room she rubbed her eyes, confused by the dream she'd just woken from.

She had been running with her brother through a forest of dead trees, everything around her on fire. She couldn't keep up with Isaac; he was suddenly too fast for her. They'd finally reached a clearing in the trees and there she found her father, only it wasn't her father, it was an eater, and he was eating the flesh from Samson's corpse.

Samson looked up at her slowly, opening his mouth unnaturally wide and screaming.

But the scream wasn't his, it was a woman's.

Veronica sat up in the bed and shivered, a chill running down her spine. The wind outside howled, slamming rain into the balcony door and windows. Thunder boomed in the sky and she wondered if it was the storm that had infiltrated her sleep.

The woman's scream that had emanated from Samson in her dream left a knot sitting in the pit of her stomach as she lie back down in the bed, pulling the covers up to her chin, listening for any other sign that something could be wrong. After a few minutes she began to feel drowsy again.

Her final thought of the evening was that they were safe; there was no reason for anyone to be screaming on the twenty-fourth floor of Emerald City.

She closed her eyes and gave no further thought to the waking world.

ALL GOOD THINGS

BOOK III

PROLOGUE

Veronica tapped her fingers on the wet railing outside Juliette's condo. She sighed heavily as she moved her weight from one foot to the other.

She's never on time.

Veronica was ready to run. Every morning since the group returned from Emerald Park she met Juliette just before sunrise for their morning workout. It helped both ladies to cope with the madness of their new world and all they had lost; plus it helped feed Veronica's obsession with running. If she couldn't run for sport anymore, she would run for fun. She gave the tall blonde another five minutes before she shrugged and took off in a sprint.

The remnants of the previous night's severe thunderstorm hung in the air. Flashes of lightning still flickered in the sky and thunder intermittently rolled past in low rumbles. The heavy rain had stopped, but even if it hadn't let up, Veronica was no stranger to running in the rain. In fact, she found it quite relaxing.

Across the full length of the outer corridor of the twenty-fourth floor she went, making her way down the interior steps to the floor below, she picked up the pace. With each pounding footstep she counted in her head: *one, two, three, four, one, two, three, four.* The numbers soon turned into beats and without even realizing, she fell into her old habit of beatboxing as she ran. Her mind free and clear of all outside influence, she continued on in perfect form and rhythm all the way down to the main lobby in record time. It had been quite a while since she'd run alone, it usually took three times as long to clear the building with Juliette alongside her. Juliette didn't have half the stamina that Veronica did, and she was a real Chatty Kathy, often times forcing the workout down to a slow jog.

Veronica stopped to stretch and take a quick break. No matter how many times she'd been in the Emerald City's enormous lobby, she always took the time to savor its luxury. Even in the low light of dawn, the expensive crystal fixtures sparkled, and no amount of dust could ever take away from the shine of the immaculate marble. She approached the main entrance and gazed out onto the pool deck. The festering pit that was once a gorgeous five-star swimming pool overflowed from the overnight rainfall. Although the group had fished out and disposed of the bloated bodies that had called the pool home, there was no way for them to drain the water. The blood and gore, bacteria and disease... no matter how much it rained, it always remained.

Veronica could see the churning gulf in the distance. The normally emerald-green waters were brown, and treacherous waves crashed against the shores. She spied the small green flags flapping violently in the wind, forever symbolizing safe swimming waters since there was no longer an attendant to change them out. Eaters stood as statues on the sand, entranced by nothing, staring listlessly into the clouded sky. Veronica, too, became entranced by nothing as she fixed her eyes on the brutal surf. Her mind wandered to thoughts of the boat they'd all arrived on two months before. The craft had survived other storms so far, but she imagined that one of these days she'd step out on her balcony and find all signs of the boat erased.

A loud slam against the glass beside her caused her to nearly jump out of her shoes. Her breath caught in her throat, Veronica grasped the large doorframe and put a hand to her chest. She'd been so deep in her own thoughts that she'd managed to ignore the rotting corpse that had made its way up to the resort. The eater snarled at her and slapped mutilated hands at the shatterproof glass. Its revolting yellow skin had an almost polished look to it from the rain. Veronica shook her head in disgust. Regardless of the safety of the tower, she knew better than to ever let her guard down near an entryway like that. She couldn't help but laugh at her foolishness and thank her lucky stars that Juliette hadn't been there. The woman would have been a screaming mess and Veronica thought it was way too early in the morning to deal with that level of crazy. She smirked; she would tell Juliette all about her encounter with the eater just to get a rise out of her and share a laugh with Ben and Clyde.

Veronica took a step to her left and the eater stepped with her. She thought about leading it off to the side until she was out of sight so it would stop pounding against the glass, but her stomach growled angrily at her. Breakfast was more important; the eater would grow disinterested over time and wander off on its own. She flipped the corpse off and turned on her heels, jogging toward the doorway and disappearing into the stairwell.

Had Veronica taken four more steps to her left, she not only would have been leading the eater away from the doors, she would have lead herself into the direct line of sight of Juliette's lifeless body splayed across the pool deck.

PART I

ALL GOOD THINGS

I

Andrew allowed his eyes to remain closed as he woke from a hearty night's sleep. He always slept the best during thunderstorms. His thoughts drifted back to when he was a child and little Clyde would come running into his room, tears streaming down his face, his body trembling with fright. He'd always scooch over and allow his younger brother to climb into bed with him during those stormy nights when he sought comfort, and the two of them would drift off into a restful slumber soon after. Although now they were both grown men, Andrew knew Clyde still had trouble sleeping during bad storms. But not him; he slept like a boulder, and that was a good thing, considering Juliette's loud, bear-like snores.

He smiled and rolled over, stretching his arm out to pull his new fiancée into a spooning embrace, but his hand found an empty space beside him. He opened his eyes and looked around the quiet bedroom, seeing no sign of her. He couldn't tell quite what time it was since the gloom of the storm still clung to the sky, but he figured it was early dawn and Juliette hadn't returned from her morning run with Veronica. Wiping the sleep from his eyes, he groaned as he willed himself from the comforts of the oversized bed and shuffled his way to the bathroom. When he had finished with his morning business, he quickly freshened up and returned to the bedroom to fetch his clothes. As he pulled his khakis up around his waist he raised an eyebrow at the sight of Juliette's running shoes sitting neatly beside the bedroom door.

Slipping his feet into a pair of flip flops, he called out to her as he entered the living room, "Hey babe?"

The condo was silent. Clyde's bedroom door was still closed and he tapped lightly. When he received no answer he inched the door open to find his brother still peacefully asleep. He made his way out to the balcony and cringed; the wind hadn't died down, and it hurled drops of rain at him, stinging his bare chest. He slid the heavy door shut and finished dressing, imagining Juliette was over at Gary's getting a head start on breakfast.

*

Andrew gave two solid knocks and let himself into Gary's condo. The smell of spam and powdered eggs greeted him along with Gary's inappropriately cheerful voice for this time of morning.

"Morning! Hungry, I take it?" Gary waved a paper plate in the air but Andrew declined. Ben and Catherine sat opposite each other at the small dining room table.

"What's up man?" Ben said while chewing. Catherine politely smiled, her mouth full of food.

"Hey, y'all," Andrew responded, crossing his arms. "Anybody happen to see Juliette this morning?"

"Veronica wasn't in her room when I got up." Ben belched before continuing. "They're probably off putting some sneaker to pavement."

"Nah, Juliette's running shoes are still in the bedroom. Catherine, Gary? Either of you see her?"

"No sweetie, I haven't," Catherine said as she began clearing the table.

Gary shook his head. "She'll turn up. Maybe she's got another pair of shoes. You know how women are."

"I'll exclude myself from that over-generalized statement, thank you very much." Catherine smirked at Gary. "Not much time to go shopping these days, but my lonely little pair suits me just fine." She placed her hands on her hips and stuck a foot out, modelling her silver and black Skechers slip-ons.

"Oh, very nice." Gary raised his eyebrows and golf-clapped.

"Yeah, I don't really pay attention to shoes." Andrew slumped onto the couch. "I'm sure she's with Veronica." He put his feet up on the coffee table and accepted a cup of instant coffee from Gary.

The four continued to chat, as if the collapse of the world beyond the Emerald City never happened. They swapped stories of horrible first jobs, wiping tears of laughter from their eyes as they poked fun at one another's accounts of teenage inexperience in the working world.

"You cried?" Catherine cackled, nearly doubling over in laughter.

"Shit, nobody ever told me how much taxes they take out of your check." Andrew chuckled. "I tried to quit, too, told 'em they were a bunch of thieves and threw some ketchup packets at the manager after I got my first check." The big man shook his head. "My mama marched my ass right back up to that Burger King, made me apologize and beg for my job back. Of course this was *after* she whooped me and called half her church friends to tell 'em about it." The room erupted in laughter.

"I guess I took the backwards route," Ben said as he grabbed his smokes from the coffee table. "Had a shot at a career and *then* got a job in food services." He pulled his lighter from his pocket and made his way toward the front door. "I'll be back."

He pulled the door shut behind him and shielded his lighter from the wind with his body, lighting his non-menthol cigarette and inhaling deeply. He leaned on the railing and gazed out on the abandoned city. It was easy to forget about all the ugliness that surrounded them. Ben remembered a phrase his mother used to spit at him when she'd scold him for his poor choice of friends in high school. "You stand by the garbage, you're gonna smell like the garbage. You're only as good as the company you keep, Benny." Her voice, like a forgotten song, echoed in his mind. She was right, though. The end of the world had proven to be much more tolerable these last few months with the small family they'd formed.

He shuddered to think back on his circumstances only such a short time ago.

Had they not all found each other, where would they all be? He thanked his lucky stars on a daily basis not only for being alive, but for the chance at creating a new life amidst the rubble of the old. He knew he might be getting too comfortable, that they'd eventually have to head back out into the streets of the dead and risk their lives one of these days to round up more supplies and scavenge what they could. Gary, although by far the most positive of the group, was definitely the last person to allow anyone to forget that they were always surviving on limited necessities.

"Borrowed time," he whispered, the words carried by smoke.

The previous night's dinner discussion was a heavy reminder of that fact as Gary and Catherine went down a list of dwindling foodstuffs and personal sanitation products. Ammunition and medical supplies were good since they'd hunkered down and begun to play house, but with the illusion of normalcy came the consequences of basic wasteful behavior of which they were all guilty. Ben did not look forward to the day that Gary showed up at breakfast with a map, a plan, and a packed bag instead of eggs.

The slamming of a door broke Ben's train of thought, he looked up to see Clyde strolling toward him. He offered a smoke but Clyde waved the cigarettes away.

"I'm about ready to thrown down on some spam."

Ben laughed as Clyde disappeared into the condo. Shrieks of laughter eked their way out before the door closed once more and the silence of the dead world returned.

Ben was not a big fan of heights, but that was one thing he liked the most about being on the twenty-fourth floor; it was the perfect height for the moans and cries of the savage eaters below to be lost on the wind.

Slamming footsteps in the stairwell drifted to him and he turned toward the source. The door clattered open and Veronica bounded into view, her pony-tail swaying. She grinned and gave him a wave as she jogged up.

"Hey there," she panted, stretching her tall, slender frame and rolling her shoulders.

"Mornin'. Have a good run?"

"Yeah, it was quiet, just how I like it. Juliette ever wake her lazy ass up?"

Ben narrowed his eyes, "We thought she was with you."

"Nope," Veronica said, siting on the ground and grabbing her feet, stretching her legs out. "She never showed up this morning. I got tired of waiting on her and took off on my own."

"You think she would have gone for a run on her own, too?" He flicked his cigarette over the railing.

Veronica giggled. "Yeah right. Juliette? She's terrified of the lower floors."

"Well, she's gotta be down there somewhere, because she ain't up here with us." He stared down at Veronica, a look of worry finally crossing her face.

"Ben, I was gone for over an hour and didn't run into her. I would have heard her, trust me. If the dead weren't already up and walking around I would have woken them. You know how quiet it is down there."

Ben shook his head slightly, a line forming in his forehead. "Something's not right. If she wasn't with you, wherever she is, she's been gone too long."

Veronica popped up from the ground with a shrug. "So let's go look for her."

II

A loud knock startled Michelle from her deep, drunken sleep. She rolled over with a groan and inadvertently slapped her hand against her forehead. She grunted and shimmied up onto her elbows, rolling her neck back and forth. "Yeah?" she called out groggily.

"It's me," Gary said, his voice muffled by the door. "Mind if I come in?"

"Yeah, whatever." Michelle grabbed a hair tie from the bedside table and sat up as he walked into her bedroom, closing the door lightly behind him. "Jesus, what time is it?" she asked him as she piled her curly mane atop her head.

"A bit too early for your liking I'm afraid." He beamed at her, his perpetual positivity too much for her hangover. "Listen, you wouldn't by any chance happen to know where Juliette could be, would you?"

Gooseflesh suddenly spread out over Michelle's body at hearing Gary utter the blonde's name and she was thrust back into sobriety. She felt a small film of sweat begin to develop on her upper lip and she ran her hand across her mouth.

"Michelle?" Gary cocked his head with the slightest bit of concern. "You alright, love?"

"I'm fine, Gary. Jesus Christ. I feel like shit, I drank too much last night, and now you come barging in here at some God-awful hour to find out if I know where the hell Juliette is?" she snapped at him, throwing her comforter to the side. "No, I do not know where she is, and I do not care." She jumped up and marched into the bathroom, slamming the door shut behind her. She leaned back against it and took a deep breath, waiting for Gary to leave.

"Sorry," he mumbled from the bedroom. "I was just checking. We're going to go looking for her, Andrew's worried sick." The bedroom door opened. "If you want to join us, we'll be over at my place for a bit longer before we head out."

A few seconds passed before he finally shut the door and Michelle exhaled loudly, dropping her knees onto the plush rug in front of the sink.

Her head swam for a moment and she closed her eyes as she tried to regulate her breathing. Just like many of her other poor choices on many a drunken night in her past, the memories of the previous evening's drunken foolishness flooded the front of her mind and made her shiver. She creased her brow as she pieced the broken thoughts together.

Alone, I was alone, always alone these days.

Her thoughts raced.

I went looking for company... looking for Gary... but he was asleep. I got confused, ended up on Ben's balcony.

That's when the imaginary knife twisted in her side and made her cringe.

"That bitch," she said as she remembered Catherine and Ben's encounter. The mix of self-hatred and envy that had stirred to the surface, the pure rage that had taken over.

Things never go as planned.

She remembered hearing Juliette's small voice from the other side of the balcony, the animal inside taking over, just as it had at the liquor store, just as it had on the highway. She remembered the look on Juliette's face, a wide-eyed mixture of shock and confusion as Michelle flipped her thin frame over the railing. The scream, the thunder, the lightning, the rain. And then finally, morning.

The corners of Michelle's mouth began to twitch and her fingertips buzzed. She pulled herself up and leaned over the sink, staring into the mirror at the cold eyes that she barely recognized. She suddenly felt lightheaded as she replayed the events over and over in her mind, a wave of heat rushing over her. She grabbed the half-empty gallon jug of saltwater and poured it over her head, relishing in the sensation as it ran down her face, her shoulders, back, and arms; she felt almost as if it were a baptism of sorts. There was no remorse for Juliette's murder, only enjoyment. Enjoyment she still didn't understand but enjoyment she had, in that moment, come to accept. She cracked her toes in the soaking wet rug beneath her feet and pulled her hair down, allowing the saturated curls to fall down around her shoulders.

She swung the bathroom door open and quickly dressed. Without further thought toward her appearance, which came as a surprise, she exited her condo and headed for Gary's. In all the years of Michelle's life, the thing she took pride in the most were her good looks. But today, for some reason, felt different. Not that it mattered, she would always be beautiful, but to say she appeared fair-minded or balanced would have been an overstatement.

She entered Gary's condominium with an air of mindful arrogance and heard the others cease their conversation abruptly as she joined them in the living room.

"Good mornin', y'all," she greeted them, crossing her arms and leaning against the wall.

"I'm glad you decided to join us." Gary smiled and nodded in her direction.

The rest of the group mumbled their hellos, with the exception of Clyde, who shot a dirty look at the sight of her hair.

"Alright, everyone," Andrew began as he got up from the couch and headed toward the door, "I'm gonna scout this building top to bottom with Ben and Clyde. Catherine, Gary, and Veronica, you startin' at the top of Central?"

The three nodded in response.

"I'll take bottom up. Central." Michelle shoved off the wall with her shoulder and followed behind Andrew, pushing passed him once they were out the door.

"Hey, Michelle," he called after her and she turned around. "I know you haven't exactly been real tight with the rest of the group or anything, but I appreciate you deciding to help."

"Don't mention it." She waved him off and continued toward the stairwell.

"No, I mean it. You know Juliette ain't well. So I really do appreciate it." His voice swelled with concern over the disappearance of his fiancée.

A shiver ran down Michelle's spine at the mention of Juliette's name again and she thought of how foolish he would feel if she decided to throw the truth at him.

"Seriously," she called back over her shoulder with steely words. "Don't mention it."

III

One by one, each unit was searched by the individual members of the group. It was a painstaking process, one that Veronica grew bored of quickly. She quietly slipped away from Gary and Catherine and headed toward the bottom floors. She was more curious about what Michelle was really doing down there; she knew the woman was lying through her teeth when she offered her help.

Unbeknownst to Michelle, Veronica had followed her quite a few timestotheunitinCentralthatshecalledherown.Callitteenagecuriosity,callitsuspicion, but something about how Michelle would disappear for hours on end, locked away in a dark room, probably drinking herself to death, pissed Veronica off to no end. What Veronica couldn't wrap her head around was Michelle's inability to readjust herself to theirnewreality.Everyonehadexperiencedsuchatragicloss,notonlyofthosetheyheld dear, but of the entire civilized world. The last few months had been do or die for everyone, but the small group locked away in Emerald City had found some sort of solace in one another. They'd found some remnant of normalcy in the things they did together to fill their time. No matter how insignificant it all seemed, there were plenty of reasons they gave one another to keep living.

But not Michelle. Michelle contributed no real amount of meaning to anyone but herself. And even then, did she really give herself any reason to keep holding on to what the world had become? Veronica hadn't liked her from the moment she'd first laid eyes on her. Not to mention how she'd been subjected to the sounds of drunken copulation on her first night in Emerald Park. She had tried giving

Michelle the benefit of the doubt when her best friend Lulu was killed, but Michelle continued to prove to Veronica that her decision to not trust the woman was a good one.

Veronica crept up to the closed door of Michelle's secret condo and pressed her ear to the door. No sounds came from the room. She slowly raised her hand to the doorknob and gripped it tightly, ever so slightly giving it a turn to check if it was unlocked.

"What's up, Nancy Drew?"

"Holy shit!" Veronica's heart nearly stopped and she felt like she'd jumped twelve feet in the air. She spun around and was face to face with a smirking Michelle.

Michelle chuckled at the spooked teen. "Damn girl, didn't think I was *that* stealthy. Whatcha doin' spyin' around down here? Am I really all that interesting that you put off looking for your friend to find out what I've been up to?" Michelle laughed again and put a hand on her hip. "Or do I just raise that many red flags for ya that you feel the need to invade my privacy?" Her smile suddenly disappeared.

Veronica, visibly embarrassed, picked at her fingernails. "I don't know... I guess I didn't believe that you were really looking for Juliette."

"Well, clearly *I* was. But you're nowhere near as quiet as you think you are, stomping around up here, so I decided to find out if *you* were really looking for Juliette." A shit-eating grin played across her face as she turned to walk away. "Come on, kiddo, let's go find schizo so I can find something better to do."

"Yeah, like what?" Veronica mumbled to herself as she followed Michelle down the hallway.

Michelle's grin was replaced with a scowl as she turned away from Veronica and led the girl away from the condo, making her way back down the stairwell to resume a dishonest search for the ill-fated Juliette.

About an hour passed and the survivors met up on the eleventh floor of the central building.

"We've come up empty," Gary said as he approached the two women.

"Same here," Veronica replied.

"We should probably head back over to the other building, meet the rest of the group downstairs. They've gotta be nearly finished searching the place." Catherine began walking toward the sky bridge.

"You don't think she went outside, do you?" Veronica asked.

Catherine turned to her as they walked, "I don't know sweetie, but I hope not.

She's been doing so well, but you can't ever be certain just *how well* someone like Juliette is really doing, you know?"

Veronica shrugged. "I guess not."

"If she was having an episode, there's no telling where she could have gone or what kind of trouble she's gotten herself into, so I truly do hope she did not leave this resort." Catherine's voice was hushed and full of worry. Her overwhelming altruism, which is what got her into practicing medicine in the first place, had motivated her to take on Juliette as a psych patient. Catherine knew she had no business taking on patients for a number of reasons; the world ending being one of them, and inadequate access to appropriate prescription medication would be another.

Veronica could see the gears turning in Catherine's head, the unease painted all over her face. "Look, wherever she is, or whatever she's got herself into, it isn't your fault. You know that right?"

Catherine smiled sweetly at her. "Thanks, hun. I think that's just what I needed to hear."

The four of them continued, making small talk. Once they reached the west building's lobby, Michelle's skin crawled; she knew it was only a matter of time before someone made the horrifying discovery on the pool deck. She threw herself into a plush chair and sighed, leaning her head back.

"Be careful," Gary said to her, "you don't want anyone to find out how overly concerned you are." He winked, completely unaware of her malicious deed of the night before.

"You're a terrible flirt," Michelle replied without looking at him.

He wandered by the other set of chairs that Veronica and Catherine had planted themselves in on the other side of the lobby, stopping at the windows just before the heavy doors. The wind whipped around violently, he could see eaters in the distance struggling against it.

"If I didn't know what time of year it was, I'd think a hurricane was on the horizon." He looked back at the group but they'd ignored him. "Sorry ladies, I suppose discussing the weather is still considered dull conversation." He grinned and turned back to the window. A clap of thunder startled everyone momentarily and Gary walked to the other side of the lobby doors to get a better look at the beach.

A lump formed in his throat simultaneously with a painful ache in his chest.

"Christ."

It was all he could do to even utter the word. Both hands went up to his bald head and he had to really concentrate in order to process exactly what it was his eyes were seeing.

There, on the ground not too far off from the disease-infested swimming pool, lay Juliette's mangled body. All four limbs were undoubtedly broken in the fall, evident in the unnatural way they were twisted. The most unfortunate part of the fall, other than her death, was that she'd landed face-down, and her head had caved in on itself. Her corpse was surrounded by a horrid amount of blood and fluids in some sort of gristly mixture. A part of her scalp kept catching the wind, flapping. The gruesome scene turned Gary's stomach.

"Jesus Christ!" he screamed this time, scaring the others in the room.

"What is it?" Catherine met Gary's horrified eyes and jumped from her seat, rushing to his side. Her hands went to her mouth as her eyes filled with tears. "Oh, God, no." She had to brace herself against Gary to keep from collapsing.

Veronica joined them and felt the blood drain from her face. Of all the things she'd seen, this was one she would never unsee. She grasped Catherine's hand and felt her eyes begin to burn, followed by chills as she thought back upon the woman's scream from her nightmare, that horrifying scream that pulled her from her sleep.

It wasn't a dream at all, Veronica thought, suddenly detached from reality. She looked over her shoulder at Michelle, who had just walked up behind her. The woman had a strangely complacent look on her face that unnerved Veronica.

"Go find Andrew," Veronica instructed her, but Michelle didn't move. Veronica swore she saw a twitch in Michelle's lips as she stared straight ahead at Juliette's deformed and mangled body. She let go of Catherine's hand and shoved Michelle hard with both hands, knocking her to the ground.

Gary and Catherine stepped away, watching as Veronica kicked at one of Michelle's legs. "I said go fucking find Andrew!" The ferocity in her voice was enough for Michelle that time. She scrambled to her feet and sprinted toward the stairwell.

Michelle met the other three members of the group about halfway to the second floor. She was breathing heavily and Andrew immediately sensed something was wrong.

"We found her," was all Michelle managed to say before Andrew pushed her aside and tore off down the stairs.

Catherine heard his heavy footsteps and rushed to meet him at the door.

"Andrew." She choked out his name, holding up her hands in a futile attempt to keep him from discovering Juliette's fate.

He stopped just in front of the small woman and shook his head. "Where is she?" he asked in a whisper. He furrowed his brow when she shook her head in response. "Cat," he said, beginning to sweat, "where is she?" He demanded the answer and a tear rolled down Catherine's cheek.

"Andrew, honey, I... I am so—"

Andrew pushed past her and headed for the exit.

Gary and Veronica stood beside the double doors, their backs to the ghastly scene. Gary had already placed a key in the door, knowing what would come.

"No, no, no."

Andrew whimpered. His breath quickened with his ever-increasing pulse. He felt his chest tighten and thought for a moment that the walls might have been closing in around him. "No!" He wailed and fell to his knees, sobs coming in short bursts, his big frame shaking.

Clyde and Ben finally joined everyone in the lobby. They knew instantly that Juliette was gone. Ben began to go to Andrew but Clyde grasped his arm. "Leave him be," he said, with tears in his eyes.

Andrew struggled with the keys in the door; his eyes wouldn't focus on anything else, just *her*. He threw his weight into the door and it flew open, caught in the wind, slamming violently against the side of the building. Had it not been for the hurricane secure glass, the door wouldn't have stood a chance. He felt the seams of his heart tearing with each step he took toward Juliette. The rain was coming down in a steady stream now, pinching his face as the wind drove it into him. He dropped to his knees beside the obliterated corpse of his fiancée and he roared. He took no care to avoid making a mess and pulled her lifeless remains into his chest.

He felt the fire inside of himself extinguish as he clutched what he could of Juliette's broken body in the pouring rain.

IV

Time stood still in the Emerald City Towers.

Clyde had finally been able to pull his brother from the macabre scene on the pool deck. Andrew had shrugged him off and disappeared into the depths of the massive building. Ben and Gary did what they could to clean her from the pavement; the fall from the twenty-fourth floor had not been graceful.

Juliette, frail and fragile in life, had proven to be the same in death, her body a shattered mess. The sheets and bedding did their part in holding the body of the young woman. The dead did their part in screaming and clawing at the glass, trapped in the east wing-turned-oversized holding cell. The rain hadn't let up, making for an even greater nightmare of a day.

Juliette was carried from the pool deck and down the cement steps that led to the beach.

Gary secured the gate behind him and joined Ben and Clyde on the sand. "You take point," he called out to Ben and motioned at the rain-soaked eaters shambling their way toward them. "We've got to make this quick."

Ben nodded and pulled his weapon, ready to fire. Clyde and Gary got to work shoveling the sand, throwing it to either side of them. The sand was wet and made for easy digging, and before long, the two men gently lowered Juliette's body into the shallow grave.

"I'm not a man of God," Gary said quietly, rubbing the rain from his eyes. "I'm not sure I have the words to say."

Clyde glanced up at the top floor of the west tower, Andrew stood watching somberly from the balcony. "He's already said them."

Gary noticed Andrew as well and nodded slowly. A shot rang out, snapping him from his quiet and he turned to Ben. The dead were getting closer, at least a dozen of them.

"I hate to be the asshole here, but we're gonna need to speed this thing up!" Ben shouted to his friends and fired another round into the closest eater's head.

Clyde and Gary hurried, piling shovel after shovel of sand on top of Juliette's corpse. Clyde needed to make sure this was right, not for himself, but for Andrew.

Ben fired two more shots and called out, "A little help, please!"

"Gary, go on. I got this." Clyde dug his feet deeper into the sand for better leverage and continued burying his brother's dead fiancée.

Gary flipped the shovel around and ran at the eater nearest to Ben. With a grunt, he swung the shovel up under the dead thing's chin and its face split open with a loud crack, its head snapping back. Gary buried the shovel into its head once more for good measure and went to work on the next eater as Ben repositioned himself further back and kept firing. The dead were dropping like flies but it was almost as if for every one that fell down dead, three more appeared in the shambling onslaught before them. A dozen quickly turned into two dozen and the pouring rain was not making things easier.

"I can't see shit!" Ben cried out as he continued to fire his weapon. Headshots he'd normally have no problem making from this distance were becoming increasingly difficult as the wind whipped rain and sand into his eyes.

Gary swung the shovel wildly, looking as if he were doing a tribal dance as he ducked and jumped, sidestepped and twirled. He breathed heavily and raised the shovel high above his head, bringing it down like a gigantic hammer, severing an eater's head entirely.

He turned quickly to take on another but lost his footing, hitting the sand hard. He went down and the wind was knocked from him. He struggled to breathe and rolled quickly to the side as an emaciated corpse lunged at him from above. Gary scrambled for the shovel and the eater grabbed hold of his leg. He cried out and tried to shake it free. It pulled itself slowly up body, growling with hunger. Gary wriggled to free his other leg trapped beneath him, but to his horror was unable to do so. He watched as the eater opened its decrepit jaws, almost in slow motion, and pulled itself closer to his thigh.

The eater's head exploded in a mist of brain and gore.

"Come on man." Clyde's light brown arms were under Gary's armpits, pulling him to his feet. "Let's get back to the resort."

The three men retreated to the steps, taking them two at a time, scurrying for safety behind the iron gates of the Emerald City's pool deck.

Gary collapsed on a lounge chair, his chest heaving. Despite the cold rain, his face was flushed and hot. "Ah, shite, that was too close."

Ben scrubbed at his bloodshot eyes with his rain-soaked t-shirt, attempting to remove all traces of sand. Clyde stood silently, staring up at his motionless brother, alone on the balcony above. He wrapped his arms around the shovel resting behind his neck and gave Andrew a nod.

Andrew nodded back. His mouth a straight line, his eyes burning from the tears that would no longer come. He gripped the balcony rail and his nostrils flared. He was past the point of sadness, a dark anger taking its place.

He felt it rush through him and his head felt like it would explode. The needle pricks of the rain numbed his skin. He stared down at the blood-soaked sand now, unable to move his eyes from the scene. He watched the rotting eaters as they stumbled over the mound of Juliette's sandy grave, and his rage reached the boiling point.

He couldn't, wouldn't, accept the fact that the love of his life, after making it this far, would have simply given up like this. He would never be able to come to terms with Juliette throwing herself from the balcony and abandoning him in this ugly, festering world.

She was still wearing the ring, Andrew thought, picturing her delicate hand. He closed his eyes, inhaling deeply. He saw her long, slender fingers. The shining diamond sitting so elegantly upon her left hand. He shook his head, he couldn't make sense of why his beautiful Juliette would leave him like this.

How could she do this to me?

His shoulders shook in anticipation of sobs that never came. He slammed his big fist down onto the railing and opened his eyes. The darkness of the day, the darkness of the world, coming back into focus.

He needed someone to blame for this.

"Catherine," he mumbled as he turned and walked inside.

V

Catherine and Veronica sat quietly in the living room of the condo that Veronica had shared with Samson. At a loss for words, Veronica mindlessly thumbed through a five-month-old women's fitness magazine. She'd never known anyone who'd committed suicide. She had an uneasy feeling in her stomach. She looked up at Catherine on the couch across from her. The woman's eyes were red and puffy. She'd taken Juliette's death hard. Of course it made Veronica sad, but after everything... she just didn't know how to show it anymore. Loss was a tiresome thing. Especially a loss that someone purposely inflicts.

Maybe that's why I'm not that *sad.*

She threw the magazine down onto the coffee table beside an empty glass candy dish. She sat back and folded her arms, crossing one leg over the other. She eyed the dish and her stomach growled.

Wish there was some candy left in there.

She sighed. "What now?" she asked Catherine.

"We keep doing whatever it is that we do." Catherine breathed deeply.

The front door opened and Ben walked in, soaking wet and covered in a number of different substances that neither woman questioned.

"There you two are." He placed his gun and extra ammo onto the countertop of the breakfast bar and rubbed the back of his neck. "We had a close one out there. There were way more of them out on the beach than we expected."

Veronica got up and went to the balcony door, standing on tiptoes and attempting to spy the swarm of eaters on the beach without going out into the rain.

"Is everybody okay?" Catherine asked, getting off the couch and going to him. She ran a hand through his drenched blond hair and another over the short growth of beard on his face.

"Yeah, everybody's fine; I can't say it was a nice burial, but she's at rest." He grabbed one of her hands and kissed her fingertips softly.

Their eyes met, Catherine's fingers still to his lips. "You need to shave. And you smell awful." She gave him a playful smile. "Go get cleaned up, I'll fix everyone something to eat. Veronica can help me."

Veronica watched the two of them from her position near the sliding glass doors. The romance that had blossomed between the two was sweet, something she felt they both needed. But it was far from enjoyable for her. Suddenly she was "the kid" to Ben and Catherine. Suddenly she was helping out with meals instead of cleaning guns and was subjected to all the domesticated boredom the tower could offer. Now that Juliette was gone, she didn't even have her running partner anymore.

"Sounds good," Ben responded. He looked at Veronica. "You alright? I mean, with everything that happened, do you need to talk?"

Veronica couldn't help but chuckle. "I'm fine, Ben. Catherine's right, you stink. Get outta here." Ben smiled at her and headed toward Catherine's to clean up.

*

Ben exited the condo, giving himself a sniff. He grimaced, agreeing with the women that he had indeed smelled better. He passed by Andrew's and the door flew open, startling him. Andrew charged out, brushing past Ben.

"Hey, man, you okay?" Ben called out.

Andrew ignored him and kept his pace toward Catherine's.

"Hey, where you goin' man?" Ben scratched at the scruff on his face, "Nobody's in there."

Andrew came to a halt in front of the door, his hand unmoving on the doorknob. "Where is she?" His voice was stern and even.

"Who?"

"Where is Catherine?" Andrew turned to look at Ben. Ben could tell there was something going on behind the man's dark eyes.

"She's with Veronica."

Andrew's nostrils flared and he clenched his fists. He took off toward Veronica's with a fierceness in his step.

"Hey!"

Andrew shoved Ben to the side again as he passed him.

"Hey man, what's the deal?" Ben's confusion turned to concern as Andrew ignored him once again.

Ben ran to Gary's and banged on the door quickly before he took off running back the way he came. He slammed his fist loudly on Andrew and Clyde's door, hollering for Clyde and then rushed back to Veronica's.

This isn't good, he thought. He could already hear Andrew shouting as he pushed the door open.

"This is all your fault!" Andrew screamed in Catherine's face. His enormous frame towered over her, a finger in her face, her back against the wall. Veronica stood frozen in the same place as when Ben had left the room. Her eyes were frantic and she seemed to be trying to sink into the sliding glass door beside her.

Catherine sobbed. "I'm so sorry, Andrew, I... I never meant—"

Andrew shoved her back into the wall when she tried to go to Ben. "You never meant what?" His voice got louder and more threatening with every word.

"Hey! Get the fuck away from her!" Ben boomed from the doorway.

"Nah, man, you need to stay outta this." Andrew didn't look at him as he spoke, his glare unbroken, and further fueling Catherine's fear.

"Like hell I will, I said get the fuck away from her, now. She's got nothin' to do with what happened." Ben stepped forward and Andrew pulled a gun on him.

Catherine sobbed uncontrollably and attempted once more to get away from Andrew. "Take one more fuckin' step," Andrew said to her in a low voice, "and you will regret it."

Ben put both his hands up. "Woah, man, hey, there's no need for this." Ben couldn't believe his eyes. One of his only friends left in the world had a gun pointed at his head. The unease in his gut was growing, practically eating him alive.

He's lost it.

"No need for this?" Andrew's brow furrowed. "*She* did this to us!" He pointed a finger at Catherine who cowered beside him.

"I didn't do anything but try to help her!" Catherine shouted between sobs.

Andrew backhanded the small redhead and she fell to the floor in a heap of pathetic whimpers.

Ben was filled with rage. "You're fuckin' losin' it man!"

"I have every right to lose it!" Andrew took a step closer to Ben, both hands on the gun, neither of them shaking. "She did this to us! Fillin' her up with all them fuckin' pills! Pills I ain't ever even heard of! *I* know what worked for Juliette, not her! I don't give a fuck if she's a doctor or not!" Andrew's face twisted and he fought back his tears.

Ben's shoulders slumped and his rage subsided. He shook his head. "Juliette did this. Nobody else did this but Juliette."

The door flew open behind Ben as Clyde and Gary burst into the room in a panic. Andrew finally broke, letting the anger go. He dropped the gun to his side and buried his face in one hand. In that same moment, Veronica swooped down, grabbed the glass candy dish from the coffee table and smashed it into the side of Andrew's head.

The big man grunted and teetered on his feet, stunned by the blow.

"*That* was for hitting Catherine!" Veronica shouted at a dazed Andrew.

Gary started. "What the—"

"What the fuck's goin' on?" Clyde yelled out, rushing with Ben to Andrew's side, helping him to the couch.

"A whole lot of bullshit," Veronica answered.

She looked back and forth between Andrew and Catherine, in their own separate worlds of chaos and misery, crumpled on opposite sides of the room. She shook her head and rolled her eyes as she trudged out of the condo.

"Michelle's the only damn one with any sense, for once," Veronica mumbled as she made her way toward the silence and solitude of the central building. She was going to find a secret room of her own.

VI

Veronica hurried across the breezeway, stomping and muttering to herself.

"Friends pulling guns on friends." She shook her head and bit her lip.

When had their close-knit group gone so mad? She understood loss, she understood the stages of grief; those things were all too familiar to her. When her mother had died, she remembered her father pulling away into silence and solitude for the briefest of times; he knew he had children to care for. Then the night in Franklin Woods, Samson lost himself in a bottle and threw a drunken fit in darkness, but he knew he needed to pull it together. Her mind wandered back to when she had lost her father and then her brother, just days apart. She'd done what she'd needed to do to survive and keep herself safe. She'd done even more than she needed to for a group of strangers that had grown to become her new family. There wasn't any time for grieving in this new world. Andrew's violent outburst had shocked her, even scared her a little. She could understand that he felt like he needed someone to blame, but she could not understand drawing a weapon or hitting Catherine the way he did.

She slowed as she approached the double doors to the central building and pulled her set of keys out. She tugged the handle and the door came gently toward her. She shrugged and chalked it up to Michelle being careless and forgetting to lock the door again. Making her way toward the staircase, she cocked her head and listened. She couldn't quite make out the noises, but they were most definitely the muffled shrieks and cries of the dead. She knew where they were kept, and she ran this building almost every day. She'd never heard them all riled up like this, though.

Curiosity got the better of her and she abandoned her mission of finding her own private condo to investigate the source of the commotion. As Veronica approached the next set of double doors on the opposite side of the long hall, she could see that one of the doors hadn't been pulled shut all the way. She crept up to the glass and peered through. Michelle was at the far end of the breezeway leading to the east building. She was stretched out on the floor, propped up on her elbows with a messy stack of papers beside her. A bottle of Malibu was within arm's reach and Veronica could hear her talking to herself. Slipping through the doorway, Veronica silently made her way toward the woman, studying her movements.

Is she drawing them?

Veronica furrowed her brow as she realized Michelle was giggling to herself and telling the eaters beyond the breezeway to be still. As she got closer, Veronica could see the stack of papers had been ripped from a sketch book.

"You still haven't mastered the art of stealth, Nancy Drew," Michelle called out.

Veronica's cheeks turned a bright shade of pink but she breathed a sigh of relief; she hated creeping around. Evidently, she was no good at it.

"Have a seat," Michelle said, rolling to her side and looking up at the blushing teen. "Looking for an art lesson?"

Veronica shook her head as she lowered herself to the dusty carpet. "How could you even hear me over all that noise?" Veronica motioned toward the rambunctious eaters beyond the glass doors.

"I didn't." Michelle laughed, clearly intoxicated. She pointed at the glass doors and chuckled again. "I saw your reflection." She sat up and exhaled loudly, pulling her wild hair up and tying it into a messy bun. Reaching for the bottle of rum she unscrewed the cap and offered some to Veronica.

Veronica scrunched her face up and she stared at the bottle. "What's it taste like?"

"Awful. I don't care much for the sugary stuff, but I'm running low on the good shit." Michelle took a swig from the bottle and once more extended her arm. "Here, try it."

"Alright." Veronica quickly took the bottle from Michelle and raised it to her nose. It didn't smell bad; in fact, it smelled sweet, like coconuts. She took a drink and coughed hard, spitting the clear liquid out onto Michelle.

Michelle laughed hard, wiping the rum from her face. "That first drink is always the worst. Go ahead," she said, waving her hand at Veronica. "Try again but a little slower this time."

Veronica's second drink went more smoothly. The warm liquor burned her throat, she could feel it as it went all the way down to her stomach. She grimaced but took another sip before handing the white bottle back to Michelle. Her mouth felt like it was on fire, but at the same time, her mind instantly felt at ease. She could see why Michelle liked to disappear on her own and drink herself stupid. It was yet another person's way of dealing with the sick world's burdens of grief.

"So what brings you to my neck of the woods, *again?*" Michelle sat the bottle in front of Veronica and stretched herself out on her side, her head resting in her hand.

Veronica told Michelle about Andrew's outburst as she took another sip of Malibu. "I just needed to get out of there. Even if I had gone to my room, someone would have known where to find me."

"They sure wouldn't think to look for you over here with me. Good thinkin' kid." Michelle noticed Veronica roll her eyes and she grinned at the teenager. "Sorry, sorry, you're not a kid."

Veronica ignored her apology. "I didn't know you were an artist."

"I'm not, it's just a hobby. I probably could have been an artist at some point, but then again, I probably could have been a lot of things." Michelle's voice seemed sad.

"What did you want to be?" Veronica reached out and grabbed the bottle, taking a quick sip. Michelle smiled at her and sat up, taking the bottle.

"I wanted to be anything but myself, I guess." She turned the bottle up again. "But I was brought up to believe that I was a nobody."

"What do you mean?" Veronica raised an eyebrow.

Michelle waved a hand at her, "My father was a piece of shit. I guess I never got over it."

Veronica thought about her last statement as she took another drink. She set the bottle down again and twisted her hair in her hand. "My father was a good man."

Michelle lay back down, hands behind her head. "Yeah, well, we can't all have perfect lives, can we, Nancy Drew?"

The pair sat silently in the breezeway, listening to the mesmerizing moans of the dead.

"So why are you hanging out with *them?*" Veronica asked, breaking the silence. She looked up at the eaters to her left. They were badly decayed and even more grotesque than she remembered. Their skin was slimy and yellow, black liquid oozed from nearly every visible orifice and crusted at the corners of their eyes, ears, noses, and mouths. Broken and rotted teeth gnashed and bit at the filthy glass, their mangled fingers clawing and grabbing fruitlessly. Howls and growls escaped their festering mouths and Veronica *almost* felt sorry for them.

"Why not?" Michelle answered with a swallow of liquor and a belch. "Who's doing who more harm right now? These guys, or those friends of yours up there?" She raised an eyebrow at Veronica, almost challenging her. "These guys listen to me. They're the perfect drinking buddies. They don't talk back or smart mouth me. If I say jump, they ask how high." She began to giggle again, rolling back over onto her side.

"You're fuckin' crazy." Veronica was feeling the buzz from the rum and cracked a smile.

Michelle shot up and covered her mouth, mocking surprise. "Who said you could use language like that, young lady?"

Veronica and Michelle doubled over in laughter and continued to drink. Michelle didn't mind the unexpected company, especially since she was already three sheets to the wind. Veronica needed the release, she needed to laugh and feel free. In that moment she didn't care that she was getting drunk with a sociopath and a group of dead people, she simply appreciated that for the first time in what felt like forever, she was getting to act like a stupid teenager.

*

Hours had passed, the bottle was empty, and night fell upon them. The breezeway darkened and Veronica relaxed against the cool glass behind her, closing her eyes. Her head spun and it felt like the earth was flying out of orbit. Michelle stood up, stumbling slightly.

"Where are you going?" Veronica slurred, her eyes still closed.

"I've gotta see a man about some sex, or... I think that's how that phrase goes."

Veronica giggled, "You're gross."

"Sleep it off, kiddo," Michelle called out over her shoulder but Veronica said nothing in response. She was already passed out.

Michelle drunkenly stumbled her way, as she always did, up to Gary's condo. When she emerged from the stairwell onto the twenty-fourth floor, she welcomed the cool December air with a sigh. She stretched her long frame and approached Gary's front door, placing her ear up to the cold surface to determine whether or not any of the others were there. When the silence finally satisfied her, she let herself in and crept her way to his bedroom. The door was open slightly and the light of a lantern leaked out through the crack into the hallway. She removed her clothes and let them drop to her feet. She slinked into his bedroom and shut the door behind her, her back against the door.

Gary looked up from his book. "You're early tonight." He tossed the book to the side and sat up, admiring her gorgeous body.

She pulled her hair from its bun and posed seductively to unclasp her bra, casting it behind her.

They giggled like children as she crawled across the bed in her panties and slid under the blanket beside him. Gary and Michelle were lost in one another's lascivious embrace. Arms and legs entwined, they reached the earth shattering climax they both looked forward to every night and lay panting on their backs.

Michelle rolled toward the nightstand and grabbed a cigarette from the drawer. The smoke curled from her mouth as she looked down at the man she both detested and desired. He gave one of her nipples a playful pinch as she crawled over him and headed for the bathroom to clean up.

She returned to the bed, passing him as he left to take his turn in the washroom. She threw herself onto the comforter and buried her face in the pillow. She thought back on the last twenty-four hours and how this might have been the longest day of her life.

"Andrew and Clyde are leaving," Gary said from the bathroom.

"Good," she muttered into the pillow.

"We tried to talk them out of it. Andrew just doesn't feel like he belongs here anymore, not without Juliette." Gary climbed into bed beside Michelle, stealing one of her cigarettes.

The familiar goose bumps licked at her naked flesh, but not in response to Gary's presence; they were once again for the mention of Juliette's name.

"Yeah? And what's Clyde's excuse?" Michelle asked, bringing her face up from the pillow.

"Ah, brothers. Where one goes, the other follows."

They sat in silence for several minutes before she rolled over onto her back and sighed. "You ever kill anybody, Gary?"

"We've all unfortunately killed someone, love. You know that."

She looked at him, her face serious. "No, I mean. Did you ever kill someone because you wanted to?"

He frowned, glancing over at her. "Why do you ask?"

She smiled coyly. "Just wondering. Doesn't everybody want to kill somebody? I wouldn't judge you if you had."

He leaned over to the bedside table and put out his cigarette. "You know, as much as I love our emotionally devoid love making sessions, you are absolutely mad sometimes." He clicked off the lantern before laying down beside her.

Michelle smiled in the darkness. "Yeah, that seems to be the general consensus."

VII

Ben stood quietly and puffed on a cigarette, half inside the condo, half on the balcony. It was beginning to get too cold at night for outside smoking, but Catherine hated the smell and insisted he not do it inside. She was sound asleep and dead to the world in the bedroom, thanks to a self-prescribed cocktail of anxiety pills.

After Veronica had stormed out of the condo earlier that afternoon, Ben wanted so badly to chase after her, to make sure she was alright. But he knew Veronica was strong; it was Catherine who needed him after what Andrew had done. It wasn't every day that the group pulled guns on each other or assaulted one another. It also wasn't every day that one of their own committed suicide. It was a lot to take in after two full months of rest and relaxation in the towers. The ugly truth was that the dead world remained dead; the small group of survivors had grown comfortable in their fortress. The sheer lack of day-to-day interaction with the crumbling world had allowed them to shut it out and almost forget that bad things could happen. They weren't ready for the losing hand today had dealt them.

Ben especially wasn't ready for Andrew's sudden desire to leave. He'd tried to talk his friend out of it. He told him that they'd all dealt with loss before, and together, they would deal with this. But Andrew would hear none of it.

"I don't have a place here anymore, man." Andrew looked up at Ben with a tear-streaked face. "Not without her. I don't belong here, not after today."

"Drew, you're not going anywhere. This is your home. We will get past this, together, I promise you." Ben placed a reassuring hand on Andrew's shoulder.

"No!" Andrew shrugged the hand off and stood up, leaning into Clyde, still woozy from the blow to his head. "This is not my home." He looked to his brother. "I can't make you come with me."

Clyde shook his head, wiping a tear from his eye. "It's stupid as hell, but where you go, I go."

The brothers turned to leave and Ben began to protest.

"Let 'em go, mate. Let 'em go." Gary clapped Ben on the back and went to Catherine, helping her to her feet once Andrew and Clyde were gone.

Catherine rushed into Ben's arms. He held her tightly and kissed the top of her head. "Are you alright?"

She nodded and looked up at him, tears in her eyes. "I'm fine. But Andrew… the pain he's feeling. I remember that same emptiness when I lost Desmond. We can't blame him for *feeling*."

Ben replayed the afternoon's events over and over in his mind. He flicked his cigarette off the balcony and slid the door shut; he couldn't wait for the next morning. He agreed to let it go at Catherine's request. And he'd also agreed to leave Andrew alone for the night before attempting to talk him out of leaving once more. That was Gary's master plan. Give the man a night to think on it, give Clyde some time to realize just how stupid leaving was, and they'd come to their senses.

"Otherwise," Gary had said, "we've got to help them on their way. We're a broken group and we've got to go out and try to patch ourselves up."

Whatever the hell that means, Ben thought as he practically dove headfirst into the bed. He tried to make as much noise as possible to see if Catherine would stir in her sleep, but her light snoring told him to give up. He drifted off and was up again the following morning, feeling like he hadn't slept a wink. He dressed and rushed out the door, leaving Catherine behind.

Clyde was on the breezeway smoking when Ben walked out.

"I was wonderin' when you'd show up." Clyde held out his pack of smokes.

Taking a cigarette and lighting it, Ben smiled at his friend. "Who knew you had the capability of getting up early for once."

"Yeah, yeah, you know I like my beauty sleep." Clyde laughed nervously before addressing the elephant in the room. "Look man, he's my brother. You gotta understand that I can't let him go out there on his own."

"I do understand that, Clyde. But what I don't get is why the fuck he has to leave. Look at this place," Ben said, making a big sweeping motion with his arms. "Why the hell would you want to leave *this* for *that.*" He pointed out over the railing at the disastrous world below them.

"Too much bad juju man, he can't deal with it. It isn't like when he lost anybody else. She wasn't just taken from him, or turned into one of them things out there. She just gave up, dude. He feels like if he stays here, he's givin' up too. He won't accept that this is as good as it's gonna get these days."

Ben inhaled deeply on his cigarette, savoring the burn in the back of his throat. He leaned forward on the cold rail and felt his eyes well up with tears.

"Don't go cryin' on me. Big pussy, white boy." Clyde flipped his braids over his shoulder with one hand and wiped his eyes discreetly with another. "My mama used to say, 'All good things, CiCi, all good things.' I used to think she meant that all good things come to those who wait. But I think we all know what it means now."

Ben nodded in agreement and looked over at Clyde as he tried to wipe another tear. "Yeah, who's the big pussy now?" The two men relished in their moment of laughter and friendship, two things that they agreed were hard to come by these days.

Ben finally did understand why Andrew had to leave. He understood that in a way, their façade of safety *was* giving up. He headed for Veronica's after Clyde told him he'd grab Andrew and catch up with everyone in a bit.

He knocked on the door softly; usually she was up and about by now. When no one answered he let himself in and the overwhelming, acidic smell of vomit hit him in the face immediately. His stomach turned and he quickly brought his shirt up to his nose. There, half on the couch, lay Veronica. She'd obviously attempted to throw up outside but hadn't made it in time. Dried vomit streaked down the sliding glass door and all over the carpet. It was all over the front of her shirt, in her hair, and on her shoes.

Ben grabbed a half-empty bottle of water from the coffee table and threw it on her face. She gasped and sat up quickly, groaning and coughing.

"Oh, my God," she said, groaning when the smell hit her. "I think I'm gonna be sick." She jumped up from the couch and ran for the bathroom, slamming the door behind her.

Ben could hear the obnoxious sounds of dry heaving and retching; he leaned against the wall beside the bathroom. "I'm gonna guess that somehow you got your hands on some alcohol last night?" he called to her through the closed door. He heard the splashing of water and the door finally opened.

"I think I'm gonna switch condos, it smells terrible in here. There's plenty to go 'round." She rubbed her temples with both hands.

"Where'd you get the booze?" Ben realized after the words had come out of his mouth that he sounded like an angry parent.

Veronica shrugged. "I don't know, I found it," she snapped, rolling her eyes as she returned to the bathroom to gather some things. "Don't worry about it. Just leave me be; I need to take a bath. Preferably somewhere that *doesn't* stink." Her head was pounding, and from the moment Ben had splashed that water into her face, she regretted drinking that Malibu with Michelle. She didn't even remember coming back to her room. All she knew was that she needed a bath, and Ben needed to leave her alone. She had no idea the impending departure of two of their own. She had no idea, and honestly didn't care, how Ben was feeling in that moment.

He grabbed her by the arm as she passed. "Hey, I'm sorry. Yesterday was one fucked up day. I'm just looking out for you."

"Yeah, well don't." She pulled away from him. "I'll be at Gary's."

His heart sunk as he watched her leave the foul smelling condominium. The group really did seem to be broken.

VIII

The crumbled group sat in Gary's living room waiting on breakfast. They'd all grown to love the smell of powdered eggs, canned meat, and instant coffee. Every once in a while, a couple of packets of oatmeal were thrown into the mix and they ate like kings. Gary returned from the balcony and served up the delicious meal to the salivating mouths.

"Can you pass the salt, please?" Catherine asked Andrew. She gave him a smile and a nod, letting him know she had moved on from yesterday's attack. He managed a smile and slid her the salt across the dining table. He kept to himself while he ate his breakfast, patiently waiting for everyone to finish. They mindlessly chatted back and forth but he knew everyone was just delaying the inevitable.

While everyone shoveled food into their mouths, Michelle pretended to be distracted by her nails on the couch, busily filing, and picking at an expired granola bar. She normally did not join the group for breakfast, but she wouldn't miss Andrew and Clyde's official departure announcement for the world.

Veronica finally joined with a towel in her hair after a much needed bath.

"You hungry, love?" Gary asked her, a plate stretched out in her direction.

She shook her head up and down, "Oh yeah." She greedily snatched the plate from Gary and it elicited a hearty laugh from him.

"I remember the first time that I—"

Ben cut Gary off with a look that said, "Don't even bring up the drinking."

"Ah, I guess I don't remember it as well as I thought." Gary gave Ben a nod and

Veronica a wink. All the while Michelle tried to hide her smirk as she continued to file.

The seemingly endless charade of a family-style breakfast finally rolled around to a good stopping point. Their bellies full and the mood lightened, Andrew stood up.

"I know an apology will never do me justice, especially for you, Catherine. But I am sorry. I'm sorry for turnin' on y'all like that. I realize now that none of it would have brought *her* back. None of that yellin' or any harm I could do to any of you would make her death any easier to deal with. Please forgive me." He bowed his head in shame and continued. "I've made my decision to leave this group not because of Juliette's death or my actions yesterday, but because I can't sit here like this anymore. I feel like all I'm doing is delaying the inevitable. We're all gonna die one day, whether it be from natural causes or from them dead things runnin' around out there, but it's gonna happen, and I want to feel like I did my part in finding something more before it does. We shut ourselves away in here and acted like everything was back to normal. Everything is one hundred percent not normal in here, people."

He elevated his voice slightly, a stern tone taking over.

"What happened to taking the city back, Gary? What happened to rebuilding and going out there and finding more survivors?" Andrew looked to him with imploring eyes.

Gary opened his mouth to speak but found no words.

"Nothing happened, that's what. We locked the doors to Emerald City and we kept all this for ourselves. Hundreds of homes for displaced people, just like us, but we keepin' it quiet for our selfish group of seven? I can't do it anymore. I deserved her death because I ain't been a good person. I gotta make that right."

Ben stood up suddenly and leaned across the table, pointing at Andrew. "You feel like shit and somehow your penance is roaming a wasteland with your fuckin' brother looking for some sort of salvation? Fuck you, man. If this is some bullshit about God then go get on your knees and say a prayer to the man in the sky. Go say a prayer to the same God that brought the dead back to life to kill everybody any of us ever gave a shit about." He glared at Andrew.

"Maybe it is some *bullshit about God* but you know what, at least I believe in God. At least I have that. What the fuck you believe in? Huh?" Andrew folded his arms across his broad chest and shook his head. "I'm makin' my soul right, man. When my time comes, I know I won't be cursed to walk around the earth feeding on the flesh of my fellow man. I will make my peace long before then and I will be gone from this hell, embraced in the arms of my Lord."

Ben doubled over with laughter and shot a vicious look at the man, "When did you become so self-righteous, dude?"

Andrew refused to respond and instead looked away.

"Yeah, that's what I thought. Go make your fuckin' peace, dude. Just get it over with and get outta here. I'm sick of talkin' to a ghost."

Ben abruptly left the table and retreated to the balcony. The silence in the room was unbearable. Michelle cleared her throat and raised her eyebrows, glancing at Gary. Gary raised his eyebrows and sighed, turning to Andrew. "I respect your decision, I really do." Andrew nodded and sat back down at the table.

Gary leaned forward and continued, "I also respect you pointing out that I did at one point have a plan. A plan I was so sure of." His voice trailed off as he seemed to fight back tears. "But people died and I no longer saw that plan as an option. I was afraid. Afraid of losing anyone else. What we've got here is solid, and I made sure we stayed here, shut away and safe." He took a deep breath before continuing, "But you're right. This is simply delaying the inevitable. I know I can't convince you to stay, so I'll see you off."

Michelle dropped her nail file in shock as the words left Gary's mouth.

"We'll take one of the armored cars and I'll drop you by the car dealership, see you on your way. I'll start looking for other survivors and scavenge the area, replenish our supplies."

"I'm going too." Catherine stood up and flashed another kind smile. "It's what Desmond would have done. He wouldn't have sat in here like this, either."

"We're all going." Veronica joined Gary and Catherine at the table. "None of this 'stay behind and wait for us to come back' crap. If any of us are risking our lives, then all of us are risking our lives. That's how it should be."

Michelle let out a cackle from the couch. "Here I was, thinking *I* was the crazy one. Just wait 'til ol' Benny-boy hears your grand plan. He'll have you locked away like Rapunzel." She leaned forward and retrieved her nail file from the floor. "Enjoy your romp in the badlands, y'all. Kiddo and I will be waiting for ya to get back."

Veronica stomped over to Michelle and slapped the file out of her hand. She wasn't sure if it was the hangover or the gravity of the situation, but she was not in the mood to deal with Michelle's bullshit. "I'm not a kid. I'm not stayin' behind, and neither are you." She stuck a finger in Michelle's face. "We are a group and we *will* do this together. So you're either with us or you're not!"

Michelle was almost stunned, but found Veronica's confident demeanor amusing and slightly impressive. She snickered. "Alright, alright. Authority looks good on you." She retrieved the nail file from the floor once more and leaned back.

Clyde shook his head and went to the sliding glass door; he noticed it had been left open a crack. He slid it to the side and stepped out beside Ben. The morning air was crisp and fresh. The smell of the dead did not reach this high up and it was refreshing to breathe in the cool air and feel the warmth of the sun on his face. He looked over at Ben. "You heard?"

"Yeah, I heard." Ben spat out over the railing, not meeting Clyde's gaze.

"What do you think?" Clyde lit a cigarette.

"I think it means we're all fucked."

IX

Guns were loaded, bags were packed, and words were scarce. Gary had the route mapped and laid out their "simple plans" on the table. Ten miles east of their location was a strip of car lots and a cluster of subdivisions and office complexes. They'd see Andrew and Clyde on their way and split up into two groups to cover as much ground as possible by nightfall. If they ran over on time, they'd at least be able to take cover in one of the homes.

Veronica grabbed her bag off the bed and readjusted her ponytail, giving herself one last look in the mirror. She frowned at her reflection. Her once-athletic frame appeared malnourished and borderline anorexic. She'd tried not to look in the mirror as much since the world ended, knowing how she felt about everyone else's appearance. She shrugged and was about to exit her condo when she stopped, spying Samson's button-up sloppily hanging on one of the dining room chairs. She scrunched her mouth up to the side before snatching it up and tying it tightly around her waist, *just in case.* She liked having a piece of him with her at all times. She'd never had the forethought to bring something of her own father's when she and Isaac fled their apartment on that fateful day which seemed so very long ago.

Veronica pulled the door closed behind her and noticed Clyde standing solo on the breezeway. She thought about simply meeting everyone downstairs as planned, but instead she watched him as he smoked his cigarette; he was clearly distracted, upset. "You know that we're only doing this because we feel bad about ourselves," she said to him.

He raised an eyebrow. "Ain't that a truth bomb."

"I know it sounds shitty, but just let it go, don't say goodbye to him. It'll only make things worse." She casually draped herself on the railing beside him. He knew she was talking about Ben.

"More truth bombs, courtesy of Veronica…" He raised another eyebrow at the teen, waiting for her to fill in the blanks.

"Williams." She snorted, "I guess most of us don't even know each other's last names, huh?"

"Sheeeit," Clyde drew the word out, "I wish I had been more clever, I would have told y'all my name was somethin' sexy, like Dante or Francisco." The pair giggled and Clyde placed an arm around Veronica. "You know, chica, whatever happens, you gonna be fine, right?"

She unknowingly picked at her nails. "I used to think so."

Clyde flipped his braids over the shoulder opposite Veronica, "Nah, I gotta good feelin' that you'll be aight."

She sat quietly for a moment longer, considering what he'd said. She looked at Clyde and tried to smile, "I think you will be too."

*

Ben stood on his balcony, anxiously waiting for Catherine to finish dressing. He gazed out over the crystalline gulf, watching *The Dockside* bob gently in the calm wake. Just a day earlier, the stormy waters had thrown the poor boat around like a toy. A part of him wanted so badly to say fuck it and get back on that boat, leaving the city of Haven and the bittersweet apocalypse behind him.

We should have never stopped here.

A knot formed in his gut and every ounce of his being screamed at him not to leave the security of the Emerald City, but he was the odd man out in a shitty situation.

Ben could no longer hold in his anger. He kicked at the bag near his feet and balled up his fists, throwing a hard punch, that he immediately regretted, at the solid, steel railing.

"Fuck!" he screamed in both pain and outrage. "We are surviving here! We are fine! What the fuck are we doing going back out there like this?!" He yelled to no one, face red with exasperation.

"Ben?" Catherine rushed onto the balcony. "Relax, what's the matter?" She moved closer and placed her hands on him, one on his back, one on his chest. Her green eyes filled with concern. "Who are you yelling at?"

He shook his head and smiled, his eyes falling back upon the boat. He exhaled and pulled the short redhead into his arms. "Everyone." He kissed her gently on the top of her head and closed his eyes, breathing her scent in deeply. He wished he could stand there with her like that forever.

"Well, nobody's yelling back." She let herself sink into his embrace as she rubbed a hand on the small of his back. "Everyone gets to make their peace. I know you're angry, but you can't take that away from him."

"Then let him go make peace on his own. Why should we go out there, too?" Ben pulled away from her and looked into her eyes.

"Because that's what friends do."

*

Andrew didn't see his departure from Emerald City as a form of abandonment; he saw it as an awakening for the group he so tenderly cared about. He hoped Ben would realize that. He knew in his heart that Ben would come to his senses once they were out there, once they found a purpose outside these walls.

"What's the hold-up?" Andrew asked Gary as he approached him on the breezeway.

"The bastards are all over the gate. We'll have to draw them away from the garage." He tossed Michelle the keys to one of the armored trucks. "You still remember how to handle that thing?"

She winked, "See ya on the other side." And with that, they momentarily parted ways.

The group, for the first time in over two months, exited the building together and stepped onto the pool deck. Gary locked the doors, slowly, as if calculating each hand movement, and led the way once again to the secure outer walkways of the building. Veronica retraced her own steps from their previous journey as she followed closely behind Gary. She turned slightly and snuck a peek behind her, knowing that Samson wouldn't be there, but imagining that he was. She instead saw Clyde's somber face. She pondered how much the group had changed in such little time. The closeness she once felt to any of them, the closeness that most of them felt to one another... she turned her head a bit more and spied Ben and Catherine, walking hand in hand.

At least some of us still feel that closeness.

They reached the end of the gated walkway and Gary repeated the same process as last time, waiting for each person to pass through the final gate and locking the padlock back into place. Once again he clawed at the earth and carefully buried the keys.

Veronica read the words once more on the novelty keychain before the dirt covered them. *Haven is home.*

She pulled her trusty PVC pipe from the strap on her bag and gripped it tightly. She charged fiercely alongside her companions and melee weapons met undead faces. She reared her arm back and thrust it forward, pipe in hand, knocking the rotting jaw off a walking corpse. She kicked forward, forcing the grotesque thing to the ground. The eater groaned and hissed, its arms stretched, fingers clawing at air. Veronica brought her foot down onto its chest with a grunt, grasping the pipe in both hands above her head.

"I didn't think I'd miss this so much," she said to herself with a smirk as she brought the pipe down in one violent, swift motion, smashing the decayed skull of the eater to pieces.

*

Michelle patiently waited for the rest of the broken group to disappear into the stairwell. She doubled back from the direction of the parking garage and headed for the entrance to the other building. Her heart pounded with excitement as she raced to the forbidden east wing's doors, grabbing one of her strategically discarded garden lights as she went.

She pulled the set of keys she'd snagged from Gary's place out of her back pocket and tapped at the glass.

"Good morning, pals!" she sang.

The ferocious dead things behind the double doors pounded against the glass in response to her voice. Before slipping the key into the lock, she slid the metal stake through the handles and made sure it wouldn't budge. The eaters' growls grew louder and the stench of death filled the air as she clicked the lock out of place.

Her heart nearly stopped as the doors buckled out toward her, but the garden stake served as a good wedge and she nodded in approval.

The eaters toward the front were desperately trying to thrust their arms through the crack in the door; decaying skin peeled and shredded against the metal as arms shoved forward. The crowd of the dead pressed up against the doors was like an ocean tide, and when a rolling wave of the eaters amassed backward, several limbs snapped off with a crack. A rancid black substance oozed from the corpses and streaked its way down the doors.

Michelle gagged and backed away, waving a hand at the garden light, "That won't hold long, don't worry. It's all yours." She spread her arms out wide to the side and spun once, smiling, before jogging back the way she came. "You're welcome!" she called out to the screaming corpses behind her.

Michelle had no plans to come back here.

X

Once the huddle of eaters was disposed of, Gary rushed the parking gate and unlocked it. The heavy galvanized steel clattered upwards and Michelle pulled the truck onto the street, stopping to let everyone pile into the back.

Ben was the last one in. He reluctantly pulled the solid door closed behind him and took a seat on the floor next to Catherine. She gently rubbed his shoulder and planted a sweet kiss on his cheek. Michelle spied their affection in the rearview mirror and rolled her eyes, her face flushing crimson with envy. She looked over at Gary, imagining sharing the same apocalyptic romance with the tan, bearded man in the passenger seat and became nauseated. She was satisfied with the meaningless, casual sex they had; that was all it would ever be.

Her eyes brightened and she grinned from ear to ear when she spotted a roaming group of eaters headed their way. She planted her foot firmly on the accelerator and let out a loud, gleeful cry. The armored truck charged down the trash-ridden street and plowed head-on into the undead. The truck barely rocked from the impact and bodies flew in different directions; over the truck, under the truck, their bones crushed and their bodies mangled. Blood, guts, and black gore covered the windshield. Michelle turned the wipers on and laughed as the grotesque mixture smeared all over the glass.

"You're sick," Gary mumbled under his breath.

"Thanks," she responded enthusiastically with a smile. She carried on this way for a few more miles, running the dead off the road in the most obscene manner imaginable. For the most part, the group was unfazed, but it began to wear on them. Even Michelle grew bored of her *Grand Theft Auto*-ish style of driving and quieted down.

"Turn left up ahead," Gary told her. "We're getting close now."

"Doesn't left take us away from the car lots?" Catherine piped in, reminiscing on the last time she and Desmond had visited one of the dealerships on the strip.

"It does." Gary turned in his seat. "But it'll also take us away from all these creatures out here. The noise will draw them all to us, we've got to stash the truck somewhere safe and double back."

Catherine nodded. "Good idea."

The truck zigzagged down empty side streets, Michelle attempted to confuse the dead by displacing the sound in as many areas as she could. About a half mile off-course from their destination, she spotted a cozy looking one-story home. "How 'bout here?"

"Yeah, that'll do. Pull around the back, there's no fence." Gary pointed and she followed directions with ease once more, veering the truck off the road and into the driveway before pulling it around to the back of the old, red brick home. She killed the engine and everyone seemed to hold their breath for a moment, peering out whatever windows they could.

"I don't see anything," Veronica said loudly, startling everyone in the silence.

"Me neither," Ben grumbled. "Don't mean they're not comin' though."

"Let's get a move on, then." Gary was the first to open his door.

The group exited the truck in silence and adjusted their bags, readying their weapons for the walk to the dealer strip.

"I think it's safe to say we know the drill," Andrew said as he checked the chamber of his weapon before holstering it.

"No gunfire unless it's life or death," Veronica piped up in sing-song.

"What *isn't* life or death out here?" Ben asked as he lit a cigarette, his voice bitter.

Ben's question went ignored as the survivors began the march to their destination. He trailed behind and smoked slowly, savoring his cigarette. His nerves sure did need it in that moment. After going for two months with barely any interaction with the undead, it was nearly overwhelming to deal with this many eaters already in such a short period of time.

There was a late December chill in the air with a bit of humidity to make the cold seep that much deeper into their bones. The previous day's storm hadn't done much to help matters, and none of them had dressed appropriately. Before long, though, the constant movement and imminent danger of the dead sped up heart rates and everyone's foreheads were glistening with sweat.

They moved quickly and quietly through the ghostly neighborhood. Remnants of the former inhabitants lie strewn about; overturned bicycles, bloodied clothing, the putrid and rotting remains of an eater's former feast. The front doors to several of the homes were ajar, allowing an eerie peek into the dark and empty houses. Each of the survivors shuddered to imagine what dangers lurked in that darkness. Close quarter combat with the eaters was something none of them were up to dealing with today.

The group approached the back of one of the massive car lots and crouched low to the ground against a tall chain link fence. Gary pulled a pair of bolt cutters from his knapsack and handed them to Andrew, who quickly went to work on the fence.

"I'm surprised we haven't seen any of them things in a while," Clyde said, a cigarette between his teeth.

"Me too." Ben folded his arms across his chest and narrowed his eyes. There was a good chance that the majority of the dead followed the maze that Michelle had run in the truck, but chances were slim they'd gotten that lucky. The knot in his stomach seemed to swell with each silent, passing second.

Andrew finally pulled the fence to the side and motioned for the rest of them to go through. They began jogging up toward the back of the main building, passing row after row of cars that would never be sold. A lone eater slowly crept into sight on their left and abruptly stopped when it noticed the group.

"See? You spoke too soon," Andrew said to his brother, pulling his golf club from its place on his hip.

The eater made a sudden movement, pulling a gun and pointing it in their direction.

"That's not a fuckin' corpse! Get down!" Ben threw Catherine to the pavement and grabbed Veronica by her backpack, pulling her to the ground with him.

A shot rang out, followed by several male voices shouting to one another. Another gunshot and more shouting, Ben could now hear that these voices sounded angry. Very angry.

"Is everybody alive?" Gary called out in a hushed whisper from behind an adjacent car.

"We're good here," Ben answered.

"Us, too," Andrew responded.

Clyde pulled both guns from his hips and readied himself for a firefight. "Can you see how many of them we're dealin' with?" he asked his brother.

"Nah, just the one, but I heard *at least* six of 'em." Andrew poked his head up and tried to get a better look. He could see the same skinny white guy with the shitty tattoos scanning the back lot for signs of where the group was hiding.

Several other tatted-up white dudes were off to the right with some heavy artillery. There was one that stood out to him as the leader; he was the biggest and hadn't left the top step to the building. He casually smoked a cigar and seemed to be yelling the loudest at his comrades. They were all muscular with shaved heads and nearly identical clothing.

"Fuck me," Andrew said under his breath, lowering himself back down.

"What is it?" Ben shimmied over to Andrew, keeping as low to the ground as possible.

"Fuckin' skinheads, man."

"Shit." Ben rolled over and pulled his gun from its holster. "Gary!" Ben tried to keep his voice low. "Gary, we gotta get the fuck out of here!"

"Where's Michelle?" The panic was evident in Gary's voice. "I can't see Michelle."

"Fuck her, dude! We gotta go!" Ben said his last sentence a bit too loudly as it elicited another angry shout from the skinheads and more gunshots whizzed by, shattering the rear windows of the car nearest them.

Unbeknownst to the remainder of the group, Michelle was already nearing the front row of cars closest to the building. She snaked between vehicles of different makes and models, strategically making her way toward the largest building in the lot. Atop the staircase stood the steroid-induced frame of a sinister looking man. She saw this as her chance.

I've done much worse, she thought as she slid her pistol into her waistband and ripped the front of her shirt slightly, exposing a good amount of her ample cleavage.

"My name is Michelle!" she called out to the men. "I'm going to come out now if I have your word that you won't shoot!"

"What the fuck is she doing?" Andrew resumed his position of peering over the hood of the car they were all hiding behind in the center of the lot.

"Nothing good for us." Gary shook his head. "Clever girl." He sucked his teeth, the hurtful pangs of her betrayal like a spear in his side.

Catherine's nostrils flared. "Should have left her back at Emerald Park."

"We can leave her now, let's go." Ben turned on his heels and started off back toward the hole in the fence.

"Ben!" Veronica cried out as the first tattooed skinny man grabbed her by her hair, pulling her off the ground.

"Where you think you're goin', motherfucker?" One of the other skinheads cracked Ben across the face with the butt of his rifle, breaking his nose. Clyde started to react and was met with a hard kick to his back. He doubled over in pain. Enemy weapons were trained on the group, rendering them completely helpless.

"This one's real cute." The skinny man leered at Veronica. "Drake's gonna like her."

"Fuck you!" Veronica spat.

"Oh yeah," the skinny man said, sneering. He leaned in and breathed her scent in deeply. "He's gonna like her a lot."

The man atop the steps sauntered down toward Michelle's voice. "Come on out, darlin'! I don't bite nearly as hard as the dead!" He laughed at his own pathetic joke and Michelle emerged from her cover, hands above her head, wild curls framing her face. If there was anything Michelle used to her advantage, it was her sexuality.

"Ain't you a sight for sore eyes?" The man sized her up; tall, legs for days, busty, unafraid. Just how he liked 'em. "The name's Drake. You mind tellin' me why it is you and your friends thought it was a good idea to trespass on private property?" He raised an eyebrow at her and took a long, hard drag from his fat cigar.

"They're not my friends."

"I see." He exhaled callous tendrils of white smoke through his nostrils, appearing even more menacing than before. "So, tell me, Michelle, what can I do you for?" He laughed again as he awaited her answer.

"Oh, I'm sure you have more than a few uses for someone like me around here."

Drake raised his left eyebrow again, turning his attention toward the rag-tag team of survivors his men were ushering toward the building. He clutched his chest and cackled. "Faggy white boys, niggers, and fine-ass women! Damn girl, 'tis the season, indeed." He winked at Michelle. "Hey Freeman, take the bitches inside. I'll deal with the rest of these losers."

The skinny man who had Veronica by the hair nodded, and another man grabbed Catherine.

"No!" Ben protested and was met with a blow to the stomach, knocking the wind out of him. Blood poured down his face from his broken nose and he gasped for air.

Catherine cried out, tears streaming down her face as she was taken to the building before them. Veronica kicked and punched at her kidnapper. She caught Freeman in the shin with a hard kick and followed it up with a punch to his jaw. Freeman ripped out a chunk of her hair, causing her to yelp in pain. He gave her a strong backhanded slap that threw her to the pavement. He kicked her in her side and she let out another pain-filled cry.

"That's enough, Goddamnit." Drake shook his head, "Jesus Christ, just get 'em inside, already!"

Freeman pulled Veronica to her feet by her hair. "Get up, bitch," he barked at her.

Veronica turned to look at Ben, she was losing everything all over again. They held each other's stare for what seemed like an eternity. Veronica flicked her eyes toward Clyde's feet and then back up at him. She held strong, her lip quivering and her eyes watering, but she did not cry. She would not cry. She could feel the rage bubbling up inside as Freeman shoved her up the steps and into the confines of the large office building. Veronica looked back once more as the heavy glass doors closed behind her, to see Ben nod.

Ben coughed and spat blood, peering to his left, noticing the knife handle poking out of Clyde's right boot that Veronica had so discreetly pointed out to him. He watched as the only women he cared about in this world were taken from him. His eyes bore into Veronica's as the doors shut, he stared until he could no longer see her. He clenched his fist and looked over at Clyde. He made eye contact with his friend and nodded. In a last-ditch effort to right some of the wrong that had come from a plan that he wanted no part of to begin with, Ben grabbed the knife from Clyde's boot and swung it upward quickly, slicing the throat of the skinhead behind him. The man dropped his rifle and grasped at his gaping wound, attempting to stop the gushing blood.

"Go!" Andrew yelled out, dropping to the floor and scooping up the rifle. He braced himself and fired two rounds into the skinhead behind Gary. "I said go!"

Gary turned and fled.

Clyde retrieved one of his guns from the downed body before him and stood up. "Shit." Six more men filed out of the building, armed to the teeth. "We gotta get out of here, man!" he yelled to Andrew, firing at the men and backpedaling after

Gary. Two shots hit their mark and a heavy-set skinhead rolled down the cement staircase, lying motionless in the parking lot.

Andrew turned to grab Ben, weapon at the ready, but it was too late. Drake had him by the throat. Bullets zipped by Andrew's head as he tore off after his brother. A searing, hot pain spread through his back and he collapsed. He gasped, bringing a hand up to the right side of his chest, the bullet had gone clean through. He looked up in time to see his brother slip through the hole in the fence, and with his last bit of strength, returned to his feet and hauled ass out of the lot.

"Let 'em go boys. They're no longer our problem, let the dead take care of 'em," Drake called to his men.

They lowered their weapons and surveyed the scene. The bodies of their fallen comrades lay strewn about.

"Well, don't just stand around!" Drake broke the silence. "Somebody patch that fuckin' hole in my fence!"

His men scrambled and he laughed. Drake stood beside Michelle, who had finally put her arms down. He stared intently at the man whose neck his fingers were wrapped around. "So darlin', what should we do with this one?"

Ben barely moved in Drake's grasp; he sipped for air, his fists clenched. The knot in his stomach was finally gone. He knew what came next.

Michelle stepped up to Ben until her face was centimeters from his. She leaned in toward his ear and whispered, "If you could go back and start things over again, with me," she said, pulling back and looking into his piercing blue eyes, "would you?"

"Yeah." He choked out and smiled at her, almost sweetly. "I'd tell you to go fuck yourself."

Drake sensed that her decision had been made. He raised his other arm and Ben was lifted off the ground momentarily as the hulking man placed both hands on his head, and in an effortless act, snapped Ben's neck.

PART II

INEVITABLY

I

Gary tore through the hole in the fence like a bat out of hell. He could hear his fellow survivors' footfalls behind him. In the midst of the firefight, he had been unable to retrieve his weapons and up ahead he spied a few straggling eaters headed his way. He darted right, taking yet another detour. His chest burned and his head swam.

How could things have gone so wrong?

Gary looked back only once to see Clyde and Andrew in hot pursuit; he waved an arm, motioning for them to follow him into one of the abandoned homes.

He rushed the door of a 1980s-style brick home and prayed that it was unlocked. With a flick of his wrist, he turned the knob and let himself in, the strong scent of rot and decay hitting him instantly. He brought his hand up to cover his nose and mouth.

"Of course I'd choose this house," he complained.

Clyde was the first to the door. Out of breath, he recoiled at the smell emanating from the foyer. "Oh, God." He brought his shirt up to his face. "This your idea of safe?" He glared at Gary as he holstered his gun and looked around the entryway for something that could be used as a more silent weapon. Andrew finally joined them, his chest heaving.

"Give me your golf club." Clyde held his hand out to his brother.

"It's back at the lot, I couldn't grab it in time." Andrew shook his head, his hands on his knees as he tried to catch his breath.

"Fucking fantastic." Clyde stormed off into the living room, alert and ready for anything. His adrenaline pumped and he spotted a heavy-duty fire poker next to the fireplace. The three men heard a thump and the creak of a door toward the back of the house. "You two, stay here."

Andrew began to protest but Clyde shot his hand up, palm facing Andrew, and raised an eyebrow. Andrew kept his mouth shut.

Clyde glanced past his brother toward the open door, wondering why Ben hadn't caught up with them yet.

The lazy shuffling of footsteps and a low moan caught his attention and he turned, stalking through the out-of-date home. Brown doors with bright gold knobs adorned the entryway to each room, and the majority of the walls were done in a dark wood paneling. A dead man stepped into the hallway and cocked his head in Clyde's direction. He opened his mouth wide, revealing a set of cracked and blackened teeth. He hissed, raising an arm and slowly started toward Clyde. The dead man had a missing eye and several missing fingers. Dried blood crusted over the left side of his face and as he got closer, Clyde noticed a missing ear, as well.

Clyde charged toward the eater and swung the iron poker, cracking the dead thing across the right side of its head. The man toppled into the wall in the narrow hallway and struggled to get back to his feet with a growl. Another moan came from farther back in the depths of the house, but no more eaters emerged. Clyde kicked the dead man in the face, just under his chin, shattering his teeth and knocking him back to the grimy floor. Clyde drove the fire poker deep into the eater's forehead, his one remaining eye rolling to the back of his head, and he finally lie quiet and still.

The poker came back easily from the decayed head with a sickening slurp, black fluids dripping from the edges.

"Disgusting." Clyde turned his nose up at the corpse as he wiped the poker off on the dead man's tattered clothes. He crept toward the sounds of the other eater in the home and found himself in the doorway to the master bedroom.

Blood, feces, urine, and God knows what other substances covered the bedspread. A woman was tied to the bedposts by her wrists, her feet free and her legs thrashing wildly when her eyes met Clyde's. She'd been gagged, but the rag did little to subdue the eater's hungry cries.

He felt the air stir and looked up as Gary and Andrew entered the hallway. The dead woman on the bed howled, her mouth opening and closing rapidly. The sides of her mouth were raw, the skin peeling and tearing around the bloodstained rag in her mouth. Her thin, decaying lips exposed rotted teeth and her whole body shook as she screeched. He entered the bedroom, followed by his brother and Gary. Despite the fact that two other people were in the bedroom with him, the eater never took her cloudy eyes off Clyde, making his skin crawl. He gripped his weapon in his right hand and drove it through her skull, putting her out of her misery. Her head fell to the side as Clyde removed the poker and rested it on the filthy bedspread.

Clyde looked toward the bedroom door and frowned. Ben had still not joined them.

He exhaled with a whoosh and brought his hands to face, suddenly feeling lightheaded. He grabbed hold of the bedside table and slid down the wall, taking deep breaths.

"You alright?" Andrew moved toward his brother.

"Where's Ben?" Clyde looked up at Andrew, narrowing his eyes.

"It was too late."

"What the fuck are you talking about?" Clyde's voice grew louder.

"He... that big motherfucker... he had him by the throat, there was nothing I could do," Andrew said with remorse.

"So you fucking left him?" Clyde shouted at his brother.

Gary looked at Andrew in disbelief.

"I had to! Believe me, I didn't want to, but I had to! I fuckin' got shot because of it! You gotta believe me, I would have never left him otherwise."

Clyde sprang up and shoved his brother back. "Fuck you," he said in a low voice, venom in each word. His eyes burned a hole into his brother. "He didn't even want to be out here today. Hell, I didn't even want to be out here today, but there's no way I would let you take on your suicide mission alone! Selfish fuckin' idiot!" He shoved his brother back again, tears welling up in his eyes as he thought of his fallen friend. "Ben, Goddamnit!" he cried into his hands before storming out of the room.

Andrew and Gary stood in silence. Gary had been the first to flee, it was a fight or flight situation and fighting was not an option. Had they stayed, none of them would be standing there in that moment. He clapped Andrew on the back, startling him. "Aren't we all selfish fuckin' idiots? That was the whole point of coming out here, yeah? Ben was a good man. Let's remember him as such. There's no point in dwelling, we've got bigger fish to fry."

Andrew wiped tears from his eyes and nodded. "Veronica, Catherine." He spoke their names solemnly.

"Aye, I'm afraid there are worse fates than death that await our lady friends." He ran his hands over his face, smoothing out his thick beard.

Andrew nodded. "I know. We've gotta get back to the tower and get some firepower."

"Now that sounds like my kind of party." Gary clapped him on the back once more. "We've got to rest up here for a bit, the dead know we're around here somewhere, those gunshots back there were like a homing beacon. It'll give us time to plan, time for Clyde to cool off. We'll get everything sorted. Don't worry, Ben won't have died for nothing."

Gary left the room, venturing back into the silent home to search for a source of nourishment.

Andrew stood before the soiled bed with the dead woman tied to it and cried.

II

The three men sat together at the brown dining room table. Clyde took immediate notice of the lack of color variety in the home. "These motherfuckers sure liked brown," he said, shoving a handful of stale cereal into his mouth.

The house had been raided, most likely by the skinheads. The only sustenance left in the home was six month old Cheerios. Gary and Andrew wouldn't touch it when they found it, so Clyde happily snatched it for himself. Their bags had been taken from them back at the dealership, leaving them with no water or food.

Gary found a first aid kit along with some other useful medical items in an overlooked linen closet. He tended to Andrew's wounds and put to good use what Catherine had taught him. He let out an accomplished sigh when he was finished. "You're all set; I've even impressed myself."

"Thanks, man," Andrew said as he pulled a clean shirt on over his head. Seems that whoever had raided the house hadn't had any use for extra clothing. They'd left every article hanging untouched in the closets.

"I don't know how much daylight we have left. We can't stay here, we've got nothing." Gary ran his fingers over the smooth surface of the table as he spoke.

Andrew agreed. "We gotta get back to the truck. If we can't make it back to the resort tonight, we can at least stay in the truck. It's safe and we've got some emergency supplies in there we can use for the night."

Both men looked to Clyde for his input, but he was a million miles away, staring at the dreary cabinets, watching a cockroach as it scurried up the wall. Clyde frowned and pushed the box of Cheerios away.

"Clyde," Andrew started, "we're all upset. But we've got to get past this and rescue the others."

Clyde's frown remained on his face. He narrowed his eyes and furrowed his brow. "Get past this?" He looked up at Andrew. "Look at the pot callin' the kettle black." He pulled his cigarettes from his pocket and looked at it. "Fuck." He shook the cigarette pack at his brother.

He pulled one out anyway and fished through the drawers, slamming them as he did, punctuating his words with the closing drawers. "Ben. Has. My. Lighter."

He found a long grill lighter and made a silent wish it would work as he pushed the button down. A small flame appeared and he happily lit his cigarette. He inhaled deeply and closed his eyes, letting his head fall back as he exhaled. He thought of Ben's goofy grin and smiled, "This one's for you, my friend."

Gary stood up and grabbed himself a smoke, joining Clyde at the counter. He lit up and coughed, holding out the cancer stick in front of him. "For Ben."

Clyde and Gary touched their cigarettes together as they would have done mugs of beer.

Andrew said a silent prayer for his fallen comrade and for everyone else they'd lost along the way, including his beloved Juliette. He realized he was responsible for this. Though he hadn't asked any of the others to come with him, he knew they wouldn't have been out here had it not been for his temporary lapse in judgment. He'd felt God was punishing him when Juliette took her own life. But he realized today that he was punishing himself, and in turn, punishing the others. Andrew and Clyde had dealt with mental illness for years with their mother. It was only in death that Andrew knew his mother was finally at peace. He hoped that that was the case with Juliette, and that God could forgive her of her transgression. Suicide was a sin.

But everyone was a sinner these days.

Gary peered out the small kitchen window that overlooked the street. It was mostly clear, only a few stragglers wandering about. His eyes fell upon a little girl, probably about seven or eight years old, standing alone in the front yard of a nearly identical house across the street. Gary could have sworn she was staring at him.

Her milky white eyes were fixated on that small kitchen window. Her greasy, blood-stained brown hair flowed down past her shoulders, just short of the lettering on her dirty white t-shirt. The lettering read: *Big Sister* and underneath it were two owls, a big pink one hugging a small blue one. Gary felt a sadness deep inside. He wondered what had happened to her, where her parents had been, or perhaps if her parents were the ones that hurt their little girl. He wondered what had become of her little brother.

And then he decided not to think about it anymore. He took one last drag off his cigarette and put it out on the already filthy kitchen counter. He made sure it was completely out before dropping it to the floor and when he looked back up, the little girl was shuffling across the street. As she grew nearer, Gary noticed the bite on her left leg. He creased his brow and wondered if maybe she really could see him through the window and moved about slightly, seeing if he could elicit a response from the little dead girl. The girl snarled, baring her teeth, and he cringed.

"I knew it. We've got to go."

Clyde peeked out the window and the frown returned to his face as he spotted not only the little girl, but a few other eaters making their way to the ugly house where they were hiding.

"Shit, yeah, let's get a move on." Clyde handed the fire poker to Gary and ran to the living room, returning quickly with two more melee weapons from the fireplace kit: a small rectangular shovel and a heavy duty set of tongs. He handed the tongs to his brother and looked at his small iron shovel as they quietly made their way toward the sliding glass doors in the back of the house. "I'll never know what these things are good for other than killin' dead people," Clyde said.

Andrew furrowed his brow at him.

Clyde shrugged and waved him off. "It's not like we ever had a fireplace growin' up. Do *you* know what these things are for?"

"Oh, who cares, keep it down," Gary hushed them as he peered between the vertical blinds of the sliding glass doors in the den. "The garden is clear, let's go." He pulled hard on the door but it didn't budge.

Andrew sighed and leaned forward, clicking the lock out of place.

"Cheers." Gary nodded and smiled, tugging once more on the door. The chilly, damp air greeted them and they crept through the fenceless yard. The neighborhood was full of similarly built homes, the majority of them one-story red brick houses with small yards and no fencing. The men navigated the yards as one, stepping in time with one another; moving at a swift but manageable pace so as not to exhaust anyone or draw unwanted attention to the backs of the houses.

As they moved between homes, the three men noticed, as they got closer to the truck's location, the streets seemed to be thicker with the dead. They climbed a small chain link fence, and there was an eater at the far end of the yard with its back to them. It kept walking into the fence over and over, stuck in an endless loop of futility.

Gary snuck up behind it and plunged the poker into the back of its skull, lowering the lifeless body to the tall grass in silence and returning to his two friends. The back door to the house hung open. "Want to chance it? We need a better look at the—"

Shots rang out from somewhere across the street.

"What the hell?" Clyde bolted into the house, followed by the others.

The smell of death had long since left this home and the men knew it was safe. They moved to the right side of the house and crowded around the window in the den. Down the road a bit, the eaters had amassed around their destination. More shots were fired.

"Goddamnit!" Clyde cursed as he lit a cigarette with the oversized grill lighter.

"Nobody was home when we parked there. Unless they were too scared to come out, the bastards." Gary paused and moved to another window, closer to the front of the large home. "I can't really tell." He strained to get a better look and sighed. "What's the plan?" He looked to the other men.

"Maybe somebody's tryin' to steal our truck." Andrew crossed his arms, shaking his head. "This is fucked."

"Nah," Gary patted his pocket. "I've got the keys, it's not a total loss. But we have to get over there and—"

He jumped as more shots were fired. "Shit, we just have to get over there. Bottom line."

Clyde noticed a car in the driveway and an imaginary light bulb appeared over his head. "Follow me."

III

Andrew stood on the front porch and aimed his rifle at the growing crowd of eaters. He watched Gary snake his way over to the next house and try the front door; it opened without incident and Gary flashed him a thumbs up before disappearing inside. Andrew nodded at his brother, who proceeded to smash out the driver's side window of the gold Buick in the driveway. The dead nearest to them turned and moaned, changing course.

Clyde put his fingers to his lips and let out a piercing whistle before wedging the iron fireplace tongs between the seat and the steering wheel. The Buick's horn sounded and chills ran down Andrew's spine; any dead uninterested in the three men before that horn went off were sure to be interested now. Clyde sprinted into the house as Andrew fired a few rounds into a couple of the faster eaters.

"Here, take this." Andrew handed his brother the rifle and pulled the chef knife he'd pilfered from the kitchen out of his back pocket, cutting his forearm open.

Clyde snatched the weapon from his brother and grimaced. "Oh, hell no, you did not just cut yourself." Andrew squeezed the blood from his left arm into his right hand and rubbed it on the front door. He made sure to drip it all over the porch and well into the foyer. He ripped a piece of his t-shirt and haphazardly wrapped his arm up as he looked at his brother and smiled.

"Sheeit." Clyde shook his head. "You nasty." The siblings laughed and Andrew grabbed his gun back. The two men made haste, running out the back door and hopping the fence, escaping into the neighboring yard.

Gary waited in the doorway and waved them inside. "It's fuckin' working!" he exclaimed, his voice full of excitement.

The group rushed to the front and watched in awe as the massive crowd of eaters shambled over to the house next door, completely fascinated by the blaring horn.

"Christ, what happened there?" Gary pointed to Andrew's arm.

"Distraction juice. They need to think there's somethin' worth eatin' in that house," Andrew replied.

"Good thinking!" Gary was pumped and ready to go.

The group, albeit their numbers had dwindled, had a purpose again, and with that purpose returned Gary's enthusiasm. "Let's go!"

The trio returned to the yard once they knew their little plan had worked and continued toward the armored truck. The howls and moans of the dead, combined with the still blaring horn, were almost unbearable. Since Emerald Park, the men hadn't seen this many of the eaters gathered in one place.

They snaked through some shrubs alongside a two-story home. Andrew poked his head out and craned his neck. "All clear," he said, and bolted across the road, Gary and Clyde hot on his heels.

As the trio ran, it seemed their destination got farther and farther away. The eaters were distracted, but the men felt as if every eye of the dead were upon them. Although their footfalls were masked by all the noise, their own feet slapping against the pavement was the most excruciating sound any of them had ever heard. Hearts pounded in chests, sweat poured down foreheads... but finally, the men were across the road and safely in the yard where the truck was parked.

"Don't fuckin' move!" a voice cried out from atop the truck.

Startled, but not stupid, Clyde drew his weapon and fired immediately. Gary took cover on the side of the house and Andrew dropped to one knee, ready to back his brother's play. The man's lifeless body toppled onto the grass, his pistol flying from his hands. Andrew rushed it, kicking it toward the house. "Gary!" he called out.

Gary peeked around the corner and spotted the gun. He rushed to the firearm and scooped it up, rejoining the group.

They noticed the sliding glass doors to the home were wide open, they were definitely shut up tight when they'd parked the truck here earlier in the day. The truck's roof hatch was also wide open.

"Stay back," Andrew warned his companions as he quietly approached the vehicle's rear. With the butt of the rifle he banged twice on the back door. "Come out now!" he ordered. "We are armed and we will shoot to kill!" There was no response at first, but Andrew, with his back up against the side of the truck, felt movement from within the vehicle. "This is the last warning!"

They could hear the eaters' moans creeping up from all around them as the interest in the car horn and Andrew's blood trail wore off. The truck's back door flew open and two women and another man stepped out with their arms up. The women were sobbing, and the man was stone-faced.

"You killed my brother," he spat at Andrew.

"No, *I did*." Clyde stepped forward, his gun trained on the man. "Now back the fuck away from *our* truck."

"You're killing us," one of the women managed to say between sobs. The women, clearly twins, held on to one another for dear life.

"And what the fuck you think you was doin' to us, huh?" Clyde grew angrier as he spoke. "I fuckin' hate thieves!"

"I second that." Gary stepped up between Clyde and Andrew, weapon at the ready. His statement shocked both of his companions; they were sure Gary would have been the compassionate one here. "You have no idea what we've been through today while you lot kept yourselves shut away nice and cozy in there!" He motioned toward the open sliding glass door as he shouted and the growls of approaching eaters grew louder. "You could have made yourself known to us when we arrived. But you didn't."

"We were scared." The women spoke in unison, their sobbing more uncontrollable now.

Gary pulled the keys from his pocket. "You made your choice. Get back to your hiding place, rabbits." He tossed his gun to the grass at the stranger's feet as the women scurried back into the home. The man didn't speak again as he retrieved his dead brother's weapon. He jumped as Clyde swung his weapon around and shot an eater, the side of its face exploding onto the brick home.

"Go!" Gary yelled at the man once more before running around to the driver's side door. Andrew and Clyde covered the stranger as he did, indeed, get back into his hiding place.

"I'm out!" Andrew yelled to his brother, tossing the useless rifle to the ground and jumping into the back of the truck.

Clyde threw himself in after his brother, Gary's foot already on the accelerator before he could pull the door shut. The undead piled into the yard as the truck bounded through the flower beds of the neighbor's home, through a fence, and then finally fishtailed back onto the road. Gary checked the rearview mirror and saw that the eaters were more focused on the truck than the cowardly inhabitants of the home. He let out a sigh.

Clyde climbed up into the passenger seat beside Gary and cracked the window, lighting a cigarette. His hands had a slight tremble to them and he was drenched in sweat. "I don't know how to feel about what just happened."

Gary noticed Clyde's anxiety.

"They could have warned us about the men at the dealership." Gary wiped his brow with the back of his hand. "But they didn't. They waited until there was no sign of us and then tried to steal from us."

Clyde nodded. "Yeah, but I still don't know how to feel about it."

Gary didn't respond. He thought of Veronica and Catherine; God only knows what was happening to them. He thought of Ben, dead in that parking lot. He imagined the skinheads pissing on his dead body… or perhaps something even worse happening to it. He felt his skin grow hot with rage as he thought of Michelle, and the sociopath who'd been hidden behind those beautiful almond eyes this entire time.

How could she do this to us? He shook his head suddenly and convinced himself that he couldn't get caught up over Michelle. Not now, not ever. They weren't going back there for her. They weren't fighting to survive for her.

"You don't feel anything," Gary finally answered Clyde. "You just can't feel anything at all."

IV

Aside from the thud of eaters rolling under the truck's tires when Gary plowed into them, the ride back to the Emerald City Resort was fairly quiet. Clyde remarked here and there about the state of decay of everything. He'd been preoccupied in the back of the truck on the trip out that morning. But now that the grizzly car accidents and gutted storefronts were in clear view, he couldn't help but be reminded of Columbia Beach and his small apartment in the city.

"It was still early," he mumbled.

"What was?" Gary asked him, eyebrows raised.

Clyde hadn't even realized he'd spoken aloud and looked at Gary, a puzzled expression painting his face.

"You said it was still early," Gary reminded him.

Clyde shook his head, slightly embarrassed.

"Oh. I was just thinking about my old apartment in the city, back when all this mess first started up. It was crazy, people killin' each other right outside my kitchen window. Lootin' anything and everything they could get their hands on. But it was still early. We left; I never got to see how bad things could get while I was there."

Gary nodded as he listened.

"I'm sure it's worse than this back home. I can only imagine what further downtown was like, or shit, the hospital. Probably lookin' like a warzone... even compared to all of *this*." His eyes moved from one burned down structure to the next as the truck passed by.

Fires gone unchecked for too long had quickly consumed every nearby home and business until there was nothing close enough left to burn. Their charred remains were grim reminders of what once was, but never would be again. The city streets almost seemed to sparkle in the sunlight, which would have normally brought a smile to Clyde's face, but he knew better than to think there had perhaps been a glitter and fun-filled parade marching its way down these streets. Everything was covered in glass, and no matter where he looked, there wasn't a window still intact along this road.

"I left my apartment door unlocked when we left. I guess as a goodwill gesture to anybody out there that was lookin' for a safe place to crash." He shrugged. "Lawd help 'em if anybody still alive in that city." He felt the familiar sting of tears force themselves into his eyes. "Ben saved us. Veronica, she don't even know it, but she saved us, too."

Gary reached out and placed a hand on Clyde's shoulder. "Ben knew. And Veronica, you'll get the chance to tell the Little Love, I promise."

Clyde managed a smile and looked over his shoulder at his brother.

Andrew sat on the floor toward the back of the truck, tossing the chef knife back and forth between his hands. He felt a pair of eyes on him and looked up. He mustered up a fake smile and Clyde turned back around to continue staring through the windshield.

Andrew sat in silence and prayed.

I lost my way, Lord. I lost my way when the devil took her from me and thought you were punishing me for my selfish ways. The dead rising, the dead walkin' around, I know this is your way of testing your children, I know that now. It's our chance to find our way back to you, Lord, I know that now. And I am unafraid. We lost one of our own today, Lord, but I know you have brought him home and that you have shown me the path to forgiveness, you have brought the evil into the light. Please forgive us all for what we've done. I am your soldier. I will serve you until you see that it is my time to be taken from this earth. Amen.

For every time that the sun streaked through the back window and glinted off the chef knife's blade, he took it as a sign from God that he wasn't alone, and that he had indeed been forgiven. He turned his face up to the small window and squinted into the sun.

Thank you.

Gary slowed the truck as they neared the parking garage. He handed Clyde his enormous key ring. "Pull up the gate."

Clyde pointed at a few wandering eaters across the road, heading for the truck.

Gary scowled at the dead. "Ignore them. Let's just get inside."

Clyde hopped out of the vehicle and jogged toward the gates of the massive parking garage. He crouched down and slid the key into the lock; it turned smoothly and he pulled up on it hard as he stood. It clattered upwards and Gary pulled the truck in. Clyde jumped slightly, catching the bottom of the gate and pulled it back down, locking it in place as an eater slammed into it.

The thing gripped at the gate and growled, its teeth clacking together with each snap of its jaws.

"Sorry, kitchen's closed!" Clyde called out as he returned to the passenger seat.

They drove up to the eleventh floor and parked, the engine finally falling silent. Clyde exited the truck once more and lit up a cigarette, pulling his long hair from its ponytail. He shook it out and scratched at his scalp through his matted, tangled braids.

Damn, he thought, *that feels good.*

Andrew laughed as he watched his brother massaging his own head and scratching at it like a puppy. He remembered when he was a kid he'd do the same thing right before bed.

"You getting sleepy on me, bro?" Andrew called out and Clyde smiled. "You should probably think about shavin' that mess off."

"Oh, you haven't heard? I'm goin' for an island look these days." Clyde laughed and continued to massage his scalp.

Andrew chuckled once more as he retrieved their supply bag from the truck before slamming the door shut.

A dry, raspy growl invaded his ears and he turned on his heels, raising the chef knife. Andrew was puzzled; he saw nothing but he definitely *heard* the sinister sound somewhere in the parking garage. He looked to his brother who'd stopped mid-head-rub and was reassured by the look on Clyde's face that he'd heard it, too.

Gary stepped up beside Andrew and put his hands on his hips, his mouth forming a grim line. "There must have been an old one lying about somewhere up here that we've missed all this time." He stroked his beard and the lines etched in his brow showed his deep concern in response to the eerie sounds.

"How the hell would we have missed one?" Andrew asked, his eyes scanning the lot. "We've made more than enough noise in this damn place over the last couple months. What's this one been doing? Taking a break?"

The familiar sound of shuffling feet preceded the eater finally coming into view. Its body drooped comically to one side as it hissed and spat in their direction. Most of its teeth were missing and it looked as though it had once been an attractive male in golfing attire.

Gary shuddered as he sized up the intruder, he couldn't quite put his finger on it, but something seemed wrong about this lone eater wandering the parking garage. It was almost as if he looked like at one point in time, he belonged at the resort.

"Take care of it," he instructed Andrew, and the former cop obliged, putting plenty of space between himself and the dead golfer as Gary worked a distraction.

The chef knife, light in Andrew's hands and not even close to being the length of his optimal weapon of choice, would have to do. He snuck up on the eater's side and kicked its left calf in, watching as it tumbled to the concrete. It attempted to rise again but Andrew gave another hard kick, this time to the back of its neck, and the dead thing let out a feeble grunt as its neck snapped before falling motionless.

Andrew couldn't help himself and fell into a fit of giggles. "Seriously?" He placed both hands on his knees as he spoke between bouts of laughter. "I thought he would have been more of a pain in my neck."

"Corny ass," Clyde responded with a smile, flicking his cigarette butt at the eater's motionless body.

Gary snorted, rolling his eyes, "You call that a joke? 'Necks' please!"

The three men erupted in laughter and Andrew shouldered the supply bag, shooting his brother a silly look.

"Now *that*, was corny," Clyde said.

The trio grinned and began their trek to the twenty-fourth floor.

V

The three men strolled across the sky bridge, still laughing at one another's silly attempts to lighten the mood with awful jokes, when a foul smelling wave assaulted their nostrils. They stopped dead in their tracks, recoiling back a few steps.

"Oh, God," Clyde coughed, grimacing. He buried his nose in the crook of his arm. "What in the world?"

A dramatic frown came over Gary's face as he put up a hand, quieting Clyde. His ears perked up and he heard the unmistakable sound of the undead lurking just around the corner of the T-shaped junction which connected them with the resort's towers. His heart raced as he took a cautious step forward, peering around the corner. Their path to the west tower was clogged with an enormous group of eaters. As if they could sense his presence, the undead collectively turned their heads in his direction and locked eyes with Gary.

"Fuck me," Gary muttered. "Run!"

Clyde and Andrew didn't hesitate, tearing off after Gary in the opposite direction of the horde. The path along the sky bridge to central wasn't clear of the undead, but it was definitely more manageable. The three men bobbed and weaved at top speed, avoiding the deadly, grasping hands. Gary was the first to the double doors and he pulled them open, impatiently waiting for Clyde and Andrew to catch up.

He kicked at a nearby eater's skinny legs, its arms still hungrily stretching toward him even as it tumbled to the floor. He plunged his fire poker through the top of its head and let out a loud cry as he pulled it back out. His companions, out of breath, scrambled through the door he held open and Gary followed through quickly, pulling the door closed behind him with all his might.

The door slammed, but not all the way.

One of the fast eaters managed to wedge itself between the double doors. The emaciated dead woman howled at the men before her in hunger. Half of her scalp had been torn away and pieces of her skull peeked through. Her teeth snapped and her cold eyes were wide with bloodlust. Gary kicked at the dead woman's face, grunting and repeatedly slamming the door on her torso. She wouldn't budge. He looked up and saw that the undead were gaining on them; a mere fifteen feet separated the humans from their slow, but persistent enemies.

"Will one of you fucking kill her already?" Gary shouted above the eater's screams.

Andrew lunged forward and buried his knife in the eater's head, grabbing her under her armpits and pulling her forward. He toppled backwards, the dead thing on top of him. The stench of rot and excrement so close was unbearable, he threw the dead body off his chest as he rolled onto his side and retched. With the door now free, Gary pulled it shut just as the mass of undead arrived. A few fingers were severed as the door made connection with the frame. Gary pulled his keys out, hands shaking, and locked the door in a hurry. He turned too quickly and snapped the key off in the lock.

"Goddamnit!" he cried out in frustration. His key ring clattered to the floor.

Clyde busied himself with bashing in the heads of the straggling eaters who were unfortunate enough to have remained in the entrance hall. One by one, he caved in the faces of nearly a dozen shambling creatures. He heard Gary's exasperated shout and turned. Gary's hands shook even as he retrieved the keys from the filthy carpet.

"Can't we make it back to our building through the lobbies?" Andrew asked, wiping his mouth and standing up.

"No." Gary punched the glass and winced. His hand throbbed and he cursed at the snarling faces pressed up against the doors before him. "It's the same key to get out of the building downstairs."

"We'll figure it out, man." Andrew put a reassuring hand on Gary's shoulder and turned toward his brother, a horrified expression taking over his face. "Clyde!"

A small framed eater, probably a young teenager in its past life, crept up on Clyde, its festering jaws open and ready for a taste of his flesh.

Clyde spun on his heels gracefully, not even flinching, and swung the fireplace shovel around in a manner that would impress any professional baseball player. It smashed clean through the eater's skull and the dead thing collapsed into a motionless pile of rotting flesh.

"Homerun, motherfucker." Clyde spit onto the corpse and looked up. "We need to move."

Gary and Andrew nodded and headed deeper into the central tower, Gary leading the way.

"This whole thing is fucked," Gary said as they moved through the dark hall. "How the fuck did they get in here?"

Neither brother responded to the man's question; they had no legitimate answer to give him.

"Where are we going, Gary?" Andrew asked.

"Michelle's little hiding spot." He cringed as her name left his lips. "She used to spend hours down there, doing God knows what, but I figured if she was making so many trips down here that I'd use it to my advantage. I had her stash some weaponry for me. Just in case. And boy am I fucking glad I did."

"Good idea," Andrew replied as they turned the first corner in the interior stairwell.

They stomped quickly down the stairs and an eater jumped from the shadows, hissing wildly, latching itself onto Gary. He cried out and tumbled into the hallway, catching the attention of more undead on that floor. Clyde swooped down and curled his arm under the dead thing's chin; its teeth gnashed and it clawed at his arms. When he'd pulled the eater a safe distance away from Gary, he tightened his bicep around its neck until he heard a satisfying crack. He threw its body to the floor and readied his weapon.

"Jesus Christ, how many of them are there?" Clyde's eyes darted from body to body as the undead grew closer, arms outstretched, moving as one.

Andrew pulled Gary from the floor. "Are you bit?"

Gary shook his head and started down the hall toward Michelle's condo. He kicked at the eaters in his way, knocking them to the floor, and pushed on. Andrew followed up behind him with his knife and finished them off. He turned once to check on Clyde.

"Keep moving!" Clyde shouted as he swatted at the approaching dead. "I've got it! Get that fuckin' door open!"

Andrew hurried after Gary and stumbled over a body he'd just disposed of. He landed hard on his side and the knife flew from his grasp. An eater crawled toward him, hissing and chomping at the air. The dead man's fingernails peeled off as he dragged himself across the floor toward Andrew. Andrew quickly rolled over, finally getting within reach of his knife as the dead man's jaws chomped down hard onto his arm.

Andrew wailed in pain, pulling the eater off of him; a chunk of his dark flesh ripping from his body. The wild-eyed dead man slurped and chewed on the fresh piece of meat. He lunged forward again with a growl, eager to taste more. Gary's fire poker sunk into its skull before it had the chance to feast.

Andrew's tearful eyes met Gary's.

Gary stared at the mortally wounded man before him, his heart torn apart at the seams with the burden he now had to bear. He raised his weapon and closed his eyes.

VI

"Step the fuck away from my brother," Clyde bellowed. He ran toward the two men, his long hair trailing behind him.

Gary, frozen in place, opened his eyes and stared down at Andrew. Clyde pulled his brother to his feet and Andrew winced slightly, blood running down his arm from the fresh bite.

"You don't touch him, you hear me?" Clyde threatened Gary. "You let me fuckin' handle this!"

Gary nodded and lowered the fire poker, too emotionally distraught to argue. The undead moans roused him from his melancholy and he locked eyes with Clyde. "I sincerely hope you *can* handle it when the time comes."

Gary rushed the others toward the empty condo and guided them inside, slamming the door shut behind him and locking the deadbolt. He leaned up against the solid door and exhaled; regret weighing heavily on his chest. He watched as Andrew flopped onto the couch and grimaced in pain.

Clyde rolled his brother's torn sleeve up to take a closer look at the bite.

"We need to clean it, stop the bleeding. Are there any medical supplies in here?"

"No. It's all up in the other tower." He frowned at Clyde. "Cleaning it will do you no good."

"Don't you think I fuckin' know that?" He threw the shovel across the room in a fit of anger, sending it crashing into a small desk.

A flat-screen computer monitor, along with a few empty liquor bottles, sailed to the ceramic tile and shattered. Michelle's sketch book flew open on the desk and a myriad of papers went flying.

Gary jumped in fright at both the pounding of the undead at the door and the effects of Clyde's rage. He thanked his lucky stars that they were encased in the safety of the condo.

But how lucky could I actually be? he wondered. *I'm stuck in here with an infected man and his 'roid-raging bodyguard.*

He understood Clyde's anger, but he felt with all that they'd already been through, it was completely unnecessary. "I need a drink."

Clyde stood breathless behind the couch his brother lay on. "Shit." His voice went soft, his shoulders heaving with each breath. "Pour me one, too."

His rage subsided and he looked down at his older brother. The tears inevitably came, as he knew they would. He leaned down and took Andrew's hand as he wept.

Andrew returned his brother's gaze and yet he looked at peace with his fate. "It's gonna be okay." He patted Clyde's hand. "Everything happens—"

Clyde put a hand up, "If you say everything happens for a reason I'll just go ahead and kill your ass right now." A smile played across his face and Andrew chuckled, wiping a tear from his eye.

"But it's true, man. I prayed this morning." Andrew sat up and turned his body toward Clyde. "I prayed somethin' fierce and I offered myself as a soldier to Him, man. And if this is His way of callin' me home, then I need to accept that."

Clyde's nostrils flared; he'd always hated his brother's beliefs. It angered him to no end how a man so smart could believe in figments of the imagination. But if this is what would put Andrew's mind at ease and make it more comfortable for him in the end, then so be it. For once, Clyde chose not to argue religion with Andrew.

Gary returned to the living room with three glasses and a bottle of Bourbon. "You're not going to like me very much." Gary said as he poured some of the bottle's contents onto Andrew's wound.

Andrew hissed in pain, cursing Gary. Gary handed him a washcloth and held up a roll of duct tape. "This will have to do as a dressing; I stripped the place clean months ago. Plenty of this stuff, though." Gary shrugged, setting the duct tape down and pouring three drinks.

Clyde thanked him for the makeshift bandages, embarrassed at how he'd reacted earlier, and tended to his brother's bite. The men then clinked glasses before downing their drinks in one gulp.

Gary raised the bottle. "Another?"

The others nodded and eagerly accepted the second helping, downing it the same as the first.

With a warm feeling in his chest and his nerves finally subsiding, Gary took a seat on the recliner across from the couch. He leaned back slightly and brought his hands up to his head, gingerly massaging his temples. His body was calm but his mind continued to race. The day's events ran rampant through his brain, playing and replaying like a marathon of the worst movie he'd ever seen.

Ben's death, Michelle's betrayal, Veronica and Catherine's capture. The strangers at the house left for dead, the roaming eaters in their only safe haven, and now, Andrew's infection.

No matter how hard he tried to push the thoughts away, they returned, reminding him of his dire situation as the undead pounded at the condo's door, their screams endless. And in the forefront of his mind, there stood Michelle; her smug face ate away at him and he wished with all his being that she was there in that room with them right then, so he could drive a knife through her heart.

After what seemed like an eternity, Gary finally spoke. "She did this."

Andrew and Clyde looked up at him, confused.

"What you mean, *she*?" Clyde raised an eyebrow as he lit a cigarette. "Who is she, and what did she do?"

Gary laughed out loud at the realization he'd just come to. "That vile cunt." He succumbed to the mounting hysteria and giggled uncontrollably. "Oh, God, I can't believe it!" He gasped for air between fits of laughter. "Oh, I mean, yeah, yes I can! I *can* believe it!"

"What in the hell are you talkin' about?" Andrew leaned forward, propping his elbows on his knees, staring intensely at the spectacle before him.

"I think he's finally lost it," Clyde said, blowing smoke up into the air.

"Michelle!" Gary cackled. "She let the fucking dead things out of the east tower!"

Andrew furrowed his brow in disbelief. "What?"

"It had to have been her! Earlier today, when I sent her to get the truck... I had a feeling it took her a bit too long to get back to us. It all makes perfect sense now!" Gary wiped the spittle from his mouth and leaned forward, staring intensely at the brothers, lowering his voice almost to a whisper. "She was always on about those damn things locked up in there, like they were puppies at the pet shop, for God's sake. I always wondered about her morbid fascination with them but ignored it because, well, she's always been a bit mad hasn't she?"

There was no argument from Clyde or Andrew.

Gary ran a hand over his bald head, laughing again. "She was all sorts of tanked up one night when she came over to my place, babbling about how she felt so powerful when she was around them."

"That is one, sick, bitch," Clyde emphasized the insulting words.

"Oh, yeah, she was tellin' me how she felt so wanted and important when she'd sit in front of those doors and draw them. I thought she was playing some sort of game with me, you know? Get me to tell her how lovely I thought she was before we got down to business. But now I get it. She's a maniac. A complete and total madwoman, and she fucking did this to our home."

Andrew leaned back slowly as to not disturb the bite on his arm. "She ain't even here and she's sealed our fate."

"She sealed that shit before we even left, homie." Clyde stamped his cigarette out on the expensive coffee table. "I knew there was more than one reason to hate that bitch."

Gary got up from the recliner and locked his hands behind his head as he paced the room, his blood boiling.

"I don't wanna die in this room," Andrew stated.

Clyde looked at his brother and shook his head. "None of us do."

Gary stopped short when one of the papers on the floor from Michelle's sketch book caught his eye: a portrait of Juliette. He bent down to retrieve it, finding it odd but thinking Andrew might want to have a look at it. Michelle's one and only talent aside from completely mastering the art of being evil was her artistic ability. The woman's drawings were so spot on, they resembled photographs.

As Gary picked up the sketch, he uncovered another of Juliette. He narrowed his eyes as he set the portrait aside and picked up the entire stack, slamming it down on the desk. He rifled through the sketches and shook his head, seething with hatred. It was almost as if Michelle had drawn out a full-fledged confession and left it there for him to find. The drawings started with the portrait, and one by one told their own individual stories of Juliette finding Michelle as she watched Catherine and Ben making love, and then plummeting to her death from the twenty-fourth floor as Michelle threw her small-framed body from the balcony.

Gary's hands began to shake again as he brought the stack of drawings over and dropped them on the coffee table in front of Andrew. Andrew looked puzzled at first but then his eyes fell upon the lifelike portrait of his dead fiancée.

He reached out and gently stroked the face in the drawing, his eyes welling up with tears. He smiled and looked up at Gary, not understanding the disgust in his expression.

“No one’s dying in this room,” Gary spoke. “And you’ll have plenty of reason to leave once you have a look through those.”

VII

Andrew's face grew hot and he felt a wave of nausea come over him. The sketches of his dead fiancée trembled in his hands and he looked from his brother to Gary and back to Clyde again. The room began to spin and he let out an exasperated cry as he began to hyperventilate. He sprang up from the couch and ran to the sliding glass door, throwing it open. He rushed out into the late afternoon sun, vomiting the contents of his stomach over the railing.

"Drew!" Clyde called out to his brother.

"Leave him be," Gary said quietly. "Let him take it in."

The two men could hear Andrew's hushed sobs and Gary moved to the balcony door. "We're right here when you're ready," he said as he slid the door shut.

Andrew allowed the door to close without any further conversation. His sobs rocked his broad shoulders and he looked up to the sky, ready to curse God. Ready to throw himself from the balcony and end his suffering right then and there. His fate was sealed, he was a dying man. A dying man who just found out that the love of his life had been murdered… and he wanted nothing more than to be rejoined with her.

But as he looked up, he couldn't help but notice an enormous white bird, flying solo, overhead. He was never a Birder, but he knew a Great White Egret when he saw one, even from such a great distance away. They were getting rarer in the Southeast, and he'd always remember the first time he ever saw one.

Andrew was five years old, visiting his grandfather on the Alabama coast. They were out fishing and hours had passed before he finally saw the end of his pole move. He jumped up and hollered for his grandpa in excitement as he struggled with the fishing pole on the small craft. He remembered the way his heart raced as his grandfather rushed over to help him reel in his very first catch.

As soon as that fish left the water it was gone. Andrew saw the shadow before he heard the wings and the biggest bird he'd ever seen swooped down and stole his fish.

"Grandpa!" Andrew hid behind the old man, terrified of the large, white bird.

His grandfather chuckled, patting the small boy on the head. "Ain't nothin' to be scared of. Come on," he picked the boy up and pointed out over the water at the beautiful thief, fish in mouth, gliding through the air. "Ain't he pretty?"

Little Andrew beamed, smile stretching from ear to ear. "He looks like an angel!"

Andrew found himself smiling again as the memory came and went. It was always one of his favorites.

He watched the bird soar, the sun illuminating the majestic white feathers that covered the vast expanse of its wings, creating a sort of halo. A final tear rolled down his dark cheek and he wiped it away. "Thank you," he said to the sky. He watched the creature until it finally disappeared from sight.

Andrew returned to the living room and rejoined his companions. The undead at the door had ceased their banging and moaning for the time being; the room was almost peaceful.

"You alright, man?"

"Yeah, all things considered… I'm alright." Andrew nodded at Clyde who was chain smoking on the couch, his knees bobbing up and down. He took a seat next to him. Clyde reached out a hand and gave his arm a squeeze.

Andrew winced in pain. "Argh, watch it."

Clyde face-palmed and shook his head. "Shit, sorry, sorry."

Andrew smiled despite the pain, appreciating his brother's gesture.

"Thank you for showing these to me." Andrew reached forward and scooped the sketches up.

"I knew you needed to see them." Gary leaned back in the recliner and crossed his arms.

Andrew bit his lip as he stared down at the life-like portrait of Juliette. As much as it was a brutal reminder of what he'd lost, it was the most beautiful thing he'd held in his hands since the day she died. A beautiful homage, made by the ugliest person he knew. He scowled at the thought of Michelle and folded up the portrait, leaning back slightly, placing it in his pocket.

"So now, the million dollar question is, what do you want to do about it?" Gary extended his hand and motioned for Clyde to toss him the dwindling pack of cigarettes.

"Me?" Andrew looked up at Gary, who lit a cigarette in response.

Andrew thought long and hard as he stared down at the wickedness before him, the picture by picture version of his worst nightmare.

He closed his eyes and found himself praying again, praying for a sign that he had not been forsaken. That the plan unfolding in his mind was the righteous path. It felt like a lifetime passed and suddenly the dead outside the door began to wail once more. Furious fists pounded at the heavy door and the sound of nails clawing to get in filled the room once more.

Andrew's eyes popped open, *Just the sign I was looking for.*

"You wanna know what I plan to do about it?" He looked from Gary to Clyde, anxiety etched in both their faces as they awaited Andrew's next statement.

He reached for his bag at his feet and shoved the remaining death-sketches inside, slamming it down on the coffee table with a bang. He stood and took a deep breath in. "The book of Exodus, 21:12 and 14." He exhaled slowly and Clyde rolled his eyes as his brother continued. "He that smites a man, so that he die, shall be surely put to death. But if a man come presumptuously on his neighbor, to slay him with guile, you shall take him from my altar, that he may die."

Clyde waved a hand in the air, "Uh... layman's terms, please?" He raised his eyebrows and looked expectantly at his brother.

Andrew turned to Clyde and smiled. "It means I'm gonna take these drawings to her," he pointed at his bag, "and I'm gonna shove them down her fuckin' throat."

VIII

Andrew's words were like music to Gary's ears. He led the way to one of the bedrooms in the condo and pulled open the double doors of a walk-in closet. "It's not much, but it's more than what we've got now."

Clyde raised an eyebrow. "Mother, may I?"

Gary swept his arm forward. "Yes, you may."

Clyde dropped to his knees and began sorting through the firearms before him. Andrew let out a laugh behind him. "You and these damn homemade explosives, man." He stepped into the closet and reached down, picking up a pipe bomb similar to the one that Gary had used a few months back. He smirked, "I should haul your ass down to the county jail."

Gary feigned shock. He widened his eyes and put his hands up in defense. "Officer, those are not mine."

The men chuckled and suddenly Andrew lurched forward, thrusting a hand out to the wall to catch himself. Clyde jumped up and put an arm around his brother's waist, helping to steady him. Clyde looked to Gary, panic in both their faces.

"Drew, you good?" Clyde tried to hide the worry in his voice.

Andrew shook his head, "Yeah, I just... my head. I got real dizzy is all." He straightened and quickly wiped the sweat from his face. He blinked his eyes rapidly, "I think I need to sit for a minute; it's kind of hard to focus."

"Right, come on." Gary put an arm around the other side of Andrew and helped Clyde half-carry him to the bed in the center of the room.

Clyde noticed the ashen tone of his brother's skin for the first time and a lump formed in his throat. He'd never been around someone that didn't turn immediately. Andrew had been acting so normal since the bite that a part of Clyde wondered, or rather hoped, that he wouldn't turn at all. But he knew sitting before him, in the body of his brother, was a ticking time bomb.

Andrew let his breath out in a big whoosh. "I can feel it. The infection. I didn't feel anything before, but now... I feel it." He wiped the sweat from his brow once more. "Like a million burning insects crawling around inside of me."

Clyde bit his lip and looked to Gary. "If we're gonna get outta here, it needs to be soon. Real soon."

Gary silently agreed and turned back to the closet. "Let's pick our poisons then, shall we?"

Andrew remained on the bed while the others loaded gun after gun, holstering what they could and packing the rest into bags. Gary grabbed a small knapsack and placed the remaining pipe bombs inside.

Once they were all packed up, the men stood in the living room, staring at the front door; despite how long the men had been in there or how quiet they'd been, the dead were relentless. They continued to pound and claw at the entrance, growling in hunger.

"We're going to have to try something *extremely* stupid," Gary announced.

"As opposed to... every other decision we've made today?" Clyde lit another cigarette and shook his near-empty pack in his hands. He looked at the delicious cancer stick between his fingers and sighed.

Gary walked to the balcony door and threw it open, letting a slight chill into the room. The sun hung low in the western sky; nightfall would be upon them shortly. "We need to be quick about this. Are either of you afraid of heights?" He looked back at his comrades as he stepped onto the eighth floor balcony.

"No, no fuckin' way." Clyde waved a hand at Gary as he followed him outside. "You're fuckin' with me, right?"

"I wish I was." Gary sighed, lowering his voice. "We can't spend the night here. Not with... not with Andrew in this condition. We don't have much daylight left, we need to get out of this building. Look." He pointed over the rail to the balcony below them. "Central isn't like the other buildings. See how the balconies are a bit staggered? I'm not saying it'll be easy, but it's our only choice."

Clyde looked back at his brother, who stood staring at the front door in a daze.

His heart skipped a beat; the change in his brother was overly apparent now. Clyde turned back to Gary, "Do you think he's strong enough?"

"I don't know, but if we wait any longer, he definitely won't be." Gary leaned forward and looked down eight stories. He whistled through his teeth. "I'm not gonna lie, I'm terrified of heights."

Clyde rolled his eyes. "Great." He returned to the living room and put a hand on his brother's shoulder.

Andrew jumped, eyes wide, he focused on Clyde's face and calmed down. "Sorry, I... I think I'm hearin' shit."

Clyde mustered a comforting smile, "We all hear shit sometimes. Now come on, let's go swing around on the balconies and try not to die."

Andrew managed a laugh. "Sounds like a good time."

The men tucked their shirts into their pants and strapped their bags tightly to their bodies. They'd stripped the beds of their sheets and braided them together, fashioning makeshift safety ropes.

Gary volunteered to go first, since the whole thing had been his bright idea. His breath quickened as he swung his legs over one by one and gripped the bars of the rail tightly, squatting and preparing to swing down onto the balcony below. "Here goes nothing!"

As Gary's feet left the platform and his full body weight now relied solely on the strength of his arms and chest, he immediately cursed himself for not being in better shape. He grunted as he swung his legs back and held his breath when they came back forward. He let go of the bars and flew legs-forward onto the cement. His heart was pounding and he didn't even realize that his eyes had been closed.

They popped open and he looked around, feeling all over his body and the floor around him.

It's real, I've made it!

"Gary?" Clyde called out nervously from above.

"Yeah! Come on down!" Gary grinned.

Andrew went next, struggling a bit more than Gary. Despite his physical stature, he was growing wearier by the minute as the infection coursed through his veins. Gary embraced the large man as he dropped to the balcony beside him.

Andrew saw Gary's smile, and raised him a grin. But both men soon scowled as Clyde gracefully descended from the eighth floor. "Piece of cake," he said as he landed. He stood tall and stretched his lithe frame.

"Yeah, yeah, why don't you go first this time then?" Gary motioned toward the ledge.

"Hmmph." Clyde grunted at him and flipped his braids over his shoulder.

The trio repeated the process for three more floors before taking a small break. Andrew began to feel woozy again, his breathing becoming more labored with each balcony they descended.

Clyde looked toward the setting sun. "Only four more to go, you got this," he urged his brother on.

When the men finally arrived on the second floor, they were drenched in sweat, despite the cool temperature.

Gary wiped his brow and fashioned a bowline knot with the sheet, securing a way down to the ground floor.

"Alright, big guy. Almost there," he comforted Andrew.

Andrew stepped up to the plate this time, eager to be finished with the physical activity. He grabbed hold of the braided sheet and carefully climbed over the final railing. He lowered one leg down but the other betrayed him, giving out from under him. Andrew slipped from the ledge but held tightly to the sheet. He cried out as the weight of his massive frame slammed his forearms into the ledge. His left arm gave out and he clung to the sheet with his right. He looked up at his brother, screaming above him. Gary's hand shot out from between the bars and Andrew tried to grasp it, but his vision was too blurry; he'd lost the ability to concentrate as a high fever set in.

Andrew's world spun and he knew he was about to pass out. His grip loosened and he dropped ten feet to the pavement below.

IX

Clyde wasted no time getting down to the ground floor. He was over the railing in an instant and slid down the sheet like he'd done it a hundred times before instead of six. He dropped to his feet and knelt beside the unconscious body of his brother.

"Drew!" He put a hand on his brother's neck and felt for a pulse, taking care not to move Andrew's motionless frame too much; his skin burned at the touch. His fever was higher than before. "Gary, we need to get him into the water!"

Gary looked down at the brothers, he frowned and sighed. *He's going to turn before we get out of here,* he thought as he lowered himself down to join Clyde.

Gary shook his head, "Clyde, we shouldn't move him. What if something's broken from the fall?"

Clyde let out a frustrated growl and threw his bag to the ground, pulling out a bottle of water. "It's gonna be alright, Drew. Drink this, please." He brought the bottle up to Andrew's lips and poured a bit onto them. This elicited a groan from Andrew, and Clyde thrust the bottle into Gary's hands. "Keep feedin' him water." He pulled a knife and hopped up, throwing himself up and catching onto the sheet. He climbed up to a safe dropping distance and began cutting away at the fabric. When it finally gave way, he landed safely and replaced the knife on his leg.

"If I can't bring him down to the water, I'll bring the water to him." Clyde quickly began unraveling the sheets.

Gary caught on to what he was doing and stood. "You stay with him, let me go."

"No," Clyde denied him. "I'll be faster. Stay here and keep givin' him that damn water. Please!"

Clyde bunched up the sheets as he ran toward the beach. He charged through the pool deck's gates, down the stairs, and stumbled when his feet hit the sand. He regained his composure and picked the pace back up. He noticed few eaters on the beach as he knelt at the water's edge, soaking up the frigid water with the sheets. He rushed back to the resort, flying past the moaning dead as they stumbled through the sand in his direction.

He returned to his brother's side and wrapped one of the sheets around his head. Gary helped wrap the others around Andrew's frame. Andrew began to stir after a few moments, the cold shock helping to bring down the fever at least to the point of his returning consciousness.

"Hey, man, we'd thought we'd lost you."

Andrew swallowed hard, squinting at Clyde. "Shit, me too." He smirked. "I felt it comin' on, that's why I let go, rather hit the pavement unconscious. But I ain't goin' nowhere. Not yet."

"Good." Clyde patted his arm. "You feel alright to stand?"

"I think so."

"Gary, help me get him up."

The two men helped Andrew to his feet and steadied him.

"We can't stay out in the open like this, we've gotta get moving, back to the truck." Gary scanned the area, checking that no eaters were in their immediate vicinity.

"I have a better idea." Clyde pointed out to the gulf. "The boat. Let's get back on those damn Jet Skis and get the fuck out of here. Those assholes back at the car lot would never expect us to come up from the water."

Andrew furrowed his brow, lines appearing in his forehead. "I don't know about that."

"I like the idea, it's solid," Gary chimed in. "We can pull the boat right up to the marina. It's not a far walk to where they are. They'll hear the truck, but on foot, we have the element of surprise on our side. Plus, we need you to get in that water, bring your fever down."

Andrew sighed, he wasn't too excited about going for a swim. "Alright, let's do this."

"My turn to disappear, give me a minute." Gary took his keys out and unlocked the padlock to the cage running alongside the building.

He quickly moved along the pathway and let himself into one of the ground-floor shops. There was nothing of sustenance left, he'd been sure to clear it out the last time he popped in. But there was a ton of plastic shopping bags inside and they'd need them to ensure the weapons stayed dry. Gary wasn't willing to take any chances with faulty firearms. He knew that what they were about to do was not only stupid, but it was one of those once-in-a-lifetime things. Veronica and Catherine were doomed to the unspeakable if they were left there. Andrew was well on his way to turning, and Gary knew it was only a matter of time. How much time, he wasn't sure, but if this plan was going to work, he needed to get Andrew to the other side of town while he was still alive.

Gary knew Andrew's fate couldn't be changed. He was also coming to terms with the fact that his home was lost, the supplies he'd worked so hard on collecting were unreachable, and he'd been betrayed by someone he'd trusted. They all had. And they'd paid dearly for it. Gary didn't just want Michelle dead. He wanted her to suffer, and Andrew deserved to be the one to make her suffer more than any of them.

He returned to the brothers, handing them the bags. "Take these, put your weapons in them."

Andrew smiled, admiring the bag in his hand. "Always thinking. Thanks, Gary."

Gary nodded and went about securing everything, and when the three men were ready to leave, Gary turned to take in the magnificence of the Emerald City towers one last time. But the trio of buildings took on an almost ghostly appearance in the dusk, their beauty suddenly fading. Gary no longer saw them as a place of grandiose solace. They had become just as poisonous as everything else in this world.

"Let's go." Gary turned and left the resort behind him for good. He led the way from the pool deck, trotting along the sand toward the Jet Ski rentals.

He pulled keys from their hooks in the beach hut and tossed them to the other men, running toward the watercrafts.

Andrew struggled with getting his to the shore line.

"Hop on back of mine, we don't have time!" Clyde shouted to his brother, pointing at a large group of eaters growing dangerously close.

Gary fired his up first. "Get a move on!" he shouted at the brothers as he took off toward the boat, a stream of water spraying in his wake.

A knot formed in Clyde's stomach; there was barely any light left in the sky. He'd ridden a dozen of these things before in his life, but never at night. He feared falling off into water and being pulled under by the bloated, hungry hands of the dead or losing Andrew off the back, somehow. But it was a risk he would have to take.

As the Jet Ski cranked to life, Andrew hopped on behind his brother and patted him on the shoulder. "Let's get out of here!"

Clyde took one last look at the approaching horde of eaters and shivered. He pulled back on the throttle and followed Gary into the night.

X

Gary leapt aboard *The Dockside* and awaited the arrival of his companions. The boat rocked gently and he looked around; it was nearly pitch-black. He shivered as the wind sent a chill down his spine. He rushed inside, flipping the lights on, making the boat easier for the brothers to find.

The whine of the watercraft grew closer and Clyde drove it around to the stern. "Get in the water," he instructed Andrew.

"Oh, man, I do *not* like this part of the plan." Andrew considered the dangers that lurked beneath the surface of the dark waters. He pulled his boots off, one by one, and threw them onto the boat. He grimaced as he dipped a foot into the frigid water and quickly pulled it back out. He imagined an enormous shark, smiling a razor-sharp grin, waiting to gobble him up. He couldn't help but laugh as he then considered the bite, his death sentence, and figured whatever could be lurking in the dark water was a far better fate.

Andrew pulled off the rest of his clothes and inhaled deeply, plunging into the salty darkness, the low temperature nearly taking his breath away. He floated, weightless, and embraced the silence. He was filled with a peace and serenity he hadn't felt in a very long time. He let his legs rise up and wished he could float there forever.

His chest began to burn and he opened his eyes. A bright, white light was before him.

God, is that you?

Hands grasped at Andrew's shoulders and pulled him toward the light.

"What the fuck you doin' down there?" Clyde hollered at his brother as he broke the surface.

Andrew gasped, gulping in air and coughing as the men pulled him aboard.

"I saw a light. I thought—"

"Ah, heaven should be so lucky to have a man like me." Gary laughed, grinning from ear to ear, the lights on the deck shining brightly behind him. "You're not going anywhere just yet."

Clyde scowled. "Get your ass up, scarin' me like that. You were down there for over two damn minutes." He helped Andrew to his feet and handed him his clothing.

As Andrew dressed, he felt rejuvenated. The soreness in his arm from the bite had subsided, and the fever seemed to disappear. His vision was clear, as was his head. He wasn't sure how long he'd feel this good, but was thankful that his brother's plan had worked so well.

Gary entered the cabin, searching for anything useful. There were still a few bottles of water left and he helped himself to one, chugging its contents. He returned to the men outside, handing them each a bottle.

They exchanged their thanks and Gary headed for the helm. He started the vessel up and inspected the instrument panel. They were lucking out left and right as everything seemed to be in working order. The only concern was gas. They barely had enough to get to their destination.

"Tear this place apart, see if there's any extra fuel on board!" he called to the others.

A short time later, Clyde brought Gary a small gas can. "Found it under one of the seats."

"Brilliant!" Gary clapped his hands, smiling. He took the can from Clyde. "I'll take care of this, you tend to the anchor."

The men readied for departure while Andrew sat quietly inside. He pulled his shirt back and inspected his wound. While the bleeding had stopped, it oozed green and smelled terrible. He hoped the saltwater had helped to clean it, but it wasn't looking so great. Not only was the wound itself black, but the surrounding area was necrotic. He poked at it and winced in anticipation of pain, but he felt nothing. He squeezed around his bicep; there was only numbness. He felt a small ball of panic begin to form as he poked and prodded up and down his arm, feeling only pins and needles.

"Drew." Clyde entered the cabin.

Andrew looked up his brother, subtly pulling his sleeve back down. "Hey. We ready to go?"

"Yeah." Clyde readjusted his hair in a ponytail as he sat beside Andrew. They were silent for a moment. "I want you to know that I love you." He put an arm around his brother and squeezed him tight.

"I love you too, man." Andrew felt tears well up in his eyes. "Who the hell is gonna take care of you when I'm gone?"

Clyde wiped a tear away and laughed. "Sheeit, I'm tryin' to figure out what I'm gonna do with myself once I don't have to take care of *your* ass anymore."

The brothers chuckled and embraced. Nothing more needed to be said. They both knew how fortunate they already were to have had each other for this long.

Gary tapped at the door. "Sorry to interrupt." His face was solemn, having overheard the exchange of words. "We should be going."

Clyde and Andrew stood up and followed Gary outside.

*

The Dockside tore off through the night toward its destination. The cold air whipped around, misting the even-colder saltwater onto them, chilling noses and ears. They grew nearer to the marina and Gary spotted a good area for them to disembark. The craft was just the right size to pull into the vacant slip and Gary killed the engine and the lights. Clyde put his fingers to his lips and let out a long whistle, hoping to draw out the dead. Gary and Andrew joined him at the bow and they held their breath, staring out into the darkness, awaiting the cries of the eaters.

All that could be heard were the gulf waters kissing the boats in the marina.

"I guess that's a good sign. Should we go ahead and tie the boat off?" Clyde whispered.

"No," Andrew said. "You're not comin' with us."

"What the fuck?" Clyde raised his voice, his hands on his hips. "What you mean, I'm not coming?"

Andrew turned to his brother, his tone soft yet serious. "I'm not comin' back,

Clyde. And if Gary and the others don't make it back..." He sighed, "At least one of us has to make it through all of this."

Clyde felt the tears struggling to return and he fought them with every ounce of his being. He thought of himself alone on that boat, in the middle of the Gulf of Mexico, at the end of the world. "Where the fuck am I supposed to go?"

"I don't care where. Just far, far away from here." Andrew pulled his brother in and hugged him tightly.

"Don't worry, mate, I'll be back." Gary placed a reassuring hand on Clyde's shoulder, even though he wasn't very sure how the night might end. "Catherine, Veronica, and I, we'd never leave you alone out here."

Clyde frowned. "Well, hurry the fuck up."

Gary and Andrew gathered their stockpile of weaponry. Andrew stepped off the boat, giving his brother a wave and a sad smile. They'd said what needed to be said in the cabin; he didn't think he could handle the word "goodbye".

Gary plaaced a flare gun in Clyde's hands. "The clock on this boat still works. You get this boat out of here and anchor a good distance away, alright? There are two flares here, you fire one in thirty minutes, the other at sixty. If we haven't returned by then, leave."

Clyde swallowed the lump in his throat and agreed.

Gary clapped him on the back, putting a hand on his shoulder. "See you soon." He stepped off beside Andrew, and Clyde watched as they walked away. He squinted and kept his eyes on Andrew as he disappeared from sight. He knew the moment would come, but it wasn't easy to deal with. He'd never see his brother, his best friend, ever again. And it broke his heart into tiny pieces.

Clyde pulled the boat out of the slip and headed back out into the gulf. When he was a safe distance away, he lowered the anchor and sobbed his heart out.

PART III

COME TO AN END

I

Ben's body fell to the ground. His head slumped to the side, his lifeless gaze falling on Michelle. She sneered before spitting on his corpse.

"Well, well. Seems like you two had quite the past." Drake pulled the cigar from his teeth and ashed on Ben's dead body.

"We didn't have anything." She crossed her arms and looked up at Drake.

"Feedin' time!" he hollered out to the men who weren't tending to the fence. He turned back to Michelle. "Well, if you're gonna be a part of my crew, you're gonna follow me."

She hesitated, narrowing her eyes, wondering if she'd really made the best decision.

"C'mon girl," Drake urged her on. "You're gonna love this shit."

Two of his men picked up Ben's body and followed. They ascended the cement steps and entered the enormous office building. It smelled like an old bar mixed with piss. Graffiti lined the glass and walls of the once-pristine offices. Each separate office was now someone's disgusting bedroom, or in Veronica and Catherine's case, their prison cell.

Veronica banged on the shatterproof glass and screamed. Ben hung lifelessly in the arms of two skinheads, his feet dragging behind him. She screamed so loud her throat began to burn, and she grabbed a desk chair from behind her. With all her might, she heaved it at the glass. With a thud, the chair bounced from the shatterproof glass and clattered to the floor.

Catherine sat on the floor, her hands over her ears. "Veronica, please stop it," she sobbed.

Veronica's chest heaved, her fists clenched so tightly she thought her fingers might break. She pounded and kicked at the glass, throwing her body into the door.

Michelle gave a sickening wave as she passed and Veronica threw herself against the glass once more, a string of curse words and insults spilling from her mouth.

"Ain't she a feisty one?" Drake remarked.

"Who? Nancy Drew? She's harmless," Michelle snickered. She looked back at the teen once more and met Veronica's eyes.

If looks could kill.

Drake led the way to a stairwell in the far right corner of the main lobby, he opened it and swept his arm forward. "After you."

Michelle stepped into the dark, her nerves getting the better of her, her stomach fluttering for a moment.

"Go on, girl, up the steps," one of Drake's men ordered.

She climbed the staircase and reached a metal door; she pushed forward on the bar and light filled the stairwell. The overwhelming yet familiar stench of death greeted her as she stepped out onto the roof. She walked forward, gravel crunching under her feet and her mouth dropped open.

"Holy fuck." She shook her head and couldn't hide her smile even if she tried as she stepped up to the ledge. "This is genius!"

"Yeah, it is." Drake replied matter-of-factly, standing beside her now, a smug look on his face. He relit his cigar and puffed his chest out. "Impressed yet?"

The entire front of the lot was full of eaters. Hundreds of them. They had nowhere to go, as Drake and his men had fashioned the area with reinforced fencing. They'd even jerry-rigged a full-height security turnstile in the center.

"How the hell…" Michelle's sentence trailed off as she gazed in awe.

"You'd be amazed at what you can steal from a prison," Drake said, admiring his handiwork. "With enough manpower, you can do anything." He pointed at the massive crowd below, "Guard dogs, I like to call 'em. 'Til that half-assed posse you were with showed up, we ain't had a lick of trouble. I guess we gotta get to work on riggin' us another one of these out back."

The turnstile let the eaters in, but kept them from getting back out, corralling them into what Drake called his homemade security system.

"The smell, the noise, all their other little dead friends draw them to the front, so I haven't had to worry 'bout the back of the lot at all." He frowned. "Trial and error, I guess."

"Well, I *am* impressed." Michelle smirked at the enormous man beside her. She had her suspicions of these men being part of a gang. They'd all dressed the same, and for the most part, had matching tattoos. Now she had confirmation that they were, in fact, prison gang members. Drake eyed her up and down and she felt the butterflies again, her nerves waking back up. She wondered if this decision was going to come back and kick her in the ass, but she shrugged off the apprehension, pretending not to notice his intense stare. She always took care of herself; if worse came to worst, she'd figure a way out of this.

"Alright fellas, the dogs are hungry." Drake looked over to the two men on the roof closest to him. He motioned toward the ravenous, screaming dead. With their arms in the air, flailing, it appeared as if they were actually begging Drake to feed them.

The two skinheads picked Ben's body back up, swinging it once, twice, and finally heaving it out over the ledge. The eaters began to wail and howl as Ben's corpse soared overhead. It landed with a sickening crunch on the asphalt and the hungry dead pushed and pulled, climbing over one another, fighting for a piece of the fresh meat.

"Hmmph," Michelle mumbled. "Didn't think they ate what was already dead."

"I'm pretty damn sure they eat anything," Drake replied.

The crowd on the roof watched as Ben was ripped to shreds. The eaters' jaws chomped down on whatever part of him they could. They tore his limbs from his torso and emptied him of his entrails in a bloody frenzy. In a matter of minutes, there was barely anything left of Ben at all.

*

Veronica sat cross-legged on the desk, finally quiet, finally still. Inside, she seethed. She watched through the glass as the skinheads beyond her office prison cell laughed and joked, smoking and drinking, some of them shooting up with filthy needles. She noticed that some of the other rooms had a few women in them. They lie half-naked on stained mattresses, barely conscious. Veronica may have never shot up any drugs herself, but she knew that's what they were doing to these poor women.

Veronica cringed. She wouldn't go down without a fight. She'd rather die than end up one of their brainless sex slaves.

Catherine had finally stopped crying. She sat in her same spot on the floor, her knees pulled into her chest, head resting against the cool glass. Her bloodshot eyes were set ahead in a blank stare, her lips cracked and dry.

"Catherine." Veronica looked at the woman. There was no response. "Catherine," she repeated, louder this time.

Catherine finally looked up at her.

"We have to do something. We have got to get out of here." Veronica dropped from the desk and kneeled on the floor in front of Catherine, cupping her hands around the redhead's face. "Are you listening to me?"

"There isn't anything we can do," Catherine responded, not looking at Veronica.

"Yes, there is. Do you see what's in those other rooms?" Veronica pointed, putting a finger up against the glass. "That's not going to be us. I'd rather die."

"They killed Ben." Catherine's eyes filled with tears again.

"I know." Veronica clenched her teeth and swallowed; she was sick with grief, but as with all other losses she'd experienced, there wasn't any time for it. Ben, just as Samson, had become her family. And now she'd lost all semblance of family and everything that came with it.

She knew in her heart that these sick men at the dealership didn't have any intentions of killing her or Catherine; they had their own devious plans for them. Her mind was made up. She was getting out of here, or she would force their hand.

"I refuse to just sit here. Ben wouldn't want that. *I* don't want that. You hear me?"

Catherine nodded, a tear rolling down her cheek. "Just tell me what to do."

II

Michelle followed Drake and his goons back down to the main lobby.

"Step into my office." Drake pointed Michelle in the direction of what was once a General Manager's office. The glass walls were covered by grimy sheets, hung haphazardly with duct tape. She crept toward the room, peeking back at Drake who was whispering something to his right hand man, Freeman. He noticed her watching and he waved his hand. "Get." He pointed at the office.

She entered the room and scrunched her nose at the smell: a combination of latex, blood, and body odor. She felt the acid creep up her throat and she swallowed it back down, willing the contents of her stomach to stay where they were. It was dark; the windows overlooking the front lot had also been covered.

Drake flipped a switch on the wall and to Michelle's surprise, harsh fluorescent lighting filled the room.

"Generator," she said, "nice."

"Have a seat." He closed the door and motioned toward one of the leather office chairs. It was stained to kingdom come.

"I'm good, think I'll stand."

"I insist," Drake ordered.

Michelle cringed as she sat, but figured she'd had worse on her clothes at some point in time.

Drake pulled two tumblers from a cabinet and a half-empty bottle of Cognac.

He poured two drinks, the brown liquor sloshing over the sides as he brought one over to her.

"Cheers." He raised his glass and she followed suit.

"Cheers," she mumbled and downed the drink, hoping it would help dull her sense of smell.

"So, let's talk shop, shall we?" He leaned against the large oak desk in the room, his arms crossed, eyeing her up and down again. His demeanor was different when he wasn't in the presence of the other men. He still had an air of arrogance and authority, but more professional. He was like a quiet storm, cool and collected on the outside, but the threat of danger was just under the surface. "You've lasted this long, so, you clearly know how to handle yourself. I don't see you as the type to rely on others. Definitely not the crew you rolled up here with, anyway."

Michelle rolled her eyes. "Clearly."

"You were sure quick to turn on them, huh? What'd they do to you?"

"They were nothing to me. It was only a matter of time before they got themselves killed, or worse, got me killed. I saw an opportunity, and I took it."

Drake squinted and nodded, pouring her another drink. She accepted it, and downed it the same as the first. He chuckled and slammed the bottle down on the desk before her. He raised an eyebrow and pushed the Cognac toward her. She was making this too easy for him.

Michelle smirked and picked up the bottle, helping herself.

"So, opportunity, huh?" Drake sipped his drink. "Tell me a little bit about this *opportunity.*"

She swallowed the Cognac, savoring it this time. "You're organized, you've got manpower. You've got a good setup here." She pointed at the ceiling. "I saw for myself up on the roof."

Drake nodded in agreement.

"You're not sitting around playing house, hoping for the best and avoiding the worst," she continued. "The world's fucked. Y'all have accepted that, obviously." She leaned back in the leather chair and crossed her legs, taking another swig from the bottle. "In fact, you're embracing the dead, using them to your advantage. You're not afraid of them. I stopped being afraid of them a long time ago." Her eyes seemed to glaze over with a sort of sadness. "They've been the only *people* I like being around."

Drake considered what she said. They'd get along just fine.

"Stand up," he barked at her.

Michelle stood up, her cold eyes bore into his.

Drake stepped toward her and kicked the leather chair away. It flew across the room and tumbled into the wall. Michelle jumped slightly but didn't take her eyes off him. He shoved her back into the wall, and she grunted as she slammed flat against it.

She shivered.

He placed his broad forearm against her chest and pushed. Fear briefly flickered in Michelle's eyes as he leaned forward, his face only an inch from hers.

"Let's get one thing straight, you and I." He sneered at her, leaning slightly to his right and grabbing hold of one of the sheets covering the exterior windows. He tore it free and daylight flooded the room, the crowd of eaters in the front lot turned in unison once they spotted the movement. Their eyes fell on Drake and Michelle and they went hysterical; fists clamored on the shatterproof glass and they snarled and screamed. The window was barely chest-level with the eaters. They struggled against one another as they tried to raise themselves up in a futile attempt to get closer to their tasty meals.

Drake turned back to Michelle. "You ever turn on me like you did your *friends*, and you'll be doing a lot more than watchin' those flesh-eating fucks out there through a window."

Michelle said nothing, simply nodding instead, a sadistic smile creeping across her face.

Drake grabbed her by the hair, pulling her mouth onto his. Michelle fumbled with unbuttoning her pants and their tongues danced as he pulled her away from the wall. He pulled her shirt over her head and turned her around, slamming her face-down onto the desk.

She cried out, whether with pleasure or pain, Drake didn't care.

As he undid his belt buckle with one hand, he pulled her head up by her hair with the other, so that she was face-to-face with the savage undead just beyond the safety of the glass.

Michelle laughed as he entered her, her eyes upon the gathered dead. Even in her solitary moments with them back at the tower, she'd never felt this way.

She'd never felt so *wanted.*

Michelle laughed until she cried.

*

Veronica watched Michelle and the skinheads emerge from the stairwell. Michelle entered a private office as Drake spoke to Freeman, their captor. Both men looked their way and sneered. Veronica felt her blood start to boil again. She glanced at Catherine, who'd witnessed the exchange, as well. A look of disgust came over her face.

"Motherfuckers," Catherine said, brushing a lock of red hair from her eyes. "They're out there talking about us."

"They're doing it on purpose," Veronica replied. "Tryin' to get a rise out of us."

Drake disappeared into the office after Michelle and shut the door.

Freeman leered at Veronica and Catherine. He licked his lips and called out to one of the other men. "Cage!"

A stocky man with no shirt, his face covered with tattoos, emerged from one of the rooms that held the unconscious women and sauntered over to Freeman.

"What's up?" He pulled his belt through its buckle and fastened it, lighting a joint.

Veronica could no longer hear the men or read their lips as they leaned close to one another, speaking in hushed voices. Whatever it was, they discussed it in great detail and Veronica soon grew bored watching them. She went back to her seat on the desk, crossing her legs. She leaned back and closed her eyes, wishing herself out of the room.

A few moments later, Catherine jumped from the floor. "They're coming, what's the plan?"

Veronica hopped down from the desk, facing the glass again. The smug men strolled toward them. "Keep it cool, we're gonna get out of here. We just need to get past them and out that back door, whatever it takes. Everybody else seems preoccupied. We can handle the two of them."

Catherine wringed her hands, "God, you sound so sure."

Veronica bit her lip. "I'm not."

The lock clicked and the door opened inward. Freeman and Cage stepped inside.

Catherine instinctively wrapped her arms around Veronica, as if trying to shield her from an unavoidable danger.

Freeman snickered. "Don't be scared, y'all. Cage and me just wanna show you around, make you feel... *more at home.*" The words rolled off of Freeman's filthy tongue in a manner that sent shivers down Catherine's spine.

"You're not touching her." Catherine stepped in front of Veronica; her short stature didn't come close to shielding the taller teen, but it was all she could do to put as much space between the skinheads and Veronica as possible.

"Ah, now that ain't fair," Cage chimed in. "We're a real close group around here. We share *everything.*" He sucked his meth-rotted teeth and moved forward, placing a firm hand on Catherine's shoulder.

Catherine pulled away and instinctively shoved Cage back. The man stumbled slightly, but countered the shove with a hard slap. Catherine's small frame impressively bore the blow, and she shoved harder this time, with all her weight. Cage fell back into the glass wall and stumbled.

Freeman reacted quickly, lunging for Catherine, grabbing her by the throat. Veronica, even quicker than Freeman, delivered a swift kick to his balls. The skinny man doubled over in pain, whimpering like a puppy. Cage rebounded off the wall and caught Catherine by the hair, snapping her head back as the woman attempted to run from the office. She fell hard to the grimy carpet and let out a cry.

The commotion in the office had piqued the curiosity of the other men in the building, but rather than join in an attempt to subdue the two captives, the men cheered the fight on. Some whooped and hollered while others whistled and clapped.

Veronica kicked Cage in the face, sending three rotting teeth flying from his mouth. She grabbed Catherine and pulled her to her feet.

Catherine pulled Veronica toward the door. "Now's our chance!"

Veronica stopped and looked down at Freeman, still reeling from the blow to his nethers. She kicked him in the side, hard, just as he'd done to her in the parking lot. The rage inside insisted that she give him another kick. So she did.

And that second kick turned into a third, and then a fourth.

"Veronica!" Catherine cried.

She saw a flash of movement to her right and it was followed by a harsh blow to her face. Veronica saw stars as she flew backwards and landed on the desk behind her. She quickly regained her composure and saw Cage upright, blood dripping from his fetid mouth. Her head throbbed from where he'd punched her and her rage intensified. Catherine screamed. Cage charged toward Veronica and she grabbed the closest thing to her left.

A pen.

Veronica let the man's heavy frame slam into her, sending them both soaring over the desk and crashing to the floor on the other side. Veronica struggled, but finally rolled atop the stout man. Cage gurgled as she pulled the pen from his neck, sending an impressive jet of blood up the wall. She plunged the pen into his neck again and again, until his eyes rolled into the back of his head and he lay motionless, the gurgling finally subsiding.

Before she could move again, there were hands on her, pulling her from his corpse. She kicked and screamed. She was an animal.

The men who had her in their grasp dragged her from the office and threw her to the tile floor of the lobby. Catherine landed next to her in a sobbing heap.

Veronica felt a sharp pain in her side as a boot buried itself in her frame. She thought she might black out as she felt her ribs crack under the weight of the boot.

A door slammed open somewhere.

Drake was screaming.

Veronica, covered in Cage's blood, looked up at him and laughed.

III

"What in the fuck is goin' on out here?" Drake hollered as he charged from his office, the buckle on his pants swinging as he struggled to zip his jeans.

Freeman, battered and breathless from the struggle, pointed at the two women on the floor. "This bitch attacked us! She killed Cage!"

Veronica giggled uncontrollably on the tile. Catherine, tears streaming down her face, urged Veronica to stop.

"You think this shit is funny, do ya?" Drake stomped up to Veronica and grabbed her under her arms, pulling her up to face him.

Veronica bit her lip and stifled another laugh. Drake, outraged, grabbed her by her throat and launched her back to the floor. Veronica landed hard on her tailbone and winced, collapsing to the tile. Catherine gathered her in her arms.

Movement caught Veronica's eye from the office behind Drake and she looked up. Michelle peered out at the unfolding scene in the lobby, her eyes meeting Veronica's. Michelle tried to hide her slight smile.

Veronica glared back at Michelle and screamed, "Skank!"

"Seems we need to teach you two a lesson." Drake folded his arms across his enormous chest and cocked his head. "Whaddya think, boys?"

Drake's men hooted and hollered as Freeman pulled Veronica out of Catherine's arms. "Looks like this is a first for us, y'all. Two feedings in one day!" Freeman egged on the crowd of men as he manhandled Veronica toward the stairwell.

"Get this one up to the roof, King," Drake barked at a muscular man behind him.

"Show her what happens when you misbehave around here. I'll be up in a minute." He motioned toward the stairwell.

Catherine shrieked as King grabbed hold of her. She called out to Veronica but was met with a slap by her captor. He hauled her off, following closely behind Freeman.

Drake reentered the office, grabbing Michelle by the waist, pulling her into him. "Damn girl, you sure know who to bring to the fuckin' party." He kissed her hard and shoved her back when he was through. "I ain't finished with you yet, but I got business to take care of." He pulled on a clean shirt, a size too small, and turned back toward the door. "Come on, lemme show you how real men solve problems."

Michelle nodded and followed him from the room. Her head swam from the Cognac and the brief sexual encounter with Drake. She attempted to smooth her wild curls back before tying them up in a ponytail. Her heart raced and she could feel butterflies in her stomach again as she climbed the steps to the roof. They were different butterflies this time, not the nervous ones she'd felt before.

She felt excitement.

She hadn't felt this alive in a very long time. Michelle felt like maybe she'd finally found the perfect home at the end of the world.

*

Up on the roof, Freeman held Veronica tightly by her wrists, forcing her to look out into the front lot at the wailing dead below her. Veronica's mouth was a line as she stared into the vacant eyes of the eaters. A grisly pile lie at their feet. Veronica refused to cry as she came to the realization that was all that was left of Ben.

After everything they'd all been through. That was all that was left.

Veronica felt a burning in her chest, thinking back on that pile of remains in Emerald Park.

Samson.

She thought of the lifeless shell, lying in the streets of Columbia City.

Isaac.

She remembered the dead eater on the floor of her living room.

Dad.

The burning in Veronica's chest became unbearable and she screamed. Freeman, startled by the outburst let go of one of her wrists. Veronica swung her fist up and it connected with Freeman's jaw. Freeman countered with a strike, splitting Veronica's bottom lip.

"Stop it!" Catherine screamed.

Veronica attempted to hit Freeman again, but he twisted her arm up behind her back, bringing her to her knees. He grabbed the back of her head and pushed it forward. "I can't fuckin' wait for you to meet your new friends."

Veronica touched her tongue to her swollen lip and winced. The eaters screamed wildly, staring up at her. She wished they'd get it over with. She wished she could leap from the roof and feed the dead herself. She had reached her limit, she was tired of this disgusting world.

Freeman greeted Drake as he finally made his way onto the roof followed by Michelle.

"She's just a girl," Catherine pleaded with the men. "You can't do this!"

Drake sighed, ignoring Catherine as he approached Veronica. She looked up at him and he brushed a strand of her dark hair away from her face. She scowled.

"What a damn shame," he said, shaking his head. "You probably would have been real useful around here." He chuckled. "But you killed one of my men and trashed my fuckin' house. That shit don't sit well with me."

"I don't really *care* how that sits with any of you," Veronica fired back, spitting on his boots.

Drake's nostrils flared as he looked down at her. He clenched his teeth and balled up his fists. Catherine continued to scream and beg behind him, only making matters worse. Enraged, Drake shoved Freeman out of the way and grabbed Veronica by her shirt, launching her backward. She rolled on the gravel and was once again in Freeman's grasp.

"Get her ass over here so I can shut her up!" he yelled to King, pointing at Catherine.

"Catherine." Veronica's voice was barely a whisper as she watched King drag her friend over to Drake.

"You want her alive so goddamn bad, then so be it, lady." Drake grabbed a fistful of Catherine's short, red hair and she yelped in pain. As Drake lifted the petite woman in his arms, ready to launch her into the growling mob of eaters, Michelle interrupted.

"Wait!"

Drake turned to her, his face twisted in anger.

"She's a doctor." Michelle put her hands up, defending her statement. "She's more useful alive than she is dead. Both of them are." Her eyes flicked to Veronica, the teen shooting her a look of contempt. "Use this one as leverage—" she pointed at Veronica, "—and the doc will do whatever you need." She nodded, reassuring Drake to trust in her words.

Drake sighed, tossing Catherine back toward King. He pulled her face toward his and raised an eyebrow. "Is this true? You a doctor?"

Catherine, shaking in King's arms, said nothing.

"Don't fuckin' toy with me. I'm done with these bullshit games, woman. Are you, or aren't you, a doctor?"

"Yes," she finally responded, her voice shaking. "I am a doctor."

"Good girl." Drake patted her atop her head and snapped a finger at Freeman. "Get them back downstairs and keep guns on 'em." Turning toward Michelle, he relit his never-ending cigar. "Think that was something you could have told me earlier?"

Michelle shrugged, "I didn't think they'd end up being such a problem. Especially Nancy Drew."

"Women are *always* a problem."

Michelle opened her mouth to say something but decided against it and pulled her cigarettes from her pocket.

"So lemme ask you somethin', did you pull that doctor card out now because you didn't want to see them two bite the dust?"

Michelle snorted, lighting a cigarette. "Trust me, I'd like nothing more than to see that ginger bitch eat shit." She exhaled a puff of smoke into the air. "But doctors are a rare commodity these days. Everybody knows that." She raised an eyebrow, giving him a sexy pout.

Drake shook his head and licked his lips. He couldn't wait to get her naked again. "I was right about you. We're gonna get along just fine."

*

Catherine and Veronica were taken back to their makeshift holding cell. Freeman and King, guns at the ready, kept watch at the locked door in case the two captives decided to make any more escape attempts.

Catherine wasn't sure how much time had passed since the morning's unfortunate turn of events, but the sky was bright as ever. The sun hid behind overcast clouds, keeping her from determining the time of day. She was almost grateful for it. If she were somehow made aware of the mere hours that had passed, she'd surely begin to believe she was truly in hell.

"I wish you would have kept your mouth shut," Veronica said, anger filling her voice.

Catherine furrowed her brow, casting the girl an odd glance.

"On the roof, you wouldn't shut up."

"Veronica," Catherine shook her head, bewildered by Veronica's statement. "They would have killed you."

"Maybe that's exactly what I wanted, Cat." Veronica said, her eyes red from both exhaustion and emotion. "This is the end of the line. Ben is dead. Andrew, Clyde, Gary, they're gone." Her voice began to waver and she paused, taking a deep breath. "I killed a man today."

"It's going to be—"

"No!" Veronica sharply countered, "Nothing is going to be okay. I've lived through this, all of this, for what? I watched my father die, my brother, my friends. Even strangers, people just won't stop dying and the dead are walking around outside eating people and what the hell is the point anymore? And now, thanks to you, God knows what the hell will happen to us here!" Veronica's voice grew in volume and Freeman shot her a nasty look through the glass.

Catherine was shocked. "Thanks to me?" She pointed a finger in Veronica's face. "I went along with your silly little escape plan. We could have gotten out of here! But no, you flew off the handle and nearly got yourself, and me, killed!"

"And now that option is out the window! Just great!" Veronica shouted back at her. "You see what they're doing to those women in there. You're a doctor, congratulations. You know what I'll be good for here. I've come this far and lived through this much bullshit just to suffer at the hands of some sick freaks. I'd rather be dead!"

"Keep it down in there!" Freeman hollered, his weapon trained on the glass.

Catherine leaned in to Veronica. "I just can't accept that, I'm sorry," she whispered. "We have lived through all this hell on earth because of one simple fact, Veronica. We wanted to. Giving up is the easy way out, but I am no defeatist, and neither are you. We keep pushing, and we keep going, until we can't anymore, but we make sure that we damn well go out with a bang. So yes, I screamed my ass off on that roof, I was willing to risk my own life on you, because I'll be damned if after all this you ended up thrown from a roof by a bunch of Goddamn bullies and eaten alive."

Veronica, angry but embarrassed, sat silent on the edge of the desk. Rolling Catherine's words around in her head.

"I won't let anything happen to you." Catherine wiped a tear from her eye.

The lock clicked loudly in the door and Freeman swung it open. "Let's go, Doc. Boss wants to see ya. This one stays here." He raised his gun in Catherine's direction when she didn't make a move from her seat. "Get a move on."

Catherine reluctantly rose from the desk and followed Freeman from the room. King shut the door and locked it, shoving Catherine forward. The redhead looked back at Veronica, but the girl had already turned her back to the glass.

IV

Catherine plodded after her captor. King was muscular with tattoos that covered his thick neck and broad shoulders. Catherine couldn't help but want to shave the ridiculous sideburns that ran down his face. She looked away from him, stealing a glance at one of the side office rooms she'd yet to visit; her heart broke for the drugged-up women inside. She locked eyes with one of them, a malnourished blonde in her early twenties. The vacancy in her eyes was even less comforting than the fact that Catherine knew what they were doing to her. Catherine hoped the girl hadn't completely checked out, but then retracted her previous thought, replacing it with the hope that the girl was completely oblivious to this apocalyptic dungeon. She thought back on what Veronica had said. Maybe she was right. She swallowed the lump in her throat as she turned her eyes away from the room and continued walking. She hoped she'd be able to keep these monsters from claiming Veronica as their own.

King rounded a corner and they made their way down a narrow hall toward the rear of the building. Drake waited near an open wooden door.

King stopped short and Catherine nearly ran into him. "Boss." He nodded.

Drake returned the nod. "Come on in, Doc." It was more of an order than it was an invitation, as King grabbed her left arm and shoved her into the poorly lit closet. The shelves were a disheveled mix of pharmaceuticals and various medical supplies. Catherine's eyes scanned the items and cringed at the unsanitary conditions in which the instruments were kept.

"Three things," Drake said from the doorway. Catherine turned her attention back to him. "Aside from the good shit, I don't know what half these drugs are. That's why you're gonna label it all in terms that we can understand. I'm also gonna need you to patch up Freeman; if you recall, your little friend did quite the number on him. Lastly, that good shit I was talkin' about, we're runnin' out of it. That's where you come in."

Catherine shrugged, rolling her eyes. "I'm a doctor, not a chemist."

Drake sighed, aggravated. He leaned against the doorframe and continued. "I don't need you to *make* the shit, I need you to go with King and replace it. We ran out of heroin a long time ago and now the morphine is in short supply."

Catherine shot him a look of contempt. "I can't believe you would even believe for a second that I'd help you harm those women any further or feed your pathetic drug addictions. Consider how stupid that even sounds! You lucked out, you have a doctor. And you want to risk that asset on a drug run? Brilliant. I'm amazed you've survived this long."

King narrowed his eyes. "I'd watch your tone of voice if I were you."

"How 'bout you consider this... you're smart. What's an addict in detox like?" Drake sneered as Catherine considered his statement. "Now imagine an entire building full of 'em. Everybody shivering and shaking, shittin' themselves and screaming non-stop. Everybody 'cept you and me. It'll be a real nice time, watchin' those girls in there seize up and die right before your eyes."

She shook her head. "There are some things worse than death. It would be a blessing for them."

"Ah, fuck it." Drake threw his arms up in defeat. "I tried, Doc. I thought you'd be easy to reason with. Michelle was right, time to use the other one as leverage."

"You're insane! Think of what you're risking by sending me out there. What happens if I get killed? No doctor for you, or anybody in here."

"Oh, it's worth the risk, trust me." Drake turned and left the closet.

King reached in and grabbed Catherine by the arm. She knew better than to pull away but still struggled against his grip. He led her back down the hall after Drake. "If you harm her, I'll do nothing to help you!" she cried out.

Drake grinned. "That's what you think."

The trio reentered the lobby and marched toward Freeman. "Open up," Drake called out to the man standing guard. Freeman obliged and grabbed for his keys.

Veronica turned her head when she heard the lock click. Drake strolled up to the glass office, looking smug as usual. King, with Catherine in tow, followed close behind.

"Grab her," Drake ordered.

Freeman leered as he pulled Veronica from her seat atop the desk.

"Hey! Get your hands off me!" Veronica shouted in protest, but Freeman twisted her arms behind her back, causing her to let out a short yelp.

Drake entered the room, his hulking frame causing her to feel as if the room had shrunk in size. "Sit Doc down there." Drake pointed toward the corner opposite him.

King bent to right the overturned chair and slammed Catherine down hard. He positioned himself beside her, his rifle just inches from her temple. Catherine felt the sweat begin to form on her back.

"Alright, Doc, last chance. You go get me my drugs and we leave Princess here alone. Not even a scratch on her."

"Fuck you!" Veronica shouted, kicking Drake in the knee. "Catherine, you don't listen to anything that they say. Don't help them!" She struggled against Freeman but feared her shoulders would be torn from their sockets. She continued to kick, even as Freeman hoisted her up and slammed her back down onto the desk.

Drake reared his arm back, seemingly unfazed by the blow to his leg, and backhanded her hard across the face. "That was for the kick." He turned to Catherine. "Last chance."

"Leave her alone! She doesn't deserve this!" Catherine hollered in protest.

Drake nodded at Freeman, who pulled Veronica's head up off the desk. Drake delivered another strike to her face, but this time with a closed fist of stone. Blood flew from Veronica's mouth as her face moved with the force from the punch. Her top lip now split against one of her canines. Veronica ran her tongue over a bottom tooth and felt it wiggle. She was sure she would lose some teeth today.

"Catherine listen to me, don't you dare help them!" Veronica yelled, her resilience renewed.

Catherine cried out in horror as Drake reared back and struck Veronica again, this time the loosened tooth flying from her mouth. Veronica dazed, stars dancing before her eyes and the sharp pain from her jaw pulsed through her body in shock-waves. She spat, a mixture of saliva and blood dribbling from her swollen lips. She shot a pleading glance in Catherine's direction and shook her head, nostrils flaring. It was not a look that asked for help, but rather warned of giving in to them.

"Hmm." Drake raised a finger to his lips and mimicked deep thought.

He reached out and snatched Veronica's left arm from Freeman's grasp, slamming her open palm onto the desk. He placed pressure down onto her wrist and Veronica squirmed. Pulling a knife from his back pocket, he flicked his wrist and the blade snapped out. Veronica's eyes went wide and Catherine's stomach fluttered. Catherine, without thinking, attempted to rush to the girl's side but was met with the butt of King's weapon. It collided with her sternum and she was knocked back into her chair, gulping for air. She threw a hand out. "Stop!" she managed to cry out between gasps.

Drake lowered the blade, stopping to hover just centimeters above Veronica's ring and pinky fingers. He looked to Catherine.

"Please, stop!" Catherine screamed, both hands held out toward the man, pleading. "I'll do it, I'll go with King!"

"Good girl." The corners of Drake's lips curled and he closed the gap between his blade and the desk beneath it, slicing through Veronica's fingers, flesh and bone detaching, like they were butter.

Veronica let out a deafening scream and Catherine lunged forward, this time meeting no obstacle.

"I think you've finally learned your lesson," Drake said to the frantic redhead as she tore the sleeves from her blouse and wrapped Veronica's trembling hand, applying pressure to the fresh wound. "King, grab Doc some supplies from the closet so she can get Princess cleaned up." He bent and retrieved Veronica's severed fingers from the grungy carpet. "Think I'll hang onto these."

V

Michelle gripped the bottle of Cognac, watching as Drake inflicted blow after blow upon Veronica. She hated to admit it, but she actually *liked* the girl. She'd put up one hell of a fight today, more than once. She could tell Veronica wasn't the type to just roll over and take it. Unfortunately for Veronica, though, this was Drake's house.

When Drake pulled the knife from his pocket, Michelle's stomach turned. Earlier on the roof, she'd made sure that Veronica stayed alive. Had it all been for nothing? Oh, how she wished Catherine were in Veronica's place on that desk.

Michelle watched as Drake brought the knife up to Veronica's long, skinny fingers. She cringed. Half of her wanted to watch, the other half, the small bit of humanity she had left, begged her to turn away. She looked down at the bottle and back at the gruesome events unfolding in the office.

The bottle always wins.

Michelle slipped away into one of the dark, filthy offices. She quietly closed the door and pulled the lighter from her right front pocket. The small flame illuminated the room enough that she spotted a flashlight near the far corner. As she crept toward it, bottle in hand, a groan off to her left froze her in her tracks.

"Hello?" Michelle called out into the darkness, her grip on the bottle tightening. There would be other opportunities to drink alone… the Cognac was now her weapon.

She heard the groan again, followed by a whisper.

"Who's there?" the voice asked.

Michelle's muscles relaxed; it was one of the captive women. She fetched the flashlight and flicked it on, pointing it toward the ceiling, casting dim light around the room.

She could see the woman's face now: bruised and swollen cheeks, eyeliner and mascara streaking her pale face. Dried blood crusted the sides of her mouth. It was eerie how much she resembled one of the dead.

"Are you the new girl?" the woman asked, curiosity mixed with hope lit up her eyes.

Michelle shook her head. "Yeah, but… not in the way you think." She pulled the top from the bottle and took a long swig.

"Can I have some?" the woman asked, licking her lips.

Michelle shrugged. "Sure, why not?"

The emaciated blonde grabbed the bottle from Michelle with greedy hands and turned it up, gulping down the brown liquor. Michelle frowned and snatched the bottle back, cleaning the mouth of it off with her shirt.

"Thanks," the blonde muttered, wiping her mouth with her frail forearm.

"How long have you been here?" Michelle asked, taking another swig.

The blonde furrowed her brow, thinking hard. She shook her head. "I… I don't know."

A scream erupted from beyond the closed door. Michelle knew who it had come from. She grimaced, wondering how much damage Drake had done.

"Was *that* the new girl?" the woman asked, staring blankly at the door behind Michelle.

Michelle ignored her question and pulled a cigarette out, before she put the pack back in her pocket, she held it out to the woman.

"Thanks." The woman accepted a cigarette and a light from Michelle, sucking in the smoke as if her life depended on it.

The two sat in silence for a moment longer, smoking, staring at one another. Michelle didn't know whether to feel pity or envy for the stranger.

Must be nice to lay in bed all day, high as a kite and unaware of what's happening all around you.

Michelle cocked her head, studying the woman's wounds. The bruises on her face were accompanied by track marks up and down both arms, and more bruising decorated her legs and thighs.

"Pity, definitely pity," Michelle said.

"Pity what?" the woman asked, eyebrows raised.

"Nothing." Michelle shook her head, not meaning to speak aloud. She finished off the bottle and let it drop from her fingertips. It fell with a thud to the filth-covered, generic office carpeting and she leaned her head back, rolling her neck from side to side. The warmth from the alcohol spread through her mid-section, and she sighed, welcoming the familiar feeling of a good, strong buzz.

"Why are you in here?"

Michelle's head snapped up and she glared at the pathetic woman sprawled on the disgusting desk.

"None of your fucking business," Michelle barked.

The woman winced in response to the tone in Michelle's voice. "I-I'm sorry. I just... I don't get any visits from other women here." The woman stared at Michelle for a moment before putting her cigarette out.

"Do you know what's going on out there?"

"Out where?" The woman was confused.

"Anywhere, dummy. Out in the lobby, in the other rooms, outside? The world? Do you have any idea what's going on?" Michelle's voice was filled with disgust.

The blonde shook her head. "I'm not sure. I remember bad dreams..." Her voice trailed off and her face went blank. She was suddenly child-like. "Demons eating people. All of the people... but Freeman... Freeman, he got out of jail early and he came and saved me." She smiled then, baring her chipped teeth.

Michelle rolled her eyes. "Freeman saved you? From what?"

"From the demons!"

Michelle dropped her face into her palm, shaking her head. "Definitely pity."

She brought her foot up and slammed it down onto the empty Cognac bottle, shattering it. The woman jumped back, startled and frightened by the sudden movement, her grin disappeared. Michelle bent down and retrieved the biggest piece from the pile of broken glass, turning it over in her hand and inspecting it.

"What are you doing?" the woman asked, bringing her knees into her chest, trying to make herself smaller.

"Freeman didn't save you from shit," Michelle said. "You might not want to admit it to yourself, but you know what's going on here. And it's a lot easier to just close your eyes and open your legs than to be out there, isn't it?" Michelle, glass shard in hand, pointed at the far wall. "I get it, I really do. Not everyone's meant for this world. I know that from experience, trust me, but this is just goddamn pathetic." She stepped forward, holding out the piece of glass.

The blonde stared at it before snatching it from Michelle's hand. Her bottom lip quivered and her eyes welled up with tears as she stared down at it. She looked back up at Michelle, tears rolling down her dirty cheeks.

Michelle nodded.

The woman gripped the glass shard in one hand and pressed the sharp end into her other wrist, dragging it down hard, ensuring that she went in deep. The blood pooled around the wound, pouring from it. The blonde took a deep breath, her hands shaking. She dropped the shard and leaned back, her head hitting the wall with a light thud. She turned her face toward Michelle, who lit another cigarette and eyed the growing pool of blood beside the woman.

"Thank you," the woman whispered. She closed her eyes and waited for the slow but welcome death.

Michelle said nothing. She heard Drake talking to Freeman out in the main lobby and wondered how many fucks anyone would give about the blonde woman's suicide.

I'm going with zero, she thought and dropped her cigarette to the floor, stepping on it.

The voices in the main lobby had ceased, and as she turned to leave, she spotted a small, yet adorable brown jacket, forgotten beside the desk. She bent to retrieve it and held it up. It wouldn't fit over her chest, that was for sure. But the blonde didn't need it.

Not anymore.

VI

Catherine tended to the trauma on Veronica's left hand. She disinfected the instruments as best she could before closing the wounds. Between her efforts to staunch the bleeding and wrapping the hand, she'd used the remaining bandages in the building. Considering Drake and his men had little in the way of medical supplies to begin with, after the incident in the office, there was much more of a need now for Catherine to venture out with King. Catherine couldn't let the hand get infected, and there was no way she'd be able to treat it with the poor excuse for medical instruments they had at the dealership. Drake knew that by injuring Catherine's friend in such a manner, it would provide the motivation for the doctor to continue making necessary trips to the nearby medical center.

Veronica lay on her side in a haze. Catherine had also depleted the last of Drake's Lortab supply, which she had to practically beg of him, in order to dull the pain Veronica felt from the beating and the forced amputation.

Catherine looked up to the high windows in the office again; dusk had fallen quickly. The events of one day felt like seven. Now that she knew just how much time had passed, Catherine accepted that this was, in fact, her new hell.

She noticed a crumpled shirt at her feet and retrieved it, immediately recognizing it as the one Veronica habitually wore around her waist. She placed it into the girl's good hand and squeezed. Catherine stroked Veronica's dark hair, terrified to leave her alone, terrified of returning to the hospital. She hadn't been back since that first day, when she'd abandoned her patients. The place had been pure chaos and devastation; she'd barely escaped with her own life. Sure, things had probably calmed down and cleared out at the medical center over the last few months, but she wasn't entirely sure what shape the place would be in once she got there, or what useful supplies might even be left.

A hard knock sounded on the glass behind her. Startled, Catherine turned to find Michelle in the doorway.

"King's ready," Michelle slurred her words slightly.

Michelle leaned against the door frame, her mane of curls sloppily gathered in a low ponytail. Her eyes were glossy and her cheeks were red.

"Drunk already?" Catherine shook her head, feeling pity for the woman.

"Take this." Michelle tossed a light jacket at Catherine's feet. "It's from one of the broads in there." She gestured toward the closed door of an adjacent room. "She doesn't need it."

Catherine scooped up the jacket and wrapped it around her frame, zipping it up. It was a bit snug, but would help shield her from the biting winter air. She muttered no thanks, instead, she brushed passed Michelle, shouldering her aside.

"Don't be so ungrateful," Michelle said.

Catherine stopped in her tracks and slowly turned, casting a look of disgust Michelle's way. "Ungrateful?" Catherine asked, moving closer to Michelle.

Michelle smiled.

"If it wasn't for her—," Catherine pointed at Veronica through the glass, "—I would rip your fucking throat out."

Michelle's smile didn't waver. "Good luck out there."

Catherine glared at her a moment longer before turning on her heels and marching down the hall.

King stood beside Drake at the rear entrance, the one the women were dragged through that morning. Eyeing the holstered pistol at his hip as well as the semi-automatic weapon in his hands, Catherine looked to Drake.

"I need a weapon."

"Not a chance in hell," Drake laughed.

"When was the last time you dropped by the hospital?" She raised an eyebrow at him when he remained silent. "The place was crawling with those things. I know how many patients were there, and I'm pretty sure none of them made it out alive. That means they're more than likely on the prowl for a hot meal. And you want me to walk back into that dead zone unarmed?"

Drake smirked. "You don't need no weapon, King here is a great shot, my best. Why you think I'm sending you with him?"

"You said so yourself, Drake." She lowered her eyes, disgusted with the words she was about to utter. "I learned my lesson."

Drake chuckled, pulling the same knife from his pocket that he'd used on Veronica. "Catch."

He tossed it to Catherine and she caught it in both hands. She looked down at the knife in revulsion but set her emotion aside and placed the folded blade in her jacket pocket.

"Don't try anything cute, and take care of it. I want my knife back," Drake told her.

She looked back toward the office turned holding cell, Michelle still looming in the doorway.

"You keep your people away from Veronica while I'm gone," Catherine warned, choosing to use the word people over men. Michelle was undoubtedly a part of Drake's group. Despite the lump of fear that she forced herself to swallow, Catherine spoke up again after receiving no response from the giant man before her. "I mean it, Drake. Keep them away from her."

Drake unleashed a hearty guffaw and patted her on the head, like a dog. He sauntered away in Michelle's direction. Catherine cringed at the thought of the two of them together; a true concoction of evil.

"Let's hit the road." King pushed the door open and the two exited into the crisp night, heading down the cement steps and toward a silver pick-up truck. King fished a key fob from his pocket and the car started before they were even near it. Catherine jumped, the remote start of the truck catching her off guard. "I always wanted a truck like this," King remarked. "Never could afford one."

Catherine ignored him and climbed inside the truck, welcoming the warmth from the heater with her fingertips, holding them up to the vents.

King slipped into the driver's seat and shifted the truck into drive, heading for the back of the lot. "Handle the gate." He handed Catherine a small set of keys.

She exited the vehicle and headed for the lock. Shivering, she fumbled with the padlock for a moment before hearing a familiar click. She pulled the lock free and moved the gate aside, allowing room for King to pull through before locking the gate back up.

King held a hand out expectantly when Catherine hoisted herself back into the vehicle. She tossed the keys back into his hands and buckled herself in.

They cautiously navigated the pitch-black streets as they headed away from the lot, avoiding long-forgotten car wrecks, abandoned vehicles, and miscellaneous trash. The hospital was only a few miles away, but with the condition of the roads, the roaming dead, and the lack of streetlights, it was a far more troublesome drive than either of them would have preferred.

They rounded a corner, heading deeper into the city. Catherine's palms began to sweat; staying on the outskirts of Haven and close to the shore had proven to be dangerous enough. Now she was on her way back to the center of Haven, in the dark, on a fool's errand.

The truck barely made it a block before a loud explosion interrupted the silence in the cab.

"What the actual fuck?" King slammed on the brakes, his eyes wide. He threw the truck in reverse and fishtailed it back onto the previous street. Smoke billowed in the distance. "Somebody just done somethin' real stupid." He slammed his foot down on the accelerator and raced back toward the dealership.

As the truck grew closer, they could see it was in fact the dealership that was burning. Flames licked up the front entrance and every eater in the neighborhood was stumbling toward the glowing structure.

Catherine covered her mouth in horror. "Oh, my God, Veronica."

*

Veronica lay still on the desk, listening to the voices of Catherine and the others down the hall that seemed so far away. Michelle stood in the doorway, swaying in her inebriation. She continued to feign a drugged-up condition, hoping Michelle would lose interest and leave. Veronica just wanted to be alone.

Drake joined Michelle at the door, whispering something to her. It caused the curly-haired madwoman to cackle. Drake disappeared as soon as he'd arrived and Michelle entered the room.

"Looks like it's just you and me, Nancy Drew." Michelle tucked a lock of Veronica's dark hair behind her ear. She pulled up a chair and had a seat. "You stick with me, play your cards right, and *I'll* make sure these assholes don't lay another finger on you. Not Catherine. She can't protect you." Michelle's eyes fell on Veronica's bandaged hand. "Clearly."

It took every ounce of control Veronica had to keep her face still, to not respond.

"I didn't think we'd ever end up like this, ya know?" Michelle leaned back, pulling a cigarette from behind her ear and lighting it. Smoke snaked from her lips. "You and me, pal. Got ourselves a new group, don't have to worry about those nasty things outside anymore. I used to get mad, how everybody fawned all over you back at the tower. But I really enjoyed our time alone at the tower; I gave you your first drink. You *are* just a kid. I know that now. You don't deserve any of this shit." She looked away, deep in thought, smoking her cigarette. "Everybody seems to have to learn the hard way." She pointed at Veronica's hand. "*That's* not your fault. That was Catherine, just like the rest of them, too damn stupid, always learning the hard way. You're like me, you're tough."

Veronica, her good hand balled up inside of Samson's shirt, clenched her fist. She was nothing like Michelle.

"I don't do the things I do because I like to." She paused, considering her statement. "Okay, maybe I do. But I wouldn't *have* to do them if everybody wasn't so fucking stupid." She shook her head in exasperation. "The man at the liquor store, he was stupid. Desmond, he wouldn't keep his mouth shut. Francis, why couldn't he just sit the fuck back down?" Michelle's eyes were wide now. "Juliette, that nosy bitch. Stupid, stupid, stupid!" Veronica's nails dug into her palm as Michelle spoke each name. Michelle dropped her cigarette to the floor and stomped it out, leaning forward, her face only inches from Veronica's. "Ben."

Veronica had had enough. Before Michelle could continue Veronica snapped her head forward, colliding with Michelle's. The blow to the head caught Michelle off-guard and she sailed backwards in the chair, toppling over. Veronica leapt from the desk onto Michelle, ignoring the pain searing through her left hand as she stretched out Samson's button-down. She straddled Michelle, her knees on both arms, and wrapped the shirt around her neck.

Michelle struggled beneath the teen, wriggling her body to get her arms free. Veronica leaned forward, pulling the shirt tighter, digging her left elbow into Michelle's chest to gain leverage. Michelle finally freed one of her arms and grabbed hold of Veronica's injured hand. She squeezed hard where the girl's fingers should have been. Veronica let out a painful wail and rolled off, clutching her hand.

The men in the lobby were now alerted to the struggle.

Michelle, gasping for sweet air, lunged for Veronica. She shoved her back against the wall with a scream, both hands gripped around her neck. Veronica punched at the side of Michelle's head repeatedly, bringing a knee up into the woman's gut, but the grip on Veronica's neck only strengthened.

"Damn, was I wrong. Stupid, just like the rest of them!" Michelle screamed into Veronica's face, spittle flying.

"Goddamnit, I can't get any peace and quiet around here!" Drake roared across the lobby in response to the women fighting. "I'm done with this shit!"

As Drake charged his way across the expanse toward the commotion, Freeman, following him, caught movement out of the corner of his eye.

"Drake, who the fuck is that?"

Drake looked toward the front entrance where Freeman was pointing.

It was hard to spot on the backdrop of writhing eaters just beyond the safety of the front door. But there stood a stranger, shrouded in darkness, holding something in each hand.

The stranger tapped hard on the glass, waving both hands, as if to show the men inside what he was holding.

"Why the hell haven't those sons-a-bitches eaten him already? Freeman, get your ass out there and handle this! I have enough to deal with!"

Freeman started toward the door, weapon at the ready. His confusion was replaced with panic, and he froze in place when the man set down the contents of his hands, lighting the ends of both fuses before disappearing back into the crowd of hungry, wailing dead.

"Oh, shit," was all Freeman could mumble before the explosion ripped through the front of the building.

VII

Gary and Andrew exited the marina with silent footsteps. They snaked their way through rows of abandoned cars in the dark parking lot.

"Just a short distance this way, come on," Gary called over his shoulder to Andrew, who was beginning to slow again. It concerned Gary that he might not see the end of their mission through.

The pair crossed the road, working their way up a small street, entering an office complex just a block from the strip of car dealerships. They rounded the corner of a small building and Gary ran smack-dab into a lone eater. Gary squawked as he hit the pavement, the eater tumbling with him. The dead thing hissed on top of him, its putrid mouth snapping.

Andrew reared his arm back, ready to crack the dead man in the head with his baseball bat, but the world tipped over onto its side and his vision swayed and blurred. His ears rang and he dropped the bat at his feet, bringing both hands up to the sides of his head and crying out in pain.

Gary writhed beneath the eater, who now dug his disgusting claws into his sides. He let out a painful wail as he finally flung the man to the side. He scrambled away and pulled his knife from his belt. The eater lunged back at him and Gary plunged the blade deep into his forehead, stopping him mid-attack. He brought his foot up and kicked the motionless body back, freeing the knife. He rested his hands on his knees, catching his breath.

Andrew groaned on the ground behind him. Gary turned, his knife up, ready to bring a swift death to his turned friend.

"I'm not... I'm not dead yet," Andrew croaked.

Gary sighed with relief. "Jesus Christ, mate, you have got to stop scaring me like that." He pulled the big man to his feet and helped him over to a bench beside the front doors of the office building. Gary pulled his shirt up, squinting in the dark. He inspected the deep gashes from the eater's nails and made a face. "This is not going to look pretty tomorrow."

Andrew wheezed, squeezing his head in his hands. "I don't know how much longer—"

A pack of hungry, moaning eaters burst through the front doors beside them. Gary jumped back and spied the baseball bat on the ground. He ran for it and swung it up to smack the first of the attacking dead in the face. The force sent the eater's head spinning, breaking its neck.

"Andrew!" Gary cried out, but the man remained seated on the bench. There was no time for concern as another eater grabbed at Gary's sleeve. He kicked the eater's legs out from under it and stomped at its head as he brought the bat down hard onto another's.

Breathless and panicking, Gary looked around in horror, realizing there were far too many of them for him to take out on his own. As he reached for the pistol on his hip, Andrew stood, his arms reaching out.

This is it.

Gary raised the gun, his finger on the trigger. Andrew let out an angry cry and grabbed the eater in front of him, twisting its head around and flinging it to the side. A look of confusion took over Gary's face as he watched Andrew walk unnoticed among the dead, snapping necks and bashing skulls in with his fists. Gary shook the confusion away and returned to disposing of eaters with the baseball bat.

The men stood amidst a gruesome pile of unmoving dead, trying to catch their breath.

"You get your second wind?" Gary looked to Andrew.

"More like my fourth or fifth." Andrew leaned forward, breathless, a solemn look on his face. "I'm one of them."

Gary nodded. "They don't attack you anymore."

Andrew inhaled deeply, wincing. His whole body hurt. "I don't know how much longer until I'm not me anymore, man."

Gary looked at one of the dead lying at his feet and frowned, imagining Andrew's face on the corpse.

Andrew straightened and put a hand on Gary's shoulder. "Come on, let's keep moving."

"Right." Gary motioned for him to follow and they continued their journey toward the dealership.

*

"That explains the smell. I was beginning to think it was you," Gary whispered in the darkness.

"Hilarious." Andrew shook his head, and although it hurt to, he was able to smile at Gary.

The two looked on in awe at the homemade security system of eaters which surrounded the front of the enormous car dealership. They'd been corralled and confined to block anyone from getting in or out of the building's front entrance.

"Amazing," Gary muttered. "I'm actually impressed. That explains why the bastards inside are in such good shape."

"There's gotta be hundreds. I don't think I've ever seen this many all together like this." Andrew shook his head.

"Get down!" Gary ducked behind a van and pulled Andrew down out of sight.

A silver truck turned the corner and tore ass own the street. Gary narrowed is eyes, turning to Andrew. "Where could they be going at this hour?"

"I don't know, does it matter?"

"I suppose not." Gary ran a hand over his bald head, sighing. "You know what you need to do, don't you?"

Andrew nodded, considering how the dead no longer noticed him. He knew there was a purpose behind the bite. He truly was going to be able to set things right before he met his end. "Everything happens for a reason."

Gary smiled and took the bag of weapons from Andrew, fishing out two of the pipe bombs, handing them to him. He placed a firm hand on Andrew's shoulder. His mouth was a hard line.

"What about Veronica and Catherine?" Andrew's voice wavered.

"Trust me, they wouldn't keep those two near any exits," Gary reassured him. "Once the deed is done, and I have a clear path, I'll make my way around back, catch them off guard. You and your dead friends, go right through the hole you're about to blow in the place. Let's end this madness." He squeezed the man's shoulder.

Andrew returned the gesture and clapped Gary on the back, closing his eyes and smiling through the pain searing through his flesh as the deadly infection worsened. "It may be that the Lord will look upon my misery; and restore to me his blessing, instead of his curse, today."

"I'll see you again." Gary returned the man's smile. He wasn't sure what Andrew's words implied, but he trusted in Andrew's belief in his God's mercy.

"Yes, you will," Andrew replied as he moved out from behind the van's cover.

As he crossed the street, he wrinkled his nose; the smell of the dead was growing stronger. He swallowed hard as he approached one of the security turnstiles.

No going back.

He slipped through, the metal clicking loudly. The dead did not turn toward the noise; they continued to mill about, bumping into one another, hissing and clawing at their own as they impeded each other's aimless walking. As Andrew grew nearer to the front of the massive crowd, the dead were more alert to the humans inside the building. The generator-powered lights shone brightly in the night, a beacon for the dead. Andrew pushed his way through the eaters. He was surprised at how calm he was amidst the rot and decay. They groaned and growled as he shoved himself past them, but quickly lost interest and returned their blank gazes to the lights.

A barricade had been set up to keep the dead from getting to the doors. Andrew chuckled to himself; the dead really were that stupid. He grunted as he moved the steel CrowdStoppers out of the way. They'd been piled atop one another, an admirable approach to fencing in the walkway that led to the front doors. One of the large pieces clattered to the pavement and Andrew cringed as the crowd of dead grew agitated. They moved forward with him to the door, bottlenecking into the alcove. Andrew noticed the large generator just inside the safety of the walkway and behind it, a long row of gas cans.

He laughed at his luck. "This is gonna be awesome."

Andrew tapped loudly at the glass doors. He recognized the leader of the group and the skinny guy with the shitty tattoos immediately.

He grinned when he saw them, waving, pipe bombs in hand. He quickly set them at the foot of the doors and pulled the long grill lighter from his pocket. Once the fuses were lit, he quickly pushed back through the vicious crowd and took cover. There was only one thing that bothered him: he wouldn't get to see the looks on the skinheads' faces when the bombs went off.

VIII

The blast briefly lit up the night, collapsing the structure at the front of the dealership. Gary didn't pause to have a look at the damage, but he sprinted across the street, seeing his window of opportunity with both the dead and the skinheads distracted. He made his way around the side of the smoking building, stopping only to scale a fence at the back lot. As he got to his feet and headed for the back steps, a man caught him off guard.

"Not so fast," the skinhead said, bringing up his rifle.

"Oh, fuck off." Gary was quicker with his pistol and quite frankly, sick of running into roadblocks. He pulled the trigger and the skinhead dropped to the asphalt, a pool of blood forming around his head, brain steam rising in the winter air.

Gary marched toward the back entrance; he was ready for anything.

*

As the truck sped toward the dealership, Catherine grew more nervous. She fumbled with the knife in her jacket pocket, sliding it open. King's eyes grew wide as he pulled the truck up and put it in park. Part of the building was on fire and eaters, crawling over the unmoving and charred bodies of others, poured into the gaping hole caused by the explosion.

"I have to get Veronica," Catherine said, tears forming in her eyes.

"Like hell you do, I'm out of here. This place is fucked." King brought his hand back up to the shifter. "You're comin' with me."

"I'm going back for her!" Catherine slapped his hand away from the knob and was met with a back-hand to the face. Unfazed by the blow and enraged for the final time, Catherine ripped the knife from her jacket pocket and thrust it into the center of King's throat.

King's hands flew up to the knife as he choked, blood gushing down his neck. His eyes rolled to the back of his head as Catherine removed the knife, a final spurt of blood spraying the steering wheel before his head slumped against the window. Catherine sat for only a moment more, staring at King's unmoving body, convincing herself she'd done the right thing. She took a deep breath and threw the vehicle's door open, charging toward the back lot.

Stray eaters, drawn to the building from all the commotion stumbled toward her; there were too many. She changed course and headed for the other side of the dealership only to run into more of the dead. She back pedaled and considered the front. The windows to either side of the entrance were blown out and too high for the dead to walk through. The fire, for the time being, was contained to one area.

"This is the stupidest thing I've ever done in my life."

Catherine breathed deeply as she crept toward the blown out windows, the eaters here far too distracted to know she was lurking just behind them. She sprinted for the large window frame and pulled herself up, minding the glass. Her jacket tugged hard, snared on something, not allowing her through. She struggled against it, from the position she was in it wouldn't be easy to slip out of the jacket.

Panicking, she grabbed the knife from her pocket and pulled the fabric tightly, cutting at the cloth. The eaters had noticed her now. Their moans grew closer and Catherine whimpered, her eyes flicking back and forth from the approaching dead and the jacket. She worked the knife, faster and harder, and the fabric finally tore and gave way.

But just a moment too late.

Rotting teeth sank deep into Catherine's calf, clean through. The grip on her foot loosened as the eater pulled back to gobble up the fresh chunk of flesh. Catherine wailed and kicked, freeing her leg and toppling into the building. She crashed to the floor, crying out in pain.

She wriggled out of the jacket and cut one of the sleeves off. She tore her pant leg and inspected the bite; it wasn't bleeding as badly as she'd anticipated, but *damn,* did it hurt. She wrapped the sleeve tightly around the wound and stood, grimacing through the pain. She was angry, but she accepted the death sentence. She gripped the knife handle and limped toward the closed office door.

"That was quite a show you just put on," Drake's voice came from somewhere in the dark office, startling Catherine. He flicked on a lantern and sat, bleeding from a head wound, his clothes tattered, holding a half-empty bottle of liquor in the corner of the room.

Catherine cringed at the sight of him, no longer afraid, just disgusted. She hobbled toward him as he took a long swig from the bottle.

He wiped his mouth and reached down beside him, grabbing his rifle. He slid the bolt back and pointed it at her.

Catherine laughed, continuing toward him. "I'm already dead, asshole."

Drake roared with laughter, putting the rifle back down and held out the bottle.

She grabbed it and took several gulps. It burned down her throat but would help to dull the pain in her leg. Her chest was filled with an instant warmth.

"Where's King?" he asked, taking the bottle back.

"Dead."

Drake sighed. "That's a shame." He took another swig from the bottle. "You shouldn't have come back here, Doc."

Catherine ignored him, and turned to leave, but Drake snapped forward and grabbed her wrist.

"Oh come on, seriously?" She pulled her wrist free and drove the knife down hard into his big thigh, giving it a twist. Drake wailed in pain. "There's your fucking knife back, douchebag." She grabbed the rifle and raised it up, backing toward the door as Drake shouted a stream of cusswords at her.

Catherine decided she'd rather know he burned to death in this shit hole than do the bastard any favors. She lowered the weapon and let herself out of the office.

*

Michelle and Veronica toppled to the floor as the explosion tore through the building, the glass walls of the office splintered and cracked. The gas cans and generator were ignited, adding to the chaos as the building was cast into darkness. Drake's men hollered all around and gunfire followed as the hungry wails of the eaters invaded their ears.

This shit-show went to hell real fast, Michelle thought as she sprang to her feet, dodging Veronica's arms as she reached out for her legs.

"Not today, kiddo."

Michelle ran into the lobby, leaving Veronica behind. She scanned the turmoil, the flames growing along the left wall lit the room enough for her to see that it was time to go. Drake's men struggled with their weapons in the poor lighting and were caught off-guard by the dead as they overran the building. She headed for the back door, some of Drake's men smart enough to do the same.

As the cluster of fleeing people neared their exit, the door flew open. Before Michelle could realize what was happening, gunfire sounded and the two men to her right dropped to the floor. She threw herself back and rolled on the carpet, hoping to dodge the gunfire as it continued, ending the lives of the other men who were escaping the blaze with her.

Out of habit, she put her hands up and her head down in surrender. She felt the barrel of a gun press up against the top of her head.

"Get it over with!" she shouted over the discord.

"Where's the girl?" A familiar English accent spoke the words.

Michelle's head popped up and she let out a chuckle, a grin spreading across her face. "Gary, you came back for me."

Gary's hands shook, knuckles whitening around the pistol grip. "Where is she?" he demanded again.

"She's dead," Michelle lied, rising from the carpet and dusting herself off.

Gary's heart shattered. "And Catherine?"

"Lucky for her, she wasn't here. Come on already, we need to get out of here!" Michelle ran for the back door, actually stopping for Gary and putting out her hand.

This was all for nothing. Gary shook his head in disbelief as he rushed toward the door. He hadn't come back for Michelle—in fact, his plans included killing Michelle—and here he was, escaping the crumbling building with her.

He looked down at her hand and shook his head, cocking his head toward the door. "After you."

The pair fled into the night, down the cement steps, and disappeared amidst the rows of silent vehicles in the lot.

*

Veronica stumbled to her feet, her throat burning and her neck sore. Her ears rang and her head swam. If she died tonight, it would not be by Michelle's hands. She crept from the office, keeping low. Michelle and some of Drake's men headed for the back entrance. Veronica darted out into the lobby, dodging eaters feasting on the remains of fallen skinheads; they barely noticed her in their hunger. The few that did were too slow, Veronica dodged them with ease and continued toward the stairwell across the lobby. She yelped as a hand shot out in the dark and grabbed her ankle. She toppled to the floor and rolled over, kicking with her free leg at the hand that gripped her.

Freeman crawled toward her, his eyes wild. Glass and other debris spiked out of his body; he'd been standing awfully close to the entrance when it blew. Veronica kicked at him again and he rolled over, wailing. Their struggle on the floor caught the attention of the eaters and the dead began to swarm. Veronica broke free from the grabbing hands and ignored Freeman's death screams as the eaters consumed him.

She retreated on hands and knees, scurrying across the floor. The pain in her wounded hand doubled as shards of glass embedded in her skin. The fire was rapidly growing, the smoke getting thicker; there were eaters everywhere. Her path to the stairwell was blocked, and without a weapon there would be no way she could make it to the roof.

A pair of strong arms grabbed her around the waist and she screamed. A hand clamped down over her mouth and she was spun around and pulled in closely to the man's chest.

"I got you, I got you." Andrew hugged her tightly.

Veronica let out a sob, relieved and overjoyed that it was her friend. Panic filled her chest again. "Andrew, there's too many of them!"

He put a finger up to his lips, still holding her tightly with the other arm. "Be quiet, or they'll know where you are."

Veronica furrowed her brow, confusion setting in. She looked around at the eaters in the burning lobby and realized they were stumbling and shuffling as they normally would, lunging at the remaining bruisers from Drake's posse. Andrew pulled her along with him as he backed slowly toward the stairwell door, all the while keeping her as close to him as he could.

"I don't understand," she whispered to him.

Andrew reached an arm around and opened the door, the two collapsing once they were safely inside. He flicked his flashlight on and handed it to her with trembling hands. "I don't have much time." Veronica shone the light on him and saw the discoloration of his once-dark eyes, the festering bite on his arm.

"You're turning," she said in shock. "How did this happen?"

Andrew shook his head in sadness. "Back at the towers, it's crawling with those things."

Veronica furrowed her brow again.

"Michelle, she... she let the dead out of the east building."

Veronica grew enraged, clenching her fists and wincing in pain.

"That doesn't matter now. I'm running out of time."

She understood now why the eaters ignored him, the infection had almost fully consumed him. The dead ate a lot of things, but they didn't eat their own.

He slid his gun toward her. "Take it. It's heavier than what you're used to, but you'll do fine." He closed his eyes for a moment, trying to focus his thoughts. "Use both hands, don't try to run and fire. You'll do fine."

She nodded her head, tears streaking her face. "Where am I supposed to go?"

"Clyde's waiting. He has the boat, but you have to hurry, he won't be waiting for very long."

"How will I find him?"

"Just get to the water."

The words echoed in Veronica's head, her nightmare, once again, repeating itself.

There was always death, there was always running, there was always the water.

Remembering Michelle's words in the office, Veronica placed a hand on Andrew's. "Juliette didn't kill herself."

Andrew smiled weakly. "I know."

Another tear rolled down her cheek. "You *have* to stop her, Andrew. For Juliette, for Ben. For Catherine."

"Michelle murdered her husband, didn't she?" he asked, that dread in his stomach from Emerald Park returning. The moment he met Michelle, something had screamed *evil* at him.

Veronica's eyes answered for her. She only wished she'd been stronger back in the office to have killed the madwoman herself.

Andrew motioned toward the steps behind Veronica. "Go on, before the roof gives way."

She hurried up the steps, throwing her weight into the door. The cold night air was a welcome relief from the inferno. She inhaled the sweet oxygen and rushed for the fire escape. She hoped she would get to Clyde in time.

IX

Andrew stumbled from the stairwell. He was already having a tough time breathing, and the smoke in the lobby wasn't helping. He only had one thing left to do: find Michelle. He pushed his way through the eaters, who were too stupid to realize there was no one left alive here, too stupid to get out of the burning dealership while they had the chance.

He heard shots and ducked out of instinct, the crack of a rifle filling the air. A familiar voice shouted insults at the dead. Andrew stood tall, squinting through the haze of smoke. Catherine swung the rifle wide, bludgeoning heads of the dead as she charged through the crowd. She stopped once more to fire another shot.

"Veronica!" the redhead hollered over the chaos.

"Cat!" Andrew screamed back at her. "She's safe! She's gone!"

He shoved his way through the horde, his big fists colliding with as many faces as he could target.

Catherine stared in disbelief as Andrew flung eaters to the side, killing them with his bare hands. She fired another shot and dropped an eater before it could get any closer to her. "Andrew!" She rushed to him, ignoring the pain in her leg.

"We gotta get you out of here." Andrew scooped her up, swaying, his balance betraying him momentarily. Catherine noticed the bite, noticed how far gone he was and wrapped her arms around him as he pushed through the dead. She wondered how long it would be until they no longer desired her flesh, how long it would take for her to become one of them as well.

They burst through the back doors, tumbling down the cement steps. The two of them yelped as they landed in a heap at the bottom.

"You're bit." Andrew pointed at her leg.

"Yeah, so are you." The two shared a morbid moment before Catherine's face became serious again. "She's safe? You're sure?"

"She's headed for Clyde. I know she'll make it. Where's Michelle?"

Catherine shook her head. "I have no idea."

"Cat." Andrew placed a hand on hers. "I need you to know something."

Catherine narrowed her eyes, lines appearing in her forehead. "What is it?"

"It's about Desmond. Michelle, she—"

"I know." Catherine bit her lip, fighting back tears. She'd had the sinking feeling all along about what really happened to her husband, she just couldn't ever accept it until she'd heard it uttered aloud. A part of her was silently grateful that her husband had been spared all this madness.

A vehicle started toward the back of the lot. Andrew and Catherine helped one another to their feet, leaning on one another for support. They shuffled toward the headlights heading in their direction.

The truck slowed to a stop and Gary flew from the driver's side. He ran to Catherine, hugging her. "Alright?" he asked, pulling away from her and looking her up and down. He noticed the bandage on her leg. "What happened there?" Gary asked.

Catherine didn't answer. She clenched her jaw, shaking her head slightly.

Gary's face dropped. "Say it isn't so."

Catherine hugged him again. "I'll be fine."

Andrew leaned forward, bracing himself on the truck, breathing heavily. "Man, am I glad to see you."

"We've got to get that gunshot wound taken care of, mate," Gary said loudly, patting Andrew on the back.

Andrew and Catherine both looked up at him, bewildered.

"Keep your face down," Gary whispered to the nearly-turned man as the passenger door opened and Michelle popped out.

"Boy, never thought I'd see you two again," Michelle said with a dark smile, lighting a cigarette. "You guys look a little worse for wear. What the hell's going on?"

"Andrew's been shot. Catherine was stabbed," Gary lied. "We should get going so we can tend to their injuries." Catherine helped Gary hoist Andrew into the backseat. Michelle stood off to the side, smoking.

Andrew's breathing slowed, he leaned in toward Gary. "Veronica, she—"

"I know, mate. She didn't make it out alive." Gary's voice wavered.

A puzzled look came over Andrew's face. "You saw her? After the roof?"

Gary shook his head. "The roof? What..." His voice trailed and he glared at Michelle. "She didn't die in that building did she?"

"No, she's on her way to my brother."

Gary smiled. "You did it." He patted Andrew on the shoulder and closed the door, turning to Catherine.

A shot rang out and Michelle threw herself to the asphalt, choking on cigarette smoke. Catherine grabbed Gary and pulled him down with her.

"That piece of shit," Catherine mumbled as she heard Drake screaming into the night.

Gary flopped over onto his side, wheezing. Catherine's head snapped down and she saw the blood glistening in the moonlight. Tears filled her eyes. "No, Gary, no, no, no."

Gary grasped her hands in his, he wheezed again when he tried to speak. He coughed hard and more blood seeped from the bullet hole in his chest.

"Ssh, it's okay. It's okay," Catherine soothed him, gripping his hands back. His eyes were wide, they bore into hers. She wiped the tears from her face and placed a hand on his cheek, glad to be there with him in his final moments. "I know what I need to do."

Gary's mouth twitched, his eyes fixed on hers. His body lie still.

"Gary?" Michelle called his name from the ground a few feet away.

"He's gone," Catherine answered, looking to the woman. Catherine swore she saw a hint of sadness in Michelle's face, but pushed the thought away. Michelle felt nothing for anyone other than Michelle.

Drake continued to fire into the night. Catherine regretted not killing him when she'd had the chance more than anything else. She grabbed the rifle beside her and jumped to her feet.

"You son of a bitch!" Catherine screamed. She aimed her weapon, but Drake got the shot off before she could.

The bullet tore through her thigh and she screamed, collapsing to the ground.

"How's it feel, Doc?" Drake yelled to her, pointing at his own thigh as he hobbled toward the truck.

Michelle stayed put, unmoving on the ground. Her eyes flicked up to Drake, whose arms and torso were riddled with bite marks. Eaters, some on fire, began to trickle out the doors of the blaze. Drake was done for.

Michelle scrambled for Catherine's rifle and raised it at the massive man trudging toward her.

"What'd I tell you about betrayal, bitch?" he spat, training his weapon on her.

She shook her head and pulled the trigger. "When are people gonna learn not to trust me?"

The rifle dug into her shoulder as it fired and she smirked, proud of herself for hitting her mark. The back of Drake's head exploded in a puff of red mist, and the giant fell to his knees, unmoving. The eaters, just a few feet behind him let loose, gorging themselves on the easy meal before them.

Michelle pulled Catherine to her feet. "Let's get outta here, Red. Don't say I never did anything for ya." She pulled Catherine to the passenger's side.

"I'm fine, the bullet went straight through." Catherine pushed Michelle off of her, her voice steel. "I'm driving."

"Alright, whatever you say. Let's just get the fuck out of here already." Michelle put her hands up, rolling her eyes.

Catherine could barely walk, but she managed to make it to the driver's side door. She spotted Andrew's overstuffed bag lying beside the truck and snatched it up. She pulled herself in with a moan and slammed the door as eaters closed in on the vehicle.

"If you're gonna drive, can you please do so?" Michelle asked from the passenger's seat, lighting up another cigarette.

Catherine could feel the fever already starting to take over. The chills rocked her body though she was drenched in sweat. Her hand fumbled on the shifter. The eaters began to pound on the doors.

"Andrew?" Catherine practically whimpered.

There was no answer at first, but he managed to croak out a response. "I'm still here."

Catherine smiled, tossing the bag onto Michelle's lap and slamming her foot down on the accelerator, avoiding the eaters picking Drake's bones clean.

"Put your seat belt on," Catherine barked at Michelle.

"Sure thing, mom," Michelle sighed, pulling the belt over and buckling herself in.

The truck rocked as Catherine plowed through the chain link fence. Eaters went flying up and over the vehicle, some crushed under the tires. She gripped the wheel tightly, trying to control the truck and herself. Not wearing her seatbelt was a necessity.

"I just wanna say, y'all fuckin' stink." Michelle wrinkled her nose at the rotten smell filling the truck cab. Her curiosity got the best of her and she unzipped Andrew's bag, snooping through it.

Catherine swerved in the road to avoid debris as the truck accelerated down the street.

Michelle turned in her seat slightly, peering at Andrew, her eyes wide with horror.

"You... like... what's in the bag, bitch?" Andrew wheezed, struggling with his words. A sinister smile spread across his face.

The bag rolled off her lap and to the cab's floor, Michelle held one of her sketches in her trembling hands.

Catherine peeked into the rearview, locking eyes with Andrew. He gave her a nod.

Michelle looked at her. "Oh, fuck."

Catherine grinned as she slammed her foot down on the brakes and cut the steering wheel hard.

The truck slid sideways, and Catherine locked eyes with Michelle as the truck clipped an abandoned vehicle and flipped.

It rolled three times, glass shattering and metal grinding, before finally coming to a stop, all four tires in the air.

No one in the vehicle moved.

X

Veronica scrambled down the fire escape. As soon as her feet hit the grass, she took off in a sprint, leaving the flaming building behind. She raced toward the beach, bobbing and weaving the eaters swarming the area. Her legs burned as she picked up speed, rounding a corner and cutting through a parking lot. The streets, shrouded in darkness, were hard to navigate. She became lost in her surroundings. Everything looked exactly the same.

She stopped for a moment, clutching her injured hand to her chest and regulated her breathing. She closed her eyes and listened. Through the unrelenting moans of the hundreds of eaters in the area, she could hear the sound she was hoping for: the sweet susurrus of waves. She broke into a run again, pushing herself on. Her pain was soon forgotten as her adrenaline took hold and she breathed in deeply through her nose; she could smell the salt on the air now.

She came upon a towering beach home and headed for the gated driveway. It was unlocked and she let herself in. She allowed a moment of rest and leaned against the lone car in the driveway. She knew a moment was even too long to stop and forced herself forward. She crept along the side of the three-story home and cringed when her foot met an empty bottle on the ground.

It clattered off to the side, the noise tearing through her ears. She shivered as she heard a familiar growl up ahead. The fence to her left was far too tall for her to scale. She heard the shuffling of feet and hoped like hell she was trapped in there with only one of them. She narrowed her eyes and focused in the darkness, the wan light of the moon doing little to help.

The eater finally came into view. It jerked toward Veronica, mouth open, grunting and hissing. Veronica raised her gun, struggling to hold it with both hands; with only three fingers on one, she could barely get a grip on the weapon. She waited for the eater to grow closer, its mouth open wide, snarling. Veronica could see the dead thing's increasing excitement as she was just in arm's reach.

The gun belched fire, and the eater's head snapped back from the force. Veronica cried out in pain, her phantom fingers aching. The shot, she was sure, had rung the dinner bell. She stood in silence, barely breathing, awaiting the death shrieks... but they never came. She sighed in relief, bracing herself against the house and taking a deep breath. She looked down at her bandaged hand, the gauze was stained with a deep crimson. She wondered if her sutures had ripped. She looked back up and forced herself back on track.

It was time to keep moving. She gripped the weapon with her good hand and started off.

Tip-toeing around to the backyard, she found it empty and raced for the gate. She was barely through and onto the sand when she noticed the beach was crawling with the dead.

"Oh, my God," she whispered.

They hadn't noticed her, *yet*.

She slinked forward, having never seen this many of them before. To say she was terrified would have been the understatement of the century. Her posture slowly diminished into a crouch and she kept close to the sea oats for cover. She scanned the black horizon and saw no signs of a boat. Her stomach fluttered and she stopped. She peered over her shoulder, back toward the beach house. She hadn't gone very far, she could still make it back unseen.

Chills ran down her spine as a long wail broke from the horde. Her head snapped in its direction and every eater she could see was looking at her. One by one they opened their mouths and roared into the night, provoking the massive crowd to move toward her.

She sprang from her spot and was running again. The soft sand slowed her down and caused her to stumble a few times but she kept on at top speed. Ahead, just a short distance away, she spotted a rental kiosk. She'd have to break through the horde, but it was her only chance. She ran forward a bit more, searching desperately for an opening. She finally saw a gap in the crowd and made a break for it, dodging death every inch of the way.

There was no safety inside the kiosk, but it was easy to climb. She scampered to the top and collapsed in a heap on its wooden roof, making it by the skin of her teeth. She still felt the burning trails the eaters' claws had grazed into her ankles, and it made her quiver in fear. She panted, her mouth dry. She tried to catch her breath to no avail. The running, mixed with the sheer terror, had not been a welcome combination. She rolled off her back and got up onto her knees. The eaters' screams were deafening, their nails scratching at the sides of the small hut.

Veronica was truly alone.

She cried as she thought of her father and brother. She was glad they'd not had to suffer through this world. She thought of Samson, of how he'd given his own life to save hers, only for her to die alone on the gulf shore. She cried harder when she remembered Ben, dead only since that morning. She hoped with all her heart that Catherine was okay, that Andrew was no longer in pain. She didn't know what had happened to Gary, but she silently thanked him for all he'd done for her and her group; even if it had all been for nothing, there had still been some good left in this world, and he was proof of that.

Veronica wiped her eyes and stared down at the gun in her hands. She looked up at the stars and wondered if hell was already on earth, maybe heaven really was in the sky. She'd fought hard, she'd made it this far, her father would be proud. She considered Catherine's words from back at the dealership.

We keep pushing, and we keep going, until we can't anymore, but we make sure that we damn well go out with a bang.

She raised her head and gazed at the dark water, sparkling in the moonlight. She felt the cold metal of the gun barrel on her temple. The last few months were spent running from an inevitable fate that had finally caught up with her, but she wouldn't die at the hands of some apocalyptic psychos. She would not be ripped to shreds by the dead.

She would be going out with a bang.

She squeezed her eyes shut and breathed in deep as she put her finger on the trigger.

ALL GOOD THINGS COME TO THOSE WHO WAIT

The sky was filled with a light so bright that she could see it through her eyelids. Veronica's eyes popped open, her heart pounding. She gasped, pulling the gun away from her head. Her chest heaved, she'd been mere seconds away from ending her own life.

The flare lit up the night and there, in the distance, was *The Dockside.* The dead faces surrounding her looked to the sky, captivated by the illumination.

This was her last chance.

Veronica threw herself from the kiosk roof, landing in a roll on the sand. She pumped her arms and threw the gun off to the side. She'd need both hands to swim. Her running grabbed the attention of the eaters again and they chased her to the shoreline.

She screamed Clyde's name into the night.

She kicked off her shoes and dove into the freezing water. She screamed again, the salt water burning her wound, but she kicked forward, keeping herself as close to the surface as possible, knowing the bloated dead lurked at the bottom. She hoped the current would help pull her out to sea.

She could barely feel her limbs, her breath getting harder to catch as the frigid water swirled around her, but she kept kicking. The boat's lights flickered to life and she heard Clyde's voice screaming for her. She choked as water filled her mouth and she struggled to stay afloat. The eaters were down there, waiting for her. Her eyes burned, but she was almost there. Just a few more feet.

Clyde threw the ladder down with a splash, urging her on. Veronica stretched her arms out with her last bit of strength but went under. Her body had simply given up.

She felt hands around her wrists, then her body broke the surface of the water and she was pulled onto the boat. She coughed and gagged, spitting water onto the deck. She collapsed as Clyde wrapped her in a blanket, dragging her into the cabin. He held her tightly and she sobbed into his chest, shivering. He wept with her in the dark.

*

Veronica woke the next morning, the light of dawn peeking through the windows, warming the small cabin. She pulled the blanket around her tightly and checked her hand. Clyde had redressed the wound. Looking around the silent cabin, she spotted her clothes. She got up and put a hand on them, finding them still damp. She peered through the window and spotted Clyde, he stood on the deck solemn faced, smoking a cigarette.

She fashioned the blanket into a dress and crept out of the cabin.

Clyde turned and waved her over. "How you feelin'?" he asked her with a sad smile.

She shrugged. Noticing the smoke on the horizon, she wondered if the dealership still burned.

The two stood in silence, watching the sun rise, appreciating the new day. Neither spoke of the previous day or the fate of their companions.

Their journey had come to an end, and a new one awaited them.

"Where to?" Clyde finally asked, dropping his cigarette to the deck.

Veronica continued to look at the sky, she repeated his question in her head. There was only one path left to take.

The way to life.

EPILOGUE

Michelle woke with a groan. Her head pounded and she could taste her own blood in her mouth. She opened her eyes and the world swayed; she was upside down. Everything hurt. If it wasn't for the seat belt, she would have surely died in the crash. She tried moving her head but it hurt too much. Everything hurt too much.

Except for her legs. She couldn't feel her legs.

And that's when she heard the sound.

The slurping, the chewing.

Michelle lowered her eyes and screamed.

She couldn't feel her legs because they were gone.

Catherine and Andrew feasted greedily on her limbs. They were so consumed by their hunger they hadn't even noticed she was awake.

Michelle screamed until she couldn't scream anymore.

NEFARIOUS

A BREADWINNER ORIGINS STORY

It was 2 a.m.

Or at least that's what the clock would have said if the power was still on.

Moira Eckhart slipped out of the coldness of her king sized bed. It didn't matter how humid and warm the house actually was on this autumn Florida evening, everything in the house that night *felt* empty and cold. Almost freezing. Her husband, Samson, had been fast asleep beside her; but even the warmth from his body so close to hers wasn't enough to break the chill she felt so deeply within her being.

She trudged into the hallway, almost in a daze, barely taking notice of the demonic howls coming from her son's bedroom as she passed by the closed door. Making her way slowly down the stairs, she brought a perfectly manicured hand up to the wall and ran her fingers along the surface as she went. She felt nothing still; only the cold.

The house was silent save for the cries of the dead that came from the upstairs bedroom. She slid herself onto the stool at the breakfast nook and placed her head in her hands, weeping softly for the previous day's events.

She'd shut herself away in the closet again that afternoon. Dancing and singing as she'd done since the start of the end of things. For each song and dance she performed for her imaginary audience she changed outfits, donning the elegant dresses that she'd never wear out of the house again. She tried explaining to Samson that this was her way of coping, it was the only way she knew how to continue to function. And he fired back at her wickedly, telling her that a good way of coping would be to take notice of her two children for once. They were all going through this together, even the housekeeper, Leti. They knew the end of the world had come and that the world they once knew wouldn't return anytime soon. They all knew, except for Moira.

She'd been mid-change when it happened. Leti's screams pierced Moira's ears and broke her from her starlet trance. She flew from the closet in stockinged feet, dressed in a blue and yellow cocktail dress that draped seductively off one shoulder. The scene unraveling before her was one plucked from her worst nightmares. Her precious boy, Robbie, was covered in blood and dying on the living room floor. He turned later that day and killed his sister. And with their deaths, died Moira's last ounce of humanity.

Moira lifted her head and opened her eyes, shaking her head violently in an attempt to pull herself from the nightmare in which she was living. She sat at the breakfast nook in the pitch-black kitchen, and yet she could see her son tearing the flesh from his sister's neck all over again, as if it were happening right in front of her eyes once more. She'd never forgive Samson. In her eyes, it was his fault that their son had left the safety of their home to snoop around the neighbor's yard. It was his fault that their son was bitten, and his fault that both Robbie and Keira were now dead.

But they aren't dead, Moira thought to herself, *dead people don't move around and scream. Dead people don't cry for help. That's all they're doing, they need my help. Oh my poor babies, they need my help.* She stood up suddenly and clenched her fists, her nails digging into her cold palms and breaking the skin. But just as before, she felt nothing.

She walked around the counter to the sink and felt around for the lantern. Her hand fell upon it and she dragged it across the surface toward her. She fiddled with the knob and finally the light clicked on. Squinting her eyes, she turned away, finding Leti in the doorway leading to the guest area of their luxurious home.

"Mrs. Eckhart," Leti whispered with a hand up to block the sudden light that filled the kitchen, "What are you doing down here at this hour? You should be resting." Moira said nothing, she simply stared with pursed lips, angry at the housekeeper's intrusion. "Mrs. Eckhart? Are you okay?" Leti stepped toward Moira, her long, designer silk robe trailing behind her. She may have simply been the housekeeper and (former) nanny, but the Eckharts paid her well. And the materialistic Moira made sure that the woman who took care of that house was well dressed at all times.

Moira slid around to the other side of the counter, facing Leti, and set the lantern town. She watched as Leti continued toward the breakfast bar, deep concern etched in the lines of her face. She took a seat across from Moira who when standing, was quite small. Even when Leti sat, she was still not eye level with the petite yet buxom blonde that she worked for. Leti let out a sigh as she looked into the vacant, blue eyes of her employer.

"Is Mr. Eckhart asleep?" she asked, but Moira still did not answer. Leti furrowed her brow and leaned in toward Moira a bit more. "Moira," she spoke again, sure to get an answer out of the woman this time; she was under strict order to never address Moira or Samson by their first names. Yet Moira remained silent, and her empty stare struck a chord in Leti's heart.

The housekeeper stood and made her way around to where Moira stood, "Alright, I think that's enough for one day, don't you think?" She spoke softly, "Let's get you back upstairs to bed." She placed her hands on Moira's delicate shoulders and tried to lead her out of the kitchen but the lady of the house wouldn't budge. "Well, it's good to see that you're at least conscious."

Leti turned her around and looked into her eyes again. "Mrs. Eckhart, I can't even begin to understand what this must be like for you. But believe me," Leti's eyes welled up with tears, "I loved those children very much. And I'm going to miss them as if they were my own children that had passed." A tear rolled down Leti's cheek and she sniffled. The fact of the matter was that Leti had been in the Eckhart children's lives since the eldest, Keira, was a baby. She did love those children like her own and knew that Moira was never a real mother to them. And now, in their death, Leti hoped that the selfish woman had some remorse to show for it. If this was Moira's way of mourning, Leti could understand, but she feared the woman had simply shut down and turned the reality of the situation off as simply as you would flip a light switch.

At the mention of her children, Moira felt a fury bubble up deep inside; when reminded of the act of her children *passing,* Moira felt that fury rise to the surface and it seemed to leak simultaneously from every single pore. She crossed the kitchen suddenly and knew Leti would follow her. All in one motion she reached forward and pulled a nine-inch bread knife from the storage block on the counter and turned, plunging it into Leti's stomach.

Leti's breath came out in one big whoosh and she hunched forward, grabbing Moira's hands that still clutched the handle of the knife protruding from her abdomen. A grunt escaped her lips when she tried to speak. She looked to her small-framed employer and grimaced through the pain, her eyes wide and frantic.

"Think of all the good you're doing for those children that you love so much, Leti." Moira smiled, finally speaking, her voice dripping with sweet condescension.

To her dismay, Leti couldn't believe just how angelic Moira looked in that moment. Leti's vision blurred slightly, and the light from the lantern reflected and framed Moira's platinum-blonde hair in such a way that there appeared to be a beautiful halo around the woman's head. Moira's perfectly large, white teeth were framed by plump lips that even in the wee hours of the morning, were impeccably glossed in a deep shade of red. Moira's smile disappeared as she grabbed Leti by her hair and shoved the knife in deeper, pulling it upwards with a grunt. Leti's flesh tore open with a sickening rip and a crimson blush spread across the silk of her robe as the crazed Moira gutted her like a fish. Leti cried out pathetically, barely murmuring. Shock and disbelief were replaced with agony and horror in response to the white-hot pain searing through her being.

"Shh," Moira leaned in close and hushed her, pulling the knife out and violently stabbing the housekeeper once more, deep into her chest, barely missing the heart. Leti's legs gave out and Moira struggled to keep from falling under her weight. She pulled back on Leti's hair, suspending the falling woman's body in mid-air for a moment, before slowly lowering her softly to the bloodied mess that was the kitchen floor. She knelt beside Leti's dying body and smiled sweetly at her, stroking her cheek with blood-stained hands, leaving a smear on the ill-fated housekeeper's face. "Just think of all the good you're doing, Leti. Think of my poor babies and how hungry they are." She sweetly cooed at Leti who tried to open her mouth in response, but could only manage a gurgling, heavy, wheeze as she desperately tried not to choke on her own blood. Moira leaned in close to Leti's ear, "You hear them up there?" she whispered. "They're crying out for their mommy. That's what babies do when they're hungry."

Leti silently plead for the ghastly torture to end; her head dropped limply to one side and it appeared she'd finally given up. Moira slid the bread-knife out and stood up with a groan, frowning at the expanding puddle of blood around Leti. She looked down at her clothes and the bloodstains that adorned them and contorted her features into her usual, haughty, expression. *Another ruined outfit,* she thought. The air around her stirred and she looked up at her husband as he entered the room.

"Moira?" Samson squinted at her in the low light and stopped abruptly when he realized what she was covered in. He looked down at the scene that lay at his wife's feet and grimaced. "Moira, what the fuck?" His jaw dropped in shock and he watched as his wife shrugged her shoulders and wiped the knife off on her pajama shorts before placing it on the counter behind her. He shouted at her again, "Moira! What did you do?"

Her expression remained apathetic and the only words she could find in that moment were, "I need you to help me feed the children."

Samson's eyes filled with tears as he glared at Moira in disbelief. "Have you lost your mind?" There was no anger left in his voice, only pity. She stared back at him and said nothing. He approached her swiftly and grabbed her by her shoulders, nearly lifting her off the ground. "Do you realize what you've done?"

She looked up at her husband as he towered over her. "Sammy, I need you to help me feed the children." Her voice was empty, just as she was. She pushed his hands from her shoulders and slipped away from him, moving toward Leti's feet. Samson watched her bend down and grab the housekeeper's ankles. She looked at him expectantly and without another thought he bent down and shooed her hands away, scooping up Leti's body into his arms. A whimper escaped Leti's lips as she stared up at Samson and his heart shattered; he thought she was already dead. Moira peered over his left arm and looked down at Leti. Smiling delicately at the housekeeper she nodded once before turning away and heading toward the staircase.

Samson felt like he'd left his own body. He didn't know who was carrying Leti's body, he didn't know who was moving his feet forward, one step at a time, to follow the hollow shell of a woman he called his wife. He knew he couldn't possibly be about to feed his housekeeper to a pair of flesh hungry eaters. He was on autopilot. His children were dead. Those things upstairs were not his son and daughter, but he knew Moira was not willing to accept that.

With each heavy step he took up the stairs he felt himself drift farther and farther away from the reality of the situation. His wife would occasionally turn around to check that he was still following. He looked down at the bloody mess that was Leti's chest cavity and then into her eyes, the life was slowly fading from them and she seemed to be slipping in and out of consciousness. He wondered if she was even aware of her current situation.

Samson glanced back up at his wife who appeared almost child-like in her adventure up the staircase. The guttural growls of the dead brought him to the brink of a panic attack. Samson felt his heart pound in his chest and despite the cool temperature in the house, beads of sweat began to trickle down his forehead. If he hadn't been holding Leti, he wasn't sure he'd have been able to control his trembling hands.

Moira reached forward and gave the doorknob a delicate turn, unleashing the once muffled cries of her undead children. She stepped into the room and the eaters went wild. They thrashed and screamed, their hands clawing at their tethers and pulling so violently against them that had they not been of the utmost luxury, the sheets that bound them to the bed would have torn. Samson lingered in the doorway, pleading internally with himself not to take another step forward.

"Sammy." Moira placed a hand on his bicep and motioned for him to follow her into the bedroom.

A film of sweat covered his entire body now, his heart thumping in his chest at what felt like a million beats-per-second as he crossed the threshold into the nightmare that was once his nine-year-old son's bedroom.

He looked into the filmy, dead eyes of the eaters tied to the bed. They were ferocious, a horrific site to see, and the smell was even worse. But the most horrid thing to the senses were the sounds that came from them; unrelenting screams of pure evil. Samson made his way slowly toward the bed and the eaters, if possible, went even wilder. Their arms reached out toward him, flailing, pathetically attempting to grab at something beyond their reach. Samson leaned in a little too close for comfort and what was once his son shrieked forward, jaws snapping a mere inch from his face. He jumped back quickly, his breath caught in his chest. He looked to his wife but she seemed mesmerized by the creatures before her, not even noticing his close-call with certain death.

Readjusting Leti's body in his arms, he looked down and whispered almost inaudibly to her, "I'm so sorry."

It appeared as if she were trying to say something, but no words ever came, only incoherent sounds. He exhaled and dumped the body on the bed between his undead children, immediately backing away. From a safer distance, Samson watched on in amazement as the eaters tore into their meal in a frenzy. He felt Leti's eyes still on him as they ripped strips of flesh from her body and devoured them. He watched as the final vestiges of life finally left her eyes and the eaters' hands methodically dug into the housekeeper's carcass, pulling and stretching her open. They harvested and feasted upon her organs like wild animals, slurping at the blood and never slowing their frenzied attack. Muscle was pulled and swallowed, fat was greedily gobbled up; the smorgasbord of the dead lasted for no more than an hour. Like a fire, they consumed all that was in front of them until only bone and gristle remained. What was once Leti became an unidentifiable mass as she was reduced to nothing more than a gory mess of a skeleton.

Samson and Moira didn't move an inch the entire time. They watched on with raw astonishment as their dead children annihilated their former caretaker. Tears streamed down Samson's face at the horrific realization of what he'd just done, and yet Moira managed to smile through it all, as if she were proud. Keira and Robbie, when finished with Leti, looked up at their parents and grunted, their mouths still full, still chewing what was left of her. Low, but what Moira believed to be tamer, growls emanated from the children and Samson and Moira crept slowly out of the room.

The husband and wife didn't speak to one another. Samson went to one bathroom to scrub himself clean of the night's horrors while Moira retired to another, singing to herself as she cleaned Leti's blood from her hands. In the low light of the lantern, Moira stole a glance at herself in the bathroom mirror. She felt like she'd aged ten years in the last few hours. She frowned and pulled the skin on her face tightly in different directions. She hoped that this whole thing would blow over soon so she could go get a face lift.

Samson was already in bed, passed out from pure mental exhaustion, when Moira finally finished obsessing over herself in the mirror. She plopped into bed beside him and took a deep breath in and exhaled with a high pitched sigh.

"I'm famished," Moira said to herself. "I think I'll make pancakes in the morning." She rolled over and closed her eyes, drifting soundly to sleep.

*

Samson slept 'til around two that afternoon. His wife was no longer in bed with him and he knew where he'd find her. The eaters had begun their howling once again and he still couldn't wrap his mind around the atrocity he'd been a part of the night before.

After freshening up, he wandered downstairs into the kitchen and found Moira. She'd obviously been through her morning routine and looked as if she'd stepped out of a magazine. Her hair was perfectly curled, her makeup flawless. She moved around swiftly in the kitchen as she cooked; no other woman could match Moira Eckhart's graceful steps in four-inch stilettos. She grabbed up some leftovers from what she'd made for herself that morning and fixed Samson a plate, pushing it across the counter at him. She could tell by the look in his eye that he wasn't proud of himself. She could tell that he probably hated himself, hated her, for what they'd done the previous night.

But then again, she thought, *he's always hated me, hasn't he?*

"It's too late today, but you'd better get a good night's sleep and an early start tomorrow, Sammy." He cringed as her shrill voice broke the silence. She tapped her long fingernails on the counter as he stared down at the lavish plate of food. "Hellooo? Earth to Samson. Are you listening to me?" He looked up at her with red eyes. Regardless of the amount of hours he'd slept, he had huge bags under his eyes and his skin was pale. Samson felt like he hadn't slept in years.

"Why, what's tomorrow?"

"The day you go out and get food for your family."

"We've got plenty, Moira. I practically cleared out Franklin Woods."

"That's not what I'm talking about, and anyway, what happens when that runs out?" She shook her head, "That isn't important right now. What's important is that you remember your role in this household." She hadn't quit tapping her nails on the counter and she looked at him across the counter with a smirk. "You need to feed your children. You need to provide for this family. You know what you are."

Tap, tap, tap, tap, tap.

Samson felt himself begin to sweat again as the tapping of her nails seemed to echo around in his head, adding more noise to the already overcrowded vault of his thoughts. The world outside really had ended. There was nothing out there but rot and decay and more death. There was danger outside the gates of their precious Franklin Woods that he'd hoped to never have to encounter.

Tap, tap, tap, tap, tap.

Last night's events replayed over and over in his mind. Moira's incessant tapping was grating on his already frayed nerves. If Samson had even an ounce more energy, he would have reached across the counter and wrapped his hands around her delicate throat. He swallowed hard and looked into her beautiful eyes, a nefarious smirk spreading across her perfect face. He hadn't been outside their gated community since the beginning of the end, yet he knew like the good husband Moira didn't deserve, but that he would always be, he would venture out into the land of the dead and risk his life to provide for her.

What other choice did he have? He knew what he was to her, what he'd always be.

"You're the breadwinner, Sammy. Don't you ever forget that."

A WORD FROM THE AUTHOR

There are no words to express my feelings in bringing this series to an end. The Breadwinner Trilogy *was my first set of published fiction and it has been an amazing journey from start to finish. The end of the world is not glamorous indeed, and I hope you have enjoyed the ride.*

None of this would have been possible without help from my friends, my family, my fellow authors, my editor, and countless numbers of others. Thank you all so much, and there are so many of you to name, so I sincerely hope you all know how grateful I am.

I am especially grateful for my readers, you're the reason I do what I do. I truly hope you have enjoyed the final book in The Breadwinner Trilogy, All Good Things. *I ask that you do me one final favor and please leave a review wherever you have purchased this book from, whether good or bad, it's the best compliment you can give.*

I look forward to diving head first into new worlds and giving my readers some new adventures to lose themselves in. And hey, who knows... maybe we haven't seen the last of Veronica and Clyde.

Again, thank you.

ABOUT THE AUTHOR

Stevie Kopas was born and raised in Perth Amboy, New Jersey. She enjoys everything horror from books to film, and is an avid gamer, caffeine addict, and apocalypse enthusiast.

Stevie is the Managing Editor of Horror Metal Sounds, an e-zine that can be found at www.horrormetalsounds.com, and she is a telecommunications professional.

She currently resides in Florida where she soaks up the sun as often as she can.

To find out more about *The Breadwinner Trilogy,* Stevie Kopas, or her other work, including her short stories *Nefarious, Patient 63,* and *Spencer Family Tradition* in the *At Hell's Gates* horror anthologies, please visit the official website, www.someonereadthis.com, become a fan on Facebook at http://facebook.com/thebreadwinnertrilogy, and follow her on Twitter @ApacoTaco.

PERMUTED
PRESS

THE JOURNAL SERIES
by Deborah D. Moore

After a major crisis rocks the nation, all supply lines are shut down. In the remote Upper Peninsula of Michigan, the small town of Moose Creek and its residents are devastated when they lose power in the middle of a brutal winter, and must struggle alone with one calamity after another.

The Journal series takes the reader head first into the fury that only Mother Nature can dish out. Book Five coming soon!

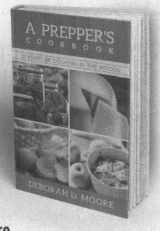